METRO

The Metro is a world in itself – in the winter it's warm down there, cool in summer. And it's always sparkling clean. No Russian would dream of spitting on the Metro's marble floor; he'd sooner spit on the coat of another passenger.

When I walked along the spotless platform under the high Romanesque ceilings, mosaics and crystal chandeliers all around, my entire body took in the sparkle of the station – my eyes, the whiteness of the marble walls; my hands, the pleasing feel of the nickel poles; my feet, the smoothness of the polished stone. Why the modernization of Russia started with the hanging of chandeliers beneath the earth I didn't know, but I did know that when I was underground, I felt free.

Alexander Kaletski

METRO
A Novel of the Moscow Underground

Methuen

My grateful thanks to:

Alan D. Williams
Lois Wallace
Alan Devenish
Michael Lutin
Scott Siegel
Pamela McPartland

A Methuen Paperback

METRO

First published in Great Britain 1985
by William Heinemann Ltd
This edition published 1986
by Methuen London Ltd
11 New Fetter Lane, London EC4P 4EE
Copyright © 1985 by Alexander Kaletski

Reproduced, printed and bound in Great Britain by
Hazell Watson & Viney Limited,
Member of the BPCC Group,
Aylesbury, Bucks

British Library Cataloguing in Publication Data

Kaletski, Alexander
   Metro: a novel of the Moscow underground.
   I. Title
   891.73′44   PS3561.A41652

   ISBN 0-413-60420-9

To my mother, Cicilia, who gave me
freedom of choice in a country
with no freedom.

To Lena, for whom I chose another
country where I found the freedom
to write this book.

To Basha, who helped me finish this
book and gave me no choice but to
enjoy the freedom.

Moscow Metro Map

Rules and Regulations
of the Moscow Metro in Honour of Lenin

In respect to your comrade passengers:

1 The Moscow Metro stations are open from 6 a.m. to 1 a.m.
2 The price for transport is 5 kopecks per person; you have permission to take one child free, under the age of seven years.
3 There will be an extra charge of 5 kopecks for every piece of luggage larger than 60 × 40 × 20 cm. or longer than 150 cm.
4 You will be permitted to take with no extra charge: skis, children's perambulators or bicycles, sleds, musical instruments, and small garden equipment. Skis, ice skates, and all other sharp or pointed objects must be in special cases or wrapped properly.
5 In order to prevent falling you must: hold on to the banister going up or down the escalators, stand on the right side facing the direction of the movement, pass on the left only, never congregate at the bottom of the escalator.
6 Very young children must be held by the hand or carried; never let them lean on the stationary part of the banister.
7 If you drop anything on the way up or down, you must ask for assistance from the platform guard.

I love the Moscow Metro, to me there is nothing better in the entire world. Some people say there is nothing better than the Taj Mahal, but I know they're wrong. In the Moscow Metro there's a Taj Mahal at each station. Anyway, what kind of name is Taj Mahal? Taj Mahal? What a silly sound, what a tongue twister! But the word *Metro* is something else. It has a special ring to it. It speaks of beauty, harmony, and hidden strength – especially the Circle Line. This line embraces the centre of Moscow, drawing its one-hour underground circle which rings the heart of the city and connects all its nerves and arteries. There is no better place to feel the city's pulse.

Throughout the day, jam-packed trains run along the Circle Line. There is no end to the river of people, as there is no end to the circle. Alcoholics worship this line. It's their haven – there's no need to worry about being dumped out and arrested at the last stop; they can keep on circling around and around until they sober up, and the best part is that the farther they go, the closer they are to where they started.

The Metro is a world in itself – in the winter it's warm down there, cool in the summer. And it's always sparkling clean. No Russian would dream of spitting on the Metro's marble floor; he'd sooner spit on the coat of another passenger.

When I walked along the spotless platform under the high Romanesque ceilings, mosaics and crystal chandeliers all around, my entire body took in the sparkle of the station – my eyes, the whiteness of the marble walls; my hands, the pleasing feel of the nickel poles; my feet, the smoothness of the polished stone. Why the modernization of Russia started with the hanging of chandeliers beneath the earth I didn't know, but I did know that when I was underground, I felt free.

The Metro was the biggest thrill of my childhood, a miracle for five kopeck. I'll never forget the day I saw it, when my mother took me to Moscow on my seventh birthday to visit Boris – my friend from summer camp – and to see the sights of that great capital. But the moment I entered the Metro, I wasn't interested in seeing anything or going anywhere else. I just wanted to ride the Circle Line.

After several station stops, my mother said we had to get off. She took my hand and led me to the platform. She told me to be a good boy and to wait for her at the station for ten minutes, because she had to go upstairs to pick up something at the bakery. (I knew it must be my birthday cake.)

Of course I could be a good boy. . . . Good boy . . . one . . . two . . . three. . . . Birthday cake . . . one . . . two . . . three. . . . I went hopping across the polished marble squares . . . on the right foot, on the left, on the right, on the left. Oops! I tumbled down onto the floor. It was smooth, cold and slippery like ice, and I slid on it a full two metres. What fun! Then I saw a train pull into the station. I jumped to my feet. The train stopped just in front of me, its open doors beckoning to me. . . . I couldn't resist, I had to see what the next station looked like and I had ten whole minutes to get back.

Once I was on the train, it was fun to guess what colour light would flash next within the darkness of the tunnel – green . . . yellow . . . white . . . yellow . . . white . . . red . . . It was easy to guess when it would be yellow or white – they were almost always one after the other. Green was at the beginning of the tunnel, red at the end, so the most exciting part was to guess when the red light would flash through the window because, immediately afterwards, the train would fly into the station.

When the train came to a stop, I charged out onto the platform and raced through the station to the escalator. But what on earth was that? I had never seen an escalator like the one at this station. For a long time I just stood at the bottom of it in wonderment. Upward went the endless stairs. If there was an end, it certainly could not be seen from the bottom. Three deep-ribbed paths soared up and, between them, bright lights shone on golden stands.

The path was long, like life.

For a moment, I was scared to step onto that escalator, but the temptation was enormous. I swallowed the lump in my throat and took the step that separates the stationary from the moving. The escalator slid under my feet, lifting me lightly, smoothly breaking up into stairs, and carrying me in an unknown way to an unknown place.

For me, the bliss was indescribable, but there were people who couldn't keep from running even on such wonderful stairs. They were rushing somewhere, passing the ones who were standing still. The funny part was that they weren't only running down, but up, too, leaping from stair to stair, stumbling, gasping for breath, but still running. And I smiled at them. I couldn't understand them – why run when you can move without any effort and just revel in the pleasure of the smooth, constant movement.

I closed my eyes. The slight vibration was all that told me I was moving. I reached out in search of the guardrail. My fingers started walking on it like the legs of a little naked man. He pranced slowly at first, then faster and faster. In the darkness of shut eyes, I had to try hard to keep him from stumbling on the metal strips. He did okay. He ran alongside me, jumping at each seventh step. All the while, the light bulbs played like red suns through my eyelids – sunrise and sunset – alternating in a measured rhythm. At one point, I had a strange sensation – I felt as if this had happened somewhere, sometime before, as if I had run like my little man up the partition between those electric lamps. I tried to recall when it could have happened, but couldn't. After all, this was my first trip to Moscow.

I don't know who tripped first, my little man or me, but both of us fell down at once. This time, it wasn't on any smooth marble, but on the metal grating at the end of the escalator.

I tried to stand up, but there was a continuous stream of people getting off the escalator. They stepped over me, pushed me off to the side, pressed me against the divider, dragged me towards the exit, and finally forced me out into the street.

3

I scurried back inside through the other door, but smacked right into a lady controller, whose indomitable stomach blocked the way.

Knowing full well that I didn't have any money, I started digging a hole in my pocket with one hand. With the other, I was busy picking my nose.

'Mrs Ticket-taker, oh please, Mrs Ticket-taker, I came up here, but I'm supposed to be down there . . .'

Silence.

'I'm supposed to be down there, but I don't have any money.'

A solemn silence.

'Mrs Ticket-taker, I was down there just now. Please let me go back.'

'Huh?'

'Please let me pass.'

'Why should I?'

'Mrs Ticket-taker, I was going for a ride on the escalator . . . came here accidentally . . . no money . . . my mother . . . she's waiting for me.'

'Go to your damned mother if she wants to see you so much!'

'But I don't have any money . . . and it's my birthday today.'

'How old are you?'

'I'm seven,' I said with a hopeful smile.

'That's too old to go for free. Get out of my sight, you little brat!' The woman said furiously. 'Next you'll be saying you left your money on the piano!'

I had no choice but to try a psychological attack. I was an expert cryer, with a high, nerve-wracking voice. Nobody could stand it, even for a minute. I gave her the full treatment – I whined, moaned, bawled, and screeched like a siren. The woman looked at me with disdain, then took a whistle out of her pocket. I don't remember her face, but her mouth was like a crack in a brick.

'Shut up, you spastic jerk, or I'll call the police.'

I burst into tears.

Apparently, the woman didn't like my performance. She blew the whistle with all her might. The sound drove me right out of the station.

In the hot, dusty haze of the day, cars and trucks roared past me. On the pavement, a thousand feet shuffled along. Fishnet bags and briefcases swung in every direction. Everyone was in an awful hurry. For a long while, I was too afraid to ask how to get to my friend Boris's street, but finally I got up the courage.

I was told to go straight past the Garden Circle. I went looking for the garden, continued in that direction for a long time, but didn't find any trees. It was very hot; the tarred pavement felt soft and shook from the trains beneath my feet. The whole way I worried that the pavement would melt and I would plunge into the Metro's abyss.

I didn't find the garden; I didn't even see the shadows of the trees, but somehow I finally found the way to my friend's house. It was night when I arrived. I was sure I would be beaten right away, but no, first I got my birthday cake.

The birthday party was one of those arranged more for the parents than for the kids. But I didn't complain, I got a lot of great presents. The best of all was an Oriental mask – maybe it was Chinese, maybe Japanese – a laughing, high-cheekboned face with tiny slits for eyes. The first time I put on that mask and did something silly with my hands and legs (my idea of a Chinese dance), the guests went into hysterics. Perhaps it was then that my love for the theatre, that wish to make people laugh, was born.

There was something magically alive about that mask – it was flesh colour, and it had so many coats of lacquer that it was as hard as wood. The mask was topped with a blue hat with a pom-pom. It had a thick elastic band, so taut that it was difficult to put it on, but once the mask was on, it stuck to my face as if it were a part of me. It made me look like a little Oriental, with a big laughing head. The guests kept asking me to dance for them again and again, first alone, then a duet with Boris, until our mothers finally put a stop to it and sent us off to bed.

I fell asleep dreaming about the show I would put on the next day in the backyard.

I didn't need anyone to wake me in the morning. I got up, got dressed, woke Boris, pulled on my mask, fixed the pom-pom, looked in the mirror to check the funniest poses, and we hurried

5

out to the backyard. There we met a disappointment – the yard was absolutely empty. It was too early; none of the kids were playing outside yet. Dying for an audience, we ran to the iron bar fence which separated the yard from the street, but the street was empty too.

'Somebody should come along soon,' said Boris. 'Let's wait.'

We didn't have long to wait. From around the corner came a man in a grey hat and a mackintosh. He seemed deep in concentration and looked rather morose. It was perfect. I couldn't wait to make him laugh. In an attempt to get the attention of the serious passerby, I bobbed my head rhythmically like a Chinese doll. The pedestrian was staring at the ground, but somehow managed to catch a glimpse of my art, stopped, crossed the street, and came up to the fence. I added hopping to my bobbing. It was supposed to kill him, but he didn't even grin. I raised my hand to salute, tilted my head in Oriental-style bewilderment, and held the pose. The man came closer and stared at me through the fence. With all good intention, I smiled a double smile – on the mask and under it. I waited for his reaction, but he just went on staring at me gloomily, his lips down-turned. As a last resort, I started up a song in Japanese – la, la, la. It moved him. He reached in between the bars of the fence, grabbing my mask by the eye slits, and pulled. I continued my la, la, la, while he slowly and forcefully pulled the mask towards himself. Believing he wanted to get a better look at my lovely mask, I kept smiling. The stranger kept pulling the mask and stretched the elastic to its limit. When I was finally squeezed against the iron fence, I stopped my singing. There was a pause . . . and silence . . . and then he let go of the mask. It smashed my face with a terrible blow, knocking me down unconscious.

When I came to, I heard giggling. I was lying on the ground; Boris stood on top of me, laughing and pointing. My mask laughed back at him, but behind the mask flowed tears. The tears were invisible to him, and that made them even more bitter.

That was my first experience with acting. I had forgotten all about it and, perhaps, would never have remembered it if life hadn't struck me again – many years later.

1 A Muscovite

I walked down the dusty platform of the Tula Railway Station checking one car after another in a search for the right conductor. Each car has a conductor, each conductor needs money, but the 'right' conductor needs money desperately and has, as I had been told, special markings – bloodshot eyes and, better yet, a red nose. It was difficult to make a choice. I had no experience in such things and, to me, all of the conductors seemed to have the same drunken look.

I had promised myself that I wouldn't be afraid, but I couldn't stop the panic from welling up inside my stomach. What if I chose the wrong conductor? Would he turn me in? And, if he did, what would happen to me? I had heard so many stories – what was I to believe? I was only nineteen years old and all I knew I had learned in my home of Tula, a provincial, industrial city 180 kilometres from the capital. But one thing I learned in this province for certain: that getting a ticket for the crowded Tula-Moscow Express was virtually impossible. Every day, half of Tula's population was climbing onto this train to go to the capital to buy food for the other half of Tula. I had tried – and failed – to get a ticket for over a week. And now there was no time left . . . I had to be in Moscow.

I choked down my fear and kept walking along the side of the train, searching for the conductor with the worst hangover. I was losing hope, when at the end of the track I finally found him.

He was swaying to and fro on the edge of the platform. I watched him as he checked the passengers' tickets. At first, he would succeed in grabbing only the air, then, when he found a ticket, he would squeeze it as if it were a bird that might fly off. With nearly blind eyes, he would attempt to examine its markings,

7

then shake his head in despair, and grunt: 'Get on.' We were meant for each other.

I manoeuvered towards him, looking around idly, feeling sure that everyone was staring at me. But I stoked up what was left of my courage, got close to him so no one could hear our conversation, and whispered: 'Can you take me to Moscow?'

'What do you mean – you don't have a ticket?' he said much too loudly.

'No, no. I have one,' I said quickly, 'but I forgot it at home, on the piano.'

'That's not too good,' he said thoughtfully.

I took my chance: 'I thought maybe we could work something out.'

He shook his head.

'Why?'

'It's illegal,' he said, not too convincingly.

'Come on,' I pleaded.

'The controllers are already aboard,' he whined. 'I can't do a thing. If not for the controllers . . . maybe.'

I could see that in his heart he was willing. He just needed a little incentive. I got closer to his ear, waited until a silence hung over us like a weight. Then I broke it with a whisper: 'I've got a bottle,' I said. The weight fell.

A long time ago in the Soviet Union, the monetary unit was devalued to bottles; one bottle equalled 3.12 rubles. The conductors know that the legal way to travel is to buy a ticket at the station for two bottles. But if a passenger pays them personally with one bottle, it may be illegal, but it's much better for them and the passenger.

'How much luggage do you have?' he asked.

'Only one bag and a guitar.'

'Step aboard,' he said, 'but watch out for the controllers. Go to the bar and hide in the crowd.'

I did it! I was on the Tula-Moscow Express!

'Express' was just a name, because this train was slower than any local . . . as we say, it stopped at every telegraph pole. But the cars of that 'express' were very modern – they had no compartments, they looked more like the inside of a bus, with

8

only one difference: all the seats faced the back, so it felt as if you were moving all the way in reverse. To avoid nausea, the passengers tried escape to the bar.

It was a lucky day for me, the bar of the train was stocked with beer. Even in the Moscow supermarkets, beer can be found only once a week. Before everyone on the train queued up, I was one of the first hundred people standing in line. The queue moved surprisingly fast and, within forty-five minutes, I was already near the counter. But then the shrill voice of the bartender rang out in the car: 'Comrade citizens, pass the word down the line that the beer is nearly gone. There is only one case left.'

I quickly sized up the situation – there were eight people ahead of me and twelve bottles of beer. The fortunate ones up front grabbed a few bottles and disappeared. Five people and seven bottles. The tension was mounting. Four and six. Just then, one woman took three bottles. What greed!

A chorus of angry voices filled the car.

'What the hell do you think you're doing with three bottles?'

'Even the men are taking only one.'

'Where did she get all that money?'

'Don't give her anything!'

'No women!'

'What is she going to do with it, wash the laundry?'

The woman knew exactly what she was doing. With three bottles, she was like a queen, and men were already making a ring around her.

Three men and three bottles! I lost hope.

Two bottles and two men!

One bottle and a mean-looking man, his face creased with wrinkles, his fist full of crumpled bills. The bartender reached out to give him the last bottle; the line froze. But the old man pushed aside the beer with his bony hand and said in a gentle voice:

'Oh no, dear boy. I haven't used beer for a long time. My health isn't what it used to be. I'm better off with a bottle of vodka.'

What a nice old man. I couldn't believe my eyes – right there in front of me stood the last bottle of beer. I touched its warm

9

neck. I hugged it tenderly and headed for the door. Everybody made way. They had all just witnessed a miracle called luck. I leaned against the train door, took a key out of my pocket, and slowly started to open my darling. I placed the key beneath the wavy cap, hooking the notch to the edge, and cautiously pulled up. The bottle whispered and bubbled.

I eased the key under another notch and another. The cap went flying; foam burst out of the bottle and, just as I raised the bottle to my mouth, I felt somebody tapping me on the shoulder. I stiffened. A controller? I turned slowly, expecting to see the stern face of authority. But no, it was a bearded, little man with a kepi on his head, dangling a tiny fish in front of my face.

'Listen, let's make a deal, huh? I'll give you the tail and fins, you give me a glass of beer, huh? No good, huh? Okay, if there's any roe inside, you get that too, huh? No? Come on. Okay, let's go halves – half a fish for you, half a bottle for me, huh? Hey, it's a real live dried fish . . . Wait, don't drink. Okay, you win. I'll give you half a fish and some vodka. Yeah, you heard me, vodka! Anyway, I can't drink vodka without beer. Let's make a "yorsh."'

I said nothing. I didn't want to draw any attention so I let the little man have his way. He quickly shoved two glasses at me, poured out his vodka and added my beer, bit into the tail of the fish and split it down the middle. What could I do? We clanged glasses and drank.

'Yorsh' goes two ways – the vodka goes straight to your head; the beer to your feet. It felt good. We smiled at each other and pressed our foreheads against the windowpane. Through the glass, amid the starting drizzle, flew the incomparable Soviet landscape – mostly bill-boards of Lenin's sayings alternating with his slogans in red stones on the hills:

COMMUNISM WILL BE THE HAPPY FUTURE OF ALL HUMAN BEINGS
COMMUNISM = THE SOVIET REGIME PLUS ELECTRIFICATION OF THE COUNTRY
THIS GENERATION WILL WITNESS COMMUNISM.

'Listen, my friend,' the stranger said, breathing on the glass. His cap, pressed against the window, was standing up revealing a bald spot. 'What's your name, huh?'

'Sasha.'

'What do you think, Sash, which generation did Lenin have in mind when he said, "This generation will witness communism," the one that lived back then; my generation; or yours?'

'I've never given it much thought,' I said tentatively. One doesn't discuss politics with strangers. Sometimes, one shouldn't discuss politics even with friends.

We continued to drink as we stared out the window.

The rain was coming down harder, and the drops were running in diagonals on the outside of the window. On the inside, the glass was fogged up by our breath, and the red sayings were turning into a blur:

EVERY DAY, LIFE IN THE SOVIET UNION GETS BETTER AND . . .
STUDY, STUDY, AND ONCE AGAIN . . .

'Where do you live? In Tula?'

'Yes,' I said.

'So, you're a Tulyak?'

'I was a Tulyak, now I'm a Muscovite,' I proclaimed proudly.

'You must be studying in Moscow.'

'I'm going to.'

'Tell me, do you know Tula well?'

'Pretty well,' I modestly replied.

'I've heard the factories there produce very good guns.'

I wondered what he was getting at. 'Yes,' I said mildly, 'they're supposed to be good.'

'What do you think, is it possible to get a rifle without permission, huh? I don't have a hunting permit, but I want to do some shooting.'

I quickly looked around to see if anybody was listening. No one was. I turned back to face the little man, wondering if he could be an *agent provocateur*, trying to make me incriminate myself. But the thought seemed ridiculous. He was just a drunk man with a loose tongue. I decided to tell him what everyone in Tula knew. I said, 'The workers at the factory steal weapons by the dozens. With a few bottles under the table, I bet you could get a machine gun, not just a rifle.'

11

'Hey, that's not a bad idea,' he said brightly. 'I think if I don't get weapons in Moscow I'll go back to Tula tomorrow and get myself a rifle *and* a machine gun.'

My curiosity got the better of me. 'And what do you need such an arsenal for?' I asked.

'A rifle for the wolves, and a machine gun for the moose. You know what I mean?'

'Not quite.'

'I'm sick and tired of them, understand?'

'Not exactly.'

'Well, I'll tell you, but first, let's have another shot, huh? A long story is always good to make a trip short.'

We drank. . . .

'I live on a collective farm a hundred kilometres from Moscow,' he began. 'Life wasn't so bad there until the day the City Council decided to raise bull moose in a nearby forest. Maybe the purpose was to provide the Party bosses with something to hunt; maybe to show the world how plentiful our wildlife is; what they really wanted, nobody knows for sure, but the fact is, our lives changed when they started their new campaign.

'First they put up statues of bull moose with antlers painted silver. Then they began to bring in live moose from all over the country. There were some moose already in our forest but, once the campaign was underway, they brought in more, from as far away as bloody Siberia. Next they posted a new law – THE KILLING OF BULL MOOSE IS EQUIVALENT TO MURDER.'

'Oh, I remember seeing a poster about it,' I said. 'I couldn't see why it was such a serious crime.'

'For us, it was a crime, but the wolves couldn't read the posters. They started pouncing on the moose. One bull moose was found ripped apart, then another, and another. The City Council was outraged, and a new law was posted – KILL WOLVES INDISCRIMINATELY.

'The bounty for each paw was one bottle. This was just what the farmers had been waiting for all their lives. They threw down their hoes and instantly took up their rifles. What an opportunity – shoot one wolf, get four bottles; shoot two, get eight. To keep the wolves from running away, they put red flags around the

12

forest. Within a week, all the wolves were lying dead, their paws amputated.

'With no more wolves around, the moose took over the forest. All day, they ambled along, knocking off branches and revelling in the sight of their statues. There were so many of them that there seemed to be more antlers than branches in the forest.

'But then, suddenly, they began to die – probably from some disease carried from Siberia. If the wolves had still been around, they would have eaten the sick moose, and there would be no problem, but instead, the sick animals roamed with the herd, spreading their disease.

'Can you imagine a disease like that so close to Moscow? Pestilence! What a shock to the City Council. It could turn into a nationwide scandal. And what official wants to end up replacing a bull moose in Siberia?

'Meetings were held day and night and, finally, those intellectuals found a solution – "The dead wolves must be replaced. WOLVES ARE THE REFUSE COLLECTORS OF NATURE."'

'You must be kidding; it's impossible!' I said, getting dizzy from the yorsh and this conversation.

'It's true, I suppose they decided that wolves had to work just like everybody else; as the Party says: "Those who don't work, don't eat."'

'Well, that's logical,' I said, thinking it's better to agree with the Party.

'Teams were set up in nearby areas where wolves still ran wild. The wolves were caught, put in cages, deprived of food, and then set free in our forest. Next, the City Council announced its new policy – THE CRIME OF SHOOTING A WOLF IS PUNISHABLE BY DEATH. THE WOLF IS A FRIEND OF MAN. A monument to the Unknown Wolf was erected on the highway.

'Meanwhile, in the forest, the wolves were in a quandary. The stench of rotting flesh was everywhere. They found the moose that were still moving unappetizing. So, instead of eating this carrion, the wolves headed for the animals on the farm.

'They attacked whole herds of cattle and the only thing the herdsmen could do was wave their shotguns at them because, as I said, shooting a wolf was punishable by death.

'The wolves' feast went well, but didn't last very long – you know how much meat there is on a collective farm. Next they started looking for something else to dig into, and set their sights on the chickens and the geese. What were the farmers to do but hide their animals inside the house?

'So you see what a lovely mess we're in. During the day, we have smelly moose milling about; at night, wolves howling in the vegetable patch and chickens flying around inside the house. But that's not all. A few days ago, a neighbour's boy was on his way to the outhouse when he was dragged into the forest by a wolf.

'That's when I decided that if anything should happen to my little girl, I wasn't going to put up with this any longer. I'd go on a shooting spree – first the wolves, then the moose and, who knows, maybe even the City Council. I just hope I'll be able to get my hands on enough bullets. I know myself; once I start shooting, I can't stop; that's why they took away my hunting permit.'

He abruptly turned away and looked out the window.

What could I say after a story like that? Was I supposed to believe it? Was I supposed to laugh? Or was I supposed to report him? Well I certainly couldn't do the last. So I just smiled innocently when he looked back at me and I said, 'Let's have another,' and I filled the glasses to the brim.

His eyes narrowed. 'Guns in Tula? Right?' he whispered.

The safest thing to do was to take his question literally. There *were* guns in Tula – factories full of them. I nodded my head.

He smiled with satisfaction and happily changed the subject, saying, 'You said you were going to be studying in Moscow?'

'That's right,' I replied, relieved.

'Where?'

'At the Theatre Institute. Just last week, I got my letter of acceptance. Today is the first day of classes.'

'I should have guessed; a good-looking young fellow like you – of course, you were born to be a film star! Why didn't you say so sooner? We've got to celebrate! Let's have the third one.'

Fourth – I thought, as we clanged glasses and drank. This time both parts of the yorsh travelled straight to my head.

14

'Sash, I heard it's almost impossible to get into the Theatre Institute. The competition must be awfully steep.'

'Yes, it's pretty tough.'

'How many applications for each place?'

'I don't know, something like four hundred, maybe more.'

'Oh boy, more than the moose in our forest! That's really some competition. How did you get in?'

'Luck.'

'Huh?'

I smiled. Losing my inhibitions in a blur of beer and vodka, I explained: 'After secondary school, I studied at the Ammunitions Institute in Tula for almost a year, but I hated it. It got so bad that in desperation I picked up a pack of cards and decided that if the first card I drew was the ace of clubs, I would give up arms and turn to art. I had dreamed about being in the theatre and films but thought it was impossible to get into a good acting school. This time I let fate decide. I placed the cards on the table, cut the pack, and, would you believe it, on the first try, picked up the ace of clubs!'

The little man with the kepi looked at me, incredulously.

'It's true. But I must admit,' I added with a laugh, 'I would've kept cutting the pack all night until I got that ace.

'Anyway, everything was settled. I went to the dean and told him I was dropping out of school. He was famous for kicking people out but, apparently, hated it when someone left on his own. "If you dare drop out," he warned me, "I'll see to it that the army gets you – and then we'll see how cavalier you are! And if you go through with this, I'll *enjoy* seeing you ruined!"

'I said, "Thank you, sir," and dropped out anyway.

'The very next day, the local Recruiting Centre ordered me to appear with my passport. I obeyed orders, like a fool, thinking I might be able to get into the Theatre Institute by the autumn, but the commanding officer took my passport, locked it up in a safe, and said I would have to enlist with a special group of recruits, and should show up in the morning with a shaved head.

'The next morning I didn't go to the barber; I managed to get a ride on a milk truck to Moscow for the first round of entrance exams at the Theatre Institute. Fortunately, I wasn't asked for documents, probably because so many people had come. I suppose I did a pretty good job of reading the prose and poetry, because they gave me a permission slip to go on to the second round. With this paper in hand, I went back to Tula to see the commanding officer at the Recruiting Centre. "Arrest that deserter!" he shouted when he saw me.

'I handed him the paper, which stated that I was a second-stage applicant at the Theatre Institute. He could not believe I had got through the exam without a passport, and kept checking and rechecking the seal on the document. Finally, he let me go with these parting words: "Future recruit and deserter, when you are thrown out in the second round and come back here, I will personally see to it that you are shipped out in an atomic submarine. In four years, you will come back bald from radiation, with no thoughts of acting in your head. Your only concern will be how to keep yourself from being shipped out on another tour of duty. And, just to be on the safe side, I'm going to keep an eye on you. A very sharp eye." He wrote something in my file that I couldn't see. Then, he looked up at me and said darkly, "We'll get you sooner or later."

'Maybe he was right about later,' I said to the little man, 'but for now, I am a student at the Theatre Institute. I was accepted after the fourth and final round. It's more than an acceptance, it means I won't be called up for four years. I won a small battle against the Soviet army!'

My companion smiled broadly and announced, 'We've got to drink to this!' He poured the rest of the two bottles into our glasses.

'To our enemies!' I said without thinking, and, on the foggy window, finger-drew the head of a moose. . . .

We clinked glasses and gulped down the remaining vodka and beer. He pulled his kepi off his head and bellowed: 'Kill them indiscriminately,' and in a flash, wiped the antlered animal from the window-pane. Through the clean window, we were astonished to see the wall of the Moscow Railway Station!

We rushed off the train and hurried out to the street to the trolleybus stop. The rain had let up, and the red sun was filtering through the clouds. On the tracks a brigade of railway employees was at work. Two men stood on each side with red flags, while ten women pounded the ties with mallets. With each stroke, their skirts flopped up, revealing blue and pink woollies. We stepped over the vibrating tracks and went to the trolleybus. It was time to part company and I felt terribly awkward. I never did like farewells.

I watched my strange friend hop up the steps of the trolleybus and, with hat in hand, he waved to me.

'Good-bye,' I shouted after him. 'Hey, what's your name?'

'Kepi,' he called back mysteriously. 'So long.'

His bald spot flashed in the setting sun; it was only then that I realized how terribly much he resembled Lenin.

The trolleybus went around the square, heading right into the sun, gobbling it up. Then it disappeared around a corner.

Something felt strange; my left arm was numb and I was dizzy. At the stop, there was a big bench with heavy metal legs. All that remained of the seat was one wooden slat; I perched on it. My strength had melted. Beads of sweat covered my forehead. I wasn't ill; I was scared. Why did I have to tell so much about myself to that man? A total stranger! What made me do it? And that toast I made: 'To our enemies!' I groaned at the memory. But maybe, I thought hopefully, I'm just drunk. That's it . . . I'm drunk. Why should I worry about a strange old man who happens to look like Lenin?

I took a deep breath to calm my nerves and looked at the brave provincials streaming in and out of the railway station. They reminded me of prospectors panning for gold as they went in search of meat, sausages, tangerines, and macaroni in the grocery shops of Moscow. These gold diggers were easy to spot, they were wrinkled and sleepy but full of nervous energy and they always carried bread, fruit in a fishnet bag, or bottles of vodka.

A smile creased my lips as I watched them, and all thoughts of 'Kepi' flew from my mind. 'Ah, country folks, country folks, today I happily tear myself away from you. From now on, I'm not a Tulyak, I'm a Muscovite!'

2 The First Day of School

I had only one friend in Moscow, Boris, who was now studying at the Architecture Institute. Without him, Moscow could be a very lonely city. I knew that for me it would take a few months to cultivate new friendships at the Theatre Institute. But loneliness never scared me. I was used to loneliness. Boris would probably accuse me of preferring that solitary state. People would come up to me and I would be friendly, but why, Boris asked me, would I never go to them first? If I only knew *why*.

Aloof, distant, unfeeling – these were the words Boris used to attack me. And those were the words against which I had no defence. But though I never spoke in rebuttal, I often wondered how Boris could still be my friend if all of what he said was true. Maybe we were friends because I was the only one who would accept such harsh criticism without punching him in the face. Or maybe we were friends because he took on trust that I did, indeed, have the feelings that I never showed. He was my oldest friend and often, very often, I wished that I could have shown him how I felt. But I just kept quiet, listened, observed – and let his friendship swirl about me just as I let everything and everybody else orbit around my world, circling but never touching me.

And though, as per usual, I didn't show it, I was glad when Boris and his friend from the Architecture Institute, Youssef, the son of the Sudanese Ambassador, came along with me on Orientation Day. They wanted to see what sort of girls were accepted by the country's leading acting school.

Youssef and Boris watched as long-legged beauties came up to me, asking my name, congratulating me on passing the entrance examination, and kissing me on the mouth! I was shy and blushed terribly. I had never seen or heard about such free expression. In

18

Tula, you could be arrested on the spot for such behaviour in public.

Youssef evaluated the flow of hugs and kisses like a sophisticated punter picking a winner at the track. He was handsome, intelligent, and talented, and sure that each girl would fall in love with him at first sight. He had everything a Russian girl dreams about – washed-out blue jeans with dark spots where pockets had once been, a foreign accent, a tape recorder, and a car. When Youssef drove his ivory-coloured Volkswagen, not only girls, but everybody would turn to stare at him, because Youssef was one of the few blacks in Moscow. Before he came to the Soviet Union, he had studied in all the best universities in Europe, and had been thrown out of each one because of his propensity for cognac.

That day outside school, leaning against the fence, Youssef was engaged in his favourite activities – sipping Pliska brandy from the bottle and checking the feminine shapes in the crowd around the Institute. Suddenly, he drew back; a golden droplet trickled over his full lower lip, across his chin, down his neck, and disappeared under his shirt. His face lit up with a blank but fiery expression as he pulled in his paunch and assumed a dignified pose. All of us turned to see what had caused the surprise. We encountered amber cat's eyes and bangs with a silver streak, belonging to a thin, captivating girl who walked in a stately manner through the crowd, neither hugging nor kissing, nor even saying hello.

'Holy sh – ' said Youssef.

'Who is she?' demanded Boris.

'I don't know,' I said.

That's how I saw Lena for the first time. Without a doubt, she was the most beautiful girl in the crowd. But that day, I didn't share my friend's awe, for I was anxiously awaiting another girl with whom I had had an unusual encounter a half year before.

I had gone to the cinema one afternoon in Tula. My seat happened to be next to a girl who certainly didn't look as if she was from around there. Tula girls always looked different – with their wrestler's shoulders, soccer player's legs, and boxer's jaw. That athletic combination could arouse fear, but never thoughts of love. This stranger was surely from another place, where the compelling force of nature was not strength, but beauty.

The film was about some rowdy factory workers who drank in solitude, fought, made peace with each other, and finally drank collectively. I can't recollect the name of that masterpiece, but I never did forget how that stranger and I touched knees. From the start, it was by accident, but then not so accidentally. It was so interesting that when the end of the film was signalled by one of Lenin's quotations on the screen – 'CINEMATOGRAPHY IS THE MOST SPLENDID OF ALL THE ARTS' – we were in absolute agreement with the vanguard of the Revolution. But the ushers, who had their own interpretation of that line, inconsiderately herded us out of the cinema.

On the street, we walked in close proximity, but I couldn't muster the courage to take her hand in mine. In the darkness of the movie theatre, our legs did everything by themselves, but in the daylight, I didn't know what to do next; I just blushed, mumbled a few words, and slipped away.

All that week, I wandered through the streets clutching a bouquet of forget-me-nots, hoping against hope to meet her again. If only Boris had seen me then. No feelings?

On Sunday night, I dragged myself to see a visiting theatrical troupe from Kiev that was on tour in our city. I expected the usual crap, but I needed something therapeutic for my pining heart.

Determined to come out of my tailspin, I finally tossed the bouquet into a litter bin in the lobby and went to my seat. But, when the curtain opened, I saw my stranger on the stage! I couldn't believe it. My eyes followed her every move. During the intermission I checked the programme; her name was J. Silver. She had a minor part, but I naturally thought she stole the show.

Right after the performance, I rushed down to the lobby for my bouquet. The litter bin was filled to the brim with smoking cigarette butts and empty bottles. I ran outside. I darted from corner to corner, searching for a flower stall. Maybe you can buy a machine gun in the middle of the night in Tula, but not a single flower. Running, and out of breath, I got back to the theatre only to find that all the performers had left. I returned the very next morning and was told that the troupe had gone back to Kiev.

I thought that was the end of it, but I met her again in Moscow at the Theatre Institute during my entrance examinations. She recognized me on the spot and surprised me by giving me a hug. I asked her what she was doing there. She said she had come to Moscow in the hope of becoming a film star, married a Muscovite to get permission to live in the capital, and, while waiting to be discovered, worked as a secretary at the Institute. But then she leaned close to me and said, 'My husband is away. Meet me for dinner tonight?'

My last round of exams was the next day. Besides, she was married. I was torn, but I clenched my teeth and turned her down. I hated doing it – and there were many nights afterwards when I wished I had made a different choice.

But now I was back, waiting for her on Orientation Day.

She came out of the main building, dressed in a brown suit. She seemed very businesslike; only her bright red lipstick gave her away. She looked my way, waved, but didn't come over. I sensed that what had taken place between us was finished. Or perhaps it was only that her husband was in Moscow now. In any event, she glanced at some papers in her hand and announced that the freshmen should line up in front of the building for a class picture.

Boris grabbed me by the arm and proposed that I come over after school and bring 'Amber Eyes.' It looked as if Youssef wasn't the only one with a crush on that girl. I replied, dryly, that I probably wouldn't be able to help them out since I didn't know who she was and had no idea how I could meet her. That was hardly a satisfying answer, but it had to do, because directly after we posed for the class picture it was time to file into the auditorium for the orientation session.

In his opening address, the Dean, who had played Field Marshal Kutuzov in the film *War and Peace* and had never got out of that role, in a tone of self-congratulation stated that we should be proud that this Institute would be our home for the next four years. He said we would be exposed to all the secrets of the Russian theatre, built on the great Method of Stanislavsky, then updated and entirely revised by the great Vakhtangov. He pointed out that in the West, minority groups such as Negroes and Puerto Ricans had no possibility of exhibiting their talent on the stage and had to resort to exhibiting it on the streets. Here in the Soviet Union, the doors of the temple of art were open to all minority groups and so, he said, the Institute had accepted, on an experimental basis, the Chechen, Filatov; the Chookcha, Mazgavoy; and the Tartar, Aliluyev, without examinations. 'Congratulate them, comrades,' the Field Marshal roared as if on parade. Everybody clapped and, in distant corners of the auditorium, three squat, dark-haired men stood up.

'We are one big, happy family here,' the Dean cried out exuberantly. 'Just like the posh, private schools of the past, this Institute provides anywhere from three to five teachers for each student – '

'Could you tell me what criteria will be used to determine the number of teachers for each student?' piped up a giant, pink-cheeked fellow sitting right next to me. 'If it depends on weight, I would like to ask the administration for five teachers.'

It was so unexpected at a formal assembly that the whole auditorium burst out laughing.

The Dean, one eye closed like Kutuzov, tried to regain command by screaming, 'No, no, young man, it will be based on talent!'

'Well, in that case, I don't need even one,' the huge fellow quipped, twisting his massive frame towards the rows behind us, then catching my eye as he turned back towards the front.

A pause lingered in the auditorium while everyone tried to comprehend the ambiguous retort, then chatter and laughter filled the room.

'Silence, comrade students!' the angry Field Marshal shouted. 'Now, for the most important thing.'

Everyone settled down.

'For the first two weeks of school, you have to contribute to the welfare of your country. This semester is going to begin at a vegetable storage house. The boys will be unloading potatoes, and the girls will be sorting and cleaning cabbage.'

22

'You mean the boys will work by the Stanislavsky Method and the girls by the Vakhtangov Method?' the voice next to me called out.

The Dean would have surely expelled the oversized student on the spot had not the entire auditorium exploded with laughter. Instead, the Dean quickly brought his speech to a close and dismissed us with a haughty gesture.

I went outside, paused on the steps to consider the best way to get to the dorm, and walked towards the trolleybus stop.

'Hey!' someone called out behind me. 'Are you going to the dormitory?'

'Yes.'

'How about going together? My name is Stas,' the blubbery giant who had sat next to me said by way of introduction. 'But you're not going by trolleybus, are you? Come on, let's take a taxi.'

I wasn't sure I wanted to get involved with – let alone be seen with – this obvious troublemaker. But he wanted to travel by taxi. This I had to see.

Getting a taxi in Moscow is equivalent to winning the government lottery – the possibility in both cases is nil. But Stas had his own system. He marched right out into the middle of the street and stopped the traffic like a policeman, then approached a cab driver who was cursing out the window. He bent down, flashed his red student I.D. card in the driver's face, and whispered, 'Keep quiet, this is government business. Trifonov Street, and make it snappy.'

The driver was quickly cowed. Stas opened the back door and got into the rear seat. The cab sank under his weight.

'Squeeze in,' he chuckled. 'Now isn't this better than the trolley-bus? Seriously, public transportation is detrimental to your health. Take it from me; health is everything.'

He opened his attaché case and took out a bag filled with plastic and glass vials bearing colourful labels. He took a pill out of one of the vials and popped it in his mouth.

'What are the pills for?' I asked, peering at his chemist's shop.

'This is for my heart; this is for my liver; this one is for my

23

stomach; this is for my kidneys; and this is for my spleen. Through these pills, I have absolute control over my metabolism.'

I laughed. Stas continued without even a hint of a smile.

'My mother is a doctor. She sends me all the latest medical innovations. Only the imported ones, of course. Our domestic medicine,' he said, stressing *domestic*, 'is only good when you're ready to die. Soviet medicine and death have a close-knit relationship.'

I had never heard anyone speak like this before; that probably went for the driver too; he kept stealing glances at Stas through the rearview mirror.

'Some people collect stamps from all over the world, but I collect medicine and even experiment on my self,' Stas continued. 'Fortunately, all my life I've had a lot of sickness – hypertension, rheumatism, diabetes, asthma, arterial sclerosis . . . ah, it's impossible to name all of them. I was a unique child; I had all the illnesses of an adult. I got over arthritis when other kids were getting over chicken pox. I was so emaciated that X-rays were unnecessary – the doctors simply held me up to the window. My transparent and twitching atrophic and hypertrophic organs always surprised the doctors by their uncoordinated and wild workings.

'Specialists from all over the Union flew around me like flies around rubbish. Each saw in my dystrophy a complete dissertation. Each tried to cultivate within me the sickness he specialized in, to the detriment of the others. But I was a clever kid and realized that only all the sicknesses together in their abominable harmony would bring about a healthy balance. That's why my mommychka and I never gave ourselves to only one specialist. You can see the results of our work,' he said, while running his fingers through his wavy hair with pride.

The cab driver turned to get a better look at Stas. Fortunately, we were stopped for a red light.

'You can't imagine how many deadly diseases are hidden within my body,' Stas went on lackadaisically. 'I bet the army could use me as a secret weapon, in time of crisis. If our military operations weren't going well, they could send me out alone against the opposition. I would cut out a few pills the night before and, in the morning, a horrendous, deadly bacteria would crawl to the enemy line, wiping them out faster than any atomic bomb. If I may say so myself, I'm a national treasure!'

While he was telling me all this, he gulped down one pill after another. After each, he took a swallow of tea from a small thermos that he kept in his attaché case.

'Okay, driver, pull over,' Stas said, leaning forward to hand the driver a three-ruble bill. But before the driver took it, Stas drew back, the bill still between his fingers. He started to inspect it and mumbled, regretfully, 'Oh, I'm sorry, I think I dropped this one in the epidemic research lab. Ugh! There is even a piece of scab stuck to the bill.' He proceeded to pick at the corner of the bill with his nail, then blew on it, and said, 'That's better. Here you are.'

'I don't need your money; keep it!' cried the driver. 'Don't touch the handles: I will let you out myself.' He jumped out, went around the cab, and opened the back door like an automaton.

'How nice,' said Stas, unperturbed, holding out his hand for the driver to support.

The driver sprang back, dived into the car, and, the moment we were out of the cab, took off at break-neck speed.

'Now,' said Stas, 'wait here for me; I have to pick something up.'

I stood there completely dumbfounded. Was Stas crazy? Or was *I* the crazy one to be standing there waiting for him? I'd never met anyone like him – and I think that's why I kept on waiting. I was an actor – and an actor was *supposed* to observe. Perhaps, at bottom, the profession perfectly suited that part of my nature. And now I was in Moscow, at the Theatre Institute, and there was so much more for me to observe. . . .

Stas rushed out of the dormitory carrying a teapot and said, 'Okay, we'll fill this with wine, let's go to the tracks.'

I had no idea why we were going to some tracks to get wine, but I didn't bother to ask. I already had some confidence in my new friend and understood I could learn a lot from him, so I just went along. We went down Trifonov Street, then turned right in the direction of Riga Railway Station. It was dark by the time we got there, and what looked like an oil tank was mounted on abandoned railway tracks which came to a dead end. Nobody was around, but as soon as we stepped onto the tracks, the glow of a cigarette emerged from under the wheels and asked with a deep Georgian accent,

'How much?'

'A teapotful,' said Stas.

'Gimme.'

Stas held out the teapot towards the cigarette light. A rubber tube reached from the top of the tank to the teapot. A tiny light darted off to one side. There was a sucking noise, burbling, then in front of us appeared the teapot, filled to the brim with an intoxicating liquid, and the glow of the cigarette returned to its place under the wheels. Stas took hold of the teapot carefully, crouched down towards the light tank, and whispered something. There was a laugh, but it was strange, it was like a woman laughing with a man's voice. The flickering glow of the cigarette jumped out onto the tracks, spraying specks of light across the railway, and then went out.

'Don't we have to pay?' I asked Stas.

'Oh, no. He's a dear, dear friend of mine,' he said with a playful wink.

'What kind of friend?'

'It doesn't matter. We have got the wine,' said Stas, changing the subject. 'Now, let's go to the supermarket for *game*, and then back to the dorm to celebrate our first day at school.'

Stas had a habit of calling poultry 'game,' and when we got to the supermarket, I found out why. Stas didn't plead with the saleslady like the babushka in front of us: 'Please, if it's not too much trouble, could you give me one little minute of your time, I beg you, the chicken over there, on the left side near your finger, yes, yes! The one that's not so blue. Ah, I see, I'm sorry, it's already been reserved. What about that one, with the ink stamp on the chest and the feathers on its neck, is that one possible?'

The saleswoman randomly poked one chicken after another, unexpectedly bumping into the right one, and the babushka screamed, 'Yes, right! How did you know? Thank you. Thank you so much. How much is it?'

The saleswoman silently flung the arthritic bird onto the scale.

But instead of watching the scale, the customer sadly stared at the swinging, bony neck, covered with feathers, and the tiny head, with an upside-down beak and frozen, glassy eyes. 'Three-fifty. Pay the cashier and hurry it up!' the saleswoman squawked, waking the babushka out of her reverie.

No, Stas's style was nothing like that babushka's. He attacked first: 'Hurry up, miss.'

The fiftyish 'miss' balked, her bloody eyes rising, her jaw twitching in forewarning.

'Don't play the coquette with me!' Stas said.

The 'miss' flexed her neck muscles and began to breathe heavily through her nostrils.

'Why are you serving me without a smile?' Stas taunted.

At the very moment the saleslady decided to bring a leg of lamb down on Stas's head, and the store manager appeared in the doorway, cleaver in hand, Stas, cool and calculating, disarmed all with a most charming smile. 'Comrade manager, I must congratulate you on your fine staff. Never have I seen such impartiality! Your saleslady here didn't give me any special treatment. She treated me like an ordinary customer, as prescribed by Soviet law. I really must tell my father that, in this store, everybody is truly equal.'

The manager and saleslady scrutinized Stas's large body and respectable, full face. They probably sensed that they had seen him before, perhaps on a poster, or TV, or maybe it was his father, whom he resembled. The fight was over, and a new performance was underway.

MANAGER: Did you find something unsatisfactory?

STAS: No! Everything down to the smallest detail was perfect.

SALESLADY: Excuse me, please. What did you ask for?

STAS: Game, that is, the most ordinary chicken you have.

MANAGER: (Taking a plump, yellow robust chicken from under the counter) Will this one do?

STAS: (Checking the label) Oh! A Hollandaise! My father likes Dutch girls. Ha! Ha! Ha! Excuse me, how much?

SALESLADY: Two-eighty.

STAS: (To the manager) Once again, I want to express my thanks. I honestly appreciate the superb service here.

Stas called it 'the reversal strategy.' He said there was only one way to win friends: through spilling blood. And he was so right . . . in more ways than I could have ever guessed.

I will not expound on how Stas cooked his game without spices, herbs, or oil – it is an arcane process, and it isn't for me to reveal his culinary craft, but the truth is that I've never seen a more appetizing, juicy, golden-brown chicken.

Stas emptied his glass of wine, winked at me, got up, and took a tiny scalpel from under his pillow. 'A gift from my mommychka,' he said ominously, and started to carve the Hollandaise like a surgeon. 'If you want, you can live in my room,' he added. 'Right now, three of these beds are free; you can choose one, but first, I must warn you,' he looked at me strangely and lifted the sharp, glistening scalpel, from which drops of juice fell, 'I have a bad habit when it comes to game – I never eat the breast; I only eat what is below the waist, so the upper part will be yours,' he said, putting a moist chicken breast onto my plate. 'Eat up, because every time I cook, uninvited guests appear.' Stas was right; in a minute there was a knock at the door. He shrugged his shoulders. 'See what I mean?' Stas stood up and opened the door.

'Good life. Good life,' said the Tartar, Aliluyev, hero of the assembly, as he came into the room, sniffing and squinting his black eyes at the table. 'Why didn't you invite me?'

'Because though the proletariat should unite, it's better for actors to be separate,' said Stas.

'What's that supposed to mean?' the Tartar flared angrily.

'Nothing, nothing,' Stas said with a smile.

The Tartar saw Stas's mocking grin. Quickly, he glanced around the room and saw that there were some extra beds. 'Are you the only two living here so far?' he challenged.

'Yes,' I admitted, much to Stas's annoyance.

The Tartar's black eyes turned to slits. 'Then I'll move in here, too,' he announced defiantly, glaring at Stas.

'That's not a very good idea,' Stas replied quickly.

The Tartar clenched his hands into fists. 'What are you trying to say, you fat pig, that you don't want a dirty Tartar for a roommate?'

I looked at Stas in disbelief as he tauntingly said, 'Look, you invited yourself in for supper – that ought to be enough. When it comes to choosing roommates, we'll make our own choices.' Stas softened just a bit then by saying, 'Now you've come to eat. So just relax, sit down, have a drink, and enjoy the food.'

'I think I will,' the Tartar said harshly, raising the teapot off the table. But he didn't pour himself a drink. Instead, he deliberately drank from the spout, his pointy Adam's apple jumping up and down, his black eyes snapping from Stas to me. 'Here, finish it,' he said, and flung the teapot onto the table. It hit the scalpel, which was sticking out of the chicken. The top of the teapot fell off, and the remaining wine splattered us.

Stas took a white handkerchief from the breast pocket of his jacket, wiped his face, smiled, and held the handkerchief out to Aliluyev. 'Wipe yourself off, my friend. Look, your shirt is all wet.'

When Ali looked down at his chest, Stas grabbed the Tartar's long nose between his fingers, and slowly pulled him down. The Tartar crouched lower and lower, his eyes rolling madly.

'Look at what you did,' Stas said, dragging him around the room, 'to the tablecloth, and to the blanket' – he shoved Aliluyev farther, farther, and farther down – 'and to Sasha's shoes, and the floor. Look at the mess you made and you tell me who the pig is in this room!' He let go of Ali's nose and fastidiously wiped his hands on his handkerchief.

Aliluyev crouched on the floor; from his nose trickled drops of blood. He wiped his nose with the back of his hand, smearing the blood and wine across his face. His lips quivered; his teeth were bared in a fierce grimace. Suddenly, he leaped at the table and yanked the scalpel out of the chicken. He pointed the knife at Stas's face and said in a hushed voice, 'Now it's my turn. I'm going to cut your nose off your face!'

Aliluyev darted around the table, the scalpel flashing like lightning. I had to do something . . . I ripped the tablecloth off the table and flung it over Ali's head. In a second, he had slashed the material and his head slipped through the slit, but his arms, entangled in the cloth, flapped futilely. I jumped on him, hurled him onto the floor, straining to wrap him up. We rolled, capsizing the chairs and table. In his rage, he wormed and wriggled out of my grip. Somewhere under the folds death was lurking. We rolled under the bed; there I pressed him against the wall, swaddling him as firmly as I could. Then Stas caught hold of his ankles and dragged him out from under the bed. We tossed him onto the mattress and searched the white mummy for the scalpel, eventually forcing it out of Ali's tight grip.

The room resembled a slaughterhouse – the walls, floor, and even ceiling were splattered with red. Knocked-over chairs and pieces of chicken were on the floor. On the bed lay a dirty sack with a man's head protruding out of it, murmuring something in its own guttural tongue. We were no longer holding him, but he continued to lie there with his eyes glued to the ceiling.

'We're out of wine,' I said. 'Let's go and get some more.'

When we got back, we opened the door cautiously. The room was clean – the walls and floor had been washed, a new tablecloth lay on the table; on one chair sat Ali.

The room was silent. We filled the glasses with wine and Stas handed Ali a drink. That night we made three more quick trips to the tracks while Ali told us his dreadful life story: after the war everyone in his Crimean village was dispossessed and banished to the cold Siberian steppes. It was the middle of February and, though they were allowed a pillow, nobody had a coat. The people ate snow and drank tears. Almost everyone died the first week, said Ali, and swore that one day he would have his revenge.

By the end of that long night we had invited him to live in our room. But it was not to be. The next day after classes, Ali was arrested. He just disappeared. No one knew who informed on him. There was a rumour that someone had picked him out of our class picture taken on the first day of school.

3 The Russian Theatrical School

As the Dean had promised, we started our theatrical education at a vegetable storage house. When we arrived, the manager of the storage house was there to meet us with a rousing speech: 'Lady comrades, comrade gentlemen, I am pleased to tell you that your mission is to provide Muscovites with fruits and vegetables. Soviet citizens are awaiting their vitamins. It's your job to give them their crunchy cabbage and clear grapes. Only your toil can quench their thirst for the life-giving gifts of nature. Let's get to work, my friends! Let's get to work, comrade actors!'

He gave us beautiful words, but he never did give us the gloves and gas masks we needed for the job. It wasn't so bad for the boys; we got to work outside unloading trucks and sorting potatoes and grapes. But the girls were stuck working in the cellar of the storage house, where it was cold and damp, like a morgue, and had the same smell. It was as dark as night in that cellar. Only very high up was there a little window, like a square moon in a black sky, and from the cement floor to that moon rose mountains of cabbage.

'Art requires sacrifice,' Stanislavsky remarked, while feasting on stuffed cabbage one opening night. The truth of his words certainly rang out in that storage house.

The girls sat on the mountains of cabbage, kerchiefs tied over their mouths to keep them from suffocating from the stench of the rotten vegetables. Their fingers dug into the gooey mess and ripped away the slimy, smelly leaves in search of a fairly fresh middle. Like divers checking thousands of shell for a few pearls, these girls checked tons of rot for a few edible hearts.

An old riddle asks: 'What has seven suits but no buttons?' Every educated Russian knows that the answer is 'cabbage'. At that storage house all the suits had turned into a rotten, murky mess. Only the very centre was fresh and pure, and the girls' job was to remove the cabbages' tattered rags in search of the purity.

From the mountain of black cabbage, the girls made a small pyramid of white cabbage, each head the size of a tennis ball. None of the girls knew what was to come – perhaps at the end of all their work, it would be necessary to form a new pile, each head the size of a pea.

One of the girls never did get to see what would happen. That was Lena, the girl both Boris and Youssef had eyes for. Frankly, I thought she was lucky when, in the middle of her work, she collapsed from an excruciating pain in her side and was taken by ambulance to the hospital.

Two weeks later, when our vegetable torture was finally finished, I was hurrying to the Institute in fear of being late for my morning acting class. Moscow had completely changed during those days; it was no longer a sunny, summer city. The trees along the boulevard were swaying in the cold breeze, the few remaining leaves rustling forlornly. Tufts of low clouds glided along over the buildings, almost touching the wet roofs.

That's when I saw Lena again. She was walking slowly, clutching her stomach, hunched over from cold and pain. She was wearing a light summer dress and walking with a pitiful weariness that made her stop every few steps to rest.

Normally, I would have hesitated over going up to such a pretty girl as Lena to engage her in conversation, but she seemed to be in such a wretched state that compassion overcame shyness. . . .

'Excuse me,' I offered politely, 'is there anything I can do for you?'

She looked at me blankly.

'You don't look well,' I nervously explained. 'Maybe I should call a doctor?'

She grabbed my arm. 'No!' she cried hoarsely. 'Please! No!'

'Okay . . . it's okay,' I reassured her, patting the hand that was squeezing my arm like a vice.

Embarrassed by her outburst, she stammered, 'I . . . I think I just need to rest a moment.'

'Let me help you,' I suggested self-consciously. And then I took her arm so she could lean against me for support.

'Thank you,' she said weakly. 'I'll be all right in just a few minutes. It's only that this is the first time I'm walking since the operation.'

'What operation?'

'Ah . . . it doesn't matter,' Lena muttered, turning her head away. 'I don't need your sympathy or your help, I can handle this myself. Yes,' she added, with a shake of her head when she saw my surprised reaction, 'you'll be late for class because of me. Go ahead.'

'I was going to be late anyway,' I replied. 'Come on, we'll walk together. Maybe then you'll tell me what happened to you during these last two weeks.'

We slowly made our way to the Institute, and Lena told me what had happened to her. And in the telling, Lena's voice was as soft and as melancholy as the sound of rustling autumn leaves. . . .

'The ambulance took me from that storage house straight to the hospital,' she said. 'Then the doctor checked my tongue, pressed on my stomach, and told me I had a tubal pregnancy.

"Impossible," I told him. "The foul air at that storage house poisoned me," I said. "I'm sure that's all it is."

'He simply grinned and told his orderlies to bring me to the operating room, which was filled with interns. The orderlies moved me to the operating table, tied my hands down, and covered me with a white sheet.

'I didn't fully understand what was happening until the scalpel came in contact with my skin. I realized, first of all, that the doctor was serious; second, that he had already cut me open; and third, that nobody was going to put me to sleep.

'"Wait! What about the anesthesia?" I cried.

'"We gave you a local anesthetic; it should be more than enough," the doctor replied.

'"Stop it, you're killing me," I yelled. "You've got to do something! Give me something stronger!"

'"How am I supposed to know whether you're dead or alive if

you're completely knocked out?" the doctor said sarcastically. "Next, you'll be asking for café au lait."

'I didn't want café au lait: I was too busy screaming because the surgeon had already begun to probe in quest of my supposed pregnancy. He was dogged in his search, too, and terribly disappointed when he didn't find any fetus.

'"Where's my glass?" the doctor suddenly demanded. "And my pickle!"

'A nurse quickly delivered his requests.

'After the shot of vodka and the pickle, he continued his search and accidentally bumped into my inflamed appendix. Fascinated by his discovery, he leaned over and exclaimed, "Hey, kid, count your blessings. One more hour and you wouldn't be pregnant, you'd be dead!" He was so pleased with his joke that he burst out laughing and couldn't get a good grip on the knife. The nurse had to take over for him. The moment she finished operating, the doctor grabbed my bloody appendix and poked it in my face to prove he'd been telling the truth.

'"Please, stop it!" I shouted.

'"It's not a baby; it's your appendix," the doctor said playfully. Then he turned to the interns to lecture them on the difference between appendicitis and pregnancy. While he was talking, he lifted the sheet covering me, pointing, at times, to my belly and, at times, a little lower. I was ready to die before he finally finished.

'"That's it, kid," the doctor said proudly. "Despite the intricacies of this operation, it was a perfect success. Even the sutures turned out adorable; they'll be perfect with your bikini. Now I hope you enjoy your stay in the most popular room in the house."

'I was put in a ward with nineteen other women, who were constantly telling tales about that very hospital. The favourite yarn was about a young girl who died after a minor operation. As the story went, the senile surgeon had left a pair of scissors in her stomach. Naturally, I immediately began to feel a pain in my stomach. I tried pressing here and there with my fingertips, but couldn't feel any metal. I wanted to see the scar, but it was covered with an adhesive bandage. The days passed slowly, the nights even slower.

34

'This morning, the doctor came to the ward and told me to come to his surgery. When I got there, he informed me that I was being discharged. Then he proceeded to remove the gauze, all the while joking about my impending pregnancy. When the last piece of tape was ripped off, I let out a scream – across my entire stomach stretched a horrible scar that looked like a purple worm, surrounded by red spots. I was horrified, but the doctor was beaming with pride. Choking down my rage, I quickly turned and hurried out of his surgery.

'"Hey, you forgot to say good-bye. You may need me for an abortion one day. I'm the best!" he called out after me.

'When I got my clothes back, the money that had been in my purse was missing. I didn't bother to report it; I just wanted to get away from that hospital as fast as I could.

'Then all I could think of was that I had to get to school. I'd missed so much! I was about to get a trolleybus, but then realized that I had no money. So I stepped back. And I've been walking ever since. But thanks to you I made it,' she announced. 'We're here!'

We walked up the last stairs to the main entrance and Lena leaned against a pillar to catch her breath. 'By any chance do you know where our class is now?' she asked.

'I'll check. Wait for me here. Better yet, wait for me in the lobby in one of the armchairs. I'll be back in a minute.'

I ran up to the secretary's office on the third floor to find out which classroom to go to. There I found Miss Silver busily applying lipstick and looking at herself in her hand mirror.

'Is this your first day of school, darling?' she said while wiping the excess lipstick from her teeth. 'You have to go back to the first floor, dear. The room schedule was posted down there sometime early this morning. Bye, bye.' She smiled sourly.

I hurried down to the lobby. In one armchair I saw Lena sitting with her eyes closed. Over the side of another armchair I saw a pair of dangling long legs. . . .

'Would you happen to know what room the freshmen are in?' I asked the legs' owner.

'Yes, as a matter of fact I would,' returned a lazy, sleepy voice.

Before I could say anything else, Lena opened her eyes and said, 'Excuse me, did you say you know where the freshmen are?'

'Of course. I'm a freshman myself,' answered the voice, and from the depths of the armchair emerged Stas's boyish face.

'I'm glad to see we're not the only two late for class.' Lena smiled. 'How are you?' she asked, clearly remembering Stas from his bravura performance at our orientation session.

'Fine,' Stas replied. 'You?'

'I'm okay,' she lied. 'Aren't there any classes today?' she asked anxiously.

'What do you mean? Of course there are. Right now, in room 45, Mr and Mrs "Kutuzov" are presenting Stanislavsky's favourite exercise, "Clapping Machine."'

'How come you're not there?' Lena asked.

'Because I can't stand stairs; they're bad for my health and, to me, health is more important than any old Stanislavsky exercises. I've already asked the Dean and Miss Silver to reschedule all my classes for the first or second floors. Until they make a decision, I'll just keep meditating according to the Vakhtangov Method.'

Lena laughed, but with the laugh came a sharp pain in her side. She moaned and doubled over. With surprising agility, Stas leaped forward, opened his attaché case, took out a green vial, removed the cap, took out a capsule, and held it out in the palm of his hand. 'Here, take this,' he stated. 'It'll straighten you out in the time it takes to say, "Twenty-four pills a day keeps twenty-four Soviet doctors away."'

That was enough for Lena. Without asking what it was, she took a capsule and swallowed it. The pain she had been suffering from disappeared almost immediately. Astonished, she thanked Stas, and as if in a cloud, rose and floated up to the fourth floor, with me close behind.

When we got to room 45, Lena made her way to the far side of the class. I stayed near the door, looking wide-eyed at everyone else as they all stood in a circle, clapping furiously. There was probably a method to this madness but, to an outsider, it was impossible to work out – like an unfamiliar card game. In the far corner sat the majestic Field Marshal on his throne of three chairs

36

– his backside on one, his arms resting on the others. Beside him, on a stool, was a petite, skinny old woman – his wife.

'Well done, students. That's enough for now,' the Dean said in a resounding bass. 'My friend and teacher Stanislavsky created this exercise to help his pupils focus on acting and keep them from losing their concentration during the applause. When you get used to Clapping Machine, you won't even hear applause. When I was a student, Stanislavsky used to clap with us for hours on end in an empty auditorium. The echo of applause would bounce off the walls, rumble in the parterre, and fly to the balcony, tinkling the chandeliers. After these exercises, even a standing ovation couldn't distract us.

'Stanislavsky was certainly a genius but, in some cases, Vakhtangov was even better. For example, take his mime exercises. Let's proceed to the next phase of the lesson, class. Now we're going to concentrate on mime.'

The Field Marshal pushed one of his chairs forward.

'Miss Kupina, would you be kind enough to take this chair and sit down in the centre of the room? Yes, that's it, right in front of me. That's fine, thank you. Try to imagine that you are a famous cellist. Have you ever had a chance to play the cello? Ah, what a pity. But that's all right; it's not very important. You're an actress, and I'm sure you have a wonderful imagination. Now pretend that you're opening a cello case and taking out a big, heavy cello. That's right, place it between your knees, yes, yes, between your knees. Don't be shy, you're an actress. Go ahead. Spread your legs apart. Yes . . . a little wider . . . yes . . . perfect!

'Now tune the instrument, Miss Kupina. Turn the pegs gently; you don't want to snap a string. Don't forget about your legs, Miss Kupina. Excellent! Now, pick up the bow. Remember, you're in a concert. Hold it gently, but firmly. Keep it in position.

'Play, Kupina. Go on, perform. Guide it, slide it in. I mean . . .

'Now, now, don't put your knees together. Keep them open, yes, that's good, let yourself go! Look at her, class. That's art! That's real art! Look at how she's playing,' the old professor crowed.

'Don't you think that's enough?' asked his wife.

'No, it's not enough! Only now she's got it. Play louder, Kupina. Crescendo! Let's hear that crescendo!' Field Marshal Kutuzov screamed, feasting his eyes under the skirt of the dumbfounded student.

'Please, stop it. That's enough,' whispered his wife.

'You're a stupid old woman. What do you know about real art? Play, Kupina, play!'

'Miss Kupina, that's enough for now, thank you.'

'No, Kupina, play. Only now I hear the music. Give me that crescendo one more time, then pianissimo . . . then – '

'Stop it. That's enough!'

'You're an idiot. You're a stupid idiot!'

'How could you, in front of the students?'

'So what. They all know you're a stupid idiot.'

'You're the one who's an idiot!'

'No, you're the idiot!'

'Beautiful! Incredible! Superb!' said Miss Silver as she walked into the room, with her hand on her left breast. 'And so natural, as only masters can do. Even for me, it seemed like a real fight. What a perfect example of the Russian theatrical school! I'm sorry to interrupt, but I have an announcement to make. It'll only take a minute.

'Comrade students, there's going to be a slight change of schedule today,' she announced. 'The next class will be Party History in room 14 with our legendary Professor Anna Ivanna.'

'That'll be all, comrade students,' ordered the Dean. 'You can go downstairs now.'

On the way down to the class, I saw Stas, still in the same position enveloped in the armchair. I had to use brute force to shake him out of his state of meditation and drag him to room 14. There, Stas and I took our seats in the last row. Lena came into the room and sat down in front of us near a fellow by the name of Barskov, who seemed always to be eating from a bag of chocolates.

'Hi,' he said to Lena. 'How are you?'

'Pretty good.' She turned around and smiled. 'Thanks to Stas's pills.'

38

Hearing this, Barskov stopped eating, looked down at the chocolates, then looked at Lena, and asked, 'Do you want some?'

'No, thanks,' Lena said.

'Okay.' He shrugged and put another piece of chocolate in his mouth.

'Say, how come you're always eating sweets in the morning?' I asked him.

'I don't know; I don't even like it but . . . if you have a few pieces of chocolate in the morning it kills your appetite, and you don't need to spend much money on lunch.'

There was an uncomfortable pause. Nobody knew what to say next. . . .

But then Stas nudged me as Professor Anna Ivanna entered the room. She was fifteen minutes late, but she wasn't in a hurry. She had been late since 1917, the year she met Comrade Lenin. That meeting changed her life and made her one of the select few who could afford to be indifferent to time. With this meeting, she became a part of history – the part called 'Party History'. The present was no longer a factor in her life, because Party History encompasses only the heroic past and the happy future. The present is of no concern, because it is short and insignificant like a human life, which is, after all, nothing compared with the business of communism.

Lenin gave Anna Ivanna a good position in that business. That was when she stopped counting the days and started counting only the years. When Stalin took over, her concept of time changed once again. She began to live according to Five-Year Plans. But this didn't satisfy Comrade Stalin. To teach Anna Ivanna more about time, he sent her for a fifteen-year stay at a labour camp in Siberia. Her education came to an end with the death of her professor. Next, she went to Moscow, where she started teaching Party History at the Theatre Institute. This job proved to be a cinch for her; it was just like the story of her life.

At the Institute, she was best known for her story about her encounter with Lenin; but her true talent lay in another area. . . .

She was short and stocky, with stubby, midget legs. Her entire body shook like jelly when she came waddling into the room, dragging a blue Aeroflot bag. She sat down on a creaky chair, put her elbows on the desk, and rested her chin on her plump fists. Large and small warts covered her face; her eyes – just two more brown warts.

She scrutinized the students in the class, then abruptly said, 'Have you ever read Lenin's book *One Step Forward, Two Steps Back?*'

'Yes, we have,' Stas called out.

'Tell me what it's about,' Anna Ivanna said.

'The way to communism,' Stas responded.

Everybody chuckled, but Anna Ivanna asked, gravely, 'What is that supposed to mean?'

'I'm sorry,' said Stas. 'Maybe you didn't understand me. I was trying to say that it was the way Lenin walked before the Revolution.' Stas peered at the teacher innocently.

'I still don't see what you mean,' said Anna Ivanna, becoming noticeably upset.

'In my opinion, Lenin wanted to show that no matter how you go, all paths lead to communism,' Stas said.

'That's a fascinating interpretation of Lenin,' she said, her eyes moist. 'Please forgive my show of emotion. Apart from the fact that Lenin is dear to my heart, my nerves are a bit jittery after my years of confinement.'

'Darling Anna Ivanna,' rang out Stas's sugar-coated voice, 'don't get upset. We all love you; we've heard so many good things about you – and your talent.'

'I don't know what you're referring to,' said Anna Ivanna, but we could see she was anxious to hear more.

'The seniors say,' Stas continued, 'that we will never be accomplished actors if we haven't witnessed the great folk art of the prison camps, of which you are the most celebrated proponent. I want to ask you, on behalf of the other students, please sing for us.'

'No,' she said firmly. 'If you want, I can tell you how I met Lenin . . .'

'Please, Anna Ivanna. We want to hear you sing.'

The whole class broke into applause and chanted, 'An-na-Iv-an-na,' with Stas conducting. It was obvious that the old communist was pleased but, at the same time, afraid.

'No, not today,' she said.

'An-na-Iv-an-na-An-na-Iv-an-na.' The chanting became louder and seemed to melt her willpower. Anna Ivanna suddenly shook her shoulders, winked devilishly, jumped off the chair, and circled around the front of the room in a prison strut called, 'Don't pick the flowers.' She stopped near the piano. We lowered our voices, but the beat was carried by the whisper and rhythmic clapping. She heaved her huge body onto the piano stool, pushed away from the instrument, spun around several times until she could reach the keyboard, spread her stubby single-jointed fingers apart, smashed the keys, whistled loudly, and, in a rasping voice, sang between the notes:

> 'Murka, my Murka, Murka my dear,
> You sold us out without fear,
> Good-bye, my Murka, and farewell,
> Take this bullet and go to hell!'

Anna Ivanna tearfully went through verse after verse of this song about a lady bandit who turned informer. When she got to the part where the treacherous Murka was lying dead on the cobblestone road, Anna Ivanna struck a dissonant chord and paused – her warts, drenched in tears, formed a tragic mask. The angel of silence flew in, then vanished, making room for our expression of bliss.

Stas led us all in a thunderous ovation. We begged her to sing more, but the old communist had already taken herself in hand. She told us not to say a word about the 'concert,' buried her warts in her hands, and went out of the room. Stas gallantly lifted the Aeroflot bag and, like the manager of a great star, went proudly marching after her. 'That'll be all, comrade students,' he said when he reached the door. 'You've just seen a perfect example of the Russian theatrical school.'

4 The Snow

Winter came and Boris and I were jealous of Youssef, who would soon be back in the Sudan, sipping chilled wine under the hot African sun. But he was jealous too, of our staying in Moscow all winter, warming ourselves with vodka.

Youssef's father, growing tired of his son's decadent ways, had decided, with diplomatic aplomb, to send Youssef home before he was kicked out of school in an embarrassing scandal. Youssef was to spend one year with his grandfather, the king of the Tukbu tribe, who would bring him to his senses in the primitive but healthy atmosphere of tribal life.

With only one week left till the day Youssef was to leave, he gave me an ultimatum: 'Either introduce me to Lena or I'll never write you a line!' I was positive he wouldn't write to me anyway, but I wanted to do something special for his departure, so I gave him my word. Boris had also been prodding me all the time about meeting Lena. I thought that this would be my chance to satisfy both of them at the same time. While Lena and I were friendly to each other – saying hello when we saw each other in the hallways – we weren't what you'd call close. I had reverted to my usual aloof style and couldn't quite break out of it; this time shyness overcame courage. But now, at least this way, I had a good reason for inviting Lena out – even if it was to meet two other men. . . .

December the fifth, Soviet Constitution Day, was coming soon. A holiday was a perfect excuse. I invited Lena to celebrate at the restaurant at the Actors' Club, on Pushkin Square. Getting into that restaurant was no easy matter – not because it was such a great place, but because it was open only to members of the actors' union. A hatchet-faced guard stood near the entrance, checking everyone's I.D. card, carefully comparing the picture on the I.D. with the face. It was simply impossible to pay him off, because behind the glass door stood the head waiter, eyeing the guard. As Lenin said, 'Trust but check!'

This system posed a problem for all but Stas, who was friends with the guard, the head waiter, and the manager of the restaurant. Thus, Stas could go there whenever he wanted and with whomever he pleased, despite the fact that he wasn't a member of any union.

This was the plan: Stas was to meet Boris and Youssef at the restaurant, get a table, and order an exotic dinner of vodka, herring, and boiled potatoes. Next, Stas would go outside, meet Lena and me, and escort us through the cordon to our table, where the festivities would begin. At the liveliest moment, Stas would recall some very important business to attend to and would ask me to help him out. We would leave Boris and Youssef on their own to woo Lena. Stas was predicting that Youssef would come out the victor, with his favourite story about his dream to build a palace for his grandfather the king and so on. . . .

The plan was simple and we were sure it would succeed. At that time we still believed that plans could rule destiny. How were we to know that destiny would change not just that plan, but our whole lives?

After class that evening, I waited for Lena outside the rehearsal hall. From the doorway, I could hear the screams of Mr and Mrs Kutuzov, who always held opposing views on art. I was wondering whether or not I should tell Lena about Boris and Youssef, but because of all the screaming and shouting, it was impossible to think. I decided to go downstairs and wait in the vestibule. On the stairs, I heard a hurried patter behind me. I stopped and turned. . . .

'What a loony bin!' Lena said, rushing after me. 'He asked Kupina to play the cello again. Let's get out of here.'

We ran down to the cloakroom. I took Lena's coat off the hook.

'Where did you get such a heavy fur coat?' I asked as I helped her into it.

'It's my grandfather's. He gave me his coat and hat when I was

43

leaving for Moscow. He knew I'd freeze here in the winter. Hold it, before I put that monster on, I have to get ready.'

She opened her bag and, to my surprise, took out several pairs of tights.

'Turn around,' she said.

I turned and heard her taking off her shoes; then, judging from the rustling, I guessed that she had put on the tights, one over the other.

'That's it. Now I'm all set. Give me my coat.'

I opened the door, and Lena went outside. Her arms resembled those of a wooden soldier because of the stiff sleeves; her legs, despite the layers of tights, looked like matchsticks under the huge tent-shaped coat.

'How come you're smiling?' she asked. 'Do I look like a bear or something? Hey, you'd better give me your hand before I slip.'

Lena didn't look one bit like a bear. Even in that absurd fur coat and man's fur hat you could sense her fragility. I gave her my arm. She leaned on it ever so slightly, and we headed across Arbat Street to Circle Boulevard.

Since we had nearly an hour, I suggested we walk to Pushkin Square. She agreed with a warm smile. And the very moment we stepped onto the snowy path along the boulevard, the lamp posts, standing erect along the way, lit up as if on command. Snowflakes, invisible only seconds before, suddenly appeared in the light of the lamps, circling among the trees like little white butterflies.

'It's funny,' said Lena, 'it's not even cold, after all. You know, I haven't been out walking all winter, I'm so afraid of the cold. Oh, look! How sweet!'

An old woman in a long, black coat was scurrying along, all hunched over, followed by three tiny black dogs, their legs lost in an inch of snow. This curious group was like a question mark and three dots on a clean sheet of white snow.

'A question without an answer,' I mused.

'Like everything in life,' returned Lena.

'Can you imagine being like that old lady some day?' I asked.

'No,' Lena replied, 'I can't even imagine being thirty.'

'Why?'

'I don't know, maybe because I was sick all the time when I

was a child and the doctors were always saying I would die. Or maybe that's not it at all. I don't know. I suppose I just can't see myself here in ten years.'

We slowly made our way down Circle Boulevard. The fresh, clean snow felt so good beneath my feet. We walked hand in hand, snowflakes dancing around us, melting on our faces, clinging somewhat longer on our lashes. We smiled at each other, and just then I got a queer feeling that we had once walked that path together.

'You know,' said Lena, 'it's funny, but I feel as if we've walked like this before.'

I didn't say a word, but it occurred to me that maybe, just maybe, I had made a terrible mistake by promising Boris and Youssef that I would arrange that meeting. . . .

Stas and I had agreed to meet right in front of the restaurant, but when we got to the square, I saw his tall, portly figure on the opposite side, near the Pushkin Monument. Besides Stas, there were nearly a hundred other people in the snow-sprinkled crowd. They were carrying posters and banners. I could make out the word *constitution* on some of the banners.

'What's going on over there?' Lena asked.

'I don't know. It probably has something to do with the holiday.'

'At night?'

'Stas! Hey Stas!' I shouted, but my voice was drowned out in the noise of the traffic around the square. 'Wait here,' I said to Lena, and dashed through the honking cars to the Pushkin Monument.

There was something unusual about the crowd at the square – the people, mostly youths, seemed almost sober. The red flags, de rigueur on holidays, were conspicuously absent. There was no podium, and nobody was shouting optimistic slogans. On the contrary, a deadly silence prevailed.

'Stas,' I said, approaching him from behind, 'what's happening?'

'Revolution!' Stas said cheerily, turning to me.

'What?' I said.

'Rev-o-lu-tion!' he repeated melodiously. 'Just a little revolution!'

He smelled of vodka; apparently, he, Boris, and Youssef had already been boozing it up in the restaurant, and he was well on his way to being drunk.

'Here! Read this,' said Stas, stuffing a piece of paper into my hand, 'and then tell me what it's all about, because I haven't read it myself!'

He laughed raucously, then went traipsing off towards the monument, zigzagging through the crowd, a pile of leaflets in his hand.

I looked down at the paper. It said something about the Soviet Constitution's guaranteeing freedom of speech to all . . . and there was also something about the arrest of Sinyavsky and Daniel. I had no idea who Daniel was, but I did know there was a famous soccer commentator named Sinyavsky. What he had been arrested for, I couldn't imagine.

I looked around for Stas. He was already clawing his way up the angled base of the monument, his feet slipping on the smooth stone, the leaflets held high above his head – a veritable cartoon of a revolutionary agitator.

Suddenly, there was a tense, nervous stir in the crowd. People started darting every which way. 'Run!' came a cry from somewhere in the crowd. At that moment, two men in grey coats grabbed my arms from behind. 'March!' one whispered in my ear as they swiftly dragged me in my bewilderment to a waiting police van along with some demonstrators.

'Black Ravens' had converged on Pushkin Square from all sides. Men in uniforms and civilian clothes had come spilling out of the vans and, in a moment, were closing in on the crowd. The operation was carried out like clockwork, like a well-rehearsed performance. There was only one snag: Stas holding steadfast at the monument. Three policemen were climbing up the angular stone after him. He kept kicking the policemen down. One, unable to hold on any longer, slipped and fell; the other two grabbed Stas's leg and were swinging from it like huge leeches. Stas managed to hold on a few more moments, but suddenly let go, and the whole group came tumbling down.

46

From the base of the monument rose a cloud of white leaflets, like pigeons circling around the statue of Pushkin. The bronze poet, his head tilted downwards, peered at the scene in silence, his hand frozen behind his back holding a top hat.

The policemen shoved us into the vans, which flew off like the ominous birds they were named after. We'd hardly gone a block before a policeman seized me by the neck.

I yelled, 'There's been a big mistake!'

My heart was beating fast with the hope of explaining the terrible error that had been made.

'What did you say?' he snarled.

'There's been a mistake,' I repeated. 'I wasn't – '

He slammed his fist into my stomach. My eyes opened wide with the pain and I thought I might throw up.

'Yeah, there's been a mistake,' the policeman taunted. 'And it was your mother who made it by having you.' I was doubled over, defenceless, when he hit me again, punching me on the side of the head. I staggered and fell.

Another policeman picked me up off the floor of the careening Black Raven and demanded, 'Who said you could lie down?'

I could hardly breathe. I certainly couldn't talk. But then there was nothing helpful I could have said.

'You know what we do to people who lie down without permission?'

I stupidly shook my head.

His answer was a knee that went crashing into my groin, knocking me to my knees. I almost bit my tongue off trying not to cry out.

'Please . . . stop,' I whimpered from the floor of the van.

He ignored me and brought his knee up again, hitting me in the throat. I started choking, gasping for air, as I tumbled backward over a huddled mass of demonstrators behind me.

Before he could hit me again, the Black Raven abruptly stopped and then dumped us all out in the yard of an ordinary-looking police station, in a drab section of the city.

I struggled to my feet, only to be herded – at the point of a gun – across the yard and then shoved roughly through the back door of the police station. After that, we were led down a corridor lined with doors, and flung, one after another, into different rooms. When all the doors were slammed shut, there were only two of us left in the hallway. Consequently, we got the royal treatment: we were thrown into the cellar. There we found, behind the iron door that was locked behind us, a dimly lit space like a boiler room, where the walls were lined with huge pipes wrapped in thick felt, and the floor covered with the wool of military coats.

'Well, students, we're going to get you warmed up for your interview,' announced a pockmarked policeman. I didn't like the way he said that as he came toward us.

'Oh, it looks like this one,' he said, referring to me, 'doesn't like our company.' There were five other policemen lounging near the locked door, and they all laughed.

I'd heard of people picked up by the Black Ravens who were never seen or heard of again. I had a fleeting thought of Ali. What had *he* done? What had *I* done?

I kept backing away from the pockmarked policeman as he continued coming towards me . . . until I found myself trapped in a corner of the room and had nowhere left to go.

The policeman laughed at me as I huddled, quivering with fear, in the corner. Then, without warning, he lunged for me. I brought up my hands to protect my face, but he never intended to hit me there. Instead, he threw me bodily towards a second policeman, who stopped me by kicking me in the kidneys and then flung me towards a third one. The third one spun me around, blasted his forearm against the back of my head, then shoved me as hard as he could towards the fourth. Only the fourth one didn't catch me. He stepped out of the way and I rammed into the pipes. I crumpled to the ground, blind with pain and fear. But they didn't stop. They just kept on passing me from one to the other and ramming me into the pipes, again and again. And though the pipes were covered with a thick padding of felt, with each ensuing smash, my ribs seemed to stab my internal organs until my insides felt like shattered glass that could never be put back together.

The other fellow was treated to a different set of rules: 'Three times toss; two times catch.' Every third time he hit the floor with a thud.

Soon, blood was trickling from his mouth.

'Okay, that's enough,' laughed the pockmarked policeman. 'We always stop at the sight of blood; besides, we wouldn't want to leave any black-and-blue marks for you to go bragging about to your mother. . . .'

I was certain that all my bones were broken as the policemen dragged me back upstairs and left me on a bench in the hallway. Whenever I inhaled, the pain was excruciating, but when I tried to hold my breath, my head would spin and I was afraid I would fall off the bench.

'Sasha K—' rang out in my head, as if in a dream. 'Sasha K— Who's Sasha K—?'

I wanted to answer, but couldn't get the words out. I raised my hand.

'That you?'

I nodded my head.

'Let's go. Comrade Captain is waiting.'

The policeman led me down the hall. He stopped near a sound-proofed door, opened the door, and with a light tap on my back, pushed me into a large office with a full-length portrait of Lenin on one wall. Beneath the portrait was a massive desk, from which shone a blinding light. Someone was seated behind the desk, but I couldn't make out who it was. Suddenly, out of nowhere, a dark spectre lunged at me. I gave a start, tried to block it with my hands, but my fingers sank into a thick fur and the beast grabbed me and hugged me. Through my intolerable pain I heard . . .

'Sasha! Sashenka! Darling!'

The voice was familiar, but I couldn't place it.

'I thought I'd never find you. Without the help of Comrade Captain, I don't know what I'd have done. What about our engagement party, dear?'

Lena kissed me, and I felt her tears on my cheek.

'Comrade Captain, how will we ever explain this to our guests?

49

They've probably left already. Sasha, Sashenka, how did this ever happen? What a calamity!'

Lena burst into tears and wrapped her arms around me, but I couldn't tell her how painful it was. I was about to pass out when the man behind the desk saved me with an order to be seated.

Lena helped me to a chair near the desk. Behind the desk, just below the legs of Lenin, sat a round-shouldered man with a tired, canine face. His outstretched arms rested on the green felt desktop. He resembled a devoted Alsatian lying near its master's legs.

'And now, comrade, explain to us how you happened to be at an anti-Soviet demonstration,' growled the captain.

'Our engagement party – ' Lena hastened to say.

'Nobody asked you, miss,' the captain intervened. 'Hurry up, comrade, I haven't got time to ask my questions twice.'

I glanced at Lena and felt a surge of hope for the first time. And then I plunged into a tale of deep love – the love that drew us to the dinner party at the Actors' Club, where, with our closest friends, we were going to celebrate the end of my bachelor life and the beginning of my family life. I then related our ardent desire to build a great Soviet family and said that the captain was the first person to be told of our secret dream to have a little son.

Here Lena stopped crying and looked at the captain coyly, to convince him that we had seriously started to make that dream come true.

'That's good, good, very good,' the captain said, 'but how did it come about that you were at the Pushkin Monument?'

'I wasn't at the monument, comrade chief. We were on our way to the restaurant on Pushkin Square, where Lena was waiting for us, and, before I knew it, I found myself in the Black Ra – I mean, in the van.'

'Who is this "we"?' the captain asked suspiciously.

'My friend and I. He's going to be the best man,' I replied, sensing trouble.

'Where is he?' snapped the captain.

'I saw him go into the restaurant,' Lena said quickly, clearly warning me to keep Stas out of my story.

'What's his name?' the captain demanded.

I did some very fast thinking, and then quickly replied, 'Boris Skobin.'

'Was there anyone else with you?' he commanded and in a more threatening voice he added, 'I can check it, you know.'

Nervously, I looked at Lena. I slowly said, 'Youssef.'

'Ah, a foreigner!' he cried, believing he had picked up the scent. 'Anyone else?'

'No.'

For the first time he broke into a smile, exposing his smoke-stained teeth. 'A foreigner!' he repeated with relish.

Lena looked worried.

'Yes,' I said, 'the son of the Sudanese Ambassador.'

'Ugh,' he groaned miserably, 'a chicken is not a bird, and the Third World is not abroad.' He leaned back, his smile disappearing within the shadow. 'She said you had reserved a table at the restaurant.'

'That's correct.'

'Who can verify it?'

'I don't know.'

'And what if I were to check right now?'

'Please, go right ahead, captain,' I said, dying inside.

He glared at me, then drew the telephone near.

Lena was very pale.

'Get me the Actors' Club restaurant on the line, yes, yes, there's only one.' He took a cigarette from a pack on the desk, all the while staring at me. 'Hello . . . who's speaking? This is the police station, comrade head waiter. I want to talk to someone called Boris Skobin. Would you check if he's there . . . okay, we can hold on . . .'

He lit the cigarette.

'What? There's nobody there by that name?' The captain's shifty eyes darted from me to Lena, and from Lena to me, as he exhaled a cloud of smoke.

'Comrade commissioner,' Lena said, trying flattery, 'maybe he's left already . . .'

The captain looked at her mistrustfully.

'Maybe he's drunk and didn't hear,' I said, imploring Lena with my eyes to help. 'Maybe you should ask for Youssef.'

She got my cue. 'Please try once more,' she said with an enticing smile.

'All right . . . Hello? Hello? Are you still there? . . . Wait a minute,' the captain said, and put his hand over the receiver. 'What does this Youssef look like?' he asked me.

'He's black,' I said, and saw Lena shoot a look at me.

'Let's give it one more try, comrade head waiter. Look for a black fellow; he should be the only one at the Russian Actors' Club . . . No, don't say it's the police calling; just say it's an urgent matter.' His eyes narrowed; his cigarette nearly burned to the end. . . .

'Hello, who is this? Youssef? This is the uh, uh . . . Sasha's friend speaking . . .What? Where is he? That's not important right now. He asked me to tell you that something came up, and the party had to be postponed. What? . . . What? . . . Okay, sure, I'll tell him,' he said with a grin, and put down the receiver.

'That Youssef, he's all right. He curses pretty well for a foreigner. He asked me to tell you that you're a . . . oh, never mind, I'm sure he'll tell you himself. You can go now.' He put out his cigarette. 'You see, the Soviet Regime is strict, but just.'

'Hey, are you okay?' Lena asked when we got outside. 'You have blood on your lips. Can I clean it off?' She took a handful of snow and held it to my mouth. The snow turned red instantly. On my lips, I felt the icy cold, but on my cheek, I felt the warmth of her palm. I took her hand and kissed it. The next second, my head was spinning, and a sharp pain washed across my body like a wave. I tried to grab the fence, but my legs caved in and I fell down in the snow. The white around me turned black.

I awoke on a couch. Beside me was a silver tray with a bottle of champagne and a can of caviar. I shut my eyes, sat like that for a few moments, then opened them again to see the same sight. Certain that I was sleeping, I didn't bother to check anymore. Just then, Lena opened the door and came silently into the room in a baby-soft cotton robe covered with strawberries. She was holding two glasses in her hands.

'Would you like some champagne?' she asked.

'Please.'

'Let's open it,' she said.

I took the bottle, removed the foil, then the metal wire, and with the thumb of my left hand carefully eased the cork up, cupping my right hand over the top. POP went the cork. Lena held out the glasses, and I poured the sparkling wine.

'Cheers to December the fifth!' Lena said.

'Hurrah!' I said, and we drank. The champagne had the light, salty taste – of blood. I realized I was awake.

'Where are we?' I asked.

'At Aunt Sonia's,' Lena said.

'Aunt Sonia?'

'Don't you remember, I told you on the way that I'm living with my aunt. She's not at home now, that's why I brought you here.'

'And where is Stas?'

'I think he's still at the police station. I couldn't be a bride to two grooms.'

'What are we going to do?'

'Drink the champagne and think about nothing. After all, you're the one who invited me to dinner,' Lena said, pouring champagne into the glasses.

'To your health,' she said.

'Thank you,' I said, and we drank.

'Why did you follow me to the police station?'

'Probably because it's the first time in my life a taxi stopped right in front of me . . . and also because I knew you didn't have anybody in Moscow.'

'Thank you again,' I said.

Lena scooped a teaspoon of caviar from the can and held it out to me.

'Eat the caviar,' she said.

'Do you have any bread?'

'No, there is nothing but caviar and champagne in this house.'

'That aunt of yours has a good life.'

'Not too bad. You know those old communists; they fought for the Revolution and now they have the Kremlin ration. Have you ever heard of the Kremlin ration?'

'I've heard of it, but I didn't know it was for caviar and champagne.'

'No,' Lena said, 'you can get everything at Kremlyovka, the Kremlin Health Food Store: salmon, sturgeon, crabs – even fruit. That's where I saw a pineapple for the first time in my life. My aunt can't eat any of those things because she's old and sick – so she eats only caviar. The doctor said it's good for her health. With her pension, she buys champagne and gives it to her doctor. That's how they live – he drinks champagne, and she eats caviar and waits for the ferry.'

'What ferry?' I asked, quite lost.

'Every spring, when the ice melts on the Moscow River, the ferry starts to run again. She waits all winter for it so she can float to the Kremlin Health Food Store and use her coupons. When she sees the first ferry, she's sure she'll live one year more.'

'What coupons?'

'They're special tickets to use at Kremlyovka. It's another world there. If you want, I'll explain it to you tomorrow; remind me. Now it's time to get some sleep. I have a rehearsal early in the morning.'

'No, first let's finish up this champagne. There's exactly one glass left for each.'

'All right.'

'Let's drink to my friend Youssef. You've never met him, but I'd like to drink to him.'

'And to Stas,' said Lena.

'And to Stas.'

'And to the Soviet Constitution,' Lena said with a grin.

'No,' I said, 'not to that.'

Lena put covers on the couch for me, turned off the light, and got into the bed, which was on the other side of the room. I couldn't sleep. I guess the events of that day had really shaken me. I realized that if it weren't for Lena, my life could have been ruined. A feeling of tenderness for that strange girl struck my heart.

'Lena,' I called out, 'are you asleep?'

'No.'

54

'I can't sleep over here.'

'Okay. You can come over here, but only because I'm freezing.'

I got up, wrapped myself in a blanket, and went to the bed. Lena didn't move. I had to climb over her to get to the empty side near the wall.

'Lie down, but don't try anything,' Lena said. 'I want to sleep.'

I couldn't seem to sleep on the bed, either. We were both lying there naked. I moved over and softly stroked her back.

'Don't pet me like that,' Lena said sleepily.

'Why?'

'That's the way you pet a dog, but I'm not a dog; I'm a cat.'

'How do you pet cats?' I asked.

'I'll show you another time, but now I want to sleep.'

I lay for a while, then moved closer and put my arm around her. My hand slid onto her stomach and met a hard, raised scar.

Lena jumped up and stood on her hands and knees. Startled, I jumped up, too. We stood so close on the bed yet a great gulf now suddenly stood between us. Her silhouette was sharply outlined in the dim window light. She really looked like a cat about to fight.

'Remember,' Lena said, her eyes glowing in the dark, 'remember,' she repeated seriously, 'when I want you, I'll come on my own, but now I want to sleep, so don't come any closer. Got it?'

'Got it.'

'So . . . good night.'

'Good night.'

In the morning, we drank champagne with caviar, then quietly slipped out of the apartment, because in the very next room lived another family – father, mother, daughter, and grandmother. Lena said it would be better if they didn't know about my visit.

We walked along the boulevard slowly. It was cold and windy, but I couldn't go any faster; my whole body was in pain. On the snow-packed surface, sleepy people were hurrying to work. None of them knew what had taken place on that boulevard the night before.

It was already light, but the lamps were still lit. Near one of the lamp posts stood an Alsatian his hind leg raised as he wet the snow.

5 The Military Coats

The rest of the winter, my life seemed frozen, like an ice crystal. Stas had disappeared without trace, Youssef went to the Sudan, Boris left Moscow for some architects' expedition to the North, and not much was happening between Lena and me, but with the coming of spring, that crystal melted and things started rolling again. I got my first job in a film. It was at the Military Studio, which wasn't very prestigious and it wouldn't have been worth mentioning except that that's where I met Andrew, or 'Andrewlka,' as he called himself.

Andrewlka was a liar, a drinker, and a playboy. In the void of his skull, a single atom bounced frenetically. There was no way to predict what Andrewlka might say or do, where the atom would land or with what kind of force it would bounce, whether it would fall upon a protrusion or an indentation, up or down, in a hard place or a soft one; nobody knew. The soft spots certainly outnumbered the hard, but just when you lost hope of hearing anything that made sense in Andrewlka's endless drivel, the atom struck a deep point, ricocheted, bounced off to the side, up again, and the sparkle from unexpected thoughts, ideas, and abilities twinkled in his protuberant eyes.

Nature, as everyone knows, encompasses both heredity and environment. Andrewlka inherited generosity and tenderness from his mother, from his father bullish manliness and stubbornness, but there was no limit to what he got from the environment. In fact, he didn't have an ego at all. He even referred to himself in the third person – 'Andrewlka is sleeping,' 'Andrewlka is eating,' and whenever he sneezed, he was always the first to say, 'God bless you, Andrewlka.' He constantly altered his beliefs, opinions, actions, routines, and manners. Even his looks were a kaleidoscope of opposites. Such changes resulted from whomever he befriended, spoke with, or simply saw. He was a carbon copy of anyone he associated with, except women. When he was around women, he didn't change, but he did change them. Unending lines of women went through him, like film in a projector. Right after Andrewlka put his mechanism in the perforation, the film would advance, and a new portrait would appear in the frame.

And what about his occupation? He switched jobs at the rate of the vibration of the Russian r – 'Andrewlka's a reporter . . . Andrewlka's a director . . . Andrewlka's an actor . . . a street cleaner . . . an informer. Andrewlka's not working, Andrewlka has never worked, and Andrewlka will never work.' What would he need to work for – he had had a two-room apartment in Moscow since the age of fifteen.

A two-room apartment?!

Two rooms?!

This was not just a big deal, it was incredible! It was as if a fifteen-year-old American boy got a gift of two million dollars tax free.

Two million?!

Tax free?!

This might be considered preposterous, but believe it or not, a Moscow boy with a two-room apartment is much better off!

What could you possibly do with two million in Moscow, when there is absolutely nothing to do with one? What could you do with it – buy lobster? It's impossible to find. A Rolls-Royce? More impossible than the lobster. Put it in the bank? There *are* no banks! But you couldn't cart all that money around with you. Stash it away? There are informers everywhere. So then, what could you get for a million? Just one thing – execution. No, a Muscovite doesn't need a million.

A two-room apartment is another story altogether. It's everybody's dream, but by law, an individual can't occupy more than nine square metres. Obviously, that's not even one room. Yes, a two-room apartment in Moscow is real wealth.

Well then, how did Andrewlka get his two rooms, each larger than the prescribed size? You would have to ask his mother that. His glamorous mother would most likely respond, 'I suffered a lot in my youth, so I want my son to have everything I never had.' Then she would probably sit down in the back of a black limousine, beside her latest husband, and be whisked away to some Party conference. But let's get back to Andrewlka. . . .

As I said, we met on the set of a military film studio where he was on the books as the assistant cameraman. As the assistant, he was supposed to be on hand to go for beer, wine, or sausages, depending on the cameraman's mood. But Andrewlka wasn't exactly your typical assistant. He sat behind the camera lazily turning the shiny knobs, drinking beer, and peering through a telephoto lens at the legs of the director's wife, while the cameraman circled around him, obsequiously inquiring if his assistant would like something to eat. Later, I learned that the cameraman was living in Andrewlka's apartment, and he tried hard to please his landlord.

The shooting took place in a top-secret military arsenal, in a forest near Moscow. The director, genius that he was, planned to film a burglary there. Which one of the heroes would perform the robbery, the genius had not yet determined, because he couldn't be sure which actors would show up that day. Nobody knew until the last minute whom he would play, what he would do, and how much he would make. The genius's basic premise was that everything should be improvised except his own salary.

The moment I arrived on the set, he began to assign parts. He handed me a military uniform and outlined what I was to do: make a hole in the barbed-wire fence, break down the arsenal's steel door, and steal, perhaps an atomic bomb or perhaps a pistol – he hadn't yet decided. As I was getting used to the role of renegade and was ready for just about any crime, the distant gaze of the director fell on Andrewlka, who was making arrangements with the genius's wife for something specific. This stirred the director's imagination and, all of a sudden, he decided to use the assistant cameraman as an actor, hoping that the force of art would divert him from his bad intentions. The director said that Andrewlka's face was better suited to the part of the robber than mine. Everyone agreed and I was immediately promoted to the good guy, without so much as changing my epaulets.

When the set was replete with two actors, the director called for the rain from the fire engines, and the wind from the huge fans. He must have felt like Eisenstein, for he screamed out in a frenzy that the impact should not be less impressive than the massacre scene in the film *Battleship Potemkin*.

'More sadism, Andrew. Tear that barbed wire as if it were a woman's dress!' he growled through the megaphone.

'Sasha, stab him with your bayonet. Don't feel sorry for him; he's the enemy.'

'More violence. Make it true to life!'

'Andrew, punch him in the gut. Knock him down and grab his rifle.'

'Sasha, fall face-down in the mud. Don't worry about the coat; it's government issue.'

'Let's have the blood in the puddle.'

'Keep down, Sasha, don't budge.'

'Now, let's see how Andrew will break through that door.'

The fire engines were spraying us with torrents of water; the fans flooding us with cool air. I was floating in the clay, like a submarine, with one eye like a periscope on Andrewlka, who was breaking down the steel door with his bayonet. For thirty minutes he fought to the death. it was a tough struggle. Finally, he stormed the arsenal with a victorious 'Hurrah!'

The director was beaming. He said the rehearsal had been a great success, and they were just about ready to start shooting. They lifted me out of the puddle and scraped the mud off me with a shovel, fixed my make-up, gave me a glass of vodka, and, once again, sent me into combat. The director cried out from joy when he saw Andrew getting into the role – ripping the barbed wire with his bare hands, really walloping me on the head with his rifle butt, and dashing over to the door to break the lock.

'Come on, Andrewlka, you're a man!' screamed the genius. 'It's like the door to your lover's bedroom! Pierce it with your bayonet!'

This time Andrewlka finished his job faster and disappeared within the darkness of the arsenal.

The crew grunted and panted as they pushed the equipment cart, bearing the frenzied director and the cameraman, who was glued to his lens. Curving around the barbed wire, they rolled towards me, took a close-up of my bloody ear sticking out of the mud, panned the wet brick wall of the armoury, lingering at the shattered bolt. There at the battered door, the scene was to come to an end, but the director, deciding to exploit his improvisational talent, ordered the crew to move the cart into the arsenal. But once they were inside, the director's talent unexpectedly ran up against the actor's talent. In the bright lights, amid plywood crates, rocking on top of a mound of machine guns, was Andrewlka's filthy back, clasped by the stark white legs of the director's wife.

Andrew and I made our way through the virgin forest. Along the way, the supple branches, with their tiny hard buds, felt like whipcords beating our faces. Our boots cracked the thin crust of ice and sank into the sticky mud, crushing an occasional island of snow.

When one of us was too exhausted to clear the path, and the other unable to endure the whipping, we exchanged forms of torture. I really couldn't understand what the devil had induced me to share in Andrewlka's punishment when the outraged director ordered the film crew to abandon him.

The order to pack up came so suddenly that we didn't have a chance to change our clothes, so there we were, trekking along in military coats and combat boots like spies in the enemy camp or deserters on home ground. That place was really dangerous – in a top-secret area like that, somebody could blow our heads off from fright, or just for fun. A Russian standing guard with a rifle can shoot even out of shyness, and then pardon himself with a bottle of vodka.

I was thirsty. I looked around for clean snow, but spring had turned all the snow into brown muck. I started to seek out a more or less clean puddle for a mouthful. There were a lot of them and, from far away, they looked blue and clear, with the inverted image of the sky and birch trees, but as I drew near, the mirrored image unexpectedly gave way to mud in which tiny worms and insects wriggled.

I stopped for a rest and leaned against a birch. My hand

squeezed the slender trunk; the bark was white and tender like flesh, and my fingers almost felt a slight pulse. Andrew came up to me, red and sweating.

'Hey, Andrewlka, do you know how to drink the juice of a birch?'

'Andrewlka knows everything,' he said, taking out a pocket knife and slashing the birch's trunk. He plunged the knife in deeper and started twisting it. It was painful to watch. He made a deep gash at an angle, and then we waited. Soon, at one end of the slit, a clear tearlike drop appeared. Then more tears welled, and Andrew said, 'Drink!'

I pressed my lips to the birch, and my tongue felt the slightly sweet spring juice. The smooth dry bark was warm, but the juice within, cool and piquant. I lost all sense of time.

'Okay, come on, Sashulka, that's enough. Leave a little bit for poor Andrewlka.'

I got out of the way. He hugged and kissed the birch firmly. His spread-apart fingers held the thin trunk and, I don't know why, but it wasn't pleasant to look at his broad back, with the white birch rising above his shoulder. I turned around and walked away; the earth began to feel harder and drier, and the forest looked sparser; there were no more of the hazelnut trees which had whipped us so cruelly.

By the time Andrewlka caught up with me the forest was coming to an end. We found ourselves near a highway, but before reaching the road, we encountered a high wooden fence.

We looked around, checking to see that there were no guards in sight, bolted over the fence, and made a dash for the highway. Luckily, a truck came along in no time. We motioned for a hitch, and the truck, which had a canvas flap over the back, came to a stop. As we were about to jump in, the cover flew open, revealing a dozen or so soldiers, all gaping. Yes, our appearance was truly something to behold – filthy coats, dishevelled hair sticking out from under military hats, and the epaulets of a sergeant. The dumbfounded soldiers raised their arms in salute; we didn't know the correct response and so I just mumbled, 'How's it going? It's okay, we're just making a check. Go ahead.' Fortunately, there was no officer among them and they simply saluted once again, put the cover back, and drove off.

Thank God a car came along next, instead of a tank. The driver turned out to be a good guy; he agreed to take us to Moscow for the price of a bottle.

All along the way, Andrewlka proceeded to narrate his tales. His most unbelievable story was that he had his own two-room apartment, with lilacs growing beneath his windows. Sensing that I didn't believe him, he suggested that when we got to Moscow, we go directly to his house, take a rest, and change our clothes. It wasn't such a bad idea, because wandering through Moscow in military garb was a sure way to prison.

We got out near a typical grey building flanked by similar boxlike structures. All Soviet architecture boils down to the various positions of a matchbox – lying down, resting on its side, and standing up. The building we came to was lying on its back – that was probably the only position that appealed to Andrew. We went in.

On the first-floor landing he screamed, 'Sound the trumpets, beat the drums, Andrewlka is home!' and, thrusting out his foot karate style, he banged open the door of his genuine two-roomed apartment. Then, dancing an African dance and belting out 'A Hard Day's Night', he descended on the bathroom and began to pee with the door open. Yes, Andrewlka was a real Russian cosmopolitan.

It wasn't easy to remove my coat; it had become stiff from the clay. I left it standing guard in the foyer, then entered the room. There were a lot of books around, a divan, a small table with a crystal bowl, a couple of chairs, a tattered Oriental rug, and a rocking chair. The walls were empty but, in the corner near the window, in a silver frame, hung a reproduction of Leonardo da Vinci's 'Madonna with Child'. Something was strange and hypnotic about this place, but what?

'Come with me. Pick out a pair of trousers,' he said, heading for the bedroom. I followed him, only to pause on the threshold; this room was quite different – the walls were covered, from floor to ceiling, with naked beauties from *Playboy*, pushing out their soft pink charm. A monstrous structure, once called a bed, straddled over the whole floor. At present, it looked more like a mountain range – there were peaks and valleys, revealing the shapes of bodies entwined in all-too-unimaginable embraces. Then it dawned on me – what was so hypnotic in this apartment was the scent, the scent of men and women in proximity, the scent of shame and shamelessness. It seeped through every pore in the room. It was irresistible. No, it wasn't the harsh suffocating smell of flesh; it was the seductive, bewitching scent of perversity.

Andrew climbed upon the bed, reached for the clothes on the top shelf, and tossed some bundles down in two separate mounds. 'These rags belong to that bastard, the cameraman,' he said. 'Stuff them in that knapsack and leave it at the front door. Today Andrewlka is signing that traitor out, but, Sashulka, you can stay here as long as you wish. Make yourself at home, this is your apartment now and these clothes are yours. You are the only one who stuck by Andrewlka through his misfortunes, and he will never forget it.'

I sifted through Andrew's clothing. We were the same size, but the only things that were clean were summer clothes – a white shirt and trousers. While I was putting them on, it occurred to me that it wouldn't be such a bad idea to stay there for a few days. I was planning to leave the dormitory anyway; I had been robbed three times, and it just wasn't the same without Stas.

'So are you going to stay?' asked Andrewlka.

I replied in the affirmative.

'Sound the trumpets,' he shouted. 'Andrewlka will arrange a great time for Sashulka. Lovely women will dance around him, and a river of wine will wash his weary limbs. Beat the drums! Sashulka will remember this apartment forever. Hey, now that you're living here, could you do Andrewlka a little favour and take the bedclothes to the laundry? There aren't any clean sheets left. Each piece is marked, and the laundry is just around the corner. When they ask for money, say it's from Andrewlka's household. Don't worry, they'll get what they deserve later.'

Andrewlka handed me a huge crocodile-leather suitcase – probably a wartime gift from America. My mother also had a large suitcase like that. I don't know what Americans shipped in them, maybe Studebakers, but who cares. Anyway, there I was, all in white, like Prince Charming, lugging that heavy, bulging, idiotic suitcase along the wet streets. The passers-by, thrilled over the free entertainment, tried to cheer me up with their pointed comments.

'Hey you, Snow White, what are you doing? Carrying your dwarfs?'

'Don't get a hernia, now!'

There was no laundry to be found at the corner. I went another block, but it wasn't there either. I kept on hauling my crocodile bag past one building after another under the fusillade of scathing remarks and jokes.

'Hey, how was the gold rush?'

'Look, an American pulling a crocodile!'

I suppose a lot of people remembered those suitcases from the war. Before I could be arrested as a foreign spy or black marketeer, I noticed a blue sign that said 'Laundry' on one of the corner buildings. I was relieved when I slipped inside. There wasn't a very long queue; after about twenty-five minutes of listening to stories about babies, sausages, and tangerines, I reached the counter.

'Are they all marked?' the woman inquired as I heaved my crocodile onto the counter.

'Yes, they are,' I replied assuredly, recalling Andrew's words.

'Clothing or bedclothes?' she demanded.

'Bedclothes,' I answered, fumbling with one of the locks.

'With or without starch?' she pursued.

'With starch,' I replied, and opened the suitcase.

The chatter in the room suddenly turned to silence. A chill swept down the line. I felt nauseated, first from the familiar smell from Andrew's apartment multiplied within the suitcase to the last degree, then from the sight of Andrew's linen, which was covered with semen and blood stains. They most definitely didn't need starch!

'How many of these?' asked the woman, fastidiously tugging at the corner of a spotted sheet.

'I don't know,' I answered.

'What do you mean, you don't know?' the woman asked sternly.

64

'I don't know; they're not mine,' I muttered, trying not to look at the suitcase.

'Don't try to vindicate yourself; you're not on trial, you know,' said the lady interrogator. 'But it would certainly be easy enough to *put* you on trial,' she said through clenched teeth as she held a pillowcase up to the light.

Everyone in the queue shrieked when the woman turned the pillowcase inside out in search of the mark. It must have been shrimp which looked like little pink crocodiles that came tumbling out. One clutched at the pillowcase and wouldn't let go for anything. The woman shook out the pillowcase, but the stubborn little creature would not let loose.

The customers laughed.

I stood here in white, like a candle, my face surely like a bright red flame. With each new piece the queue roared. They were stupefied. In front of the stunned audience was a show of purity and impurity, tenderness and cruelty, love and death. This was no suitcase, it was a human comedy.

Hoping to subdue the queue, the woman at the counter said, 'We won't be able to wash this with the other linen, so there'll be an extra charge of one ruble. That'll be four rubles, fifty-three kopecks. But this lady's panty, take it back, it isn't marked,' she added in a reproachful voice.

Once again the queue laughed heartily. I tossed the panty into the empty suitcase, closed its snout, and said coolly, 'These are Andrew's bedclothes; he'll take care of the bill later.'

'What?'

'I said it's Andrew's linen.'

'What?'

'He'll pay you later,' I repeated with emphasis.

'What Andrew?'

When I realized that I didn't know his last name, I just winked at the woman and whispered, 'Andrewlka. You know?'

'I don't know any Andrewlka. Are you off your rocker? Let's have the money. That's four rubles, fifty-three kopecks.'

There was no money in my new trousers. I started to stuff everything back into the suitcase. It didn't fit. I pressed down on the cover, the copper locks clacked, but the crocodile refused to close its jaws. I jumped on top of it and grappled with it, but to no avail. So, I charged at it, grabbed it from both sides, and pulled it out into the street. The cover was flapping, the sheets and pillowcases flying. I flung the suitcase onto the pavement, leaped on top again, this time snapping the locks shut.

The suitcase felt even heavier as I pursued my way back. I was totally exhausted when I reached the group of grey buildings – but which one was Andrew's? I had forgotten the number! With dusk sweeping the sky, all of the buildings looked like crooked matchboxes. I started to wander among them, like a ghost dragging a coffin. Pedestrians fled from me; children pointed at me and cried out in fright. I myself nearly cried as I passed the entrances to the same apartment dwellings again and again. I had lost all hope when I unexpectedly came across a door that looked familiar because it was covered with footprints. I summoned all my strength, attacked the door with a fierce samurai hit, nearly knocking it off its hinges, and staggered in. A blond girl was standing in the foyer holding a tray with china cups, a coffeepot, and a sugar bowl, all of which shivered, and shook, and shuddered, and fluttered.

I realized that the only way out was a quick retreat. Mumbling 'Sorry,' I started to push the crocodile onto the landing. The animal resisted, but finally I managed to drag it outside. I paused in thought.

The dusk was turning to night. The spring breeze wasn't a bit springlike as it touched me with cold fingers through the white summer cotton clothes. There wasn't one star in the sky – only the lights in the windows, teasingly winking the warmth of home at me. Thick bushes lined the building, and the buds on the branches were just burgeoning, playfully sticking out their tiny green tongues. I wanted to pull the branches down and touch them. I loved the smell of fresh greenery; it had never failed to clear my head and awaken my hopes. I reached up, but stopped because of what I saw between my fingers and the leaves. Looking down at me from the first-floor window were the pensive eyes of the Madonna with Child.

'Sashulka, where are you?'

'I'm here.'

'What are you doing there?'

'Nothing.'

'Looking at the lilacs?'

'Are they lilacs?'

'Yes, they are.'

'When will the flowers be coming out?'

'In two weeks.'

'So soon?'

'You don't believe it?'

'I believe it.'

'No, you don't. Come over here.'

'Okay.'

'Sound the trumpets, beat the drums! Andrewlka has found Sashulka, and now there will be a big celebration. Tanya said some robber broke into the apartment . . . She wanted to give herself to him (what an insatiable puma), but he ran away. Where did you disappear to all this time? The company has already started to arrive. Did you drop the linen off?'

'No, I probably went the wrong way.'

'Andrewlka forgives you, even though you forgot to take the military coats.'

6 The Lilacs Blossomed

The arrival of guests was, in fact, under way. I soon discovered that the law of Andrewlka's household was that nobody comes empty-handed. The golden-haired nurse, Tanya, who had come first, brought Takaji – 27.6 proof; next, two Georgians, Goga and Voga, brought Chacha – 160 proof; then a scientist brought experimental vodka, produced from petrol – 80 proof; next a famous cosmonaut brought 'Turtle,' aviation alcohol in a huge wicker bottle – 192 proof; three Japanese girls brought sake – 40 proof; then the butcher, an old friend of Andrew's, brought Bull's Blood – 24 proof, White Horse scotch – 86 proof, and filet mignon – sixteen pounds; then a man in a grey suit brought two girls, about fourteen or fifteen years old, who acted shy but were heavily made-up. After seating them on the divan, he took out a walkie-talkie, spoke into it, and in a few seconds, his chauffeur, also in a grey suit, brought in a case of sixteen-year-old cognac – 80 proof.

While the meat was roasting, the scientist quickly calculated the quantity and proof per person. He discovered that the average proof was 76.2, and there were 1.35714285714∞ bottles each. Everyone agreed that it was sufficient for the time being, and began to drink. We got off to a good start – we drank hot sake for friendship among nations; then White Horse scotch for our livestock; then gold Takaji for Tanya; then vodka for atomic energy; then potent Chacha for sunny Georgia; then cognac for the man in grey, for his work with juvenile delinquents; then pure alcohol for the conquest of the cosmos, and then it was impossible to understand what we were drinking, and for whom, or for what.

There was so much smoke in the room that you could hang an

axe on it, as we say. But anyway, in that polluted environment, life went on – the wayward girls sat on the grey man's lap, scanning the room with pencilled eyes, giggling, and downing shot after shot like grown-ups. The cosmonaut and the nurse drank to their new friendship, then he picked her up and carried her off to the bedroom, explaining the principle of the docking of spaceships. The Japanese girls were attacked by the united forces of Andrewlka, the scientist, and the butcher until they dispersed to different corners of the room, where they fell into action like kamikazes. All the while, the Georgians were running to the kitchen to check the meat and then back to the room to see if any girls had become available.

I sat on the rug, leaning against the wall, observing a translucent forest of empty bottles springing up around my legs. Through the blaring music and the sighs and moans came the ring of the doorbell. 'It's open!' Andrewlka screamed. The cameraman from the Military Studio entered the room sheepishly, a bottle of wine in hand. Andrewlka got up, walked over to him, whispered something in his ear, and then picked up the knapsack left on the floor, slapped it over the cameraman's shoulder, motioned to the door, and jauntily walked back into the room. The poor fellow came after him, gesticulating madly, as in a silent film. Andrewlka, looking exasperated, marched up to the window and began to study a bunch of lilacs attentively. The cameraman stood behind him, continuing his pantomime. Andrewlka flung the windows open and whirled around. A fresh breeze came into the room, sending the curtains flying behind Andrewlka like white wings. He stretched out his arms, took the knapsack from the cameraman's shoulder, and, without wasting words, threw it out the window. The knapsack tumbled down, snapping off several branches, and plopped onto the pavement.

'My camera's in there!' screamed the frantic cameraman as he lunged at Andrew, grabbing him by the throat. Without much interest, Andrewlka watched the cameraman's attempt to strangle him. Then, with a grin, he took the cameraman by the elbows and sent him the way of the knapsack.

We heard a thump and then a scream of unending pain. Then came silence. The bushes I had been admiring not so long

69

ago showed their broken branches sadly through the window. Andrewlka closed the curtains theatrically and said in a tragic tone, 'He would have gone far if it weren't for my lilacs.' Everybody applauded and started to drink Bull's Blood. Andrewlka went around filling glasses. When he got to me he asked, 'Wine or vodka?'

'To tell you the truth, I've had enough.'

Andrewlka sat down nearby and regarded me with concern. Our stretched-out legs were like paths in the bottle forest.

'Are you mad at Andrewlka?' he asked.

'What for?'

'This crazy bordello.'

'No, I've just had too much . . .'

'Andrewlka understands you, but you should understand Andrewlka, too. He is not the master of this house; he is the slave. Don't laugh; it's true. Every day, at the crack of dawn, the telephone starts ringing – "Andrewlka, old pal, could you help us out? Please, Andrewlka, be a dear." Andrewlka has such a big heart, he can't say no. Everybody needs his apartment – where else can you take refuge in Moscow? This is the only door that's always open.

'Take that top-secret scientist over there – where can he go to forget about his bomb? Not into his wife's arms; she's worse than radiation! And that cosmonaut – where is he supposed to take a girl when he wants to have a little fun? You know the Moscow Hotel bars Muscovites. Besides, he'd lose all his medals if he were seen playing around. And that plainclothesman over there – a few words into his walkie-talkie and he could wipe out half the city this very moment. But deep down inside he trembles – today it's them, but tomorrow maybe it's him. Only here can he forget this "maybe". You know, right now, Goga and Voga have a bundle on them from their tangerine business, but if Andrewlka didn't let them sleep on his kitchen floor, they would ride around in a taxi all night long rather than take a chance at some other place.

'So that's how they're drawn to Andrewlka's hearth. They know that here, nobody will sell them out. Everybody sleeps peacefully in Andrewlka's bed – the just and the unjust. Everybody finds repose here, everybody except Andrewlka! He has all Moscow in his hand, everyone's secret in his head, but he never has a minute's peace. He has told himself a thousand times, "It's time to turn over a new leaf," but again the telephone rings, and again the wheels are turning. Andrewlka is tired of these troops. Oh, how tired. Sashulka, old pal, today you're the man of the house. Just say the word and Andrewlka will throw all of them out the window, one after the other.'

'No, don't bother.'

'You don't believe Andrewlka would do it?'

'No, I believe you.'

'No, you don't. Let's make a bet.'

'No, I believe you.'

'You have very strange eyes, Sashulka. When you're laughing they are serious, but when you are serious they are laughing. Are you in love, by any chance?'

'You've guessed it.'

'Is it serious?'

'Maybe.'

'How come you didn't invite her?'

'She said she would come to me on her own, when she wants to.'

'And?'

'And she still hasn't come.'

'You're a funny fellow, Sashulka. If a woman says she'll come to you on her own, it means she wants you to go to her. Trust Andrewlka, nobody knows women better than he. Since his early childhood he's been interested in only two things, and both of them belong to the female body – one, from where Andrewlka came into the world; the other, where he first put his mouth. A woman is to Andrewlka like spring to a lilac bush; its bark can be ripped off, its branches broken, but come the spring, it will blossom. You'll see in two weeks; Andrewlka's lilacs will be the first to bloom in Moscow. You want to make a bet?'

'No, I believe you.'

'No, you don't. Nobody ever believes Andrewlka.' Just then he leaned over and whispered in my ear. 'Do you believe that Andrewlka will die the same day his lilacs die? Let's make a bet.'

Before I had a chance to respond, he leaped up and screamed at the top of his lungs, 'Sound the trumpets, beat the drums! Look who's here!'

A new couple appeared in the foyer.

'Get up, Sashulka, let's go, I want to introduce you to a big shot – Eyebrows' secretary and interpreter. Don't bother asking from which language to which; Andrewlka doesn't remember – maybe from Ukrainian to Russian, maybe from Russian to Ukrainian, but anyway, he is our leader's interpreter. Come on. You don't believe Andrewlka?'

I was drunk and didn't want to meet the interpreter or even the leader himself, but Andrewlka yanked me up and shoved me toward the latest arrivals.

'Yuri Petrovitch,' said the well-dressed, well-fed man, by way of introduction. Next to him stood a heavy-set lady with an unappealing face and very large breasts.

'How do you do,' she said. 'I'm Galina. Where can I wash my hands?'

'In the kitchen,' said Andrew.

'I'm referring to something else,' she said haughtily.

'Oh! You want to pee!' he screamed. 'Andrewlka's not so stupid; he can take a hint. You're right next to the bathroom. Go on in, as long as nobody is fucking, oh I'm sorry, screwing, in there.'

The lady laughed and shut the door, noisily locking herself in.

Without removing his raincoat, Yuri came into the room, took a bottle of French champagne from his pocket, stroked his wavy, glossy hair, and announced, 'Whoever wants to drink Dom Perignon, get in a circle.'

Everybody took a seat excitedly. Tucking his raincoat under him, the interpreter sat down in a cross-legged position between the two juvenile delinquents, then placed the bottle in the centre and set it spinning.

Yuri had begun to play the Russian folk game The Bottle, a cross between strip poker and spin-the-bottle. The game is quite simple: just give the bottle a spin and wait to see who it points to.

Then the person the bottle is pointing to has to take off a piece of clothing – a jacket, shirt, skirt, or stocking. What could possibly be more simple? But many generations have sat up all night in hopes of seeing that first bit of naked flesh.

Getting a Russian to expose himself in front of others is simply impossible; nothing but the finger of fate can break down his inhibitions. But if the spinning bottle selects him, a Russian will readily give in. For fear of angering Providence, he will show anything to anybody.

Only two people didn't play that remarkable game – the lady who came with Yuri Petrovitch, and I. She didn't because she had been busy in the bathroom, and I didn't because I was already totally drunk. The lady was sitting on the divan staring at me. I was busy concentrating on the pattern on the wallpaper over her head in hopes of stopping my dizziness.

The bottle spun faster and faster, lustily searching out a victim. The sneaky Japanese started by removing their necklaces and bracelets; the scientist started with his glasses; the butcher with his boots; the hot-blooded Georgians with their sweaters; the teenagers naively started with their skirts. Yuri Petrovitch, in spite of his clever plan to begin in his raincoat, was soon down to his underpants. His blubbery flesh, tumbling over the elastic waistband, looked like stretchy dough in a pot.

Passions flared. Each time the bottle stopped, the participants laughingly threw themselves at the loser, helping him remove his clothes. The excitement and tension were reaching a peak when the bottle slowed down and unmercifully pointed its green-gold neck right at Yuri. There was a hush. In the stillness Andrewlka started to perform a drumroll, as if announcing a dangerous number in the circus. With an imperious gesture, Yuri cut off the drummer and said in a concerned tone, 'Comrades, I sincerely hope that my dear boss will not get wind of tonight's next event. It could jeopardize détente.'

Everyone roared while Yuri, feigning seriousness, started to take off his underpants, without coming out of his guru position. Grabbing the elastic band in the back, he slowly pulled the briefs down under his fat thighs, but somewhere along the way, they got stuck. He tugged at the elastic; it slipped out of his grip. He lost his balance, clumsily fell backward, flapping his arms, and presented his bare, hairy backside straight to the ceiling. Everyone fell over in hysterics. Yuri, sensing the thrill of success, didn't hurry to change his pose.

At this point, the abused bottle of champagne was opened with an explosion and the party officially began.

Andrewlka lugged the sixteen pounds of steaming filet mignon from the kitchen and started beating the interpreter on his naked rear with it. Red drops splashed everywhere. Yuri shouted that he couldn't stand rare meat, but Goga, who apparently wasn't so fussy, yelled, 'Ara!', rushed over to Andrew, grabbed the filet mignon from his hands, bit off a chunk, and threw the rest to Voga. Voga took a bite and passed it on to the butcher. The steak moved around the circle, from hand to hand, and from mouth to mouth. While teeth were sinking into the meat, hands were reaching out for bodies covered with drops of juice, smearing the juice over the shoulders and breasts, moving down, stroking the belly and legs. . . .

'Sashulka!' Andrew called out as he came toward me through the haze of cigarette smoke. He was wearing only one white sock, and drops of blood trickled down his bare chest.

'Go to sleep, Sashulka. Go while the bed is still empty. Nobody will bother you there.'

'Good idea,' I mumbled.

When we went to the bedroom, Andrewlka got down on the floor, rummaging under the bed, and pulled out a sheet. He looked it over very carefully, glanced at me, examined it again, and said, 'It's the last one. I've been keeping it for myself.' Then he spread it out, covering the bed's hills and mountains, and went out, closing the door behind him.

I took off my clothes and cautiously lay down on one of the mountains. The next second I was sliding down a deep, soft cliff. The hills surrounded me with caring caresses; the valleys cradled my body gently. No inventor could even hope to create a masterpiece like that bed, shaped and moulded by the lovemaking of hundreds of bodies.

I don't know how long I slept, but I woke up to a hushed conversation coming through the door.

SHE: No, Andrew, no.
HE: (An indistinguishable murmur)
SHE: I said no, that means no.
HE: (An indistinguishable murmur)
SHE: I told you, I want to go over there.
HE: (An indistinguishable murmur)
SHE: You know what I'm talking about. Let go!

I heard the door of my room open quietly. Soft footsteps approached the bed. I couldn't see a thing in the dark, but felt the bed slump down and a large, warm body lie near mine. I didn't move. For a little while my guest didn't move either; I just felt short breaths on my shoulder, then a hand slowly easing its way under my neck, a leg moving under mine. Suddenly, with one swift movement, I was flipped over, and landed on top. I found myself resting on ample thighs, my face exactly between two breasts, one of which slapped against my cheek. Judging from its size and weight, I guessed that it was the woman who had come with the interpreter.

'Hello,' I said.

'Hi there,' she said.

'Everybody left?' I asked.

'No,' she replied, 'I'm still here.'

She started running her fingers through my hair, then slid her fingers down my back, leaving a trail of gooseflesh.

'I think I'll go take a shower,' I said.

'I'll be waiting,' she said.

While getting up, I clumsily stuck my elbow into her flabby flesh, and the woman cried out loudly. I apologized and left the room.

For quite a while, there was no hot water in the shower. I stood under the chilly spurts while I pondered the silly question Lenin posed the morning after the Revolution. 'Now what?'

Before I was able to find the answer, I noticed movement through the translucent shower curtain. I stretched out my hand to draw aside the curtain. Just then a large hand flung the plastic to one side. The rings jingled and bloodshot eyes confronted me. It was Andrew.

'So?' he asked.

'So what?' I asked.

'How was it?' he asked.

'How was what?' I asked.

'How was she?' he asked.

'I don't know,' I said.

'How come she screamed?' he asked.

'I poked her with my elbow,' I said and, at that moment, I found the answer to Lenin's question.

'Listen, Andrewlka,' I said.

'Andrewlka is always listening.'

'Do you like her?' I asked.

'What's the difference?' he said.

'Then splash a little water on yourself for good luck and get over there.'

'Why water?' he asked.

But the next second, the atom of Andrewlka's brain struck a deep spot, and without asking any more questions he put his head under the nozzle for a second, shook out his wet head like a dog, wiped off his face, whispered 'Sound the trumpets, beat the drums,' and quickly pattered barefoot to the bedroom.

I got out of the shower, dried myself off, went into the living room, lay down on the divan, and closed my eyes. As I was near dozing I perceived a recurring thud coming from the adjoining room. At first, it was like a heartbeat. Then it became louder and louder. Each beat was followed by a scream. From the start, each scream was unclear, but then, much to my surprise, I made out the words:

'Sasha, my precious! Sasha, my sunshine! Sasha, my genius! Sasha! Sashenka! Sashulka! Sashulichka! Sashulionok! Sashulion-ichik! Oh! Oh! Oh!'

I buried my head under the pillow and crawled beneath the blanket, but the vibration passed through the wall and floor. The sledgehammer was shaking the whole apartment. The sound resembled the rumbling of a distant earthquake.

'Sa-Sha-Sa-Sha-Sa-Sha-Sa-Sha-Sa-Sha-Sa-Sha-Sa-Sha-Sa-Sha!'

I didn't know how to make myself sleep. I was suffocating under the pillow. I tried counting, but against my wishes, I fell into the rhythm that Andrewlka was providing and found myself recording his heroic feat. Succumbing to the heat and lack of oxygen, I lost the count. I had no more strength. I flung the useless pillow off to the side and was surprised to find silence. There was no more pounding, but directly over my head somebody was breathing heavily. I looked up. Above me stood Andrew, naked and sweating profusely, his arms dangling by his sides. He stood there, sadly looking out the window, the pink rising sun playing in his eyes.

'Sound the trumpets,' he said softly, 'beat the drums. The lilacs have withered; Andrewlka is dead,' and with these words he came crashing down onto the divan.

When his feet landed beside my face, Andrewlka was already sleeping peacefully, the heavy stench of his production enveloping the divan like a cloud. It was impossible to lie down nearby. I got up and paced back and forth for a while.

Through the window, I saw the fiery sunrise between the matchboxes. Through the bedroom door, I saw the woman lying behind the mountain. I was dying to get some sleep. There were only two choices, and it wasn't a very difficult decision. In order not to wake the woman, I tiptoed towards the bed, chose a peaceful valley at the foot of the mountain, and curled up, falling asleep instantly.

I saw a garden of lilacs where ladylike hands grew in place of flowers. When a lazy breeze filled the garden, the hands swished against each other, and the flowers fell like lavender snow. One bush gently bent over and stroked my cheek, whispering, 'Sasha, you were wonderful. Good-bye; see you in two weeks,' and the whole garden of lilacs waved bye-bye.

I woke up. The whole room was bathed in sunlight coming through the open window. The wind teased the paper beauties on the walls. Some were falling down onto the bed, rustling and wiggling coyly. I looked around. I was alone. I got up, found my white trousers, put them on, and went to the other room, leaving the paper harem behind.

Andrewlka was sitting on the windowsill. There was a heavy pan beside him filled with hot fried potatoes mixed with eggs and scallions. Two sparkling crystal glasses and two frosty bottles of beer stood beside the pan.

'Sound the trumpets, Andrewlka meets Sashulka after a fun-filled evening,' gaily announced the hero of the previous night. 'I trust that Sashulka had a good night's sleep and is ready for breakfast. His faithful servant, Andrewlka, cleaned everything up as quietly as a mouse, gathered up the bottles, turned them in for cash, and, with the money, bought beer and potatoes. Andrewlka hopes that his best friend and master will not refuse to try a very simple dish called "Village Potatoes."'

I sat down on the windowsill across from the Madonna.

We drank the beer and dug in. It was awfully good. The potatoes were cooked masterfully, and I told Andrewlka so. He immediately began to brag that he knew one thousand and one ways of cooking potatoes, and that maybe 'Love is not a potato' as we say, but potatoes are his love. The atom in his head had a good night's sleep, and now it bounced easily and happily. I followed its speed and intricate trajectory with amazement, until it ricocheted on me.

'But anyway, tell Andrewlka, honestly, how the perverse ladies' man Sashulka liked that nymph with the big tits? Huh?'

I didn't answer.

'She wasn't as slim as the birch, was she?' laughed Andrew.

I kept quiet.

'But why is there always such injustice around? Poor Andrewlka was as busy as a bee in the garden of love all night, but his reputation as a sex maniac, built up over many years, was taken over in one night by shy Sashulka. Isn't it ironical? Isn't life senseless? Why, you probably don't even know who she is.'

'No, I don't,' I replied.

'I thought so,' Andrew said. 'She has a short but impressive last name. She is . . .' He took a sip of beer, poked the potatoes with a fork, broke off a brown, crunchy piece and a bit of a scallion, put it in his mouth, chewed it with relish, took another sip of beer, smacked his lips, and said:

'She's the daughter of our leader!'

'What?' I asked.

'She is the daughter of our dearly beloved Brezhnev,' proudly announced Andrewlka.

He was a liar, a drinker, and a playboy, but when it came to the most unbelievable things, he always turned out to be right; in fact, in exactly two weeks, beneath his window, the lilacs blossomed.

7 My Wooden Castle

Every night at Andrewlka's apartment was about the same and after a few weeks I felt that the only way to stay alive was to find my own place. . . .

In the centre of Moscow, just off Arbat, tucked away in a quiet side street just three minutes from the Institute, was a picturesque log cabin. This little wooden castle appeared to be from some long-forgotten time, resting as it did between two modern brick monstrosities.

From top to bottom, the castle was covered with lacy fretwork. According to legend, the house was built in 1872 by a wealthy merchant who had a penchant for Russian fairy tales. The only tool employed in the construction was an axe; not a single nail was used. When the work was completed, the gingerbread house was so beautiful that, to ensure that nothing like it would ever be built again, the eyes of the craftsmen had to be gouged out. In 1889 the log cabin was sent to the Paris Exposition as an exemplar of the finest Russian openwork. Its delicate fretwork pleased the Parisians much more than the metal rivets of the Eiffel Tower, built for the same Exposition.

The log cabin was full of riddles. When seen from the street, it looked like only one storey; from the backyard, it looked like two storeys; but from the inside, when you ascended the stairs, it seemed like at least five storeys. How so many stairs could have been packed into such a small house was a secret that died with the blinded builders.

Whether that dreamy merchant passed through the labyrinth of rooms and corridors alone, or whether he shared the joys of that fairytale castle with a wife, I can't say, but the beneficent Soviet government gave the same pleasure to at least twenty families and, believe me, each family member who resided in that castle could have been an exhibit at the Paris Exposition.

There, on the second floor (as seen from the backyard), was my first room in Moscow. After Andrewlka's, it was even easy putting up with my new landlord, Toilik.

Each morning, through the plywood partition, I would hear my landlord's gravelly baritone. Before even taking the sleep out of his eyes, he would be singing his favourite song – hoping to convince himself that he was still alive after the previous night.

'*Rise up, poor people, you the world's hungry ones . . .*' With this line from the 'Internationale,' Toilik would fall out of the bed onto the floor. Through the plywood, I could hear my landlord struggle with a revolutionary impulse to get up on all fours and crawl into the hallway. '*We are ready to go to the deadly war!*' he sang, stumbling on the landing.

'*This is our final fight!*' his voice thundered on the stairs. The whole wooden house would vibrate and hum like a cracked contrabass, as Toilik defiantly crawled through the maze of corridors en route to the toilet, the only one for all the tenants. As for a bath or shower – we tenants had to go to the public baths five blocks away.

The jakes was in the busiest place in the house – at the intersection of all the corridors. Each morning, the citizen-tenants scrambled out of every hole in the wall and formed a long line, as if queueing for tickets to a concert. And it really was a concert, featuring Toilik's revolutionary rhapsody, with a finale in which all nations promised to rise up.

'*Rise up, people!*' Toilik sang, accompanied by the sound of flushing, then the door flung open, and the performer, closing his fly, emerged facing his captive audience.

Toilik was a real star – not only in his own house, but in the whole city. He was one of the top ten on the long list of Moscow alcoholics picked by the police to be expelled from the capital as part of the present Five-Year Plan.

By waiting for the liquor shop to open, by queueing for vodka, by gradually switching from vodka to port wine, and from port wine to cologne, cologne to tooth elixir, little by little, Toilik won the respect and honour of the legions of ordinary Muscovite alcoholics.

Those who made it to the top of the list had a right to call themselves the cream of the crop in our society. As a rule, they were all well educated and, at some point, had held respected positions as professors, actors, captains, doctors, and scientists. But every one of them relinquished his post, without a moment's hesitation, all for the pursuit of his passion. Inevitably, all of them wound up working as loaders in a vegetable market, the only job they could get, because who else would apply for a job where there is nothing worth stealing?

In keeping with the traditions of his clan, Toilik too worked in a vegetable market. In his previous life, he was a well-known test pilot, in fact, a Hero of the Soviet Union. He had even had a wife and daughter and, because of his reputation as a family man, the government gave him a room in the wooden castle. With a hero's instinct, Toilik divided that room into two narrow rooms, then partitioned one further. If the original builders could have known how many nails Toilik used for the renovation, they would surely have regained their eyesight. When the construction was over, Toilik had two small square bedrooms and one rectangular living room. It was quite an accomplishment because each member of the family acquired a room, but such an uncommon luxury seemed to destroy the family unit. Toilik's wife and daughter stopped supporting his drive to be in the top ten, and left him.

This domestic disaster propelled Toilik from an aviator-hero to an alcoholic-hero. He then became the leading dissident in the fight for freedom to drink, not only in lobbies, but in all public places. For all this he needed regular funds, but since when did dissidents have money? So, the revolutionary Toilik decided to compromise himself and became a landlord. He rented out his daughter's bedroom, and I was the first tenant. Toilik wasn't quite sure of himself in his new role as landlord and, hoping to please his tenant, he decorated my room with his collection of antiques – a bronze candelabra and a bearskin rug.

Blue wallpaper sprinkled with tiny white daisies covered the walls of the room. Near the window stood a hand-carved desk. The candelabra rested on the desk. There was a bookshelf over the desk, and against the opposite wall, a little bed. Flush against the bed was a wardrobe, and, on the floor, the worn bearskin rug – that was it. There were no lights in the room; in fact, there were no electric outlets. When it was dark I just lit a candle.

Late one night, Toilik banged on the partition and grunted something about a phone call. I went downstairs to the only phone in the house. It hung on the wall near the most popular place – the toilet. As usual, a long line of tenants stood in the hallway, shifting from one foot to the other in anxious anticipation. Each one held the newspaper, *Pravda*, in his hands. *Pravda* provided both entertainment and practical function.

As I walked down the line, each of the residents put down his copy of *Pravda* and said, 'You've got a call.' The last one in the chain, holding *Pravda* in one hand and the receiver in the other, said, 'Did you know it's for you?'

'Yes, thank you,' I replied, and took the phone.

'Hello,' said a familiar voice.

'Boris!'

'I just wanted to let you know my new girl friend, Mashka, and I are back in Moscow,' Boris said.

'New girl friend? That's great!' I exclaimed. 'When are we going to get together so I can meet her?'

'Actually,' said Boris, 'we're near your house right now. Could you come out for a little while?'

'Why don't you come over here?'

'No,' said Boris. 'We don't have time. Mashka is trying to get me to go with her to her father's dacha, but I've got something I can't take there and I'd like to leave it with you. Is that all right?'

'Sure,' I said. I put down the receiver and went outside.

There, on the corner, I saw two figures. One was Boris, tall and skinny with his long, thin neck; the other was Mashka – she didn't seem to have any neck at all. She was squat and mannish-looking. They stood together near the telephone booth and, despite their different heights, they swung in perfect synchronization, like two metronomes. They held a big, dark sack which rocked between them to the same rhythm.

'Welcome back,' I said.

'Nice to see you,' Boris said, and hiccupped. Then he turned to the young lady next to him and said, 'Mashka, I want you to meet my oldest friend, Sasha.'

She took my hand and said, 'I'm happy to finally meet you.'

'And I'm very happy to meet you,' I warmly replied.

'Have a drink!' offered Boris, taking a bottle out of his pocket.

'How much have you had already?' I asked.

'Not much. Just one or two bottles,' said Boris.

'Two or three,' corrected Mashka.

'How's everything up north?'

'Dead,' said Boris, frowning and glancing at me with his slanted milky grey eyes. His face was red as a beet, but he managed to speak in a steady voice: 'We were floating down the river and there were deserted villages on both sides. The houses were black from the rain, and damp inside. You could stop, walk into any log cabin, and take whatever you wanted. But what poverty! There wasn't a thing worth taking, except for this,' he said, motioning to the bundle.

'Do you think you could hide it for us at your place?' Mashka asked as she joined Boris in hiccupping.

'What is it?'

'The end of the earth,' said Boris. 'You'd better take it before we take it back.'

'When you get it upstairs, pick out whatever you like,' offered Mashka.

'All right,' I said, 'I'll take it.'

The heavy bundle was wrapped in a woollen blanket and tightly fastened with a clothesline. They helped me lift it onto my shoulder.

'So long,' said Boris.

'Hey, wait, when are we going to make plans for our holiday?'

'How about tomorrow night?' asked Boris.

'No, tomorrow is the last day of school, and there's a party at the Institute.'

'Okay, the day after tomorrow, then.'

'Okay,' I said and, stooping under the jagged-edge sack, went inside.

Going up the rickety stairs in the dark with that awkward sack wasn't easy. Each stair was a different height. I still didn't know all their secrets by heart and stumbled a few times. Though covered with the blanket, the bundle dug into my shoulder. I was on the verge of dropping the damned thing when I got to my room. I lowered it from my shoulder to my arms and heaved it onto the bed. I lit a candle and went about untying the cord in the wavering light. I came across some sailor's knots, but not being a seaman, I couldn't loosen them. Eventually, I got fed up and cut the cord in several places. The package, which had felt like a rectangular crate moments before, fell to pieces with a strange, wooden sound. I drew back a dirty corner of the blanket and found, staring up at me with unflinching eyes, a dark face framed in black, wavy hair.

A real icon!

Never in my life had I seen a real icon before, but here were one, two, three, four, five . . . more than twenty of them. I spread them out on the bed carefully. I put some on the table and on the bookshelf. I looked for any nails on the walls and the wardrobe and hung the icons on them. The room took on the aura of a country church. The icons were cracked and blackened with smoke. In the darkness, my candlelight captured St George killing a dragon; the Saviour bleeding on the cross; an old man staring with weary eyes; and the Virgin holding her Child.

The last icon mesmerized me; it was Our Lady of Tenderness cradling her infant, serious beyond his years. From top to bottom, a deep gash was cut through the Madonna's face, but somehow it didn't mar her beauty.

That Madonna brought to mind Leonardo's Madonna, though they didn't look alike. The painting by Leonardo was a jovial one, with a homely touch. I could speak with that woman about anything – life, music, or love. It seemed to me that if I asked her, she would be pleased to let me touch the pink, plump leg of her son.

The Madonna from the North was rather different. A dark red cloak covered her head and fell on her shoulders in heavy folds. The infant resting in her arms was a son, but no child. Both of them looked right through me, viewed the world with seriousness

85

and serenity. I felt no desire to chat with that Madonna; I simply stared at her and felt happy.

Suddenly I got an irresistible urge to share my delight over the Lady of Tenderness. I took hold of the icon, blew out the candle, and before the zigzag smoke had faded, I was already on the street.

I ran along the boulevard, the icon firmly pressed to my side. It felt good to touch the warmth of its time-dried wood. It was weightless – it seemed that if I let go, it wouldn't fall down, but would simply hang there in the air and be carried along by the spring breeze. I smiled and held my icon tight.

When I found myself at Lena's house, I realized it was very late. Perhaps she and her aunt were sound asleep; maybe she wasn't even at home. Standing in the middle of the street, I took a few steps backward and looked at the building, hoping that her room would be lit up.

There was a supermarket on the first floor of the building. Its large windows displayed cans of fish in tomato sauce, boxes of laundry detergent, and frozen meat.

I remembered that Lena's aunt's apartment was on the second storey. The entire floor was in darkness except for one window – the one above the meat section of the supermarket. There, level with the windowsill, deep within the room, bobbed a woman's grey head, resembling a puffball. I truly hoped that the puffball was Aunt Sonia. The woman scooted back and forth several times, then disappeared within the room, and the light in the window went out. I passed the icon from one hand to the other, rubbed the warm wood, but it didn't change a thing. I waited a little longer, but still no change. When I was about to leave, the light flashed in the window again – and there, in the window frame, stood Lena. It was suddenly as if somebody had switched on a slide projector. For a little while I didn't budge, fearful that the picture might change when I went charging towards the building. On the pavement I searched for a small stone but found nothing but two bricks. I scurried around in front of the supermarket window, like a squirrel searching for a nut, and, near the stairs, I saw what I was looking for – a small, smooth grey stone, something that could be found only at the seashore.

Without bothering to figure out how such a pebble from the sea could end up near a Moscow supermarket, I simply seized it, moved away from the building, took aim, threw the stone, and followed its path, only to discover that Lena was no longer at the window. The sound of the impact was unexpectedly loud, and I was afraid the window might break. In the window frame appeared a portrait of Lena with a surprised expression. With her hands shielding her eyes, she pressed against the glass. We stood there staring at each other for a moment. I held up the icon and motioned that I had brought it for her. She smiled. The next minute she was gone from the window.

I stood there looking up, my neck craned. I thought my appearance with the Lady of Tenderness in the middle of the night must have seemed ridiculous. It occurred to me it might be better to slip quietly away, but just then another window was thrown open, and Lena's voice rang out in the darkness.

'Are you crazy?'

'Yes,' I said, placing the icon on my head and ad-libbing a few dance steps.

'What is it?' Lena asked.

'An icon,' I said, stopping my dance.

'You're completely crazy,' said Lena.

'I want to show it to you.'

'You came here at twelve o'clock at night for that?'

'Yes,' I said.

'Get closer to the light; I can't see a thing.'

I moved closer to the shop window.

'I still can't see it.'

'Come out here,' I said.

'Wait,' she said.

My visit didn't seem to be so stupid after all. I headed for the entrance to meet Lena, but from above, her hushed voice sounded once again:

'Hey.'

I looked up.

'Catch this,' Lena called in a whisper.

She balled something up in her hand and then threw it from

the window. It opened in flight and slid down the store window. Right near my feet landed one end of a silk ribbon.

'Tie the ribbon around it.' Lena laughed in the darkness.

I did, and gave the ribbon a tug.

'Pull,' I said.

Slowly and silently, the Madonna rose, hugging her son. Behind her, in the shop window, smoked pigs' legs and red frozen beef hung on big metal hooks.

Lena's hand reached out the window, caught the icon, and disappeared. The light in the room went on; I saw Lena standing in the middle of the kitchen scrutinizing the painting. She was in profile and her thin figure in her strawberry bathrobe was sharply set against the white tile wall. She slowly turned to face me and mouthed, 'It's beautiful, it's very beautiful.'

The light in the room went out, but I went on standing there looking up.

'Hey,' sounded Lena's voice.

'What?' I asked the window.

'What are you looking at? I'm over here,' Lena said, peeking out the entrance door. 'Come over here; I don't have any shoes on,' she said, flashing her socks out of the door.

I went into the building. The gloomy entrance was lit up by a dirty, paint-spotted bulb. A heavy spring slammed the door shut behind me, and I jumped. Lena laughed and, without a sound, came toward me in her thick white socks on the chipped tile floor. She stood on tiptoes, leaned against me, and kissed me gently. Her lips were soft and dry. I closed my eyes and let myself go in the head-spinning wonder of our first kiss. She had nothing on beneath her lightweight robe; I carefully opened it and tentatively kissed her small, warm breasts. Still surprised over our unexpected closeness, I didn't hear the door open, and a dog and a senior citizen come trampling into the building.

'Ruff, ruff, ruff,' said the dog.

'What are you doing here?' barked the old man.

It was written all over his grey face that he was not only an old man, but a retired civil servant.

'Ruff, ruff, ruff,' repeated the dog.

'I'm asking you in plain Russian who you are and what you're doing here,' growled the old man.

'We're kissing,' Lena said.

'I'm going to call the police this minute! Show me your documents,' the senior citizen snarled viciously.

'Documents?' asked Lena, going up to the civil servant. 'Okay, I'll show you. Oh, where is my passport?' She checked her naked body, searching for a pocket. 'Where did I put my passport? Where is it? Don't worry, I'll find it. Can you hold on a minute?' Her bathrobe flapped, exposing now her thigh, now her breast.

The civil servant's face went into contortions. He howled some gibberish about his medals, his work for the KGB, and our imminent arrest. Then he leaped into the lift, dragging the dog in by its chain. The dog wanted to add something himself, but the metal door rolled shut, preventing him from putting in his two kopecks.

The lobby became quiet. Again we stood in the dingy entrance lit up by the dusty bulb.

'It's cold,' Lena said, snuggling up to me. 'I'd better go.'

I wanted to say something to her but she had already turned around and was on her way up the stairs. Her white socks jumped from step to step noiselessly, like soft rabbits. They fluttered around the iron banister, reached the top of the stairs, and disappeared.

What I wanted to say to her was – 'I love you, Lena . . .' I would tell her the next day . . . the next day . . . I thought as I went running through the night to my wooden castle.

8 The Beginning

As I had told Boris, the next day there was a gathering at the Institute to celebrate the end of the freshman year. The evening was unusual – no pompous speeches and no pep talks about self-discipline; on the contrary, the party was unofficial and homelike. We were even permitted to bring wine.

In front of the plush crimson curtain, all the tables in the auditorium were lined up in a row, covered with lamé tablecloths from the performance of *Othello*. The abundance of food on that long table brought gasps from all who entered the room. There was everything – roast turkey with a glazed, crisp skin; sturgeon in jelly garnished with carrot stars; stuffed duck with appetizing, golden-brown legs jutting upward; a whole broiled piglet, fat and pink, on an enamel platter; fruit baskets laden with grapes and ripe yellow bananas; and on each plate, slices of white and dark bread had already been laid out.

The bread was real but everything else was papier mâché, brought from the props room, at the request of the Dean, to create a festive atmosphere. He believed that the most important thing for young actors was to have a vivid imagination and, according to his theory, there was no better place to enrich the imagination than at the table. His imagination had already grown sufficiently over the years and so on his plate there was a genuine and juicy beefsteak with sautéed onions, ordered out from a nearby restaurant by his secretary, Miss Silver.

We drank wine and each one imagined eating whatever entrée his heart desired; fortunately, there were many good examples on that table, and our fantasies, accelerated by alcohol, flowed without limit. We gallantly offered each other the meats and fruits, but everybody was so full in his imagination that he politely refused.

Lena took a seat next to Misha Limshitz, the class Romeo. All evening they took turns feeding each other huge bananas and laughing heartily. I didn't think it was very funny – I just sat there drowning myself in wine and didn't even pretend to eat.

The silver-lamé tablecloth, with its shiny sequins, shimmered and dazzled me. It seemed to me that the turkey was beckoning the piglet, and the piglet was staring at her rear, twitching its nose and winking at me mockingly with its fried eye. I sensed it was time to get up from the table and make a visit to the men's room.

Trying hard to walk straight, I left the auditorium with a heavy head and nauseous stomach and stumbled into the bathroom. Near the urinal, the Field Marshal was standing with his legs spread apart. With a dramatic flair, he shook the last few drops onto the cement floor.

'Oh, Sasha! Congratulations on successfully completing your first year! I congratulate you with all my heart,' he said in his deep voice while majestically transferring the wrinkled, purple flesh to his left hand and holding out his right to me. . . .

When I got back to the auditorium, the dancing had already begun. Polkas alternated with rock, but it didn't make a bit of difference to the dancers; nobody was paying attention to the music. A flashing garland of multicoloured bulbs seemed to be the only thing setting the rhythm.

I was making my way through the jumping crowd when someone came up from behind and put their hands over my eyes.

'Lena?' I asked, feeling my legs go numb.

'Wrong,' said a hot whisper in my ear. I turned to find myself in the embrace of Miss Silver.

'Did I surprise you?'

'Yes,' I said.

She placed her hands on my shoulders and started shifting from one foot to the other. I stayed put, but she was gliding to the left and to the right, and so, it turned into something like a dance. The country folks considered this a tango. It's a good dance – you can hold each other, or not; you can shuffle along the floor, or not; you can listen to the music, or not; it's very easy and extremely popular.

'How this year flew!' she said, tilting her head to the side.

'Yes,' I said. 'It's hard to believe.'

'It seems like yesterday that we sat at the cinema, remember?'

'Yes,' I said. 'I remember.'

'What are you doing after the party?' she said, pressing her breasts right up against me.

'I don't know,' I said.

'I heard you rent a room in that strange log cabin. I'm dying to see it from the inside. Let's go there, drink tea, and reminisce about the past.' Her legs moved forward and backward, adroitly slipping between mine while we danced.

'How about it?' she asked.

'About what?'

'About the tea.' She smiled, brushing her cheek against mine, then whispered with a sigh – 'You know, this is your second chance, but I warn you, there won't be a third.'

'Then let's get going,' I said.

'Where to?' she asked.

'To the third one, which won't be,' I replied.

Somebody stopped the music and in front of the scarlet curtain, in a bright light flashing nervously, appeared the Field Marshal, his arms folded in front of him. He stopped in the middle of the stage, took a handkerchief out from under his lapel, wiped his bald spot, and announced that this would be the last dance.

Everybody started grumbling – the dancing had just begun, they clamoured, why did this have to be the last dance? The Dean held up his hand with the white handkerchief. It looked as if he were weakening, but just when the student victory was imminent, Miss Silver intervened. She went up to the Dean, said something to him, and walked off the stage, her heels pounding in syncopation. The Dean's handkerchief wilted in his hand and he slipped it beneath his lapel.

'Comrade students,' shouted the Field Marshal, to silence the crowd, 'I'm asking for your cooperation. Comrade Silver must ready the auditorium for tomorrow's performance of *Othello*, and she requests that you vacate the premises. That's why this will have to be the last dance.'

I went to look for Lena. She was leaning against a column, surrounded by Misha Limshitz and a bunch of the class intellectuals. They were crossing wits to see who would get the last dance with Lena. Each witticism was weighed by the group and occasionally someone would say, 'Good joke; twenty kopecks.'

It would have been inappropriate for those intellectuals to laugh – that was for Lena to do – but somehow she wasn't laughing either. I slipped inside the circle and said, casually, 'Somebody's got real sausages over there!'

The intellectuals stared at me, not knowing whether or not to take it as a joke – I wasn't from their clique. I didn't go into details; I merely smacked my lips. That worked better than any words. Marx was right when he told Engels that matter comes first, the intellect second. When the chords of the last waltz sounded, there were only two people near the column – Lena and I; the brains were scurrying around the auditorium in search of the sausages.

'Twenty kopecks,' said Lena.

'Let's dance,' I said.

She was wearing a green knit dress, and her tanned body shone through the loose stitches. She was always brown, even in the winter. It was as if the sun from her southern city on the Black Sea followed her around all year. My fingers, dipping into the holes of her dress, tingled as they touched her smooth, lithe body. My head was reeling, but now, it was not from drink.

'It seems like we didn't even say hello to each other tonight,' said Lena.

'Yes,' I said, 'you were so busy with the bananas, you didn't notice who was sitting across from you.'

'Yes, I did,' said Lena, smiling as if in a dream. 'You weren't across from me, though; you were off to the side a little. How come you weren't sitting beside me?' she asked.

We circled the room; everything around was a blur – only the amber lights of Lena's eyes were fixed in the whirl of the movement.

'What are you doing after the dance?' I asked, stupidly getting onto Silver's track.

'What do you want to know for?' Lena answered with a question.

'You've never been to my house and I thought . . .'

'Sorry,' said Lena, 'I've already been invited somewhere else.'

'Okay,' I said, 'I was also invited somewhere – for tea at my house. I guess I'll have to accept that invitation now.'

'Is this your usual style?' Lena asked.

'What do you mean?' I asked.

'To protect yourself like that.'

'Yes,' I replied, 'with girls like you, it's safer that way.'

The whirling stopped abruptly. I felt a sudden slap. I was stunned. Who could imagine that a fragile girl like Lena would have such a powerful right hand. The pain and insult coloured my cheek. Before I knew it, I had slapped her back. For a few seconds, Lena just stood there in front of me, her eyes tightly shut, her hands down at her sides. Then she opened her eyes wide and looked at me, questioningly. I, too, wanted to know what was going on, and I stared back at her. Lena shook her head in resignation, then burst out laughing. Her laugh was contagious and I joined in. She leaned on me, put her arms around my neck, and the dancing started all over again. We waltzed around and laughed nonstop.

'I see you've mastered Stanislavsky's Clapping Machine,' Lena said, struggling through her laughter.

'Now I know why we were learning that stuff all year,' I said.

'Stanislavsky really knew what a good fight was,' shouted Lena, circling faster and faster.

'Hooray for Stanislavsky!' I roared.

Somebody behind me must have thought the sausages had arrived and took up the 'Hooray'. After him somebody else chimed in and, in no time, the whole drunken class was going hoarse shouting 'Hooray!'

But Lena and I were already outside, walking along quiet Arbat Street. We didn't want to scream; we didn't even want to speak; we simply wanted to walk in the night air. For once, we didn't have to think about rehearsals in the morning. Vacation was to begin the next day.

When we got to the wooden castle, Lena hopped onto the carved porch, touched a wooden ornament on the cornice, and asked, 'Is this your house? You really live here?'

'Yes,' I said.

'How lucky you are, living in the centre of Moscow in this wonderful house! It's like a dream,' she said, putting her arms around one of the posts.

I stood on the porch, gazing, not at the house, but at Lena. I thought to myself – if she doesn't back out, I'm really lucky!

She was flying around the porch, leaping from one carved post to another, like a green bird.

'Lena,' I said, hoping to interrupt her flight, 'do you want to see the rest of the house and drink tea from an antique samovar?'

'Tea?' Lena said, as she flew around me. 'Tea is good for getting me inside.'

I opened the oak door before she had a chance to change her mind. We crossed the threshold and started on our trip up the stairs.

'Which floor are you living on?' Lena asked anxiously.

'The second,' I replied.

'I don't understand. By now, we should be on the third floor, at least,' Lena said, and grabbed my hand.

'There are only two flights left,' I promised, not quite sure myself.

When we reached Toilik's apartment, I realized that I hadn't prepared Lena for the greatest 'wonder' of the house.

As I opened the door, I hoped with all my heart and soul that we would not meet him . . . but no luck.

The Wonder was standing in front of a mirror, dressed in his Sunday best. With undivided attention, he stared at the reflection of a gold star pinned to the lapel of his jacket. In one hand, he held a glass of red wine; in the other, a cigarette and a pickle. In all probability, he was getting ready for the next dissident meeting at the liquor shop. He was checking his appearance carefully and critically from every angle. He had put another mirror on a chair behind him and the two mirrors reflected his ridiculous figure, multiplied a hundred times. His diminishing frame went down the mysterious mirror-corridor; the gold star of the hero became smaller and smaller in each new reflection and vanished somewhere, consumed by the darkness. It seemed to disturb the hero. Deep in concentration, he tried to fathom the unfathomable. His entire visage showed that he was very close to discovering where the star went, when, out of the corner of his eye, he spotted us. This seemed to bring him back from his ruminations. He raised his glass and immediately hundreds of hands in the mirror also raised their glasses, hundreds of stars twinkled, and hundreds of mouths exposed broken teeth.

'Ha! . . . Ha! . . . Ha! . . . Nefertiti . . . Nefertiti . . . Nefertiti . . . Has come . . . come . . . come . . . To drink . . . drink . . . drink . . .'

'That's okay, Toilik. We've already had enough for today,' I said.

'I can't drink alone,' he said. 'I can't, that's all. To be more specific, I can, but I don't want to.'

'Drink with them! Look at how many of you there are,' I said.

'Who?' asked Toilik in confusion.

'Them,' I said, 'drink to their health.' I took his hand and pushed it towards the mirror. The real and the reflected Toiliks clanged glasses. The wine splattered the mirror and red drops trickled down all the reflections.

'No,' he said, 'I want to drink with Nefertiti.'

A hundred Toiliks sneered at me from the mirror.

'With what Nefertiti?' I asked.

'With that one,' he said, indicating Lena in the mirror.

'No way,' I said.

'Why not?' piped Lena's voice from behind me. 'I have no objection to drinking with him.' Lena went up to Toilik and took the glass out of his hand.

'To your health!' she said, and drank bottoms up while Toilik watched her with amazement.

'Nefertiti,' he said after a brief pause, 'you're a good fellow. Here, have a bite,' he said, and pushed the pickle under her nose.

'Thank you,' Lena said, 'but you're not supposed to eat after the first shot.'

'Then let's have the second one,' Toilik said.

'Later,' Lena said. 'Bye-bye, Toilik.'

'See you soon, Nefertiti,' my landlord offered with a friendly wave.

We went into my room. I closed the door and lit the candle. Without a second thought, Lena kicked off her shoes and jumped onto my bed.

'Are all these icons yours?' she asked, looking around the room.

'No, some friends asked me to keep them for a while, but I'm not so sure this is the safest place for them. "Your" friend Toilik might trade them in for a few bottles when he goes on his next drinking binge.'

'I'm not so sure the icon you brought me yesterday is safe at my place either. When my aunt found it this morning, she started yelling that they didn't throw the icons out of the churches during the Revolution so that their children could take them in.'

'Is she so anti religion?'

'No, it's more like the blind faith in the Party. Tomorrow, if there's an article in *Pravda* that says that God exists, Sonia will be the first to place a cross around her neck but, until then, you'll have to take your icon back. Actually, I think you had better take it tomorrow morning, because in the evening I will be flying home to the Black Sea.'

'Ah,' I said, trying not to sound too sad, 'I hope you have a good time.'

'What will you be doing this summer?' asked Lena.

'My friend Boris invited me to Koktebel. He found a house on the water. I may go there in a week or so.'

'Where is this Koktebel?' Lena asked.

'I don't know exactly, somewhere in the Crimea.'

'I wish I could go there instead of going home,' Lena said.

'Don't you want to go back home?' I asked.

'Only to see my grandfather.'

'What about your parents?' I could tell from the look on Lena's face that it was a question she didn't want to answer. I didn't pursue it. An uncomfortable silence followed.

'Who plays the guitar in this house,' she suddenly asked, motioning to the guitar in the corner, 'you or Toilik?'

97

'Both,' I said.

'But if I wanted to hear a song, who should I ask, you or him?'

'Me,' I responded.

'Why?' Lena asked.

'Because Toilik knows only one song, but I know two.'

'Would you sing for me?'

I picked up the guitar and sat down on the bed, near Lena. When I lifted my hand to strum the guitar, my arm brushed against her leg. The candle on the table flickered, and the night air rolled into the room through the open window.

I sang a song about the Metro:

> To me, on my Metro, it's never crammed,
> From childhood on it's like a song –
> Keep to the right if you're standing still,
> And keep to the left if you're moving on.

I don't always sing well, and it's hard to say what it depends on, but that night, it was impossible not to. It seemed as if the song flowed with the night breeze. All I had to do was finger the strings and listen to the song, rather than sing.

Lena kept watching the dancing flame of the candle. I went right into another song, with words by Mandelstam, a poet who died in one of Stalin's prison camps.

> The Greeks captured Helen by the sea,
> As for me,
> Only salty foam on my lips,
> Only salty foam on my lips.

'I didn't know you could sing,' said Lena when I stopped.

'I didn't either,' I said.

'Do you write your own songs?' Lena asked.

'One time I tried to write a song about Mandelstam. He had such a terrible life that I wanted to do something for him, but it just didn't come.'

'Why don't you try again? I'm sure you can do it.'

'You think so?' I asked.

'I don't think, I know,' said Lena confidently. 'I feel it. By the way, where's the tea you promised me?'

'Wait a minute.' I went to the kitchen to light the samovar. I had brought it from Tula and used it only on special occasions. It was very old, made of copper, and it burned either coal or wood. If any of the tenants caught me lighting a samovar in the kitchen of that wooden house, all hell would break loose, so I had to carry it to the back staircase, where I rested it on the top step. I gathered some chips of wood which were scattered around the house, put them into the samovar, lit it, and waited for the water to boil. I couldn't wait to bring the shiny samovar into my room to enthrall Lena. When it began to bubble and hum, I took hold of the handles, and just then heard . . .

'Nefertiti's a good fellow.'

I was taken aback. It was Toilik. After a fruitful meeting at the liquor shop, he was making his way up the stairs, on all fours. He was clearly in a revolutionary state – his body couldn't follow orders, and his head couldn't give them.

'Did you hear me?' He repeated. 'Nefertiti's a good fellow.'

'I know,' I said.

'You don't know a damn thing,' he muttered. 'She's a good fellow. She wants to drink with me, and here I am.'

'No,' I said.

'But she promised.'

'No,' I said.

'Yes!' said Toilik, and he crawled to the top stair. Only then did he see the samovar, not exactly the samovar, but his gold star, reflected in it. He was mesmerized. He reached out for his medal in the reflection.

'Don't touch; it's hot,' I cried, moving the samovar away from Toilik just in time.

'Give it to me,' he said, grabbing my arm.

'What for?' I asked.

'It's none of your business. If you don't give me that samovar, I will not give you a minute's peace all night. But, on the other hand, if you give it to me, you won't have the pleasure of my company.'

'Take it,' I said, 'but first let me pour two glasses.'

Toilik gave his permission.

I put a pinch of tea and a spoon in each glass and turned the

99

spigot. Smoke billowed from the samovar, covering the glasses with steam. Before the tea could settle to the bottom, Toilik had grabbed the blazing samovar by the handles and was lugging it downstairs. He stumbled on each step, moaning, groaning, and cursing. His medal clanged against the copper; the top of the urn jiggled. Smoke and steam rose from the hero's shoulders. It looked as if he were descending into Hades. God knows how many bottles he got for my samovar, but from that day on, I never saw it again.

When the clatter on the stairs subsided, I took the red-hot glasses by the rims and rushed into the room.

I don't know how I managed not to drop the precious tea when, from the threshold, I saw Lena lying naked on the bed, her straight dark shoulders across the white pillow. Her amber eyes looked with devilish interest at my confusion.

I stood there, arms outstretched, holding the glasses. I didn't know what to do with the tea, with Lena, or with myself.

'Do you want sugar?' I asked, hardly able to recognize my own voice.

'Sugar and lemon,' Lena said.

'No lemon,' I said, through clenched teeth.

'Put those glasses down!' cried Lena.

Mustering every bit of self-control, I sauntered over to the desk, where I placed my tools of torture, praying that they wouldn't fall over at the last second. I did it – only the spoons betrayed me by their tinkling.

'Show me your fingers,' Lena said.

I went up to her. She took my hands, blew on my fingers, and kissed the fingertips lovingly. A sweet pain pierced me. I bent over and kissed her lips; they opened slightly and her tongue, hot and wet, slipped into my mouth, circling around and around, making me dizzy. I tentatively fingered my way to her breasts. Her breath came in short, steep gasps and I realized she expected more, much more. . . .

I was paralyzed from love. I didn't know what to do. Worse than that, I found that I couldn't do anything. . . .

'No,' I said.

'Why?' she asked, astonished.

'I can't,' I admitted with shame. 'I never had a woman.'

Lena moved out from under me and sat at my feet, watching the candle fade in the depths of the candelabra. The candle went out; only a tiny spark was somehow wrestling with the darkness. Each moment looked like the last, but minute after minute, the light continued to smoulder within the bronze.

For a long, long time we both kept staring at that firefly flame, but never really saw the moment it went out. Dawn had come, and the tiny flicker just dissolved in the morning light.

Lena sat motionless on the edge of the bed. Her refinement captivated me.

'Lena,' I called out.

She didn't answer. She just went on staring at the light which no longer was. Then, in strangely measured tones, she asked, 'Why did you hit me?'

I didn't know what she meant.

'When?'

'At the party.'

I thought she was kidding, then realized she wasn't, and said, 'But you hit me first!'

'I just tapped you!'

'No, you hit me very hard. No one ever hit me so hard.'

'I'm sorry,' I said. 'I didn't mean to. But believe me, you hit me very hard too.'

'I hit you like this,' Lena said, turning towards me and slapping me across the face with her powerful right hand.

Once again everything was happening on its own. Without knowing what was going on, I slapped her back and cried out, 'And this is how you hit me!'

I tried not to strike hard, but the sound was quite loud. For some time we sat in shock. Then Lena jumped off the bed and ran around, looking for her clothes.

'I'm sorry. I didn't mean it,' I screamed, going after her.

She shoved me away, but in the process, the bearskin rug slipped beneath her feet, and she fell down on her knees. I rushed over to her. We stayed on our knees, hugging and crying.

'I love you!' I cried.

'I love you too,' Lena laughed through her tears.

I kissed her wet eyes, and she kissed me back. Then I took a bottle of Pliska cognac out from under the bed. It was the last remnant of Youssef. He had left it for me in his will before departing. We drank the cognac from the tea glasses, kissed, caressed each other, lost ourselves in love, drank again, slept, woke, and again threw ourselves into each other's arms. Our shadows, cast on the wall by the sunrise, flitted about the white daisies, like clouds pursued by the wind, colliding and separating, colliding and separating. . . .

I woke up with the sensation that somebody with tiny feet was walking on me. I lay there a while longer, trying to grasp what was happening, but I could only understand one thing –

Somebody with tiny feet *was* walking on me!

I attempted to open my eyes; it was difficult with the bright light streaming in through the window. Squinting, I finally saw that the room was filled with bright yellow dots, which at times were still, at times, jumping and chirping. I thought I must be delirious; I had heard that when you're delirious, devilkins come, but I had no idea they would be yellow. Through the power of concentration, I tried to drive out those little devils. They didn't want to go away; on the contrary, they became more and more playful. There was nothing else to do but open my eyes, which is what I did.

They were everywhere – on the bed, on the table, on the shelf, and on the windowsill.

'Lena, look,' I called out.

She opened her eyes.

'Oh, we have company,' she said without a bit of surprise, as if she always woke up with little chicks around. Dozens of them were scrambling all over the blanket, chirping comically. One of them, I noticed, had a piece of paper tied to its leg. I waited till it came closer and cupped my hand over it. It cheeped in fear. I untied the paper and let the chick go. It ran off as I read the note:

Dear Friend,

I arrived as planned, but was greeted by cries and moans coming through the door. I didn't know who was killing whom but, believe me, I was tempted to come to your aid. But soon I found that my wish was blocked by the locked door. I decided, therefore, to frighten your enemy with an army that could fit beneath the door. They were recruited in a pet shop, but I believe my brave soldiers will rescue you. When they become full-grown they will transport you on the wings of freedom to the Black Sea. See you there, in Koktebel.

> *Your loyal friend,*
> *Boris*

'Who is Boris?' asked Lena, looking over my shoulder.

'You almost met him,' I replied with a smile.

'Really? You'll have to tell me about it later, but now I have to go.'

'I'll take you home. But first, can you help me round up these chicks to take back to the pet shop?'

Once again we stood in the entrance to Aunt Sonia's building. It was getting to be a routine to say hello and good-bye in that paint-chipped lobby. To keep out of sight of the dogs and senior citizens, we stood behind the lift shaft. The lift would creak up and down, compelling us to raise and lower our heads in a mournful rhythm.

'What's with you?' Lena asked.

'Nothing,' I responded, with mindless concentration on the thick rubber cable chasing the lift.

'Don't be so sad; we'll be swimming in the same sea,' Lena said. She smiled and kissed me.

'Yes, but we'll be sunbathing on different banks,' I said out of the corner of my mouth.

Lena put her arms on my shoulders. I hugged her and held her. Our separation was coming all too fast; our closeness had been much too short. We stood facing each other, leaning against the metal cage, which shook and rattled. Lena said something, but I couldn't hear it with the noise.

'What?' I asked.

'You heard me,' she said.

'No,' I said, 'I didn't.'

'Don't pretend. I know you just want me to repeat it.'

'I really didn't hear you.'

'I don't like to repeat things,' she said.

'Then don't,' I said.

The grating near my shoulder shook; the elevator rumbled and chased the cable, which scurried downward.

'Don't get angry. I just don't like to repeat a joke,' said Lena.

'I'm not angry. I just didn't hear you.'

'Well, all I said was that if we miss each other, you can swim towards me, I will swim towards you, and we'll meet in the middle of the Black Sea. You see, it's not funny the second time.'

'It may not be funny, but I like it.'

'And do you know where the middle of the sea is?'

'Of course.'

'Where?'

'Where we'll meet.'

We laughed. In response to our laughter, the lift appeared once again, but didn't fly off that time; it stopped just above our heads.

'Shhh,' said Lena. 'It must be Aunt Sonia coming back from Kremlyovka.'

'How do you know?'

'She's the only one who goes to the second floor by lift. Wait here a minute. I'll go and get your icon before she throws it away.'

I waited about ten minutes. I don't know how many times the lift and cable chased each other up and down, but she still wasn't back. I thought perhaps a battle had broken out between Lena and her aunt over their beliefs. I was getting nervous. Just then I heard the shuffle of feet on the second-floor landing. Next, I saw long legs, followed by a short green dress, and then all of Lena appeared. She had a large brown paper package in her hands. On top of it stood the icon, held in place by her chin. In front of the icon there was a pineapple, its green leaves pointing upward. With her view totally obstructed, Lena approached the stairs cautiously. With each step she comically stuck out her foot, feeling for the next stair.

'Where are you?' she asked. 'Help me, for God's sake.'

I tore up the stairs and caught the heavy bundle. The icon tumbled onto the pineapple, which scratched my nose and cheek with its spiny leaves.

'What are you doing with this?' I asked, annoyed with the fruit.

'My aunt got it for my parents, but I want to give it to you,' Lena said.

'What is it?' I asked, regretting my tone.

'It's a gift from the Party and the Government. One time you asked me what the Kremlin ration is. I forgot to explain it to you, but now you'll see for yourself.'

'Thank you,' I said, getting a better grip on the package. 'What do you think, could I be arrested for walking around Moscow with an icon and a pineapple?'

'Let me put the icon facing you,' said Lena, 'and don't let anybody open this package, or you'll wind up in jail for sure.'

'Listen,' I said, 'do you know anybody I can leave those icons with while I'm away?'

'The people I could trust don't even have a room, but you need somebody who's got his own apartment.'

'Somebody who's got his own apartment!' resounded in my head. Of course, somebody with his own apartment!

'I've got it,' I said.

'You're kidding,' said Lena, 'such a person doesn't exist.'

'There *is* somebody. Maybe there is only one in Moscow, but I know him. You're a genius! Can I give you a kiss?'

The pineapple leaves pricked me once again and we kissed. I was positive that that bristly kiss would be the last one that summer but, at the same time, I had the feeling that it wasn't the end, but, rather, the beginning.

9 An Unscheduled Car

'Sound the trumpets, beat the drums, Andrewlka's eavesdropping on you!'

'Hello,' I said, 'you know who's calling?'

'Andrewlka knows everything.'

'And does Andrewlka know what I'm calling for?'

'Of course. Sashulka is the only one who still hasn't asked Andrewlka if he could leave something at his apartment over the summer.'

'Do you think he'll let me, while I'm at the Black Sea?'

'Sashulka is insulting Andrewlka. What kind of question is that? And what are you asking permission for? Andrewlka told you before – his home is your home. You can bring whatever you want – even if it's a hippopotamus. Your humble servant Andrewlka is like a mosquito; he can always find some crack in the plaster for himself.' (Andrewlka loved similes from zoology.) 'Come over as soon as you can. Andrewlka will have a nice surprise for you when you get here,' he said, ending the conversation abruptly.

Yes, there certainly was a surprise waiting for me when I got to Andrew's – and not only one.

First, I didn't recognize the door of his apartment. It had been washed clean. There were no more footprints; instead, there was a sign nailed to the door which said: PLEASE DON'T DISTURB ANDREWLKA NEEDLESSLY.

When I came in, I found a second surprise – Andrewlka had grown a walrus moustache, which he tugged at and curled pensively. Beneath the moustache protruded a Stalinesque pipe, which he moved lazily from left to right and from right to left with the hand that wasn't busy with the curling. He was elegantly turned out in a black three-piece suit. Instead of his usual manic self, this new Andrewlka was languid and downcast.

Without even glancing at my bundle of icons, he simply opened a cupboard and motioned for me to deposit my sack beside the other suitcases and trunks. It was obvious that such a request was nothing new to Andrewlka.

Without a word he brought a bottle of mineral water from the kitchen, poured some into a crystal glass, sat down on the rocking chair, blew a smoke ring, and covered his eyes with his hand.

He sat in this fashion for quite some time. At one point, I reached out for the mineral water, but a voice from the rocker stopped me.

'Oh, how cruel and indiscriminating life is. Indiscriminating and cruel,' Andrew repeated with a funeral tone. He blew a new smoke ring which he tried to position right above his head, like a halo, but the ring wasn't willing to remain and flowed off to the side.

'What's happened?' I said, picking up his tone unwittingly.

'Sashulka is going to the Black Sea to swim and sunbathe, to eat shish kebab, and to breathe the fresh sea air, but his best friend, Andrewlka, is destined to stay here eating potatoes and suffocating on the dusty Moscow streets all summer. Life has punished that fool Andrewlka for his generosity, his frivolity, and yes, his lechery. And so it was, and will be, forever and ever. *C'est la vie! Cherchez la femme!*'

At first, I didn't understand what he was driving at and I swallowed the bait.

'I'm sorry,' I said, lowering my guard. 'If I had known you wanted to go to the south . . .'

'If you had known, would you have taken Andrewlka with you?' he said.

It would be folly to bring this 'mosquito' with me, I thought, but said aloud, 'Of course I would have taken you!'

'Andrewlka feels better now, much better,' he said with a twinkle in his eye.

'I would have taken you, but it's too late now. Actually, I've got to get going this minute. I'm on my way to the railway

107

station,' I said, trying to cover myself, but it certainly was too late.

'And Andrewlka is on *his* way to the railway station!'

'But I don't have time to wait for you to pack.'

'Andrewlka never has to pack; he's always ready,' he said with pride as he dragged out his famous crocodile and Turtle bottle from behind the rocking chair.

I knew I was snared, but I gave it one more try.

'It's too late to buy a ticket, Andrewlka!'

'Andrewlka never buys a ticket and hopes you don't either,' he returned crisply.

There was no escape; we were products of the same law – the Law of the Bottle.

Andrewlka sprang out of the rocker, spat out the pipe, pulled off the suit, changed into plaid trousers and an orange shirt with green palm trees, stuck a pack of Marlboros in his breast pocket, scooped up the crocodile in one hand, the Turtle in the other, and screamed, 'Sound the trumpets, beat the drums,-Andrewlka is taking Sashulka to the south!'

We crossed the street to the Metro station, took the Circle Line, and got off at Kursky Railway Station. We went through the underpass to the platform. We had arrived in time – according to the timetable, the Comsomol Express was leaving for the Crimea in fifteen minutes. This would give us enough time to locate the 'right' conductor.

We fought our way through the crowd to the first car. The day's surprises were only beginning – instead of the men's drunken faces we were expecting, we were met by the clean, sparkling, flawless faces of youthful Comsomol girls.

When we checked the timetable, we hadn't fully grasped the meaning of the 'Comsomol Express' – Communist Youth Express. Who would have taken it literally? With the name 'Comsomol Express,' the conductors could just as well have been from the Civil War of 1919, but on this train, real live Comsomol girls stood at attention beside the door of each car. And paying them off was out of the question.

108

Our summer plans were in jeopardy. We held a brief conference, then grabbed our belongings – Andrew took his suitcase and jug; I, the package, my bag, my guitar, and the pineapple in a fishnet bag – and went to face the worst.

Our first attempt failed miserably. It seemed that the girls hadn't even heard about the monetary value of the bottle. Yes, it is difficult to speak with amateurs.

We found that time was running out. We would have to change tactics. We split up: Andrew took the even cars; I took the odd ones. I used my special cherubic smile; he employed a burning, rousing stare, but the result was the same: 'Get back, comrade. Where is your ticket? There's no room,' the Comsomols said, raising their hands in warning, their red armbands in full view. 'Don't you understand? You want us to call the police? There is no room!'

There really was no room. Swarms of people hurried towards the cars, throwing their valises and food baskets aboard in a mad rush, poking their tickets under the Comsomols' noses, bumping into each other, and cursing.

Our scheme was turning into a catastrophe. We had already met rejection at twelve cars; there was only the last car left, which was somehow unnumbered. Nobody was getting on board. Most likely, it was already jam-packed. Two girls who seemed totally impossible to deal with were stationed at the door of the car. I had never seen such bright faces, such clear eyes, or such pink cheeks. They were dressed in new, navy blue uniforms, and pinned to the bulge of their Comsomol blazers was the gold, bald head of Lenin.

'Comrade passengers,' intoned the loudspeaker, 'the Comsomol Express will be departing in one minute. All well-wishers please stand clear of the train.' Andrew and I were beginning to feel like the well-wishers who would be left behind. Andrewlka flung his crocodile onto the platform, gave it a good kick, and proceeded to open the Turtle. I stood there, twirling the fishnet bag with the pineapple inside, turning over in my head the question Lenin asked himself the morning he discovered he had syphilis: 'Now what?'

As I stood there, I sensed that somebody was staring at me

from behind. I turned around to find the Comsomol conductors from the last car eyeing me intently. Andrew nudged me and said, without moving his lips.

'Get over there fast. Those girls are giving you the eye.'

I walked over to the conductors, adjusting my guitar strap along the way to hint that I could serve as an accompanist for Comsomol songs on the trip. The strange part was that the closer I got, the more they lowered their eyes, as if they weren't one bit interested in me. When I got up close to them, I truly didn't know what I had come for, or what I should say, because they were not looking at me at all.

'What is it?' one girl spoke up unexpectedly.

'Where?' I asked.

'In your hand,' she replied.

'It's a guitar,' I said, perking up.

'No,' she said, 'in the bag! It's a pineapple, isn't it?'

'Yes,' I said, 'it is.'

'Hooray!' the girl screeched happily. 'I told you so, I told you it's a pineapple. She said it was an armadillo, but I knew it was a pineapple!'

'Yes,' I said, 'it's a pineapple.'

'It's so weird!' said the second girl. 'I was sure it was an armadillo.'

'No,' I said, 'it's a pineapple.'

'How beautiful it is,' said the first girl, 'it's just unbelievable.'

'It sounds as if you're crazy about pineapples,' I said.

'Yes,' she said, 'no,' she said, 'I don't know,' she blushed. 'I've never tried one. I've heard they are very sweet. Is it true?'

'No,' I said, 'not really. Would you like to taste it?'

'How?' she asked in utter confusion.

My next words should have been something like 'If you want to taste the pineapple, you'll have to let us come aboard,' or 'When we get to the Crimea you will get your pineapple,' but much to my surprise, what I said was, 'Take it!'

'Wow!' yelled the Comsomols. 'Really?'

'Really!' I said, holding out the fishnet bag with the pineapple.

All four hands grabbed the gift, all four eyes were popping.

They couldn't even say a word, they were so surprised. I turned around and walked towards Andrew.

'Well?' he said, leaping off the suitcase. 'Are we going?'

I didn't respond.

'Did you make a deal with them?'

I didn't know what to say.

'Are we going or not?'

'No,' I said.

'What the – '

The wheels of the train screeched and rolled backward, shutting out Andrewlka's most expressive words. The train seemed to exhale; then it lurched forward, and slowly rolled south. Andrewlka exhaled too, and headed north on the platform.

'Hey,' we heard.

As the last car was passing us, the rosy faces of the Comsomol girls appeared in the open door of the train.

'Where are you boys going?'

'To the Crimea,' screamed Andrewlka as he changed his course and hurried after the departing train. 'We've got to get to the Crimea. We don't have any tickets. We left our tickets at home on the piano, and now we have no tickets, understand? We don't have any tickets, blast it!' His words chased the accelerating train.

Laughter came from the car.

'Hop on, comrades! Hurry!'

We charged for the train. Andrew got near the door and tossed his immense crocodile inside. The Turtle followed close behind at a speed unknown to that animal. Then Andrewlka jumped onto the footboard and vanished within the car.

I was running down the platform, the guitar in one hand, the package of food and my bag in the other; well-wishers waving goodbye were blocking my way.

'Let me through,' I roared as I ran towards the car door. I hurled the brown package and my bag inside; they landed with a thud.

'Watch out!' I cried ominously and, raising the guitar above the crowd, attempted to pass it into Andrewlka's hands. I made it on the third try.

I was freed of all encumbrances, but I couldn't catch up to the train. I pressed ahead, but the train also went ahead. It was only a step away, only one stride, but it felt like a mile.

'Grab it,' Andrewlka shouted from the train.

I saw the net bag with the pineapple thrust out to me like a lifeline, the three of them holding the bag tightly by the handles. I grabbed at the mesh and the spiny pineapple leaves, attempting to pull myself to the door. The black end of the platform was zooming toward me like a deadly cliff. Just one more step and I'd be over the edge. I took it – somehow. At the last second, I managed to push off the edge and, in that desperate jump, flew on the net bag, as if on a vine, and found myself on the footboard.

Before I could catch my breath, Andrewlka was ushering me into the car. There, a new surprise awaited me. The car was empty, absolutely empty! How could a train going from Moscow to the Crimea be empty? Empty . . . empty . . . pounded the wheels. How could that possibly be? People reserve tickets for the trains south months in advance. They stand in queues for days and sleep near the ticket counter by night in hopes of obtaining a ticket for even the rottenest upper berth. But without any tickets, there we were, travelling in a perfectly empty railway car with two lovely Comsomol Girls.

'What are you so surprised about?' one of the girls said. 'This is an unscheduled car. According to the timetable, it should not be going from north to south, but from south to north. That's why it was attached to our train and is now being sent south. There, it will be hitched up to the right train and will go from south to north as scheduled. There's nothing very surprising about that.'

'How come they weren't selling tickets for this car at the ticket counter?' I asked.

'Because this is an unscheduled car,' the conductor softly reminded me.

They brought us to the last compartment, where mattresses were piled up from floor to ceiling.

'Get yourself a mattress,' said the Comsomols, 'and pick out any compartment you want.'

'Listen, girls,' said Andrewlka, still trying to comprehend the situation, 'are you saying that there will be nobody but us in this car the whole way?'

'Of course,' replied the girls, 'we've already told you that this car is unscheduled.'

'Sound the trumpets,' whispered Andrew. 'If the whole car is empty, Andrewlka chooses this compartment for himself. It has the softest bed – in fact, it reminds Andrewlka of his very own little bed.'

Andrew took the pineapple from the girls' hands and threw it onto the pile of mattresses, then climbed to the top. From the ceiling came his sweet, seductive voice, 'Hey, you down there, come on up here. Let's eat this pineapple. Andrewlka welcomes you with open arms.'

The Comsomols looked at each other, giggled, kicked off their shoes, pulled up their skirts, and climbed up, their plump legs brushing past my face. I went after them. Up on top it was dark and stuffy, but at the same time, it felt good – it was fun to sit on a bed with your head nearly touching the ceiling.

We all found a spot around our benefactor – His Majesty, the pineapple. The conductors looked with trepidation at the scaly body, unable to muster the courage to touch its leaves. Andrewlka, on the contrary, viewed the alien fruit unceremoniously. He took out his old faithful pocketknife, wiped the blade on his trousers, seized the pineapple, positioned it between his knees, and got a good grip on the knife. The girls held their breath, but Andrewlka put his knife down and whined, 'Hold it. Andrewlka never cuts pineapples without a full glass in front of him. Girls, go and fetch some glasses for Andrewlka,' he said, reaching for the Turtle.

The Comsomols huddled together and whispered to each other, then one of them said, looking into Andrew's eyes pleadingly, 'I'll go if you promise not to start cutting the pineapple without me,' then jumped down and went pitter-patter through the car.

Andrewlka hadn't even had a chance to pull out the cork when the Comsomol, as if she had wings, flew back. Andrew proceeded to pour the alcohol, whereupon he discovered that the Comsomol had brought not four but six glasses. He stopped pouring and looked at her inquisitively. The girl stuttered, 'I invited the girls from the next car. They were the ones who gave me the glasses.

They aren't going to eat. They will just drink a little bit and watch how you cut the pineapple. You're not cross, are you?'

'Not at all,' Andrew replied, 'the more maidens, the merrier. Andrewlka considers quantity much more important than quality. Summon your friends; the Comsomol meeting is about to begin!'

'We're here,' high-pitched voices sang from below and, before we knew it, two more Comsomols had joined us beneath the ceiling.

Andrewlka bowed the Turtle's head. Those with the red armbands got half a glass of the clear liquid; those without got full glasses.

'What is this?' one of the Comsomols asked.

'Aviation alcohol,' came the answer, simple and clear.

'Oh!' said the Comsomol. 'I'm afraid.'

'Don't be afraid. There's nothing to be afraid of,' said Andrew.

'It must be very strong!' said another Comsomol.

'It is, but it's good for you and absolutely necessary when you're eating pineapple,' said Andrew.

'Is that true?' asked the Comsomols.

'Andrewlka always tells the truth. The pineapple is a tropical fruit and therefore it requires something strong and hot. It's not like herring, which you can eat with any old champagne. This is a pineapple, and you shouldn't mess around with it if you don't want to get a tropical fever. Before and after eating a pineapple you should always disinfect your stomach with at least 192-proof alcohol. Besides, this combination puts you in an equatorial mood.'

'What's an equatorial mood?' the Comsomols inquired enthusiastically.

'It's when it is extremely hot and clothes become absolutely unnecessary,' explained Andrewlka in a pedantic tone.

The girls grew silent. All at once, Andrewlka plunged the knife into the pineapple, separating the leaves from the prickly body, then he sliced it into even circles. He dug a hole in the bottom section of the pineapple and filled it with the alcohol. Then he removed the skin from each piece, distributing the slices, and put the brown rings back together again, forming a pineapple once more, but with thin horizontal slits across the fruit. Andrewlka lit a match, tossed it into the hollow pineapple, and covered the opening with its hat of green leaves. The pure alcohol blazed, and the pineapple glowed like a lantern in the compartment.

'Andrewlka never eats without fire,' he announced, then took a bow.

'Bravo!' cried the Comsomols, and everybody drank. The interesting thing about it was that this didn't look like the girls' first experience with such a potent drink. They followed the shot with the juicy pineapple slices, the aromatic juice trickling down their freckled faces, onto their uniforms.

We drank the second shot. It grew hotter. There was nothing else for the Comsomols to do but remove their blazers and ties. In their blue uniform blouses, the top buttons open, they looked even younger than before.

'Now, Sashulka,' said Andrew, 'let's take a look at what we've got here from the Kremlin tropics.'

I opened the brown parcel; the girls oohed and aahed and began to play a guessing game. It was clear that the Comsomols had never seen crabs, sturgeon, pork loin, caviar, or ketchup. They held up each delicacy, checked the label, smelled it, poked it, and asked what it was called and how it was eaten. Somehow, the most successful item turned out to be the ketchup, maybe because its label was in English. Andrewlka attempted to explain to them that the ketchup was for the pork, but they refused to listen, and insisted on putting ketchup on everything – from the crabs to the pineapple.

We drank the third shot. It was really getting hot in the compartment. The heat must have stirred Andrewlka's atom, for he plunged into a yarn about the last film he had directed. He said the film was shot on an island in the Pacific Ocean where it was hot, like in the compartment, and so, all the natives were walking around naked and making love freely, without a bit of shame. While relating his story, he smoked one Marlboro after another – obvious evidence of his trips abroad.

Little by little, the tropical fever was spreading. I don't know how Andrewlka did it, but an aura of sexual madness always sprung up around him. By the end of his story, the Comsomols were thoroughly hypnotized by his artistic credo, his shirt with the palms, and, especially, his pack of Marlboros. They came right out and said that the islanders were nothing compared to Soviet girls and, if we blew out the light in the pineapple, they could easily prove it.

The pineapple, apparently understanding the Comsomols' words, went out on its own that very second. The girls laughed and scrambled around in the dark, daring each other.

'What is going on in here?' roared a voice with a thick Ukrainian accent. It was like thunder in the middle of the night. And then, like lightning, a match illuminated our bed. Up on the mattresses, the half-naked Comsomols froze while two heads in uniform hats gaped at our tropical kingdom.

'Comrade Chief . . . Comrade . . .' the Comsomols sputtered in confusion, as they covered themselves with their skirts and blouses.

'I've been a railway chief for twenty years, but I've never . . .'

'We . . . we . . . you . . . you . . .' the Comsomols stammered.

'Comsomols, would you please calm down and speak clearly! Ouch, fuck your mother!' Comrade Chief yelled as the match burned his fingers. 'Stanislav Konstantinovitch, turn the night light on.'

The assistant flicked a switch on the wall; the compartment was lit up by the intense blue light. As his huge frame towered over me, my eyes went wide with surprise. The assistant smiled and quickly shook his head.

'What do we have here?' said the chief. 'Who might you be, and what are you doing in the "spec" car? Let's see your tickets, comrades.'

'How do you do, Comrade Chief.' Andrewlka slipped into the conversation. 'What an unbelievable thing happened today. We went to the railway station, but my friend here, just a few days ago, bought a new piano, and five minutes – '

'Okay, if you don't have tickets, show me your documents, comrades,' the chief cut him off. 'I've been a railway chief twenty years, and I've heard all this before.'

'Believe me, this was something unbelievable!' Andrewlka continued. 'First, he was playing the piano, then he was playing his guitar, and when there was one minute left before the train pulled out – '

'Young man, I assure you that very soon you will be watching this train pull out. Stanislav Konstantinovitch,' he addressed his assistant, 'what shall we do with these ticketless citizens – telegraph the police or hand them over to the guard at the next station?'

'That's a tricky question, Comrade Chief,' said the assistant thoughtfully.

'Why?' the chief raised his eyebrows in surprise.

'You see, if these ticketless citizens were in any other car of the train, it would be a crime, but since they are in an unscheduled car, it would most likely be a crime if they *had* tickets. It's very difficult to say what to do from a legal point of view. Only you, as chief, can take responsibility for a decision like this,' the assistant said gravely, then whispered something into the chief's ear.

'But what does it say in the regulations?' asked the railway veteran in confusion.

'That's just it, there is no such ruling,' said the assistant. 'It seems that you'll have to determine it yourself. But first, take a look at what they're eating.'

'How could there be no rule?' the chief pursued the point. 'There are rules for everything.'

'For everything but unscheduled cars, Comrade Chief. Of course, you can create one. After all, you've been on the railway twenty years. But first,' he repeated, 'look at what they're eating.'

'What?'

'Take a closer look.'

'Big deal. A coconut.'

It was a serious moment, but the girls couldn't control themselves and giggled into their skirts.

'You know everything, Comrade Chief,' said the assistant, glaring at the Comsomols.

'They are grown on our Ukrainian farms as feed for the pigs.'

'And what about sturgeon?' asked Andrewlka in a timid voice, holding out a shimmery piece on waxed paper.

'On the Ukrainian bank of the Black Sea, boys wallop them

117

with poles,' said the chief, eyeing the yellow strip of fat which contoured the fish.

'How about some pork loin with ketchup, Comrade Chief. Why don't you check to see how it compares with Ukrainian pork?' suggested Andrew.

'Try it, try it!' yelled the girls. 'Just to make a comparison, just to make a comparison. Come on up here, Comrade Chief. Come up!'

'If it's only to make a comparison, then I just might. Stanislav Konstantinovitch, give me a hand. That's it. That's fine. Now climb up yourself. There is enough room here for everybody.'

When the chief's assistant made it to the top, the mountain of mattresses sank down appreciably under his weight. With their bosses in such close proximity, the girls hurriedly began to pull on their entangled uniforms.

'Comrade Comsomols,' the assistant interrupted authoritatively, 'first, I'd like to remind you that you are on duty. Keep in mind that our beloved chief disapproves of noise and disorganization. Second, you're working on a special car; therefore, your clothes are unimportant except for two things – our red armband should be on your arm; your Comsomol pin, on your breast. This is what the instructions require – the symbols of this express.'

The girls proceeded to put the red armbands on each other and take Lenin from their blazers and pin him to their bras.

'Okay, that's good. You can go ahead with the tasting now, Comrade Chief,' said Stanislav Konstantinovitch.

'Surely you won't refuse a glass of spirits to whet your appetite,' said Andrewlka.

'It's a possibility. It can't hurt,' replied the chief, loosening his tie and unbuttoning his jacket. 'It's hot here. Open a window, somebody.'

Stanislav Konstantinovitch, surprisingly agile for his size, slipped between the Comsomol bodies, sat across from me, and opened the window.

In the fresh breeze, the chief swiftly downed his shot, then gobbled up a piece of pork loin smeared with ketchup.

'How is it?' asked Andrewlka, now offering a slice of bread topped with black caviar to the still-chewing chief.

'I must admit, it's good pork, very good,' the chief said, nodding and smacking his lips. 'I'm sure it's from the Ukraine. Give me one more piece. Pork is my downfall. Take your time with that caviar, ticketless citizen. The caviar can wait. What do you think, I never saw caviar before? No, no, no, don't take it away! Hold it! I've got a good idea, let's put it around the pork and pour that tomato sauce on top. Don't be stingy now, don't be stingy, you bastard.'

'It's not tomato sauce,' laughed one of the girls, 'it's ketchup, Comrade Chief.'

'It's all the same thing. Anyway, it's made from Ukrainian tomatoes,' said the chief.

'But the label's in English,' the girl said, unrelenting.

'A Ukrainian export,' said the chief, settling the argument once and for all. He chugged another glass, stuffed the pork and caviar into his mouth, and continued with his mouth full:

'You still didn't answer me, you louse. Where did you get this pork, huh? Where did this lovely thing come from? I bet it's from the Ukraine.'

'I bet it's not,' said Andrewlka.

'What do you mean, it's not? There is no place on earth with better pigs than in the Ukraine,' the chief railed at him.

'Let's drink to our dear chief's native land,' proposed the assistant, diplomatically.

'To the great Ukraine,' the Comsomols cheered.

'To an independent Ukraine,' bellowed the chief, revealing his dissident side. 'Tell me the truth, you scum, let's not play cat and mouse, where is this pig from – the Ukraine?'

'No.'

'Then where?'

'From the Kremlin,' Andrewlka replied.

'Then I was right all along,' cried the chief triumphantly. 'The pigs in the Kremlin are the same as the ones in the Ukraine.'

'No,' said Stanislav Konstantinovitch, 'here I beg to differ with you, Comrade Chief. In the Kremlin, the pigs are bigger.'

As always on a trip, it was drizzling outside. The patter on the roof of the train, along with the tropical atmosphere in the compartment, made everyone lazy and relaxed. The thoroughly drunk Comsomols lay down between us like Tahitians. The assistant to the chief sat across from me, near the window, lazily tossing a vial of pills into the air. Then he opened it and began to fling one pill after another into the darkness.

'What's that, Stanislav Konstantinovitch?' asked one of the Tahitian Comsomols, resting her head on his knees.

'It's Tigrin,' the assistant replied.

'Tigrin?' echoed the Comsomol. 'What's that?'

'The latest tiger repellent.'

'What? Who ever saw tigers on the railway?'

'Works well, doesn't it?'

'Oh, you're always teasing,' said the Comsomol, slipping away from the assistant and crawling towards the chief.

'Hello, Stas,' I said quietly.

'Hi,' said Stas.

'Where've you been all this time?'

'Shh,' said Stas, nodding in the direction of the chief, 'wait a while.'

The chief and Andrewlka were sitting arm in arm, smoking Marlboros. Between puffs, Andrewlka was boasting about his two-room apartment in Moscow with the lilac bushes beneath his window. The girls doted on every word.

'Come on, stop trying to pull the wool over the girls' eyes with your silly tales,' Comrade Chief said amiably. 'If you want to sleep with one of them, just pick one; she'll go with you for an empty pack of Marlboros. What do you have to lie for? It hurts my ears.'

'Nobody ever believes Andrewlka,' the raconteur said glumly, staring out the window.

Outside, the rain was coming down heavier; warm drops were sailing into the car through the open window.

'A tropical downpour!' gushed Andrewlka. 'Beat the tom-toms! We're crossing the equator! Now we're in the jungle. Oo-lu-lu-lu-lu! We left the pigs on the other side of the equator. On this side, there are only tigers and monkeys. The Tahitian holiday is about to begin. Male tigers are hunting for female monkeys. Oh-lu-lu-lu-lu!'

Andrewlka tore off his shirt and threw himself on the naked Comsomol monkeys. The monkeys shrieked. When Comrade Chief started taking off his hat and growling like a tiger, Stas winked at me and we crawled over the mattress to the edge of the bed. We climbed down and headed for the rear of the car. We came to the last door of the train. For a while we stood there quietly watching the heat lightning in the stormy sky.

'Where were they holding you?'

'Lefortovo.'

'What was the charge? Political?'

'Of course.' He smiled. 'That and homosexuality.'

'What?' I was shocked.

'Didn't you know?' he said with a grin.

I shook my head.

'Only you, with your provincial naiveté, could have missed it,' he chuckled.

'How . . . how did you get off the hook?' I managed to stammer.

'Somebody helped me out: you'd never believe who.'

'Who?'

'Our beloved history teacher, Anna Ivanna. She has a lot of connections with the secret police. Believe it or not, we're living together. She's fascinated by men like me.' He laughed. Then, more seriously, he added, 'But I don't have Moscow propiska, and without that stupid permit I can't live in the city more than a few days at a time. That's why I took this job. Only it's so boring; I'm sick and tired of it. I've had enough of that Ukrainian pig, too.'

'Why don't you come along with us?' I offered. 'We're going to Koktebel.'

'Sure. Why do you think I didn't arrest you?'

We both burst out laughing. I never laughed so heartily with anyone as I did with Stas. Somehow, we had our own mutual understanding of the rules of the game somebody had called life.

'Who is that with you?' asked Stas.

'Andrewlka.'

'He's funny. Seems like a good fellow.'

'Oh yes, he certainly is,' I agreed.

'Sound the trumpets, beat the drums!' we heard coming from behind us. 'Who is talking about that scoundrel Andrewlka? Who is speaking of him in good terms? Instead of talking about him, you should be helping him. Right now, he's in danger. You must save him from that flock of monkeys.'

A naked Andrewlka with wet, gooey hair came up to us and pressed his forehead against the windowpane.

'What day is today?' asked Andrew.

'Monday,' said Stas.

'Thought so,' said Andrewlka.

We stared out the window, watching the black night gradually turn into a wet, foggy morning. The familiar sayings ran through the rain and fog:

THIS GENERATION OF SOVIET PEOPLE WILL SEE COMMUNISM . . .

THE COMMUNIST PARTY IS OUR RULER . . .

EACH DAY LIFE IN OUR COUNTRY IS GETTING BETTER AND BETTER . . .

From time to time, within the car, came the screeches of the monkeys.

'What a zoo!' said Andrew. 'The whole damn country's a zoo!'

'A circus,' said Stas.

'No,' said I, 'an unscheduled car.'

10 Arctic Light in a Hot Southern Night

The house at Koktebel was a low, reinforced-concrete structure, three of its walls dipping into the sea, the fourth clinging to the cliffs on the sloping bank. Some time ago the building had served as a bathhouse. Guests would come here to spread medicinal mud all over their aching bodies and take in the sun. All the aches and pains were supposed to ooze out of the body and into the mud.

More recently, with each Soviet citizen having the constitutional right to good health, it was decided that such charlatanism as mud baths be put to an end. So, the bathhouse had been boarded up for the last few years. Boris had come upon this building during one of his architectural escapades. He cleared away the dried clumps of mud and moved in, enjoying two cool rooms and a verandah. This summer he had invited me to take advantage of the second vacant room. Of course, he had no way of knowing that I would arrive with company.

Andrew, Stas, and I had a rough time finding that concrete structure, so naturally did it blend in with the landscape. Its roof, level with the ground, was almost completely obscured by a strange tree, something between a weeping willow and a palm tree, growing on a hill. Its drooping branches swayed in the sea breeze, sweeping the roof's cement surface with a hushed rustle.

I asked Stas and Andrew to wait for me under that tree while I went into the house. I hopped down onto the verandah and went up to the door – actually, there was no door at all; the entrance was covered with a red-and-white-striped towel. I lifted the towel and peeked in. A cosy coolness lingered within. Against the dark grey wall the windows stood out like bright pictures, each one depicting a different seascape: one was of the sea and the far-off green mountains; another was of the sea, the sky, and a white ship on the horizon; the third, the sea, sand, and gulls. The furniture in the room was built from oddly shaped snags and brownish-grey driftwood. There was nobody around, but I heard a rustling in the far corner, which was cluttered with large cardboard boxes. I went in, crossed the room, and looked into the boxes. There, behind the boxes, was Boris. He was deeply involved in cutting the cardboard into pieces and gluing together a sort of cupola-like structure.

'Hey,' I said. 'Hello there, labourer.'

Boris looked up at me. His burned, pointed nose gleamed in the centre of his sun-tanned face as he smiled. He trampled over the mound of excess cardboard, wiped his hand on his trousers, and held it out to me.

'Hi there, sponger,' he said. 'How was the trip?'

'The usual,' I said. 'Nothing special. How's everything with you?'

'Nothing special, the usual,' Boris returned.

'What a good life you live here,' I said.

'I try to,' said Boris.

'Where did you get such beautiful furniture?' I asked.

'Contraband from Turkey. It came through the Black Sea.'

'What are you doing now? Unpacking the contraband?' I asked.

'Wrong,' he said, 'building a church.'

'Ah, I see. I suppose the local government's planning on baptizing the Party members now?'

'Wrong again,' said Boris. 'I need the church for a wedding.'

'Ah,' I said, 'I see. What are you going to make the bride and groom out of?'

'I don't have to make them; they'll show up on their own,' he said.

'Are they on their way from Turkey?' I asked.

'No,' said Boris, 'from the Black Sea.'

'Now everything is clear,' I laughed, 'but perhaps you need a priest and a deacon for such an affair.'

'You know,' he said, 'that's not a bad idea.'

There was no better moment to introduce my pals. 'Hey,' I shouted out the window, 'Stas and Andrew, come over here. I found a job for you.'

The towel on the doorway flew up, and Stas entered the bathhouse, ducking his head. Andrew followed close behind, peeking over Stas's shoulder.

In the bright light streaming in through the doorway, Stas's figure looked larger than ever, and Andrewlka's cunning face even sneakier.

'Let me introduce you,' I said. 'This is Stas. I think you met him once. He's a reliable and extremely serious person – a saint, you might say. Because of his many good traits, he would make an excellent priest. And this is Andrewlka, an honest and dedicated person. He's nearly a monk. He'd make a fine deacon. He was a monastic chef, at one time. They're both absolutely essential for a Turkish wedding.'

Seeing that Boris was at a loss for words, my partners launched into their attack.

'As far as the wedding goes,' rumbled Stas's voice, 'I can see to it right now. I don't even need the bride and groom.'

'I don't need the groom either,' Andrew added rapidly. 'As for the bride, I'll have to get a look at her – who knows, she might come in handy after the wedding dinner. Speaking of dinner, all I need is a couple of potatoes; for the drinks we have aviation alcohol left over from yesterday.'

Andrewlka then held out the Turtle to Boris. It was an instant success. I could see the two new arrivals wouldn't have any trouble making themselves at home; they were already drinking with Boris to their friendship and slapping each other on the back. It seemed they had completely forgotten about me.

'Hey,' I said, 'are you planning on inviting me to that wedding?'

'What do we need you for?' said Boris. 'Why don't you go on out in the fresh air.'

'Can I leave my stuff here?'

'Can't you see there's no room for you here; you'll have to stay on the roof.'

'What?'

'Don't worry, the nights are warm,' said Boris. 'Now get lost.'

'Where should I go?'

'Why don't you go for a swim. Don't disturb us. I need

125

to discuss the details of the forthcoming ceremony with these sextons.'

I walked out onto the verandah. The sea was an emerald blue flecked with glistening spots of the midday sun. On the edge of the blue, slowly, almost imperceptibly, floated a white ship. Closer to me bobbed an apple core, which looked exactly the same size as the distant ship, between the apple and the ship, there was a dark dot – a swimmer's head. Near my feet, a light wave tenderly licked the steps of the verandah. On the bottom step, I saw a few bottles of champagne chilling in the water.

I took a deep breath of fresh air. A gentle breeze enveloped me like a blanket of tranquillity. I liked it here, it was very different from the other resorts on the Crimea, where it's impossible to see the sand on the beaches for the thousands of bodies. Bodies of workers and collective farmers baking themselves in the sun. Koktebel was different, with its number of empty little coves. A private resort which was kept as a retreat for Soviet writers, who didn't want to share the sand and water with simple people and did everything in their power to protect their domain.

I stripped down to my pants, placed my clothes on the roof of the bathhouse, and walked towards the water. The verandah was covered with smooth grey pebbles, hot in the sun. I picked up a small stone and went down the stairs into the water, tossing it from one hand to the other. The stone looked just like the one I had found some time ago near Lena's house. In its dark oval form, I could see nothing but uncertainty. I drew back my hand and, with all my strength, flung the pebble into the sea. It skipped across the smooth, shiny water, jumping among the sunlit spots. It hopped over the apple and skidded off in the direction of the swimmer. It was too late to scream; the pebble was flying lower and lower, in shorter jumps, then simply slid across the surface of the sea and disappeared beneath the water so close to the swimmer's head that, in the blinding sun, it was impossible to tell whether the stone had struck or not.

I dived into the water and swam out. Each time I came up for air, I checked the direction beneath my arm. I was getting closer and closer to the victim of my attack. My heart was pounding. I raised my head out of the water, but the swimmer moved away awkwardly and swam behind my back.

'I'm sorry . . . it was an ac – '

Before I could finish, the stranger had jumped on my back, grabbed me around the neck, and dunked me under the water.

'An accident?!' a voice gurgled in my ear, 'that was no accident. You have a weird habit of throwing stones at women!'

Her legs were clasped around my stomach, her hands strangling me. I desperately wanted to break loose, but couldn't. We were sinking into the depths. Just when I resolved to fight for my life, the deadly embrace weakened, and the swimmer came to face with me. There, in the emerald water, pierced by the shiny needle of the sun, appeared Lena's face, laughing soundlessly and emitting silver air bubbles. I reached out for her. She took my hand in hers, and we swam in a spiral to the air and light.

That day we learned how miraculously our bodies are suited for love – we have skin, wonderful skin, smooth and tender; we have fingers, wonderful fingers, so good for touching; we have hair, wonderful hair, which you can run your fingers through; we have lips, warm lips, which you can kiss so tenderly; we have a tongue, inquisitive yet cautious; we have arms and legs that can be cosily entwined in an embrace. We loved each other in the sand and sun. We loved each other in the sea and sky. We loved each other in each other.

We lay there on the narrow strip of sand. The sun warmed our bodies, the waves cooled our legs.

'I don't believe you're here!' I whispered.

'You're the one who set the time and place.'

'No, I didn't.'

'All right, I did.' She smiled.

'I thought you were to be with your parents all summer.'

'I couldn't stand the thought of it,' she said.

'When did you get here?'

'This morning. I came by ferry. I found your friend Boris, and he's arranged everything.'

'What do you mean?' I asked.

'Our meeting in the middle of the sea,' she said.

'Wait a minute! Tell me, whose wedding is he preparing for? Ours?'

'I don't know.'

'What if it's our wedding . . .'

'What?'

'Will you go along with it?' I asked.

'If it's for fun.'

'And if it's for real?'

'Then . . . I'll still go along,' she said.

We swam in the sea nearly until sundown. We swam out so far that the beach disappeared. The hills and cliffs, still lit by the sun, were all that showed us the way back. So far out the water was colder, but Lena didn't want to go back. In the sea, she was never cold.

When the red sun had already dipped halfway down the water, the sound of a whistle sailed to us from the embankment. On the edge of the sunlit cliff, we saw three figures waving us in.

Then came the wedding. The altar was erected and painted by Boris; the mass was celebrated under a cardboard dome by the priest, Stas; the table set and decorated by the monk, Andrew; and the flowers, lots of flowers, had been picked by all on the neighbouring hills. While Stas placed the silver-plated rings on our fingers, Andrew swung the soup-can censer; and Boris held aluminium-foil crowns over our heads.

We drank the champagne and ate Andrewlka's 'Wedding Potatoes,' and it was much tastier than the Kremlin delicacies we had left with the Comsomols.

That night, Lena and I slept on the roof of the bathhouse. Our friends had placed candles on its four corners – north, south, east, and west. Wild flowers served as our bedclothes, our blanket – the southern night punctured by stars. The willow's canopy of branches rustled above our heads, while unseen waves beat against the concrete walls, and our black ship, lit by the four candles, floated along the Black Sea towards the unknown.

That night, I wrote my first song. The words and music came simultaneously, with God's help. But back then, I didn't believe in God, and was thrilled by my incredible luck.

I will wrap you in cobwebs of tenderness,
Carry you to ponds of peace and goodness.
Where the dreams of butterflies gleam,
I will lay you down on hills of green.

Dreams, only dreams,
We will take with us,
As a light cover.
Only dreams . . .

Lena listened, gazing at the sky, then asked me to sing it again. While I sang, she chimed in, sometimes very high, sometimes very low, and the song became very beautiful. Our friends came up on the roof and asked us to sing it one more time. Of course, we did. Later, Andrew went down and, with the remaining champagne and spirits half and half, mixed the world's strongest cocktail, 'The Arctic Light'.

I never wore my ring after that night. Lena wore hers but lost it, then took mine and lost that, too. Many years later, we made our marriage official in a civil ceremony, but the real one for us was always that wedding in the cardboard church – a wedding with an Arctic Light in a hot southern night.

1 Knock . . . Knock . . . Knock . . .

Why do we love to sing? What compels us to do it? Why would we even want to take a deep breath, open our mouths, and send a mysterious melody into the silence?

Where do we get such strength and will? After working all day, riding on a jam-packed trolleybus, waiting in the grocery queues, we whistle on the street, hum in the kitchen, sing in the shower, and even wail on stage.

But it's not just that everyone sings – some even have the will to listen, and there aren't only one or two fools like that, but hundreds. Yes, everybody wants to get into the act – if not to sing, to listen; if not to listen, to sing.

That winter night, the auditorium at Moscow University was packed with listeners, and the stage was not empty either – thirty Comsomols, in white shirts, their top buttons open, were singing:

> Lenin is always alive,
> Lenin is always with you,
> In sadness, in hope, in happiness too!

Lena and I were not in the audience that night, nor were we in the chorus; we were backstage, because we were to sing the next number in that concert.

My hands were cold as ice but, at the same time, I felt hot. My throat was dry; it seemed impossible not only to sing, but even to whisper. I attempted to find a chord on the guitar, only to discover that I had completely forgotten where to place my fingers. I wanted to ask Lena, but stopped myself – she was hugging her lute and whispering something, maybe she was trying to remember the words to the song. Her eyes had turned green, like seawater, and in the depths of that water hid endless fright.

Why had we got involved in that silly concert? How much better it was to sing at home, in private, but no, we had to go on stage, and all because of Stas. Every time we had something to do with Stas, there were fateful consequences, though at first, it always seemed as if some kind of fun was on the way. So it went with this concert, which had begun with crayfish, to be more precise, with beer, yes, with beer. . . .

One snowy night, Andrew had shown up at the wooden castle with two suitcases of Zhiguli beer. Later, Boris arrived with live crayfish, wrapped in newspaper. Andrewlka tossed the crayfish into a pot and started rounding up all the spices he could find in the communal kitchen. While the crayfish were cooking, Lena and I sang a few songs.

Our audience was always the same, so we had to sing new songs all the time. Eventually, there were so many songs that, to keep things straight, we started calling each twelve an album. Our friends knew our albums by heart and, depending on their mood, or their drinks, would simply request song five from the first album, or number eight from the second.

'The feast is about to begin,' Andrew announced as he brought a tray of steamy red crayfish into the room, his face the colour of the crustaceans.

He placed the tray on a stool. Everybody took his usual place. Boris sat on the desk; Andrewlka, now sporting a goatee, and a black leather jacket, sat in the open armoire, his hand reaching out and snapping up the crayfish by their long antennae. I sat on the bearskin rug. We ate the body and tails and, by common consent, left the claws for dessert.

Lena didn't join the group; she sat on the windowsill, as far as possible from our 'barbarian food'. Even though she grew up near the sea, she had never liked water creatures like crayfish, eel, or octopus. Her fingers tinkered with the strings of the lute to block out the sound of the shells cracking. Suddenly, she stopped playing and said, 'Somebody's coming.'

We paused from our intense work and listened. We heard the stairs creak. Thinking it was the Wonder coming home for his night's sleep, I motioned to everybody to keep still. If Toilik knew I had company, he wouldn't miss the chance to join the party. We sat motionless; nevertheless, the door was flung open without the usual knock with the head and, instead of the gloomy, green face of the hero, we saw the happy, pink face of Stas, sprinkled with snow.

'Stas!' we shouted.

'Oh, how I hate stairs,' he said, panting.

'Hurray for Stas,' we cheered.

'What's up? Just hanging around?' he asked, brushing the snow from his sleeves.

'Yes,' we said.

'Singing?' he asked.

'Drinking,' we said.

'"A drink and a shiver is bad for your liver," my mommychka always said. You know, you people don't give a damn about your health. You've got a concert coming up in a week, and you're sitting here wrecking your organisms,' Stas said.

'What concert?' Lena asked.

Without stopping to explain, Stas crossed the room, leaving a trail of wet footprints behind him. He sat down on the bed, and tried our patience by yanking a little green box out of his pocket, taking a white pill out of it, snatching a bottle of beer, popping the pill into his mouth, and drinking the beer from the bottle to make the pill go down.

'At Moscow University,' Stas said, taking a swig from the bottle, 'in the name of Lenin.'

'And what will we be doing at this concert?' Lena asked.

'Singing,' said Stas, 'what else?'

'Sound the trumpets! Sashulka and Lenulka are going to be famous! Beat the drums!' shouted Andrew from the wardrobe, accompanying himself with a drumroll.

'No,' said Lena.

'What do you mean?' said Boris.

'Why not?' asked Andrewlka.

It was evident that our friends liked Stas's idea.

'Because we're not ready,' Lena said.

'What do you think, you're a crayfish? When they're ready, they may look great, but they're dead. What's the sense of always

133

singing to friends who know your imaginary records by heart? It's high time you crawl out of the communal pot, before you're overcooked.'

There was a silent pause. Stas pulled the stool with the tray over to the bed, picked up a red claw, and continued, 'In one week there will be a convention of journalists at the University. Correspondents, writers, and reporters will flock there from all over the Union. I can think of no better time for you to launch your career. There will be photographs, interviews, and articles. I will make you famous overnight. This is your last term at the Institute; before school is over, all the theatres and film studios will be playing tug-of-war with you. That's the way to establish a career!'

'If you know so much about establishing a career, how come you're not in the theatre yourself, instead of hiding out behind Anna Ivanna's breakfront?' I challenged.

'Because,' responded Stas, thrilled to have the chance to explain his profound philosophy to simple folks, 'I have no need for the theatre. There's only one theatre in the world for me, and its name is – life! That's a real theatre, with a premiere every minute, and every day – to be or not to be. And what productions – where could you find a stage like Moscow? And what actors! Talent by the thousands, scrambling from store to store. And what costumes, my God! And decorations. Is the human imagination really capable of this? Who could dream up so much red?

'Only recently, the West came up with the Theatre of the Absurd but, in our country, in our cities, in our apartments, absurdity goes all the way back to 1917.'

'What an avalanche!' said Boris.

'Andrewlka's orchestra is still,' said Andrew.

'I'm toying with an idea,' continued Stas, 'a funny plan, a production to be called the "Performance of the Century." I have thought it over and come to the conclusion that for such an event, I need some stars. I already have one great pianist, but that's not enough. I need more and I've decided to use you. Not because you're my friends, no, but because the Performance of the Century necessitates song.'

'Why?' asked Boris.

134

'Because songs are the exception to the rule, the exception to the Soviet system.'

'Andrewlka wants to know what you mean,' said Andrewlka.

'Because,' Stas said, waving a claw as if it were a conductor's baton, 'there is nothing more powerful than songs. Books, films, and television shows are subject to strict controls; only songs can slip through the censorship and spread across the country. That's why songs are the exception to communist theory. Perhaps this is the only area the theory bypasses.'

'That's impossible,' said Boris. 'The theory covers everything.'

Stas stopped waving the claw, threw it on the tray, and said, 'Right, let's take a look at what Marx said about songs.' He began to fumble through the heap of crayfish, found a large one with a broken head, looked at it from all sides, and said, 'Nothing! Marx said nothing about songs.'

'You're right,' Boris said.

'Well, maybe Lenin touched on this.' Once again, Stas burrowed through the pile and took out a tiny, curled-up crayfish, which looked more like a shrimp. He straightened the tail, staring at it for some reason, and then asked, 'Did Lenin say anything about songs? No.'

'You're right again. He said that art in general was necessary for propaganda, but he didn't say anything specific about songs,' Boris playfully replied.

'So, maybe Stalin said something more explicit,' said Stas, getting fired up. He tossed Lenin into the pile, fished around, and pulled out a huge body by the antennae. Its black eyes scrutinized us as if it were alive. 'No,' said Stas ponderously, 'it's better not to touch Stalin.' Stas let go of the antennae, and the body of the crayfish tumbled onto the red heap of broken legs and bodies.

'Yes, it's a ticklish question for the Party,' Stas said, looking at the pile of crayfish thoughtfully. 'How can the Party control songs if it's impossible to get people to sing bad songs? Singers may sing, but the masses will not chime in. So, it is quite clear that a good song is more powerful than the system, and is, in fact, outside the theory. The whole theory concerns the science of domination, but songs, by their very nature, are free. How come you're so quiet, comrades?' Stas asked us and the crayfish.

'Anyway, that's enough theory. To get things moving, I've arranged for you to be in a concert at Moscow University. To become stars, you've got to start somewhere,' Stas said, putting a piece of crayfish into his mouth.

'What are we supposed to sing?' Lena asked.

'The one dedicated to Mandelstam,' screamed Boris, spurred on by Stas's revolutionary monologue. 'The concert will be for journalists and writers, and that one is about a poet, a writer.'

'Listen,' said Andrewlka, 'you'd better not sing that, if you don't want to suffer Mandelstam's fate. You've got to choose the most impartial songs – like the ones about nature, or love, or – '

'You're right, but not entirely,' said Boris, cutting him short. 'Mandelstam was killed when Stalin was in power; things are different now, and I think there is no harm in trying.'

'I don't know,' I said. 'I don't want to spend the rest of my life in prison talent shows.'

'Stas, what do you think? Come on, stop eating for a minute,' said Boris. 'What's the censorship going to be like, very tough?'

'Nonsense,' said Stas, cracking a claw. 'I have friends on all the commissions. I know what they like.'

'Hold it,' said Lena. 'Sasha and I should be the ones to decide what we're going to sing. I think we should be asked first.'

'No! Andrewlka should be asked first,' shouted Andrew. 'The issue isn't what you want or what you don't want, but what you must do; and Andrewlka is the only one who can tell you that. He says you must sing number two from the first album and number one from the second.'

'Horseshit!' muttered Boris. 'Both of those songs are about autumn, but it happens to be winter outside!'

'Nobody ever believes poor Andrewlka. Andrewlka's a part-time informer, you know, a "knocker," for the KGB. He knows which way the wind is blowing. He has connections, and if he says number one and number two . . . that's the way it's got to be.'

Andrewlka really was working for the KGB, not in the capacity he aspired to, but as a porter, and the opinion of a porter, even one who was cleaning such special floors, couldn't be decisive. Bedlam broke out.

'Shut up for a minute,' Stas said, finishing the last crayfish. 'What's all the arguing about if the commission will make the decision anyway,' he said and stood, drawing himself up to his full height. 'Give me a dozen songs; I will put them into the right hands, and everything will be as smooth as butter.'

And, in all honesty, everything did go smoothly. The next day, Stas took the twelve songs, and passed them on to his friends at the Comsomol Commission at Moscow University. The Comsomols liked the songs. They discarded only those which mentioned: *the Mother of God; thunder; scalpels;* and *diamonds.*

The eight songs that were left were passed on to the Party Commission. The communists also liked the songs. They discarded only those which mentioned: *wine glasses; candles; kisses;* and *blackbirds.*

The four remaining songs were passed on to an 'unnamed commission,' which asked us to bring our guitars to the School of Journalism at Moscow University, where the final decision was to be made.

The 'unnamed commission' was composed of only two comrades, of indeterminate age, who were waiting for us in their office overlooking the Kremlin. Both of them were dressed in grey suits – one was in a light plaid; the other, in dark grey stripes. Without much preliminary discussion the indeterminate comrades asked us to sing our repertoire. We sang the four remaining songs.

'Good,' said the comrades, 'very good, but not very suitable. Don't you have any songs about Lenin?'

'Unfortunately not,' I replied.

'Too bad,' said the comrades, 'that's too bad. Don't you have any songs about cosmonauts? We're expecting a cosmonaut to be in the audience for tomorrow's concert, and a song like that would be very appropriate.'

'No,' Lena said, 'we don't have any songs like that.'

'What a shame,' they said. 'Don't you have any songs about the Comsomols who were crushed to death by Fascist tanks during World War Two?'

'No,' I said.

The comrades lit their cigarettes.

'Hm,' said the striped one.

'Hm,' said the plaid one.

'Perhaps you have a song about the boy scout who was strangled to death with his own red necktie by his treacherous father?' one of the comrades asked.

'No, but we have a song about a red-haired fireman.'

'All right, let's hear it,' the commissioners said without much enthusiasm.

We sang:

> The red-haired fireman in his red fire engine
> Rushes through the blazing forest,
> To put out the autumn's fiery leaves . . .

'That's enough. Not bad,' said one of the indeterminate men. 'The rhythm's a bit strange, but you've got a lot of red in there, and that's always good. I like what you said about autumn – it will remind people of the plentiful harvest this autumn. By any chance, would you have something specifically about our heroic collective farmers?'

'We have a song about a farmer, Ivan, who fell in love with a milkmaid called Marie,' I said. 'The only problem was that their affair had a bad effect on productivity. It's really a funny song.'

'That's not funny!' the plaid one said, 'not funny at all. It sounds like love is destroying communism in our villages. It's not appropriate. By the way, what's that instrument?'

'It's a lute,' said Lena.

'It's not a Russian instrument, is it?'

'No, it's Italian.'

'You mean it's foreign, huh? How come you don't play a Russian folk instrument? You should be playing the balalaika and the melodion, and singing Soviet folk songs about important things like the harvest. Can't you change the song about Ivan and Marie so that their love affair makes productivity go up? That would be good and funny, too.'

'I'm sorry, but there's no time,' I said. 'The concert's tomorrow night.'

'Yes, the concert *is* tomorrow night, but the issue is who will perform in that concert,' the plaid one said ponderously. 'One last question – don't you have any songs about Soviet holidays like December fifth, May first, or November seventh?'

'The only one we have is about a holiday of autumn flowers,' I said. 'It's Lena's music.'

'What? Lenin's music?' both comrades cried.

'Yes,' I said, not wanting to disappoint them. 'Would you like us to sing it for you?'

'That won't be necessary,' one of the comrades said. 'It must be a fine song. It's just that we had never been informed that Lenin wrote music. Anyway, it's precisely what we need. Okay, we'll put down that Sasha and Lena will sing two songs. The first song will be the one with the strange rhythm about the communist on the fire engine. By the way, what kind of rhythm was that?'

Rock 'n' roll, I almost said. 'A very fast march,' I uttered instead.

'Perfect,' they said. 'So, we have written down the Communist March and Lenin's Song. It will be a sensation for the journalists. Good luck, comrades.'

So, as always, Andrewlka turned out to be right; we would be singing the first song from the second record and the second from the first – both songs about autumn.

The Comsomol chorus sang, for the last time, that Lenin was always with them. The applause sounded thin and reserved. Lena and I were nearly in a panic – if forty Comsomols with an orchestra got an applause like that, what would we get?

'How should I announce you?' asked the distraught compere, running up to us as the Comsomols were marching off the stage.

'Just say that Sasha and Lena will sing two songs about autumn,' Lena said.

'About autumn?' the compere repeated in confusion as he fixed the parting in his hair, and went up to the microphone with a jaunty step.

How the compere finally introduced us and how we began to sing, I don't remember. I could never have imagined that it

139

would be so terrifying to sing two songs about nature. The stage was nothing new to us – we were in our last year at the Theatre Institute – but we were more nervous than ever before. Maybe because it was the first time in our life we were going before an audience with something of our own, something we loved.

Only when we got to the last stanza of the song about the red-haired fireman did I understand what we were doing. I discovered that we were both singing the right words and even in sync. My fingers were strumming in a strange fashion but, somehow, everything turned out right. The song ended with the open bass string – it was difficult to make a mistake. I struck the string and made it sound like a departing fire engine.

Earlier, before going on stage, we agreed not to wait for the applause, which might never come, and go right into the next song. My guitar didn't have a chance to quiet down when Lena softly started up the next song on the lute, and we swiftly made the transition from the rock beat to a waltz. In this song, Lena soloed, and I even got up the nerve to glance at the audience.

The audience was one huge smile. In the first row, in the middle, between the two grey suits, sat the cosmonaut. He was looking at Lena and rocking slightly from side to side, as if he were weightless. I recognized him right off – he was the one at Andrewlka's party.

When we finished, the cosmonaut was the first to stand up and clap. After him, the whole auditorium began to rise; only the two grey suits remained seated. We bowed and hurried backstage. Lena threw her arms around my neck and sighed, 'That's it! Thank God it's over! Thank God!'

But Lena was wrong; that was only the beginning.

The compere appeared out of nowhere. 'What are you doing here? The audience doesn't like to be kept waiting. They're calling you. Hurry. Hurry.' He took us by the arms and nearly dragged us onto the stage.

We took four more curtain calls. The frantic compere, trying to restore order, requested that the lights in the auditorium be turned on to signal the end of the concert, but this only emboldened the audience. They were clapping, stamping their feet, and shouting: 'Bravo! Encore!'

'What should we do?' Lena cried when we went backstage.

'I don't know,' I said.

Then the compere popped up like a jack-in-the-box. Apparently, he had lost all hope of subduing the audience. 'Maybe you can do an encore,' he pleaded.

'Anything but the same songs,' Lena said. 'I can't sing like that the second time.'

We went out on stage and, when the audience quieted down a bit, I asked if they wanted us to sing one of the same songs again, or another one.

'Another one!' came the cry from the auditorium.

'What should we sing?' I asked Lena, turning away from the mike.

'Mandelstam,' Lena said. 'Sing Mandelstam.'

'But we decided – '

'Please!'

'Now we will sing,' I said into the mike, 'a song dedicated to the poet Osip Mandelstam.'

There was a strange silence in the auditorium, a silence so pervasive that it was possible to sing without a microphone. The audience's smile was strained, frozen like a mask. I had seen that kind of mask somewhere before. . . . I began to tap out the rhythm on the guitar and sing:

> The fire of insomnia is burning my brain
> Thoughts spinning senselessly ingrained
> Rushing cavalry endlessly galloping
> Iced sweat and hearts walloping.
>
> Idiocy, idiocy, hellish idiocy
> With a constant torturous drive
> We dare expect happiness from this life
> Where somebody's ear is always listening
> And then to find your friend is whistling.
>
> Swollen veins implore me painlessly
> To end this world's affairs aimlessly
> But to spill all this blood on the bathroom floor
> To no avail and no one to implore.

We don't need verses about death
Death alone steals breath
Ah, I will wrap myself in a downy quilt
And then perhaps, in the morning, peace will knell.

The fire of insomnia still in my head
Thoughts whirling, endlessly dread
Rushing cavalry galloping
Only . . . Knock . . . Knock . . . Knock walloping.

Mandelstam. Open up.
Knock . . . Knock . . . Knock
We know you're in there.
Knock . . . Knock . . . Knock
Open up! We're your friends. Don't try to resist.

Useless.

We finished the song but the silence was still there exactly as at the beginning, as if we hadn't begun at all. We didn't move. It was as though someone had pulled the pin out of a grenade. The tension moved through the entire auditorium all the way to the back exit. Suddenly, there came a knock. Everybody froze; the knock was repeated; nobody moved. The door began to open slowly with a sinister creak, and a head in a security guard's hat peeked into the room. The guard looked from one side to the other, trying to work out what was going on in that silence. He came in and went down the aisle with a baffled expression on his face. He walked over the wooden floor carefully, trying to keep his boot heels silent, but they resounded anyway – knock, knock, knock.

And then the grenade exploded into a thunderous laughter. It found its mark – the guard. The audience laughed at him openly. The poor fellow didn't understand what was happening. Feeling like the object of tremendous attention, he hunched his shoulders, backed up to the door, and disappeared. We hurried backstage. The last thing I saw before going off stage was the cosmonaut winking at me.

'Why did you suddenly decide to sing Mandelstam?' I asked Lena.

'Because you solo in that one, and I join in only at the end of each stanza.'

'So?'

'So, I was afraid my voice would crack if I had to sing a solo.'

'But weren't you afraid to sing Mandelstam?'

'Oh my God, I didn't think about that!'

The compere came up to us, coughed into his fist, fixed his part, looked off to the side, and said, 'Come with me, comrades. Somebody's waiting for you.'

In the dressing room sat the two indeterminate men. Something had happened to them; somehow they looked different. Maybe it was their suits – the one who had been in grey stripes was now in grey plaid; and the one who had been in plaid was now in stripes. Maybe it was something else.

'Sit down,' they said, interrupting my thoughts.

We sat down.

'How did this happen? You were told in advance.'

'Told what?' I asked.

'How do you like that – he's got the nerve to ask what. I'm talking about the song you were supposed to sing by Comrade Lenin.'

'The second song we sang was Lena's,' I said.

'What do you mean?'

'That the *music* for that song was written by Lena.'

'Lena, Lenin, let's not twist things around. What do you mean to say – that Comrade Lenin wrote that rubbish about water and grass dancing? Don't tell me those were Lenin's lyrics.'

'No,' I said. 'I wrote the lyrics.'

'Okay,' they said, 'that's clear, but tell us who wrote the words to the third song with that "Hey, Mandelstam, open up, knock, knock, knock" stuff?'

'I wrote that one, too,' I said.

'I see, now we understand everything. But we'd like to ask you one more question: who gave you permission to sing that song?'

'You approved only two songs, but the audience was asking for more,' said Lena.

'Why didn't you repeat one of the songs we had given you permission to sing?'

'You heard it yourself,' Lena said. 'He asked the audience what they wanted. They said they wanted a new song.'

'Who gave you permission to ask them what they wanted? How do they know what they want? That's our business to decide.'

It was useless to argue.

'And, by the way, where did you get the idea of writing a song about that Jew poet Mandelstam; are you Jewish?'

'No,' I said.

'We'll check that,' said the plaid one. 'But if you're not, why did you hide that song from us, like a sneaky Jew?'

This is it, I thought.

'We didn't have that song when we spoke with you,' said Lena. 'We've just written it; it's our latest song.'

'It's more like your last song!' the striped one said.

'I never heard such nonsense,' the plaid one said. 'You didn't have time to change a few words in an approved song, but you had enough time to write a new song.'

We remained silent.

'All right, that'll be all, comrades, but remember, a mistake on the Soviet stage is like a mistake in a minefield – it can be made only once,' the striped one said.

The commissioners stood up and walked out of the room. Just as the door closed, a knock came. I saw Lena shiver.

'Who is it?' I asked.

'Open up, we're your friends. Don't try to resist.'

The door was thrown open, and Stas ploughed into the room, followed by Boris and Andrewlka. Each one held a bottle of champagne.

'Salute!' Stas ordered, with a wave of the hand. They all raised the bottles to their shoulders like rifles and shot simultaneously. The salute seemed more like an execution, with the corks whizzing over our heads.

A stream of people came into the room, congratulating us and pulling bottles out of their pockets and briefcases. At first, there was much talk of magazine articles and TV and radio broadcasters, but as the evening wore on, the promises died out altogether and were soon forgotten. The more we drank, the more the thrill of success vanished, as if it had never been. Then a drunken wave rolled over us and all was lost. . . .

We found ourselves out in the snow and cutting cold, guitars in hand, at the trolleybus stop. It was too late for the Metro, so we went out in the storm, hoping to catch the last trolleybus. Lena was not in her unique fur coat, but in a flimsy jacket she had pulled on in a hurry, before the concert. Beneath the jacket, she wore only a cotton dress. On her feet were high-heeled sandals, making her look as if she were standing on tiptoe in the snow. She seemed about to cry at any moment.

'Lena,' I said, 'come over here.'

She came towards me, stepping over the piles of snow, carefully. The wind nipped at her dress mercilessly, and it looked as if she would be blown away in the darkness. I opened my coat. She squeezed in under my arm.

'It's cold,' she said pathetically. 'It's awfully cold. Sasha I'm afraid. What's going to become of us?'

I hugged her tightly and murmured through chattering teeth, 'Maybe everything will be all right. Let's hope.'

Far off in the distance, we saw headlights, then the whole trolleybus, enveloped in snow like an icehouse. It drew near with the clatter of chains on its wheels.

It was the number 11. We were really disappointed; we needed the number 31. The icy doors banged open, spraying us with a cloud of snow and frost.

'Is the 31 still running?' I asked the driver.

'Who knows,' he said, through a wool scarf wrapped over his mouth and chin.

'Where are you going?' I asked.

'Where are *you* going?' he replied.

'To Arbat,' we said.

'Are you musicians?' he said, looking at our guitar cases.

'Sort of,' I said.

'Get on,' he said, 'I'm a musician myself.'

We got on.

'All right, folks, this trolleybus is taking a special route. Next stop – Arbat!'

The number 11 made its way through the storm, along the dark streets of Moscow. From time to time, the driver stopped at the intersection, jumped out into the street, ran the length of the snowy trolleybus, pulled down the frozen electric poles, which looked like two huge icicles, switched them to another cable – blue sparks flying about – and there we were on another route. Even in the strictly organized system of Soviet transport, there was room for an independent trip.

Knock . . . Knock . . . Knock . . . the chained wheels clanged on the icy street. Knock . . . Knock . . . Knock . . .

2 To Live

After that night at Moscow University, I kept feeling that something was wrong and out of joint, but I couldn't put my finger on it. There was a chill in my spine. I expected something bad to happen. I kept mulling over the concert – the songs, and the conversation afterwards – trying to convince myself that it was all behind me, but the feeling wouldn't disappear; it just dug in deeper, like a troublesome splinter in the flesh of my soul.

There were only a few months left until graduation and the last thing I needed was trouble. I knew how easy it was to lose my chance for a job at a Moscow theatre and, by so doing, destroy my career forever. The only way to success for a young actor was to stay in Moscow after graduation. Once you left the capital for the provinces you could never come back. Your 'propiska' – permission to live in Moscow – would be lost for all time.

Four years of school had flown by faster than it was possible to imagine, but long enough for Moscow to become my home. I felt comfortable there. I loved the big city. I loved its museums, exhibitions, ballet. I loved its high-rise buildings and our log cabin. I loved wide squares and narrow side streets. I loved Arbat. I loved boulevards. And, most of all, I loved the Metro. I didn't want to lose it like the station I lost in my childhood and had never seen again. I forget the name of that station, but was sure that living in Moscow sooner or later I would find it, because I took the Metro almost every day. Strangely enough, in all those years I had never had time to look for it. I was too busy learning the secret art of acting according to the Stanislavsky Method.

My own short definition of the Method was that it was about how to act natural and be free on stage. Perhaps that sounds too simple, but here is the secret – for Soviet people it's almost impossible. Even in everyday life we can't act natural and feel free, but to be free, to be uninhibited on stage is as hard as feeling natural in a police lineup. So the Stanislavsky Method is probably the only way for us Russians to become professional, accomplished actors.

It was a long way from Clapping Machine to mime exercises, then from improvisation with short lines, to short plays with long monologues, but, finally, after four years we came to our diploma performance, produced and directed by the Dean himself. It was an 'optimistic tragedy' called *Storm*, by Bill Bilotsirkovsky.

All the last term we were busy in the student theatre working on this extravaganza about the Revolution. We weren't just acting workers, peasants, soldiers, and sailors – the great living witnesses of the Revolution – we were also working backstage day and night. We built the sets and dragged around walls, hills, bridges, and ships, all of which were laden with dust – probably stowed away since the day of the Revolution itself. In the midst of all this activity, Field Marshal Kutuzov bellowed orders punctuated by filthy cursing. He saw himself as one god in three persons: teacher, director, and stage manager. For each of these jobs he collected a salary which, all told, probably surpassed the salary of the real Field Marshal in the Czar's Army.

There was another good reason that the Dean considered himself a god. He could create a world – light and darkness, earth and water, thunder and lightning – not in seven days, but in seven minutes.

Those he liked, he named angels, those he didn't, devils. The easy jobs, such as lighting the sky and hanging the clouds, were delegated to the angels, of whom Miss Kupina was the favourite. Little Barskov was the number-one devil, and his group was subjected to working on the earth and under the earth. Naturally the worst jobs were always given to Barskov. The Field Marshal didn't for one minute believe the stories about his weakness and poor health, and every day he made a point of giving Barskov a little checkup which entailed carrying a bookcase filled with books from the basement to the stage. Life wasn't much easier for the rest of the devils, either.

Kutuzov was no advocate of discrimination and he always

treated the devils and the girls as equals. The girls, with the exception of Kupina, of course, had to sweep the stage floor, make adjustments in the costumes, and practise how to move the props in the dark. It was no easy job. Everything had to be done with precision – the girls had to change into the decrepit costumes of the workers, dash out onto the stage to see their sailors off, rearrange the props again, slip into peasants' clothes, say farewell to their soldiers going off to war, switch the furniture, then change into black for the finale, where a wounded commissar would chant his parting words before going to another world which he didn't believe in.

His speech, repeated day in and day out, lingered with all of us like a nightmare. Swaying, and almost falling down from exhaustion, we prayed for the commissar's speedy departure. But he was a solid, stalwart fellow and didn't want to be hushed. Each time he raised his bandaged head and opened his mouth we held our heads in our hands expressing grief, but in truth we were covering our ears to shut out the endless ravings.

When the day of the premiere arrived, all the actors and actresses, if you can call us that, were on the verge of a nervous breakdown. The Dean constantly pestered us, driving everyone crazy and railing at the angels and devils with his choice and mostly profane words. So when we heard a barrage of filthy words coming from high in the wings, everybody knew that it was time for the curtain to open.

The lights in the auditorium waned and the revolutionary activities commenced. The performance rolled on flawlessly; we switched sets and costumes like robots. Applause rang out in the auditorium frequently, but the seniors, trained in the Stanislavsky Method, didn't pay heed. The spirit of the Revolution filled the room. As it got closer to the last scene, the tension mounted; the sailors were already carrying the listless body of the commissar. They cautiously placed him stage centre and drew back in expectation of his parting words. With intense determination the commissar forced open one eye, then the other, then slowly and painfully began to lift his bandaged head. Silence permeated the room when . . . suddenly, from above there was a thud. Everybody froze. Nobody was expecting it. It had never happened

149

during rehearsals. The commissar was mute and, for the first time, missed his cue. Just at that moment, from on high, rang out the thunderous voice of the Field Marshal.

'Eh, you "mudaks"! What shithead locked me in up here, when I have to be on stage for a curtain call? I'm asking you once and for all, you fucking devils and you stupid angels!'

There was a chilling silence.

'No answer, you fucking Stanislavskys and you triple-fucking Vakhtangovs? Right, then I'll come down by rope and show you soldiers and sailors what a revolution is really like!'

In his uncontrollable rage, the Field Marshal turned on the switches for thunder and lightning. Blood-red flashes of light blinded us. A rope tumbled from the sky, and the absurdly kicking legs of the god of thunder appeared. Apprehension and confusion were written all over the actors' faces. Only the number-one angel, the number-one devil, and I smiled knowingly.

Amidst a blast of thunder and lightning after the kicking legs appeared a torso in a crazily flapping jacket, then hands and a head. The rope was too short and Field Marshal Kutuzov dangled from it, swinging to and fro. Then there was a wild scream – he lost his grip and tumbled down, crashing through the bridge, knocking over the factory smokestack, and smashing through the trap door. The earth parted and from the abyss an angry, distant sound arose above the thunder: 'Now you virgin-fuckers know what the Stanislavsky Method is! Your classes may be over, but I'm not finished with you yet . . .'

After our disastrous diploma performance at school came the tense time for auditions at the theatres. I was surprised to find that it was Miss Silver, my pursuer, who was most concerned about setting up jobs for our class. She voluntarily and zealously contacted the directors of the theatres, checked if they needed young actors and for what roles, set up appointments, met with the theatre managers after the auditions, and was the first to know the fate of each one of her protégés.

The only thing she asked of us was that we not make any appointments without her approval. She took it upon herself to divide our class into groups and set up a schedule for group auditions in order not to wear out the directors. She told students of each group to help each other out and stick together like a close-knit family.

Our family group was composed of Misha Limshitz, Barskov, Kupina, Lena, me, and our minority students – the Chookcha and the Chechen. After four years of studying the Stanislavsky Method, we were even able to act a part in a few plays. This, of course, had nothing to do with Kupina, who stuck with Vakhtangov and was still playing the cello after all those years. She had so refined the movement of her hands and legs that, when one was observing her, it seemed as if not only a cello, but a full symphony orchestra were playing. If Paganini could command the attention of his listeners playing only one string, then Kupina could hold the attention of her audience without any strings. It was easy for Kupina to decide what to present at the auditions – she didn't know anything except her invisible cello, and she didn't need anything else.

It was more difficult for the rest of us. Shy Barskov decided to read a monologue from *The Living Corpse*, by Leo Tolstoy. This was the only part that gave him any confidence. Misha Limshitz acted a part from *Christmas at Señor Cuppello's House*, by Eduardo De Filippo. With his big nose, curly hair, and dark, sad eyes, Misha was positive he looked Italian. Lena prepared a one-act play, *The Conversation*, by Jean Cocteau. In that act, she was fighting with her lover, who sat in an armchair the whole time, reading the newspaper. I played the part of the lover and I also prepared the part of the gentleman caller from *The Glass Menagerie*, by Tennessee Williams. The Chookcha and Chechen had prepared their own menagerie – 'The Dance of the Trained Bears'. Their folk instinct told them to dance so nobody would know how poorly they spoke Russian.

After the first few auditions, it became evident that language wasn't very important in the Moscow theatre. What was really necessary was Moscow propiska. The first question asked at each audition was whether we had Moscow propiska or not.

Unfortunately, none of us except Misha Limshitz had a permanent Moscow propiska. All we had was permission to live in the capital temporarily – while we were students. And so we would inevitably have to leave the capital after graduation if we didn't land a job at a Moscow theatre. But the theatre had no right to give us a job if we didn't have Moscow propiska. It was a vicious circle. We continued to go from theatre to theatre like a gypsy caravan and, everywhere we went, we came up against the same sharp question, as sharp as a razor cutting out our hope – 'Are you a Muscovite?'

During our years at the Institute we considered ourselves Muscovites, but our documents never forgot where we were really from. It became quite clear that the purple stamp in our passports was considerably more decisive than how we acted at the auditions, and the directors seemed to view all of us as 'living corpses'.

The end of my performance was always followed by an uncomfortable pause – I looked at the directors; they looked at me; I smiled with a masklike smile; they looked at me gloomily, deep in concentration. The silence stretched like the elastic of my Oriental birthday mask. Then came the blow:

'You aren't a Muscovite, are you?'

'No,' I replied.

'No Moscow propiska?'

'I have a temporary permit for studying.'

'You need permanent propiska to work.'

'I can get it if you give me a job.'

'We can't give you a job if you don't have propiska.'

'If you give me a paper saying that you intend to give me a job, I could apply for propiska.'

'We can't give you such a paper unless we have a place for you to live. Why don't you audition at the academic theatres; they have dormitories.'

'Thank you,' I said and smiled, knowing that the academic theatres rarely scheduled auditions; they had their own acting schools and didn't need actors from the outside.

At each theatre they hit us with the same questions; they hit us mercilessly, but we simply smiled and said, 'Thank you.'

Misha was the only one in the whole group who had the right stamp on the propiska page of his passport. That isn't to say that all his problems were solved; he had trouble with another page.

Each and every director said that he didn't look the least bit Italian, and even less Russian. They said his nose was too big; his hair too curly; his eyes too sad; and that all these things together exposed his true nationality, which never was much help. If there had been a Jewish theatre, they would have taken him for sure.

The noose was getting tighter, and our group was beginning to feel not like living corpses, but dead ones. There were almost no theatres left, and what was the point of going for auditions if we didn't have propiska? Nevertheless, we kept trying. Our temporary Moscow permit was good for a few more weeks, till school was over. After that, nobody would even speak with us. We would be considered 'provincials.' It looked as if life was putting me back in my old place as a Tulyak. Everything was starting all over again. Even the army was becoming a threat, and the officer from the Tula Recruiting Centre rose in his atomic submarine from the dark recesses of my mind. A four-year tour beneath the water! My head bald from radiation! I had to come up with something, but what?

We were locked in our passport-prison by the purple stamp of propiska. There was nothing to do but pray for a miracle.

Kupina's prayers were answered first. Distraught over the endless rejections, the cellist ignored Miss Silver's rules and went by herself for an audition at the Theatre for the Deaf and Dumb. Kupina hoped that there, in that cathedral of silence, she would not hear the despised word *propiska*.

Kupina turned out to be a sensation at the Theatre for the Deaf and Dumb. The deaf director, crying from joy, cooed and waved his hands to show that, for the first time in his life, he had heard music. Immediately after the audition, he offered Kupina his heart and his hand, thereby giving her Moscow propiska, an apartment, and a job in the orchestra for the deaf and dumb.

This event opened the eyes of the Chookcha and Chechen. Once again, they followed their folk instinct – they found Moscow brides and paid them a thousand rubles each. The money had been sent by their parents as a wedding present. So, they too became Muscovites. Unfortunately, there were only two theatres left where they could apply for a job and present 'The Dance of the Trained Bears' – the Bolshoi Theatre and the Children's

Theatre. Because of its conservatism, the Bolshoi refused to view the folk art, but the Children's Theatre was always in need of such divertissement to keep the kids from smoking in the toilets. The Children's Theatre expressed interest in their folklore, and a date was set for an audition.

Lena and I didn't want to marry Muscovites for the sake of propiska. Besides, we didn't have that kind of money. But our chance came, too. One morning, Stas called to say that the Academic Theatre of the City Council would be holding open auditions that afternoon. Nobody knew why, but young actors were being sought. Stas said he'd stop by to pick us up at one o'clock.

It was a true miracle! An academic theatre in need of young actors! Hurray for the academics!

Stas came for us by taxi. We jumped in.

'How did you find out there were auditions today?'

'I just knew.'

'Did Anna Ivanna tell you?'

'It doesn't matter.'

'Did you tell anyone else about it?'

'Come on! That's the whole point. Nobody from the Theatre Institute will be there.'

The first thing we saw as we rode up to the Theatre of the City Council was the Chookcha and Chechen, pacing back and forth like bears in front of the entrance. On the steps stood Misha Limshitz, a dour look on his face, staring at the clouds floating along in the sky. All around the pavement, on the grass, and even spilling into the street, standing, walking, and practising, was not only our entire class, but every young actor who had graduated from the other theatrical schools within the last few years. There were also some other people – probably from other cities. I think Kupina was the only one who wasn't there.

This was even worse than it had been for the entrance exams because now, not a full class was to be accepted, but only one or two people, and every one of those who had shown up that day was no newcomer to the theatre business, but a professional, fighting for his place in life.

Competition?! We didn't care. Our group was happy to be able to compete. This was an academic theatre; it had a dormitory where we living corpses could lie down legally. Here nobody would ask us about propiska.

The audition at the Theatre of the City Council was the first audition in which somebody actually looked at us, not at the purple stamp in our passports, and since they were watching, we were going to show those academics how we could act. We would show them Stanislavsky and Vakhtangov, and the trained bears. We would make them laugh, and we would make them cry. Those academics would look into our eyes and see that we weren't merely actors without propiska, but real people.

I had never seen Lena act with such inspiration. How she yelled at me as I read my French newspaper. How she screamed that she loved me, though I was sleeping with all the whores of Paris! Oh, how she was acting!

Oh, how all our group was acting!

At the end of the day, after all the auditions, the actors were summoned into the lobby and thanked for coming. We were told that everyone had performed extremely well but, regrettably, there were only two openings, for one actor and one actress, so everybody was free to leave except so and so, who were to go to the director's office for a talk. 'So and so' were Lena and I.

'Tell me a little about yourselves,' the director began.

'We aren't Muscovites,' we said sheepishly.

'It doesn't matter,' he said.

'You know we don't have propiska,' we said.

'Don't worry, we'll give you propiska and a room in the dormitory,' he said.

'I might be called up,' I said.

'We'll get you out of it,' he said.

'When do we start?' we asked.

'I'll ring you in the morning,' he said.

'Tomorrow morning we'll be in class. Can you leave word with the school secretary, Miss Silver?'

'All right,' he said. 'I'll contact her.'

The news of our miraculous achievement travelled through the Institute like fire. Everybody congratulated us, though they were all a bit jealous of our good fortune. It was impossible to take one step without some classmate or professor dashing over to us, hugging us, then dragging us into a corner to ask how we had pulled it off; what we had done for it; and who had put in a good word for us. We replied that we hadn't done anything special. They stared at us incredulously, promised not to say a word to anybody, and, when they still didn't hear what they were looking for, they stormed off in a huff. It seemed that we had run into the whole Institute, everybody, that is, but Miss Silver, and so we headed straight for her office at the end of the day.

'Hello,' she began. 'It's a good thing you came to see me. I have something to ask you. How did you happen to set up an audition without me?'

'I'm sorry,' I said, 'but it all happened so suddenly.'

'It wasn't very nice, but what's done is done,' she said. 'Oh, I have a message for you. Somebody just rang from the Theatre of the City Council. They said they wanted to take another look at you tonight.'

'Again?' said Lena, blanching.

'Yes, dear, again. Did you really think it would be as simple as that? Yesterday, somebody couldn't be there, and so they said that if you're free tonight, you should go there and put on your little show all over again. Then they will make their final decision.'

'But yesterday they said everything had been decided,' Lena said.

'What was decided?' Miss Silver queried.

'That they're taking us.'

'Oh, you two still don't know a thing about the theatre. Intrigues abound backstage. But don't worry, I'm behind you.'

That night we performed the whole thing once more. They said we were even better than the first time, and promised to ring Miss Silver the next day.

In the morning, Miss Silver congratulated us. She said she had had positive feedback; the Theatre of the City Council was thrilled with us. But again they requested that we go to see them to present everything we had done before, plus something from another play. This was to be the last time.

'I can't do it any more. I can't do it,' Lena said with a shudder as we left Miss Silver's office.

'It's okay,' I said. 'Relax, this is the last time.'

'Something's wrong, I feel it,' Lena whispered.

'It's okay. Everything will be okay,' I said.

'I can't act the same role every day in front of the same people. I can't do it. And the worst thing is that I don't even want to! And when I don't want to, nothing goes right.'

'It's okay,' I said, 'relax. Everything is going to be all right. This is the last time.'

We performed for the academics one more time. I thought we had done a pretty good job; at least they said it was good. In fact, they said it was very good, but there were some complications with the dormitory. It was being renovated for the holiday, May the first. When the construction was over and the rooms were ready, we would be contacted and our propiska would be issued. Until then, we could take it easy.

Take it easy? We didn't want to take it easy. We wanted to work. We wanted to stay in Moscow. We wanted to live!

3 Why the Theatrical Mask Has Two Faces

Toilik, apparently sensing our predicament, brought home a kitten to distract us from our heavy thoughts. The kitten was white all over except for its snout, which had a black spot, just like Charlie Chaplin's moustache. The kitten was funny and we wanted to call him 'Charlie Chaplin,' but Toilik was up in arms, and said, 'What's the idea of naming a kitten. Who knows, tomorrow it may run away or fall out of the window.'

Our kitty loved to gambol but would tire quickly and would take long naps. Lena thought he might be sick. She took good care of him – moved the dish of milk right near his moustache to feed him, combed him and stroked him continually, but, nevertheless, the kitty's fur became dull and matted. We told Toilik that the kitten should be taken to the doctor, but he merely laughed it off and said, 'What – a doctor for a kitten? There's nothing wrong with him! He just hasn't got used to his new home . . .'

We decided to wait a few days, and if the kitten hadn't improved, we'd take him to the vet.

In the meantime, I went for my last audition – this one at the Children's Theatre. I wasn't planning to work in that theatre; I was there to help out the Chookcha and Chechen. The ethnic actors, realizing that it was their last chance to justify their wedding expenses, took the audition very seriously. They invited me to join their act as the animal trainer. I was supposed to come up with some funny lines to cover up their inability to speak Russian.

The audition went well. The bears were uproariously funny,

and I said some funny things too. There was nothing to lose; I just babbled whatever came into my head and everybody was in stitches. The director, a rosy-cheeked old man with small blue eyes, sat at a table drinking green Uzbek tea, eating a napoleon, laughing, and wiping his eyes with a handkerchief. Finally, the director laughed so hard that a piece of napoleon got caught in his throat and he went into a coughing fit. Everybody rushed over to him, hitting him on the back, nearly killing the old man. Choking and panting, he pushed back all his rescuers and drove everybody out of his office but, at the last second, motioned for me to stay. I was about to summon the bears, but the director signalled that he wanted to talk with me alone. For some time, he went on coughing and gasping and lacked the strength to utter a single word. Then he resumed drinking his tea.

Powdered sugar formed a white circle around his mouth and covered his navy blue jacket with a silvery dust. On his head there was a halo of white hair. In fact, the director looked like a pink, old angel, sitting under the laughing and crying masks.

'Are you looking for employment?' he finally asked.

'Where?' I asked.

'Here,' he replied.

'The City Council Theatre have promised to hire me,' I said.

'I didn't ask you about the City Council. Do you want employment in the Children's Theatre?'

'I don't know. Why, do you want me to perform something else?'

'No, that's quite all right. Do you want to destroy me altogether? Listen, I'd like to offer you a job.'

'I don't think it's possible. This isn't an academic theatre.'

'You mean you don't have propiska?'

'No.'

'Why don't you marry a Muscovite?'

'I can't, and I don't want to.'

We sat quietly for a little while.

'Whom can I get in touch with at your Institute? I want to check about the City Council Theatre.'

'You can call the secretary, Miss Silver. Here's her number.'

'All right,' he said, and picked up the phone to dial. 'May I speak with Miss Silver? . . . Thank you . . . Hello. This is the director of the Children's Theatre speaking. My name is Dudin. How do you do. I'm considering hiring one of your students . . . yes, of course . . . but I need some information about him. Can you help me out? It has to do with the City Council Theatre . . .'

Dudin placed his hand over the receiver, looked at me mischievously, and whispered, 'What's your name?'

Before I could reply, he motioned for me to keep still and went on with his conversation.

'Ah, you know whom I'm talking about. Right, that's him.'

Dudin took a pen from the desk and wrote my last name on a clean sheet of paper. 'Yes, I know. He told me he doesn't have propiska. . . . Yes, he said that too. . . . Mm? . . . No, I didn't know about that. . . . What? No, I didn't know that either. Really? . . . Very interesting. What happened after that? Oh no. Is that so?'

Dudin continued in this vein for the next few minutes. His hand was automatically pushing the pen on the piece of paper around my name, developing the outline of some bird. 'Oh no. At Lenin's university! . . . Who's a Jew? . . . Oh, Mandelstam; that's not so bad. . . . Anti-Soviet? That's bad! . . . Why didn't they lock him up? How was that? . . . I see. . . . He could be arrested any day now? I see. . . . That's right. Right. I'm glad you told me. You've really been a big help.'

I sat stone still. Dudin put down the receiver and began to drink his tea, following it with what was left of the napoleon. He ate heartily, his little finger held up diligently. As he finished eating, Dudin realized that his suit was sprinkled with powdered sugar. He brushed it off his sleeve, then meticulously dotted the sides of his mouth with his handkerchief, cleared his throat, and finally set his tiny blue beads on me and said, 'You have a good impresario.'

I didn't respond.

'Miss Silver told me a lot of fascinating things about you and your girl friend. A lot of things! Hm, it certainly was interesting. You know, that Miss Silver knows what to say and how to say it but, the problem is, she doesn't always know to whom. She was probably hoping to scare me, and that's where she made her mistake. There was only one person who could scare me, but that was a very long time ago.' Dudin stirred the spoon in the glass; it sounded like a chime. 'I'm an old man. I like to talk about the past and I have a story that might be of help to you, young man.'

I sat back, repressing my impatience.

The director smiled mischievously at my discomfort and began his story:

'A long time ago, before the war, I was sitting at home one night when I heard a knock at the door. I opened the door to find a military man standing at the threshold. He handed me an envelope which contained an invitation to a banquet. There was no date, or time, or place on the invitation. I asked the officer when the banquet would take place. "Now," he replied. "I'm to take you there." "I'm busy," I said. "I can wait five or six minutes," he said. "Tell me, who sent the invitation?" I asked, guessing something was going on. "Comrade Stalin," he said. "I don't need the five minutes," I said, "let's go."

'A large banquet for all those engaged in the arts was in progress at the Kremlin. The place was packed with people, mainly film directors, theatre managers, writers, playwrights, and, in general, a whole mélange of Socialist Realists. We ate, drank, and talked but, to be perfectly honest, we were anxiously awaiting Stalin. He was late. Actually, he wasn't late, he was never late, he was always "tied up" somewhere. That night, he was tied up for quite a while, so long, in fact, that everybody got completely drunk and forgot where they were. Then at the most unexpected moment he arrived, making an entrance as only he could do. Naturally, when he appeared, everybody stopped talking. It was as if somebody had tugged on our strings. We then formed a line to make it easier for him to be introduced to us. He moved along, puffing on his pipe, holding out his hand to each one, and calling each by his last name. Sometimes he stopped and asked – "What's your name?" The response would come out in a stutter: "M-my name is so and so, Comrade Stalin." "How do you do, Comrade so and so," he would say, and go on. Eventually, he approached me, stopped, and asked, "What's your name?" I replied, "My name is Dudin, Comrade Stalin." "How do you do, Comrade Dudin," Stalin said, going on. Then he came to a stop, turned around, removed the pipe from his mouth, and said, "That's strange," and came back to me. "Your name's Dudin?" he asked, jabbing his pipe into my chest. "Yes, Dudin," I said. "Strange," he said, "haven't you been arrested yet?" "No," I said, "not yet, Comrade Stalin." "That's strange," he said, and kept going. The line around me scattered like dominoes. The party continued, but there was a dead zone within a radius of ten metres from me. Everybody avoided me. I kept standing in the middle of the hall so as not to embarrass anybody. Suddenly, I heard footsteps behind me on the parquet floor. At that moment, I nearly died of fright. I turned to find Stalin standing in front of me. "What's your name again?" "Dudin, Comrade Stalin." "I'm so sorry, Comrade Dudin. It was Meyerhold who was supposed to be arrested, not you." "Thank you, Comrade Stalin," I said. "Since you still haven't been arrested, perhaps you could organize a concert for me at the Kremlin, if you're free, that is." And so, after that night, I arranged six concerts in a row for him at the Kremlin. Nobody did more than that. By the way, after that banquet, I have never been afraid of anything; so your friend Miss Silver tried to scare me with that story about your concert at the University for nothing. The worst part is that obviously she has told that story not only to me. After hearing an intriguing tale like that, I have a feeling the City Council Theatre will no longer be interested in taking you. But don't worry; I consider everything she said to be like this – ' Dudin held up a piece of paper on which he had drawn a funny-looking bird over my name.

'But there are other problems. You know, propiska is propiska. We aren't exactly an academic theatre; we don't have a dormitory, and so we're allowed to give only one person a job without propiska – our street cleaner. It's too bad you're not a street cleaner.

'I'm not going to promise you anything. I'll think about it and if I come up with something, I'll ring you. Good-bye for now. If I haven't contacted you by the autumn, then farewell. Oh, give me your home telephone number. I don't want to ring Miss "Thirty Pieces of Silver" anymore.'

'Now what?' It was the same question Lenin asked after his first stroke.

When I got back home it was very late. Lena was sitting in bed staring at the kitten in the candlelight. At first, I didn't want to say anything, but then I thought about how long it had been since I'd seen her smile, so I told her the story about the bear dance and the funny director, Dudin.

'What did Dudin say?' Lena prodded.

'He said he would like to give me a job if he could work out the propiska.'

'Really? What else?'

'Nothing.'

'Tell me everything.'

I could no longer hide it. 'Miss Silver's an informer,' I said. 'She knows about the concert at the University.'

'What else?'

'She informed the City Council Theatre about it. And added something of her own. I don't know what she knows about the rest of our group, but it looks as if she set us up so that all of us are hanged together.'

'I knew something was wrong. It was torturing me.'

'Lena?'

'What?'

'Are you sorry you're with me? Maybe things would have been better with someone else. You could have had an apartment, propiska; it would have been easier for you.'

'I've never looked for the easy way out and I'm not sorry about anything. Let's not talk about it,' she said.

'Why did you decide to be with me?' I asked.

'I liked your nose.'

'What?'

'It was your nose.'

'My nose?'

'You're really too soft with me, too cute, too easygoing, too quiet. I've never liked that type. But once, when I glanced at your nose – crooked and slightly off to one side – I believed in you; I believed you were strong, and I loved you.'

'When was that?'

'The day after the demonstration.'

163

'But that was the day they broke my nose! That's why it was off to one side.'

We laughed.

'So you're not sorry about anything?' I asked.

'I'm sorry about only one thing – that we wasted so much time with all those auditions and forgot about our cat. Have you seen him? He's in bad shape. We've got to call the vet before he dies.'

The kitten was lying in the doorway. He really was ill. His fur was matted; his eyes glazed. When we drew near him, he tried to get up to meet us but couldn't, and lay down once again. He looked with a smouldering gaze at a white feather lying in the corner. I pushed the feather towards him. He touched it with his paw, listlessly. His paw was thin and light, it too was like a feather.

We went downstairs to call the vet. We found the number in the phone book but there was no answer. We phoned another place and it just kept ringing. We phoned a third, and a fourth, but again nobody. Finally we phoned an emergency number. The cleaning lady answered.

'What? . . . The doctor? No doctor here. Nobody's here. That damn epidemic broke out again. First the moose and now the wolves are dying, who knows what's next? Don't you read the paper? They're looking for peltchers. An ambulance? You want an ambulance for a cat? Listen, ring after the holiday. Ring after May the first.'

The kitten died on May the first. We kept the door closed so we wouldn't see him suffering. He squeezed his paw and nose with its black moustache beneath our door and, with his last bit of strength, tried to play with his feather. And so, with his glassy eyes wide open and with his little paw under the door, the kitten without a name died on International Workers Day.

The next day the City Council Theatre called to say they couldn't do a thing for us because we didn't have propiska and construction was still going on in the dormitory.

So the theatrical mask struck once again. It hit painfully, with a sharp sting, even more painfully than the Oriental mask, the one from my childhood. This is when I realized why the theatrical mask has two faces.

4 A Long Summer

With the help of Miss Silver, the artistic destiny of our group was finally set as follows:

The Chookcha and Chechen gave up art and turned to business. They divorced their wives, thereby gaining the chance to sell their Moscow propiska to girls who wished to settle in Moscow. This minority group organized an international company, which was, according to rumour, joined by the recently released prisoner, the Tartar, Aliluyev. The company was in the black-market business of selling jeans and tangerines.

Misha Limshitz had no desire to join that multinational corporation; he was too busy dealing with his own nationality problem. Eventually, he managed to get himself married to the daughter of a Politburo member, but this didn't solve a thing. The Politburo wouldn't forgive their member for giving away his daughter to a Jew; the member ceased being a member, and Misha was left with his untitled wife and inseparable nationality problem.

The biggest sensation of all was quiet Barskov. Tired of the fight for propiska, he finally asked the Ministry of Culture to send him somewhere far away, as far away as possible. He was sent to Sakhalin Island, where he hanged himself immediately upon arrival.

Lena and I decided that if our fate was to die we didn't have to go that far, we could do it right here in our home on Arbat Street. But we weren't giving up until we heard from Dudin.

We weren't studying or working that summer, we had even stopped waiting for a miracle, so I often found myself on Arbat counting the steps. I worked out that the length of Arbat Street is one kilometre exactly and there is nowhere in the world such a heavy concentration of alcoholics in a single kilometre. While doing my research I was also looking for money on the pavement. I wasn't doing it for fun. Lena and I had no money at all, and to find thirty or forty kopecks in one day was a major event. It meant we could buy a roll and a container of milk.

There was no other way for us to get money. Finishing school, thereby making us lose our temporary propiska, eliminated the possibility of obtaining any job, not only in the theatre, but anywhere. Furthermore, it was even illegal to beg without propiska, but there was no law that said you had to have propiska to look for money on the street.

During this desperate time, I began to hate myself for coming to Moscow. I began to hate Moscow itself – that arrogant capital of the communist kingdom where no one was allowed to live unless born with the mark of Moscow on his documents. I began to hate Muscovites, those lucky elite (Soviet aristocrats). From the look in their eyes, you never know whether they will offer you a bottle, or whack you over the head with one.

But I never hated Arbat. I couldn't let go of the tiny scrap of hope that Arbat would not let me down. And so I went on searching the street for the glint of lost kopecks . . .

Looking for money was a passionate affair – something akin to hunting. You had to be alert every second, because you never knew where and when it would appear. At the same time, you had to learn not to strain yourself too much, not to concentrate only on what was under your feet, but to let your eyes take in as large an area as possible. Sometimes, you had to listen for your prey. People often drop coins and, if you hear it in time and are the first to rush in and help pick them up, while giving them back you can hide ten or fifteen kopecks between your fingers. This didn't make me feel one bit like a thief. It was rather like a game of Finder's Keepers. Sometimes the hunt was unsuccessful all day; such is the hunt. But once, as I was walking along Arbat, out of the corner of my eye I spotted some fool who had dropped five whole rubles while waiting in a queue for cabbage. The note didn't have a chance to land when I had already stepped on it. I jabbed a few people in the side, just for effect, and asked what was for sale, then bent over to tie the laces of my boots and grabbed the five imperceptibly, then vanished. Finder's Keepers!

But other times I would see a shiny circle in a forest of legs and, dashing over to it, would push the pedestrians aside only to discover a bottle cap or just spit shining in the sun. These were the sad moments of the hunt in the centre of Moscow, on a street whose length is exactly one kilometre.

While I was making a living by hunting, Lena was out fishing. She was stealing Aunt Sonia's caviar. Fishing required skill; it was more dangerous than hunting because Sonia kept strict control on fishing rights in her refrigerator. In this way, the issue of food was resolved.

Bathing was worse. The summer was hot and dusty. Hunting and fishing were tiring jobs and, as I mentioned, there was no bathtub in the wooden castle. There was nothing else to do but go to the city's bathhouse, and, everybody knows, such pleasures cost money. The baths for men and women were on different floors, which meant that we had to buy two tickets. Such expenses, even if only once a week, were incompatible with our income. For that reason, we worked out our own system. We would go to the bathhouse early in the morning, at opening time. I would buy a ticket for the men's showers. Then Lena would slip into my cabin and we would enjoy a shower for two, for the price of one.

One time, we got caught. The guards dragged us to the manager of the bathhouse, who asked us for our documents right off the bat, but of course, we had forgotten our passports at home on the piano. The manager threatened to call the police. If the police came, we would have been forced to produce our passports, and that would have been a catastrophe. For living in Moscow without propiska, for sneaking into the bathhouse, and for engaging in sex in public places, we could easily be sent to a correctional institution for a couple of years.

'This is it,' I thought, but Lena, who always kept a clear head at such moments, told the manager that we would rush home to pick up our passports, leaving our watches with him as collateral. The manager wasn't exactly convinced, but took the watches anyway. He wasn't stupid, after all. Naturally, we never returned to pick them up.

Living without propiska made each day more dangerous. The longer we lived like that, the worse our crime became. It weighed on us till our lives were filled with constant fear. We were afraid of being caught for some minor offence like getting on the trolleybus without a ticket; or in a spot check of documents. We were afraid of phone calls, creaking noises, a knock on the door, the plumber, the electrician, any unfamiliar person who came to the house. We were afraid to sleep and afraid to wake. We were even afraid to fall ill, because no hospital would admit us and no doctor would treat us without propiska.

All our friends were away, there was no one in Moscow we could ask for help. Things got worse towards the end of summer. Aunt Sonia went to the hospital for a checkup, and Lena's fishing was over. Because of the weather, my hunting wasn't going well either. It rained frequently. I trudged across Arbat, raindrops splattering around me on the wet pavement. They would glisten like silver coins momentarily, then, as if to tease me, disappear. There were fewer people in the street and, with their hands kept in their pockets, they almost never lost any money. With each succeeding day, Arbat seemed longer and longer. The trees along the boulevards were rapidly turning yellow, and our hopes shrivelled and fell. Dudin didn't ring. We were starving. Lena became terribly thin. When you looked at her face, all you saw were her frightened eyes. Life was becoming unbearable, but we would joke that we couldn't kill ourselves because, without propiska, we couldn't even be buried.

In August, we practically didn't eat at all. We were in a state of drowsiness. . . . One morning, Toilik knocked on the door and said that a letter had been lying on the floor downstairs for two days. He slipped it under our door. It was an offer to be in a film. An offer to be in a film? Both of us got an offer to be in a film! Just one day of shooting, but each of us would get seven rubles!

A Moldavian film director by the name of Vasya Vasilevitch was shooting a picture called *Bread*, something about conserving grain and wheat.

The day of the shooting, we were taken to a large bakery with glass walls. Vasya, a pimpled genius, placed a string of bagels around Lena's neck, stuck a long loaf of French bread into my

168

hands, then instructed us to walk out of the shop as if we had just made our purchases.

Lena went first. Through the shop window I could see a plump woman with a microphone pushing the crowd aside and bumping into Lena. Behind the woman came the cameraman and Vasya. The woman stuck the mike into Lena's face and asked her something. Lena turned away, her searching eyes met mine. She began to play with the bagels on the string, but didn't respond. The sound-woman pushed the mike under Lena's nose. Lena followed the mike with her eyes but remained silent as she fiddled with the bagels. Vasya came up to her and shouted something. Lena laughed nervously. She went on soundlessly laughing for some time, and it looked as if she would never stop. Then her face became distorted, she raised her hands, covered her face, and began to cry.

I couldn't watch it through the window any longer.

I charged out of the bakery, but the director, sound-woman, and cameraman blocked my way. The camera aimed its glass eye at me, and the fat sound-woman put on a serious face and asked what I thought of people who feed farm animals bread.

I stood there staring into the camera, in my hand the loaf of white bread which I desperately wanted to bite into. There was Lena, crying from hunger, bagels strung around her neck, and that fat fool was asking my opinion of overfed animals. I was getting crazy. I looked right at her and said, 'One day, at the zoo I saw an elephant in a cage. In front of the cage a sign proclaimed that the elephant could eat 150 loaves of white bread and 340 loaves of whole wheat bread in one day. I asked the zookeeper: "Can this elephant really eat all that?" "Of course he can," replied the zookeeper, "but who will give it to him?"'

The fat lady stood agape. I bit into the crisp loaf and began to eat.

'Stop!' shouted the director, 'stop! Don't let him chew on camera. Take that bread away from him. We need it for tomorrow. That's enough for today; the shooting is over.'

The sound-woman yanked the bread out of my hands, gave me a slip to sign, and said they would send me the money later. The director gave Lena her money on the spot, without even getting

169

her signature. Then the genius brought her over to the film truck to talk. He said that her silent scene with the bagels had moved him so much that he wanted to develop this tragic scene further. He intended to film Lena in a Moldavian village where fascists were to have killed her father during the war for a mere bagel. He said that at that very moment he was searching for a heroine, a starving young girl, and that Lena fitted the part to a T. The shooting was to begin in three days in the village on the border, between Moldavia and the Ukraine. Lena would have to be there from the start. The director would put her on camera immediately and make her the Soviet Audrey Hepburn. He gave her a one-way ticket and in a few days Lena left for the Moldavian capital, Kishinyov.

I was left in the city alone, but my heart was now much lighter. It wasn't for nothing that we had stayed in Moscow. Maybe not for me, but for Lena everything was beginning more or less to work out. Who knew what was going to be after the film.

I couldn't give up. Moscow was still my home. Arbat would not let me down, my glorious, perfect street. A kilometre of sadness, love, and dreams. A monument cast in concrete!

On Arbat, on the last day of that summer, I worked out how to repay my debt to Miss Silver.

EXCHANGE SILVER FOR GOLD!
From 9:00 A.M. to 5:00 P.M. call 746-16-11 (work)
From 5:00 P.M. to 9:00 A.M. call 285-65-14 (home)
Ask for Miss Silver.

I wrote out thirty or forty announcements like this and went on a real hunt. I glued them to the telephone poles along Arbat. The advertisements would draw crowds and, seconds later, the people would disperse to the nearest telephone booths.

At the end of the day, when I had finally finished my job and I was at home, Toilik shouted that I had a phone call. I went down the stairs, said 'Hello' to the line of *Pravda* readers waiting for the toilet, and picked up the receiver.

'Hello,' I said. Nobody answered but I got the feeling it was Lena. 'Lena?' I asked. 'Lena, is that you?' It sounded as if she was laughing. 'Are you laughing?'

'I'm not laughing,' Lena replied quietly. 'Can you meet me at our Metro stop?'

Before I could answer, she had already hung up.

Lena didn't say where I should meet her – upstairs at the gate, or downstairs on the platform, and, if it was downstairs, near which car? I decided to go down to the platform but, not knowing which side she would be coming from, I stopped in the middle of the station. Every other minute, trains rolled past from the left and from the right. The doors clanged open, and crowds of people poured out onto the platform. There they divided into two streams, which flowed to opposite ends of the station. I was spinning like a top on the polished stone but to find someone in a subway crowd is no easy thing. Train after train, crowd after crowd . . . Had I missed her? No, there she was, walking slowly near the end of the platform, her head down, her hands in the pockets of a long raincoat which nearly reached the floor.

I rushed after her. The crowd blocked my way. Lena approached the escalator, where something strange took place. She grabbed the handrail of the down escalator, stepped on, and tried to make her way up. I let out a cry. She went up a few steps against the flow of traffic, swayed as if she were drunk, then stopped. The escalator carried her back down and threw her into the crowd. As if she hadn't noticed a thing, again she stepped onto the moving stairs and was again thrown back. People began to laugh, but Lena, as if in a daze, went against the flow once more and, amid increasing jeers, was thrown right into my arms.

'Lena!' I screamed.

She stared at me as if she didn't know me, like the dead stare of our cat.

'Lena! What's the matter with you?' I said, pushing aside the crowd and leading her down the platform. I found an empty bench near the wall. We sat down. I could see that she was starting to come around.

'So, how was your trip,' I said, pretending not to notice anything.

'Trip?' Lena repeated, devoid of any expression.

'Did something happen? Was it something to do with the shooting?'

'There was no shooting.'

'What?'

'Sasha, don't ask.'

Her lips and hands were shaking. Tears welled in her eyes even though she was making every effort to keep herself from crying. I took her hand to make her relax but found that I was beginning to shake.

A train thundered into the station, expelled its passengers, shut the doors, and pulled out.

'All right, all right,' I whispered. 'There's no need to say anything right now. Maybe later.'

'No, I don't want to talk about it later. It's better if I tell you now. Then we can both forget about it and that will be that.' She grew silent.

I waited. She stopped crying and smiled bitterly.

'I don't want you to feel sorry for me. I hate it when people feel sorry for me, because then they always start to attack me.'

'Lena, what are you talking about? Everybody loves you – '

'What everybody?' Lena cut me off. 'Oh, it doesn't matter. I wish everyone would just leave me alone, I mean, except you and my grandfather.'

'What is this all about?'

'Let's get out of here. Those people are making fun of me – my short hair, this long raincoat . . .'

We walked toward the escalator. We stood in silence as we rode up. I kept one arm around her slight shoulders as we walked outside.

It was foggy and starting to drizzle. The street lamps were teasing me with their reflections, like golden coins in the black puddles. I still didn't know what had happened to Lena, but I already knew there couldn't have been a worse end for this long summer.

5 There Has to Be an Exit

Lena never talked much about herself, but this time she really opened up. She talked all the way home and all through that rainy night.

She said that it all started a long time ago, when her mother left her with her father. She grew up with a cold, miserable stepmother and her fat, ugly daughter. Lena was a skinny, sickly, lost child and all her childhood she felt it was a mistake that she had been born. She was lonely. She felt abandoned.

The same feeling came to her when she got to Kishinyov. She strolled around the airport to see who was there to pick her up, but found nobody. The other passengers went their separate ways. She stood there alone thinking they must have been late. She waited forty-five minutes, but nobody appeared. One hour passed, still nobody. She found the number Vasya had given her. She dialled the number. Nobody answered. She asked some people where the film studio was in Kishinyov; they had never heard about it. She inquired at the information desk at the airport. They checked in some books, made some calls, and, finally, when she had lost all hope, found the address and even told her which bus to take to get there. When she reached the studio, she realized why nobody knew about it. The entire studio consisted of nothing more than a low barnlike structure surrounded by a dirty, slatted wooden fence.

At the gate a guard was sitting in a guardhouse. Who knows what he was guarding. She began to explain her situation, but he interrupted her: 'I don't know anything, and there's nobody around to ask. You should have come earlier; the work day is over.'

'Is it my fault that nobody met me at the airport? Can't you ring the director of the studio at home?' Lena asked.

He just looked at her with open disdain, then said: 'The director is on holiday. He'll be back in two weeks. Anyway, that's not my job.'

At that point she became furious. She realized it wasn't his fault, but her head was reeling and she couldn't control herself. 'It's not your job?' she shouted at him. 'Where am I supposed to sleep; nobody gave me any money for a hotel. If you don't do something, I'm going to spend the night in this guardhouse.'

He got scared, made a call, then said: 'The film company is on location, but you're in luck, the truck with the costumes is still here and will be leaving any minute. Wait here. They'll be coming along shortly, and maybe they'll take you with them, you crazy woman!'

The truck appeared in fifteen minutes. The driver stuck his head out the window, waved at Lena, his arm tattooed with an anchor, and shouted, 'You that actress from Moscow? All aboard! The ship's about to sail!'

Lena climbed into the truck. That lady, the fat one, was there too. There was nobody else in the truck but there was nowhere to sit. There were boxes everywhere and, on top of the boxes and all over the floor, there were dirty suits and coats. When the woman saw her she started rattling away, 'Oh, Lena. Hello. You don't know how glad I am to see you. I'm Iraida, remember me? The sound technician. We've been waiting for you. Vasya will be so glad to see you. Come, sit beside me. Don't worry, you won't get dirty. Tell me, how's the weather in Moscow? The rain never lets up here. By the way, I'm not just the sound technician, I'm the bookkeeper and treasurer, too. If you need any money, I can give it to you this minute. Did you bring your passport with you?'

Lena didn't want to give her her passport, so she said she didn't need any money then.

They drove for about four hours to this village. It was almost halfway between Kishinyov and Lena's hometown. It wasn't too bad on the highway, except for the big bumps, but when they turned onto the country road it was hell. Actually, there was no road at all. What had once been a road had blended in with the

174

mud in the fields. The truck got stuck about ten times. The driver shouted: 'My boat doesn't like to carry women. Get out.'

Iraida and Lena got out. Iraida pushed the truck from behind. Lena put boards and cornhusks under the wheels. Clumps of dirt flew up in her face. The seaman yelled curses at them, the truck roared and rocked and, in that fashion, inched its way through the soaking fields of beets and corn. It became clear why the driver on this road had to be a seaman. Iraida gave Lena a pair of huge rubber boots, but they weren't much help because she wasn't up to her knees in dirt and mud, she was up to her waist in it. She was soaked to the skin and freezing.

'It's okay,' said Iraida, 'soon we'll be coming to the hotel and you'll be able to get warmed up there.'

It was pitch black when they finally arrived. The hotel turned out to be a village school, given to the film studio for the summer. Military cots had been set up in the classrooms. When Iraida walked Lena to her classroom, the first thing she saw was a four-letter word on the blackboard. She picked up the cloth and erased it. Iraida laughed and said. 'Don't bother, they'll only write it again.'

When Lena wanted to change into something clean, Iraida chuckled and said, 'You don't need to change; we're only going to the dining room.'

When they arrived at the dining room, Lena found out why Iraida had said not to change; it was the school gym, under construction. The paint was peeling from the walls and ceiling. The floor was strewn with pieces of fallen plaster and boards. Everything was covered with dust and, in one corner, near a jungle gym, there were three pots among pails of paint. On one pot was written in chalk – 'flotilla borscht'; on another – 'macaroni à la carte'; and on the third – 'compote'. Trays, aluminum bowls, and spoons were scattered about. Iraida poured borscht into one bowl and the dried-fruit compote into another. In the third, she dumped the macaroni with black specks of meat, and said 'Dig in!'

Iraida didn't eat. She simply sat there staring at Lena, who ate everything and even drank the compote.

175

'Bravo!' said Iraida in amazement. 'I never eat this stuff. If I tell Vasya, he won't believe it.'

'Where is Vasya? When can I see him?' asked Lena.

'He's out shooting. When he's through, he'll come back here.'

'What's shooting? It's dark outside.'

'Oh, Lena, Lenochka, you don't know our Vasya. He works at night, exclusively. You'll see for yourself,' and again she laughed.

Soon the film crew filtered into the gym. They were unbelievably dirty, as if they had been working in a coal mine. When they spotted Iraida and Lena, they came up to their table, sat down without asking, cracked some stupid jokes, and showered Lena with compliments. They had a ball introducing each other to her and shaking her hand. Their hands were wet and dirty.

Then Vasya appeared, wearing a raincoat with a hood, and rubber boots rolled down. She was relieved; things would finally start moving along. She could tell that Vasya was aware of her. He came in, his eyes searching for her, but it was strange – as soon as he saw her, he looked away, turning his back to her, and went to get some food. He took a seat at the farthest table in the gym. He sat bent over his plate, eating some stew Lena hadn't been shown, while speaking with his assistants and fingering his pimples. When he finished his meal, he jumped up and went to the door. Lena couldn't believe her eyes. She was on the verge of running after him, but she didn't want the others to see.

She waited for a while, got up, and went to her room. In the corridor, she bumped into some of the crew – her 'new friends'. She asked whether they had seen the director.

'Sure,' they said, 'he just went to pick up some wine. Why don't you come with us, we've already got wine.'

'Thanks, but I'd rather not,' she said. 'I'm too tired.'

She went upstairs to her room, put the hook on the door, and turned on the light. Iraida was right – somebody had already rewritten what she had erased.

She felt dirty. There was a cold-water sink in the room. She got undressed, ran a towel under the tap, and sponged herself off. She was chilled to the bone. She turned off the light and hopped into bed. The bed was wet, the sheet coarse, the blanket itchy. She lay there in the darkness.

Suddenly she heard a man's voice.

'Lena, Lenochka, it's me.'

She jumped up. She wanted to turn on the light, but couldn't find the switch. She wanted to get dressed, but the only things she could find in the dark were wet, dirty clothes.

'Lena, open up, it's me,' came a whisper through the door.

She stumbled on her bag and took out the first thing her hand touched. It was her old wool dress, the green net. She pulled it on, slipped her feet into the rubber boots, and went to the door. She was afraid to take the hook off the door. The whispering continued, 'Lena, it's me, open up.'

She just stood there. She couldn't get herself to open the door or to answer. It was very strange – why the whispering? It sounded like Vasya, but why did he have to whisper?

'Who is it?' she asked.

There was no answer. She moved away from the door and sat down on the bed. What was going on? What kind of film crew was this? What were they up to? She felt that it could be dangerous to stay in that room. There was only one rusty hook on the door. She decided to wait till the person left, then go to the vestibule and stay there until morning. In the morning, she would beg them to send her back to Moscow.

She didn't hear anything. She tiptoed over to the door and listened – there was silence. Whoever was there had probably gone away. She carefully unhooked the hook, opened the door a crack to make sure that nobody was there – but somebody was standing right beside the door! She slammed the door shut, tried to jam the hook back on, but it wouldn't go into the loop. Somebody punched in the door. She gasped and jumped back in the room. It was Vasya. He stormed in, hugged her with his big, bony hands, dragged her all around the room, then threw her on the bed.

'Why wouldn't you open up? Why were you hiding from me?' he said straight into her face, the smell of wine on his breath.

'I wasn't hiding from anybody!' Lena screamed.

'Don't scream. Don't scream. Don't be afraid,' he whispered.

'I'm not afraid of anybody. Just let go of me,' she said, trying to defend herself from his hands.

'Yes, I know you're not afraid of anybody. I saw you in the dining room with the crew. You couldn't even wait for me, Lenochka. You couldn't wait long enough for me,' he said, his fingers plunging through the holes of her dress and crawling across her body like cold snakes.

'Let me go. What are you talking about?' she said, feeling nauseated from his smell.

'I will fire all of them . . . all . . . believe me.'

He attempted to kiss her on the mouth.

'Let go of me. I've got to talk to you.' She struggled.

'Talk? What do you have to talk about?'

He pressed against her harder and harder. She pushed his pimpled face away. He pinned her hands down on the bed.

'I'm going to scream,' she said emphatically.

He lay there on top of her for a while, breathing heavily, then rolled over on his side, and sat up, his back leaning against the iron frame of the bed.

When he got off her, she jumped up and stood up against the blackboard.

'All right, let's talk,' he said, taking a cigarette from his pocket.

For a long time he couldn't light the cigarette, then he finally got it. The cigarette glowed and lit up his angry face.

'What are we going to talk about? That nobody was there to meet you? Is that what you're so annoyed about? What am I supposed to do? It's impossible to rely on anyone. I've got to do everything myself, but I'll show them. Come over here, my little birdie, come here.'

He held his hand out to her, waiting for her to go to him on her own.

'Don't be so afraid. We're not going to be able to work together like this. How can I make you into Audrey Hepburn if I don't get to know you better?' he said, grinning.

'Is this what you invited me here for?' she asked.

'What's the problem. Is there anything wrong with this? What are you pretending for? We'll see how you're going to survive in this dump with those idiots around. You'll go mad. You'll be running to my bed in no time.'

178

He was starting to get angry again. He got up and walked over to her.

'You're probably the type that needs to be raped,' he said, and grabbed her with his iron grip. Again she was suffocating from his drunken breath.

'I heard you went for wine,' she said, hoping to divert his attention.

'Oh, would you like some wine?' he said, growing happier. 'Come with me. It's in my room.'

'Why not bring it here? That'll give me time . . . to fix myself up.'

'Nonsense. You don't need . . . Okay. All right,' he said abruptly, as if he had just realized something. Then he whispered in her ear. 'But don't close the door. I don't want to have to break down the door next time.'

Waiting until his footsteps were out of earshot, she quietly crept through the corridor and ran downstairs. She ran right into Iraida, who was in the vestibule unpacking some boxes.

'Iraida,' Lena cried.

'What's with you?' Iraida asked suspiciously.

'Help me, quickly!' Lena whispered.

'Ah, I see, the nighttime shooting has begun,' Iraida said, and smiled.

'Fast, help me. Hide me,' Lena said nervously.

'All right, come on, don't cry. Let's go to my room.'

Iraida led her down one flight to the basement. That's where her room was – the chemistry lab in the cellar. In the middle of the laboratory, there was a huge lab table, with test tubes standing on it. Iraida brought Lena behind the table. Between the blackboard and the table was a fold-up cot.

'You can sleep here,' she said.

'What about you?'

'I've got to get some work done. Don't be afraid; I'll send somebody to stay with you. What a beautiful dress you're wearing,' she said, reaching out toward Lena, hooking her fingers on the net, pulling it out, and giggling. 'Beautiful!' she repeated, and left the room.

Lena didn't lie down. She walked over to the lab table and

looked at the chemical solutions. The flasks of multicoloured liquids stood on metal stands. Soon she heard footsteps on the stairs. She froze. Without knocking, the seaman-driver entered the room, a bottle of wine in his hand.

'Hi,' he said. 'Iraida sent me to keep you company.'

He stumbled over to the lab table, placed the bottle on it, and began to search the vials for something. The vials clanged, the liquid rolled, sending red and blue reflections across the walls.

'Do you know, by any chance, if there are any glasses around here?' he asked. 'I can't drink from test tubes. Oh, here they are. I found them,' he said cheerily, as he pulled two glasses out of the lab table.

'Not for me,' Lena said, 'I don't want to drink.'

'It's not for you,' he said.

His words froze her blood. Just then, Vasya walked into the classroom, closing the door behind him. She stood on one side of the lab table, they on the other. It was as if they were at a bar. She was like the barmaid; they were the customers. They drank and stared at her; she felt totally naked in the net dress. Nobody uttered a word. When there was about one glass of wine left in the bottle, Vasya intercepted the hand of the seaman pouring the wine and said, 'That's enough. Leave the rest for Iraida.'

They downed their last shot, looked at each other, and drew near her. Vasya took one side of the table, the seaman the other. There was no use screaming; in the basement, with the door closed, nobody would hear a thing.

They came up to her simultaneously. The driver squeezed her arms and pressed her against the table. Vasya grabbed her legs. They placed her, boots and all, on the lab table as if it were an operating table. Somehow, she didn't care what happened to her at that point. The driver, seeing that she wasn't resisting, pulled her dress over her head.

'Oh, the birdie's been caught in the net!' said Vasya with a chuckle. 'Look at the lovely scar she has here.'

His words penetrated Lena like an electric shock. Where she got the strength from she didn't know, but she suddenly slipped her foot out of the rubber boot and gave the vials in the stand a good kick. The liquid from one flask hit Vasya right in the face.

The blue, slimy, smelly solution slid down his face. Vasya screamed violently, then charged around the classroom as if he had been blinded. The driver let go of Lena, ran over to Vasya, and pulled him up to the sink. She hopped off the table, flew out of the lab, and ran upstairs, the one huge rubber boot on her foot like a manacle on a prisoner's leg. She ran down the corridor. An animalistic cry rose from the basement. The doors along the corridor opened and half-naked men peeked out.

Only when she was up to her knees in mud did she understand that nobody had stopped her. She was running in the dark. With each step, the rubber boot got stuck in the mud, slowing her down. Finally, she pulled her foot out of the boot and ran barefoot. She didn't know what made her turn off the road and hide among the cornhusks, but thank God she did. When she looked back, she saw the crew running out of the 'hotel'. Somebody had climbed into the van with the projector and turned on the light. Bright rays pierced the rainy night, lighting up the road. If she hadn't hidden in the cornfield they would surely have spotted her and caught her. They drove back and forth on the road, lighting up the field. She was lying face-down in the mud, afraid to move.

When the projector was switched off, Lena made her way through the field to the highway. There she was picked up by a truck from a collective farm. Luckily, the truck was headed for her home town. The driver, a young Moldavian, was so embarrassed to look at her he gave her his raincoat to cover herself.

In this coat, barefoot and filthy, she showed up at her parents' house, early in the morning. She knocked at the door for a long time before they finally heard her. When they saw her at the door, they started running around like chickens with their heads cut off. Nobody expected her, but there she was, and what a scary sight. Her head was spinning, and she had the chills. They put her to bed, covered her up with every blanket in the house; the chills didn't subside. She was choked up with anger at the whole world and felt like a hurt animal. She wanted to sleep but nobody would leave her alone. They sent for her grandfather. Before he arrived, they began their investigation of what had happened. She didn't want to tell them anything, but they

181

squeezed it out of her anyway. It was turning into something like a Party meeting. . . .

'How could you have run like that all alone at night? You could have been killed on the road,' shouted her father, the great logical thinker.

'What was I supposed to do, stay there and get raped?'

'You should have been more firm with that film director. If you had said no more emphatically, he would have left the room. Then he wouldn't have tried to compromise you.' These were the words of her stepmother.

'For God's sake,' she screamed. 'How was I supposed to say no if he didn't ask me?'

'I don't believe something like this could happen at one of our Soviet film studios,' said her 'little' sister. 'After all, you went there to work, didn't you?'

'There's something fishy about all this,' said her father. 'I just can't imagine this happening.'

'You don't have to imagine. Just believe me, for God's sake,' Lena pleaded.

'What are you always saying "God" for; you know we don't believe in God. There must be something else. How come you didn't call the police? How come you didn't report him? It would be better if you told us the whole truth.'

'What truth? How they pulled me onto the lab table and . . . How could I have gone to the police? They would have arrested me for not having propiska. I hate you, all of you!' Lena screamed.

'You have no right to speak to us like that. We're your parents. We devoted our lives to you. We fought the war so you could go to school and work!' shouted her father.

'You don't like anybody. You criticize everybody, you despise everybody. You want to be different from everybody. You've always had your own opinion about everything!' screamed her stepmother.

Lena wanted to respond but suddenly she was unable to utter a single word. She opened her mouth, but nothing came out.

'Tell us the truth. Tell us the truth.'

'Leave her alone,' Lena heard her grandfather's voice saying. 'Can't you see she's ill.'

But they kept pressuring her more and more.

'We're not going to leave her alone until she tells us everything. What propiska were you talking about? How come you could be arrested? Why don't you answer? Tell us the truth. Answer!'

How could she answer when she couldn't even speak? She felt like she was strangling. The room was spinning. But they kept it up: 'The truth! The truth!'

She wanted to run away. She bounded off the bed onto the floor, but the room was circling, and she fell down. Her father called an ambulance. But when she was being taken to the hospital, she went berserk and nearly wrecked the ambulance. It was like an explosion; she started screaming that she wanted to run away, that our motherland was like a stepmother, that in 1917, all the princes' throats were cut and only informers were left, and, in general, she cursed the whole Soviet Regime. So, after all her ranting, the ambulance took her, not to the hospital, but to a psychiatric clinic.

There, she got the 'wrap-up' treatment; they wrapped her first in wet canvas, then in warm blankets. When the canvas dried, it contracted, and the pain was blinding. This went on for about two days. Then the doctors came with their pills and injections. But Lena wouldn't let them get near her.

'I know your tricks,' she exclaimed. 'You can make healthy people crazy!'

With that, they put away their needles and began to pose questions on diverse subjects. She thought they intended to release her, that they had realized that she was normal, but this wasn't the case.

At the end of the week she had a piece of luck. She was going to the toilet, which was in the corridor. There was only one for all the patients on the floor. It was always kept locked, and so, when they wanted to go, they had to be accompanied by a nurse. That day, the nurse had given the key to the cleaning lady, and she took Lena. The cleaning lady opened the toilet but, instead of waiting outside as usual, she came in with Lena. She swiftly locked the door behind her, put her finger to her lips, and said: 'Shhhh.' Lena was frightened stiff. Anything could happen in a psychiatric clinic.

'Don't worry. I'm not crazy,' the cleaning lady whispered.

'I know,' Lena said, 'I know,' but thought to herself that she was mad for sure.

'I've got something to tell you,' the cleaning lady continued.

'What?' said Lena.

'I was cleaning the doctor's office and I came across your medical history. It stated: "Angry dislike of environment. Unable to accept reality. Preliminary diagnosis – schizophrenia. Transfer to Dnepropetrovsk Special Psychiatric Hospital."'

'Schizophrenia?!' Lena was stunned. 'But I'm not crazy.'

'You don't accept reality. To them, that's schizophrenia. While you're still here, you'd do well to run away. Later, when you're transferred to Dnepropetrovsk, there'll be no chance to get out. I know, my husband is there. They've been giving him sulfazin injections and now he can hardly walk.'

'How can they send a healthy person there?' Lena said, terrified.

'You're not healthy if you aren't happy with your environment. Anybody who doesn't like the Soviet Regime is sick. I know this because my husband went through the same thing. We're artists . . . or at least used to be. We organized an illegal exhibit, and I wound up here; he was sent there with the violent ones. You must run away before it's too late. But don't go where you have permission to live.'

'I don't have propiska for anywhere.'

'You're lucky,' she said, 'in your case, with only a preliminary diagnosis and no propiska, they might not even look for you, and if they did, it would be hard to track you down without propiska. Do you have anybody you can trust? Write him a note, and I'll get it to him. Have him come at night. I'll let you out; I've got all the keys. It's unbelievable, how lucky you are not to have propiska!'

'Yes,' Lena said. 'I suppose I'm lucky not to have propiska, after all.'

'Here's a pen and paper,' said the cleaning lady. 'Write the note immediately. Who knows, maybe they'll send you away tomorrow.'

Lena had a thought that maybe this was a trap, but she had to trust someone and didn't have much choice in a psychiatric clinic.

She wrote a note to her grandfather and he helped her run away that very night. The cleaning lady let her out as she had promised.

'. . . Now I'm cursing myself for not even getting her name. I'm always doing things like that,' Lena said bitterly. 'And that's the whole story. I've bothered you enough.'

We looked out of the window at the backyard. The rain had let up and the fog rose above the ground.

'It's getting cold, and we have the whole winter ahead of us. I'm afraid of the winter,' Lena said; her voice cracked and she looked away. 'The summer isn't even over, and I'm already dying for the spring to come. I think I really am crazy. You know, I did a lot of thinking these days, maybe even too much thinking. Everything that happened to me was no accident – the film studio and the psychiatric hospital. I asked myself what would have happened if I had been in that film. Would I have been happy? I know for certain the answer is no. And what if I were to be in any other film? No, again. I don't want to struggle all my life to play the lead role in a film about fascists, communists or alcoholics. I don't want to be party to "the greatest tool of totalitarian propaganda," as Stalin called it. I realized that I hate Soviet films, Soviet theatres, all Soviet art . . . Forget about creating what we really want. You saw what they did to us for singing a song about Mandelstam – we can't even get a job! I'm worn out, tired, cold, frightened. Tired of shuddering at the sight of a policeman, tired of making up reasons for not presenting my passport, tired of worrying about opening the door. What is there to live for – they've already maimed my body, crippled my mind, and ruined my career. Now I'm going to say something terrible; I hate my native land. I know it's horrible and wrong, but it's a fact. And once I came to know this, I realized something else – when I was in the ambulance I was screaming about running away because I really wanted to run away, yes, I want to run away!'

'Where?' I asked uneasily.

'Abroad,' Lena shouted. 'I want to go away from the Soviet Union. Of course, you'll say that everything will pass, that life will get better, but I want to go, not because I want a better life,

185

but because I simply can't live in this country any more. I feel as if I'm dying every minute I'm here. I don't want you to see how I'm dying and I don't want to see you become an alcoholic, if you're not one already. We're different from others – in our looks, in our manners, in our music. It's precisely what the Party has been fighting against since the Revolution. I'm certain they will kill us. They will kill us if we don't run away. They are killing all the young people who are trying to be free; this is a country of senior citizens. We've got to save ourselves. I ask you, I beg you, to promise me that we will go away from here.'

'I promise,' I said.

'You mean you agree? You don't know how afraid I was that you wouldn't agree with me. But you're talking as if you had already made up your own mind.'

'Do you think I really spent the whole summer checking the length of Arbat?' I said. 'All those months I was tormented by one thought – could it be that we, the third generation after the Revolution, can't beat this system? I think we can. But I don't want to run away like a loser. I want to walk away like a winner. Don't worry, we'll leave here before we're thirty.'

'How?' Lena asked.

'There *has* to be an exit.'

6 A Street Cleaner

It's always like this – when you're expecting something, counting the days, wearing yourself out trying to predict when it will come, you never get what you're waiting for; but the moment you stop waiting and get involved with something else, and stop expecting it, that's the very minute it will come to you.

Fate doesn't like the grey routine of everyday life. It likes to surprise, to play, to teach us not to be tenacious in our decisions and long-drawn-out plans. It calls on us to live for the moment. Fate teaches us not to lose faith because of delays and changes, but to have more faith. Everything comes at the right time, not when we decide we need it, but when it is really needed. 'Don't play with fate; you'll wind up in jail,' Toilik used to warn his friends when they decided to break down the door of the liquor shop ten minutes before opening time.

The call from the Children's Theatre came in this way. I had been waiting for that call all summer; it never came. But when I stopped waiting and began to think about more important things, Dudin rang early one morning and asked me to come to see him.

Nearly half a year had passed since my initial contact with him, but it was as if I had never left the room – Dudin was sitting behind his desk, drinking tea and eating a napoleon. He wore the same expensive, dark blue blazer, sprinkled with powdered sugar. Everything was the same in his office; only I wasn't the same.

'How's everything?' Dudin asked between sips of tea.

'Fine,' I said, smiling weakly.

'Have you heard from the City Council Theatre?' he gently asked.

I nodded. I'm sure the desperate look on my face told him everything.

'I hope you haven't changed your mind about being employed here,' he said.

I kept still, holding my breath . . . hoping . . .

'So,' said Dudin, 'everything is quite simple; it just takes a little time. I felt, even back then, that the resolution of your problem was imminent; all the ingredients were available, but the issue was how to put them together. The key point, which would integrate all of them, was missing. What do you think it was?'

'I don't know,' I said.

'What is the most important thing in Soviet life?'

Hopelessness, I mused, but naturally didn't say a word.

'The most important thing is holidays,' Dudin said. 'Holidays give us the impetus to live and to work. As soon as we finish celebrating May the first, we have to stock up on vodka for November the seventh, and when we finish celebrating November the seventh, we've got to run to get in the queue for champagne for December the fifth. Haven't you noticed that everything in this country is related to the holidays?'

'Yes, I have,' I said.

'Good,' Dudin said and went on. 'All you need to do is pick a holiday and dedicate a project to it.'

'Which holiday could possibly fit propiska?' I asked.

'That's it. That's precisely it; that's where you've been lucky. Your holiday is unusual. It comes only once every hundred years – it's the centennial anniversary of the birth of Lenin. Yes, the jubilee of Vladimir Ilyich is the holiday suited to your propiska problem.'

'I don't follow you.'

'Our theatre is currently working on a play called *The Brothers*, a performance about Lenin and his brother, Alexander.'

'But what does that have to do with me? Do you want me to play Lenin?'

'No,' said Dudin without smiling. 'We found the perfect Lenin. You will play the brother.'

'But how can you take me without propiska?'

'That's no problem. As you know, we can't take an actor without propiska but we can employ a street cleaner without propiska. Understand?'

'Not quite.'

'It's no problem,' Dudin repeated. 'I am going to hire you as a street cleaner for now, then I will give you an appointment as a stagehand. Once you are on stage, I can have you not only move props around, but read lines too, and in that way you will become an actor who will act the role of Lenin's brother. Then I will ask the City Council to give a room to Lenin's older brother. How can they say no? Once you have a room you will automatically get propiska! Simple, isn't it?'

'Yes, it is!'

'Okay, that's enough talk, let's get to work,' Dudin said, finishing his napoleon and brushing off his sleeves. 'Get a broom and go and sweep the front stairs. I want to see how Lenin's brother sweeps; it should be nice. Hold it. I forgot to ask you about your friend, Miss Silver. I heard she was arrested for selling gold or something, is it true?'

'It's true,' I said.

'Do you know how that happened, by any chance?'

'No, I don't,' I said. 'Where can I find a broom?'

'I don't know either,' Dudin said, smiling, 'that's your job.'

'The theatre starts with the cloakroom,' the great Stanislavsky once said to the great Vakhtangov when his coat was stolen. For me, the theatre started with the stairs, to be more precise, with the stairs outside the theatre. It was here that my career in the theatre was launched early that autumn morning.

I started out as a street cleaner, at a salary of 120 rubles a month, was made a stagehand, at 90 rubles a month, and finally became an actor, playing Lenin's brother, whose salary was 75 rubles a month. So, in this way, I climbed the ladder of success, and, with the same alacrity, I slid down the salary scale, finding myself in the lowest-paying job in the theatre – a 'Young Actor'.

A Soviet actor's salary is in no way related to his talent, the role he is playing, or how well he knows the Stanislavsky Method. In the theatre, there isn't even any talk about the Stanislavsky Method or the Vakhtangov Method. In the contemporary Russian theatre, there is one and only one Method – the bottle method.

189

The classification of actors and their salary is determined exclusively by this method.

The standard for a 'Young Actor' is generally agreed to be one bottle a day. That should be enough for him, and with the tax for being childless, it comes to twenty-five bottles a month or 75 rubles. The next category is the 'Renowned Actor'. These actors, after years of working in the theatre, should have learned to drink more. Their standard is two bottles a day. After taxes, this comes to fifty-eight bottles a month or 150 rubles. The last and practically unattainable category is the 'People's Actor'. His standard is almost beyond belief – three bottles a day! With holiday bonuses, it comes to ninety-six bottles a month or 400 rubles.

Changing from one category to another had to come slowly – no less than ten years. It was necessary to prove over and over that you had high standards. For example, if somebody drank two and a half bottles during a performance once, don't get the idea that he's a Renowned Actor. Maybe it was just beginner's luck. Maybe he just forced himself in order to get a rise. The Young Actor is carefully watched over the years – how he acts on stage, how he behaves after one glass, after two, three, et cetera; whether he can kill the smell with coffee beans; if he tears the curtain when he falls down; whether he confuses the door and the fireplace.

It's not art to guzzle down a bottle of vodka and chase devilkins on centre stage or, even worse, to throw up green slime in the orchestra pit. You call that art? In Tula, maybe people will go wild over tickets for such entertainment, but in Moscow, it has been a long time since you could surprise anyone with slime on a violin.

Art in the capital is different. There, an actor tries to intrigue his audience by making them wonder if he's a genius or just drunk to the gills. How pleasant it is to see a People's Actor weaving on stage! He would never let out a hiccup or burp like a Renowned Actor. He would trudge across the stage, forgetting all his lines, but would not bump into anything. The astounded audience, holding its breath, would follow his every movement, waiting for the moment he would lie down and snore, but he would balance on the edge of the stage as if on a tightrope, and would never fall down. Then how appreciatively the audience would applaud him for such mastery, and the People's Actor would ever-so-slightly lower his head in a well-deserved bow. This is professionalism honed to perfection.

This was exactly the kind of art needed at the Children's Theatre when the audience was composed of tender, impressionable youngsters who came to the theatre to forget the amateur performances of their violent fathers, or the foul domestic art of their drunken mothers. They came here and paid for their tickets not to see a fat man burping on the stage. They can see such art in their own homes, free.

In the Central Children's Theatre I came to realize that Toilik's lessons were much more practical than the great Stanislavsky's. Between drinking bouts, the cast rehearsed the play about the Ulyanov brothers. There was nothing in this play about what Lenin and his older brother, Alexander, were going to do about the Russian national problem – alcoholism. The entire focus was on their intense desire to kill people. The play was based on the differing views of the two brothers regarding this matter. Each one had his own revolutionary theory.

Alexander was a confirmed terrorist. His idea was to play on Russian idealism and blood-thirstiness. He was convinced that murder should start at the top and work down to the bottom – first the Czar should be killed, then his ministers, then the civil servants, and, only then, those who were left.

Vladimir (later known as Lenin), though he was younger by a few years, realized, even back in elementary school, that large numbers of people cannot be eliminated by singular acts of terrorism. And so Lenin took a different approach. He wished to play on another Russian trait – jealousy. With this as a basis, he would have the rich and the poor kill each other.

The whole performance was about how the brothers checked their theories through practice. In the first act, Alexander was on stage all the time, but Lenin was thinking backstage. Alexander didn't do much thinking. He did more acting – he made a bomb in the shape of a book and planned to throw the book into the Czar's carriage. The Czar didn't like to read while moving, so

Alexander was seized by the gendarmes and put on trial. Pleased by the prospect of being heard, Alexander delivered a brilliant speech. The speech was a success and so the young revolutionary was not in the least saddened by the court's decision to hang him. There was only one thing which worried him before his death – that the rope to be used for the hanging might break, thereby spoiling his heroic end. He didn't want to have to repeat the words of another revolutionary Decembrist who had to be hanged three times because of the weak rope – 'Oh Russia, what a country where a man can't even be hanged right!' The worries of Alexander were in vain, and he was very successfully hanged the first time. Act One ended with this scene.

The whole second act was devoted to proving that the younger brother's theory was the right one. After Alexander's sad experience, Lenin concluded that it was too risky to be personally involved in such villainy, and that it was much better to use other people. He organized the Party, collected money, and went abroad. From quiet Switzerland, he began to send letters, articles, and books in which he promised to give the poor everything the rich had. These books turned out to be much more effective than the book-bomb of his naive brother. Lenin provided the spark, and folk jealousy flared up into the fire of the Revolution. The poor began to kill the rich indiscriminately. Before the masses had a chance to discover that they had been fooled, Lenin passed through all the countries of Europe in a sealed train and returned to Russia to take power. The performance drew to a close with Lenin's coming from Finland to Petrograd. Huge crowds filled the railway station. Lenin emerged from the train, leaped onto an armoured car, and gave a fiery speech. The crowd caught their leader up in their arms and carried him backstage. Rachmaninoff's 'Bells' rang out, and the performance came to an end.

Something wasn't working in this scene during rehearsal, and Dudin couldn't work out what was wrong. During the whole scene Lenin remained backstage, and when he made his entrance at the end of the play, he was supposed to be met by elation. But somehow, everything turned out to be the exact opposite – no matter how much effort the director put into it, it just didn't work. The more rehearsals there were, the sadder the crowd at the railway station became. The actors carried the leader across the stage with less and less enthusiasm.

At first, Dudin thought it was because there weren't enough people on stage, and Lenin was pretty heavy. The director ordered all the actors in the theatre, even those not involved in that performance, to pitch in for the final scene, but this didn't change a thing. Then Dudin ordered all the stagehands, electricians, and even the cleaning ladies, to show up at the railway station to carry Lenin. But it didn't help. The finale was even more solemn. There wasn't the slightest thrill of the Revolution present in this scene.

The day of the premiere was approaching rapidly but, if there were any changes, they weren't for the better. When all else had failed, Dudin called a meeting of all the actors and workers to ask what the problem was. Here something incredible came out.

The embarrassed actors eventually revealed that they were unable to act because, during each rehearsal, the money they left in the dressing room was disappearing. Of course it wasn't a lot of money; they didn't have all that much, one or two rubles, but each time they went on stage they weren't sure if they would have enough money to buy a bottle after the rehearsal. It made them nervous and prevented them from concentrating on the joyous arrival of Lenin.

Theft in the Central Children's Theatre! What could be more distasteful. Dudin promised to take the situation in hand. He asked the actors to mark their bills with a secret sign which would help catch the thief. It seemed as if everything would be all right after that, but instead things got even worse. The marked money disappeared just as swiftly as the unmarked money had. The People's Actors suspected the Renowned Actors, the Renowned suspected the Young, the Young suspected the stagehands, the stagehands the cleaning ladies. . . .

April the twenty-second, Lenin's centennial and the day of our premiere, Dudin told me to come to his office. He said he had worked out that there was only one moment in the second act when the thefts could be taking place. He said that only I could help uncover the crime because my part as Alexander ended in the first act. So he asked me to go to the dressing rooms during the final scene and watch. I agreed to do it.

There wasn't the usual excitement that opening night, even though Miss Furtseva, the Minister of Culture, was expected to be present.

The first act went from bad to worse. The actors were so nervous they forgot their lines, and the workers got the stage sets all mixed up; I felt relieved when I was finally hanged.

The second act was even worse. The actors couldn't care less about the Revolution or Lenin's letters in which he promised to give poor people everything. It was easy for him to make promises; it wasn't coming out of his pocket. But what were you supposed to do when your last ruble was disappearing? So, they all looked at each other mistrustfully and said their lines mechanically.

When the gloomy crowd went to the railway station to meet their leader, I stealthily made my way to the corridor. There, near the wall, stood a clothes rack – a long metal frame on wheels, packed with costumes of birds and animals from the morning performance. It was impossible to find a better place to hide. I slipped between the bright silk costume of a rooster and the grey felt costume of a mouse. Crouched there, breathing in the dust from the costumes, I was feeling a bit foolish when I heard hurried footsteps in the corridor. I kept still. I heard the door of one of the dressing rooms open with a creak and then close noiselessly, but I didn't see a thing. The corridor had a bend in the middle and from my position I could see only the doors on one side. I waited a while, then inched the clothes rack forward. The wheels rolled without any sound; I kept going until I had a view of the whole corridor. My heart was pounding and I was trembling so, that the silk feathers of the rooster near my chest and the mouse tail behind me were quivering too. Suddenly, one of the doors, the second on the right, was flung open and, from there, crept Lenin!

He peered from side to side, tore his kepi off his head, placed something there, threw the kepi back on his bald spot, adjusted the brim, hunched himself over, and sneaked down the corridor and onto the stage.

There was nothing more to wait for; I leaped from the clothes rack and hurried backstage. There, in the darkness, somebody grabbed me by the arm. I shuddered.

'Who is the thief?' Dudin asked.

'Lenin,' I said.

'That's what I was afraid of,' said Dudin. He turned and whispered something into the ear of a stagehand. The next moment the crowd at the railroad station stirred nervously, and the workers, peasants, soldiers, and sailors passed the holy word, 'Lenin,' down the line.

The locomotive's whistle sounded hauntingly; the train wheels screeched to a halt. For a second, the stage was enveloped in a cloud of steam. When the steam vanished, the leader of the World Revolution was already standing on the armoured car, his arms outstretched.

'Lenin!' sighed the crowd in unison, 'Lenin!'

Vladimir Ilyich Lenin had hardly begun his speech when the crowd started pulling him down by his coattails. Lenin regained his balance somewhat, then fell down, and the stream of people triumphantly carried him to centre stage.

'Perfect!' whispered Dudin. 'Perfect! It's exactly what I've been looking for!'

Lenin launched into his line that the bourgeoisie was stealing from the people and would have to face cruel punishment. But the white arms of the crowd, like foam on the crest of a wave, kept carrying him around the stage. Lenin sensed something was wrong in that tumultuous atmosphere and turned silent. He began kicking and thrashing his arms like a swimmer trying to stay afloat, but nevertheless, he went under, his worn-out boots flashed momentarily in the air, and then Lenin disappeared. His kepi surfaced on the angry sea and was passed from hand to hand.

In the kepi was found a one-ruble bill and a three-ruble bill. Both bills had been secretly marked – the single in the corner, and the three-ruble bill right on the picture of the Kremlin.

The workers and peasants were furious. If it were just the three rubles for vodka, the proletariat could have made peace, but the sight of that extra ruble drove them wild. They wanted to kill their leader on the spot; right there at the railway station, they wanted to kick him to death, and they would have done it if Dudin hadn't taken swift action.

'No luck with Lenin,' Dudin whispered in my ear. 'You've got to go out there and save the show.'

'What should I do?' I asked.

'Repeat some of your lines,' he replied, and shoved me out on the stage.

In one leap, I jumped onto the armoured car and, amid the bells of Rachmaninoff, surprised myself with the cry, 'Oh Russia! What a country, where a man can't even be right!'

Somebody screamed 'Bravo!' from the audience, and the curtain fell.

An impromptu Party meeting was called immediately after the performance. The first to speak was Furtseva, an attractive grey-haired woman, the first (and last) female to be a member of the Politburo. She announced that the performance was to be cancelled, not because of the actor who played Lenin, as many had predicted; Furtseva liked that actor – she said he had given a fresh interpretation of the role of Lenin. The performance was cancelled because of me. To be specific, because of my final line, which thoroughly annoyed Furtseva.

'Who says we can't hang people? Who says we can't do it better than anyone?' she said, and walked out of the meeting.

At that point a debate began. The actors were divided into three camps: the Young Actors proposed that Lenin be named a Renowned Actor; the Renowned suggested that he be named a People's Actor; the People's Actors asked Dudin to throw him out of the theatre. Dudin made a King Solomon decision – he gave Lenin a rise and the vacant post as the theatre's street cleaner.

7 The Prince

After my unsuccessful attempt to kill the Czar, my career as a terrorist was over, and my career as an aristocrat began. I never again played a revolutionary; I moved into the realm of princes. I constantly changed accents, wigs, and capes, but always and everywhere wore white gloves. Dudin had the firm conviction that there was but one way to make a Russian man an aristocrat – to put snowy white gloves on his hands. In these very gloves, I played German, French, Russian, and English princes, sometimes the heir apparent, and sometimes imposters. The gold crown was often beside me on a velvet pillow, but was never placed on my head. I was always walking around the Czar's throne but never seated on it. I became a professional prince, but never played the king.

The king always had palaces, slaves, and armies, I had nothing but my white gloves. I don't want to say I felt bad about this; I had no desire to change places with him. Who needs such a nervous life? Who needs the burden of daily decisions – to declare war or keep the peace; to build a new jail or repair an old one; to hang the queen or simply cut off her head? Who wants to sit all day on a throne, lie awake all night, assume tremendous responsibilities, and know that all you'll get anyway is the people's wrath?

A king's end is always disastrous – either poison (Italian style); decapitation (French style); or even worse, an invitation to have his picture taken, and then execution (Russian style). Believe me, as the son of a monarch, I can say it is a rotten destiny to be a king.

To be a prince is another story. He has no power but also no responsibility, no decisions to make. He doesn't care about the present. His whole life centres on the future; his head is filled with the romantic dreams of something even more romantic to come. What could be better? There are, of course, those who would disagree. They would say that the life of a prince is nothing compared with that of a king. The fact is, a prince doesn't own anything – he walks in a marble palace, but that palace is not his; he reclines on a golden coverlet, but it is also not his; he sits on an Arabian mare to chase his bride, but, of course, she is not his either (not the bride, the horse, naturally). So, if you use the Marxist-Leninist theory, the prince is like the proletariat, poor as a church mouse, and by law he has the right to *nothing*.

But that nothing is what opens the door to the land of happiness. That's what gives him the freedom to make his romantic wishes – to find a crystal castle; to fight a dragon; to fly across the sea on a magic carpet. That's how it was before the Revolution.

With the coming of socialism, there were to be no more kings, but every young Soviet man became a prince. Naturally, Soviet princes are more realistic. They won't be fooled by tales of crystal castles or magic-carpet rides. They're not floating in the clouds. They don't believe in Pushkin fairy tales. Ask any Soviet prince to make three wishes, and he will most definitely say:

First – to have propiska and an apartment in Moscow.

Second – to get out of the call-up.

Third – to take a long trip abroad, preferably forever.

There they are, the three doors that open the way to happiness in Soviet life.

These three doors are securely guarded by three dragons. The door that leads to Moscow propiska is guarded by the police; the door that leads to avoiding the call-up, by the army; the door that leads abroad, by the KGB. Thus, to slip through any of these doors requires a vicious battle with the attendant dragon. Here it is not enough to be a romantic prince; here you've got to be a valiant knight schooled in Marxism-Leninism.

To get propiska, you must know whom to pay off, how to falsify your documents, and whom to sleep with. Even so, there is no guarantee of victory. The Soviet prince spends years hacking at his dragon. Finally, he manages to chop its head off and get Moscow propiska, but the next day, just when he gets his new apartment, he also gets his notice from the Call-up Board and, toodle-oo, he's off to the army. What did he need that apartment for if he was going to be killed on the Chinese border?

Another prince takes a chance and starts with a different dragon. He successfully pretends that he is insane, gets out of the call-up, but his victory is tarnished – as a schizophrenic he will surely never get an apartment in Moscow or ever be able to go abroad.

As for going abroad, it's better not to think about this, even if you are healthy. On the way to this most cherished of all doors, the competition is severe; you will be slashed and trampled by competition even before you confront your beast. For a trip abroad, people go all out. Years before, they kiss their boss's arse, join the Party, become informers, and cut each other's throats. To be perfectly honest, I have never met anyone who conquered all three dragons.

Never considering myself sufficiently ready to enter into the fight with the beasts, I studied them, got to know their routines, and bided my time. I kept waiting and waiting until they pounced on me and there was no choice but to take on all three simultaneously.

I was still awaiting the decision of the City Council regarding a room and propiska when I received a notice from the Call-up Board ordering me to appear immediately for a medical. That was a bad year for Moscow actors – there were renewed skirmishes with the Chinese – everybody was being called-up. Comics and tragic actors, singers and dancers, jugglers and tightrope walkers, all those who hadn't reached their twenty-seventh year were called up. Even the Bolshoi Ballet wasn't able to protect its stars that fatal year.

It was precisely what I feared most – if I were to go into the army, I would lose out on propiska and so, after completing my military service, I wouldn't be able to return to Moscow. Over and over I repeated the question of the paralyzed Lenin when Stalin dragged his wife into the other room: 'Now what?' I don't know what Lenin finally did, but I decided not to go for the medical and, as quickly as I could, to move from the wooden castle to Andrewlka's place.

In one week, all the young actors except me were swept from the theatre. I was still safe because of the confusion over my whereabouts, but this wouldn't continue for long. Late one night a military patrol descended on Toilik's house. The soldiers couldn't get a thing out of him. They searched the whole house, checked the cupboards, turned the mattresses upside down, then took their position and waited all night in ambush. In the morning, they threatened the sobered-up Toilik that he would lose everything if he was protecting me, then they went to catch me at the theatre. Toilik, having nothing to lose, immediately phoned me at the theatre, and by the time the recruiters had blocked all the entrances to the theatre, I was already attending an anti-call-up meeting hastily convened at Andrewlka's apartment.

Andrewlka's apartment had been fully redecorated. There were no more *Playboy* bunnies pasted on the walls. Instead, the walls were covered with Boris's icons, the ones I had left there some time ago. Andrewlka, too, looked different. He had shaved off his goatee but made up for this by letting his hair grow shoulder-length. He was in sandals, jeans, an Indian shirt covered with flowers, and beads strung around his neck. This was the new Andrewlka – the hippie-pacifist.

Andrewlka's cooking habits hadn't changed much – he prepared 'Potatoes in Olive Drab,' put the Turtle on the rug, and the whole command sat around warming their insides with that hot combination. At this meeting we discussed the eternal question of how to avoid the call-up.

Boris started things off with a bold proposal – he said he would take it upon himself to hack off the index finger of my right hand, thereby making it impossible for me to pull the trigger of a gun.

Andrewlka said politely that that trick no longer worked, for the button on an atomic rocket could be pushed with any finger, or even an elbow. He said it was much better to feign insanity.

Stas said he had heard somewhere that the safest way out of the draft was to join the army and, once there, to pee in your bed every night. He said that after a few wet months, I would undoubtedly be discharged for a sick, urinary bladder. However, he warned that soldiers don't like bed-wetters in their barracks and they just might smother me in my own bed.

Lena said she had heard from her grandfather, who had been in three wars, that by straining the muscles of the feet, it was possible to raise one's blood pressure to a critical point and, once diagnosed as having hypertension, I wouldn't be drafted.

'Hypertension!' cried Stas. 'Of course! That's my speciality – high blood pressure. I will make your blood pressure go so high the doctors have never seen anything quite like it, and that's without straining even one toe!' He opened his attaché case and held out to me a translucent box of fiery red pills. 'Here, take these pills, only please be careful with them. Look out not to take an overdose, because my mommychka still hasn't sent me the antidote. I don't know how, but you've got to determine the right dosage.'

'Where can I go to find out the dosage? I can't go to the theatre's clinic,' I said.

'There's no need to worry about finding a clinic; Andrewlka will take care of that,' Andrewlka interposed sweetly. 'Do you remember Tanya, the nurse? She's working right around here in a hospital. She's one of us; she's all right, but you know, she's insatiable. First you've got to give yourself to that puma, ha, ha, ha! Don't worry, Lena, it was just a joke. Andrewlka likes silly jokes. Anyway, Andrewlka won't abandon a friend in need. Sound the trumpets, beat the drums, Andrewlka offers himself as a sacrifice for Sashulka!'

Everybody gave his or her approval. We drank one last shot, and Andrewlka and I left for the hospital. The hospital was one stop by Metro or one by bus. I wanted to take the Metro, but Andrewlka said the bus stopped closer to the main door of the hospital. Andrewlka never walked any farther than he had to, so we took the bus.

The insatiable puma invited us into an office, hung an out-to-lunch sign on the door, showed me how to use the blood-pressure apparatus, and went behind the screen with Andrew. While I was getting practice measuring the blood pressure in my body, behind the screen, Andrewlka was measuring the pressure in the nurse-puma's body. Her panting and moaning kept me from concentrating on the column of mercury, which bounded up and down madly.

When I was beginning to see the effect of the pills, the puma's appetite must have been satisfied to a certain extent, for she came out from behind the screen. With a limp hand she closed her white uniform, fixed her hair, sighed, sat down on a chair near me, assumed a professional pose, took the reading from the apparatus, and asked me to strip to the waist.

I proceeded to unbutton my shirt, but Tanya stopped me and said that she had to check the bottom half. From behind the screen came Andrewlka's giggle, but there was nothing else for me to do but follow the nurse's orders.

She fingered everything she could and announced authoritatively that I was as strong as a horse. She said that my blood pressure was high enough to kill me, but it wasn't high enough to get me out of the Soviet army. She explained that the general state of my health was too good and, until the reason for my hypertension could be made clear, there wasn't one doctor who would take it seriously.

'What should I do?' I asked Tanya.

She licked her lips and said, 'You need some other sickness which can bring about high blood pressure.'

'Like what?' I asked.

'It's got to be something that's impossible to diagnose,' she said with a yawn.

'Where am I supposed to get something like that?' I asked.

'The best thing is a verified concussion,' the puma said, sleepily.

'But how do you get a verified concussion?' I inquired.

'You need to be involved in an accident,' said Tanya, 'and a doctor should come and file a report.'

'What kind of accident?' Andrew asked, coming out from behind the screen.

'Make something up,' the puma said, rising. 'Like a brick fell on your head, or something like that. Just remember, there are two symptoms of a concussion – high blood pressure and vomiting.'

'Thank you,' I said.

'The pleasure was mine . . . By the way, make sure they don't take you to the Sober-up Centre instead of the hospital,' Tanya said, pulling Andrew toward the screen.

'Time's up, *c'est la vie!*' Andrewlka whispered, releasing himself from the puma. 'Andrewlka's got to go prepare the accident!'

When we got back to Andrewlka's, I ate a bowl of borscht, then swallowed Stas's pills and chased them with the aviation alcohol. Next we all went out of the apartment onto the staircase, where Boris positioned me at a frightening angle – one leg draped over the banister, my head resting on the stairs. I shut my eyes, and then Andrewlka tossed a second bowl of borscht in my face. At the same time, Lena was calling an ambulance and telling them, her voice cracking, about the dreadful accident on the staircase. Her voice must have created the right impression, for an ambulance appeared immediately. A doctor rushed toward me, pushed my friends aside, checked my pulse pounding from the alcohol, sniffed the surrounding air, asked what I had eaten, and said that he would have to take me to the hospital because I had concussion.

'How can you diagnose it so fast?' Stas asked in amazement.

'The vomiting,' said the doctor proudly, pointing to the borscht with sour cream artistically running down the steps.

At the hospital, the doctors fought for my life: they X-rayed me; examined my skull; checked my pulse; struck my knees with a hammer, took blood samples; gave me injections; and used all the powers of their science to bring down my stubborn blood pressure, while I used all my power to keep it high – three times a day I took the red pills and the alcohol smuggled in by Lena, Andrewlka, and Stas. This struggle over my health went on for a week but my hypertension finally won out. I left the hospital, holding my head, the brain of which had been brutally damaged according to the official medical report which I presented at the Recruiting Centre.

A sergeant with blood-shot eyes took a cursory look at my papers and shot his first question at me: 'Reason for being late?'

'It says right there; I was in the hospital.'

'The military hospital?'

'No. Skulifasovsky Clinic.'

'That's no reason. We don't accept civilian hospital reports. Consider yourself lucky that you got here by today; tomorrow you would be considered a deserter; and the day after tomorrow you would be arrested. Soldier Petrov, take this criminal to the barber.'

'You can't lay a hand on my head,' I protested. 'It says right there that I had a concussion.'

'Where does it say that?'

'There, on that paper.'

'I don't believe that phony document,' the sergeant said, tossing my papers into the wastepaper basket.

'But – '

'Shut up. You should be proud that your country needs you. You should be proud, understand? Perhaps you think this is peacetime? Well, it's not. Communism still hasn't been victorious throughout the world. While there remains even a single capitalist country, the war goes on. No, this is not peacetime. There was never peace and there never will be, that's why we need people, young healthy people. And according to your file, you're to receive special training for submarine duty. Congratulations!'

'But I'm not healthy.'

'What's that, you don't want to serve?' the sergeant shouted. 'You mean you don't want to defend your motherland?'

I don't want to defend a regime I hate, I thought, but said, 'I'm a sick man. Trust me, I can die any moment.'

'Comrade Petrov, take these documents and this liar next door for a medical.'

This was it. I didn't have any red pills, I didn't have any alcohol, and I didn't even have any borscht.

The doctor had a round face, round eyes, and round wire-rimmed glasses. He was dressed in a once-white gown, now fully covered with red and brown spots, something like camouflage. Most likely, he had put in his time on a submarine: his head was polished to a mirrorlike shine, but there was a chip in the mirror – on his forehead, on the right side, was a tremendous cavity.

'Occupation?' he asked.

'Actor,' I replied.

'You can entertain the soldiers in the trenches,' he said, and made a note in my file.

'But I just had a concussion!'

'Everybody has a concussion at some time,' the doctor said, scratching his cavity with his fist.

'But I've got lethally high blood pressure,' I cried.

'Remove your clothes,' the doctor said.

I got undressed.

'Sit down.'

I sat down.

'Give me your hand,' the doctor said.

I held out my hand.

'No, the left one,' he said.

He placed the black rubber bag on my arm and began to pump air into it. What was I to do? What to do? What . . .

'Don't stiffen up; relax your arm,' the doctor said. 'Don't strain your muscles.'

Here I recalled Lena's story about her grandfather. I relaxed my arm but, with every bit of strength, strained my toes.

The air began to come out of the rubber bag with a snakelike hiss. The rubber softened its grip. I knew that the mercury would descend slowly, then bounce, then plummet. I couldn't see where the mercury was hitting and I inadvertently stared at the doctor. He glanced mistrustfully at the column, scratched his cavity, peered at me, and, once again, pumped in air. My legs trembled from straining my muscles. The doctor looked at me and asked, 'Why are you shaking?'

'It's cold,' I said.

'Is your father alive?' he asked unexpectedly.

'No,' I said, 'he's dead.'

'When did he die?'

'A long time ago, when I was thirteen.'

'What did he die of?'

'A heart attack.'

'Get dressed.'

He jotted something in my medical file and said, 'Listen carefully. I can't release you just because of the hypertension and the concussion. However, I don't want to take responsibility if you die during combat. My only alternative is to write here that you're insane – to say that the accident caused brain damage. But you must understand that a record like that sticks with you all your life. Of course, I'll have to send a report to the theatre's clinic. It's your choice.'

'I'm crazy,' I said.

'You're free,' the doctor said, and smiled.

One of the dragon heads was cut off. I went outside. I walked along the red brick building which housed the Recruiting Centre. A string of new recruits, stepping in unison, came out of the gate. For a few blocks, we walked together, only they were on the street with the trucks, I was on the pavement with the people. At the Metro, we went our separate ways. As I went down the escalator, from the street came a popular wartime song:

> I wish you, this day
> My fellow soldier,
> If it's death on its way
> Let it be fast.
> If it's only a wound,
> Let it be your last.

Thank God I'm not a soldier, I thought, it's much better to be a prince.

8 Death Comes Only Once

I expected my return to the theatre to astound everybody and make me the centre of attention for at least half a year. I expected my return to stir up a commotion not less than a dead man's return from the other world. I expected a barrage of questions. In anticipation of this, I made up a convincing explanation for my reincarnation. To get even more mileage out of my story, I devised a special way of walking called the 'alternating limp,' and added a slight twitch of the eye and cheek. What could I do – I couldn't just blurt out for all to hear that in the other world I was deemed insane and so was sent back. But all my preparation was in vain.

When I got to the theatre, there was a surprise, but I was the one who got that surprise. I was met with complete indifference. No one even noticed my limping. I expected anything but a welcome like that. My fellow actors stood around in groups and, from within these groups, not the familiar gurgle, but something rare for our theatre – the sound of human speech. The look of the actors was strange, distracted. Am I in the right theatre? I wondered. Even the smell was different; not the familiar vodka-port wine scent, but some delicate, nostalgic aroma supposedly called the 'smell of the stage'. Hm, what changes! Forgetting my limp, I hastened to see Dudin.

The director's office was in half-darkness. As usual, Dudin was sitting at his desk and, as was his custom, gently stirring green tea in a glass with a golden spoon. A lone ray of sunlight, slipping out from behind the heavy drapes, played on the silver hair of the director.

At least something in the theatre is still the same, I thought, brightening up. Limping on both legs, I hobbled to the desk like the Hunchback of Notre Dame. After all, I had to show somebody what I had been rehearsing.

'How's it going?' Dudin asked, stirring his tea.

'Permanently exempt,' I said with a twitch.

'That means freedom,' Dudin said.

'That's right,' I said with a heavy sigh.

'Freedom is good,' Dudin said. 'Sit down.'

With one leg jutting out, I slowly lowered myself into a chair. Dudin looked on silently. I kept still. He kept still. Both of us were still. In a pause like that, a policeman is born, as we say. The teaspoon, clinking against the rim of the glass, signalled the end of the silence.

'There's been a lot of changes around here,' Dudin said.

'Yes,' I said, 'I thought I had come to the wrong theatre.'

'Have you talked with anybody yet?' Dudin asked.

'No,' I replied. 'They didn't see me.'

'Did you notice that nobody's drinking?' Dudin asked.

'It's hard not to,' I said.

'What do you think could get actors to stop drinking?' Dudin asked.

'I can't imagine,' I said.

'Guess,' said Dudin.

I thought. It was difficult to find a reason. Silence seeped into the office once again.

'Give up?' Dudin asked, preventing the birth of another policeman.

Squinting one eye as if from pain, I said, 'I give up.'

Dudin stopped stirring the tea, raised his hand with the teaspoon. As the spoon glistened in the sun's ray, Dudin looked at me like a hypnotist and said, 'We're going abroad. Our theatre is going on tour – first to India, then the United States. We're going to America!' Dudin tossed the teaspoon onto the table triumphantly. 'How do you like that! But here's the catch – there's a strict rule in the Ministry of Culture about not taking anyone who drinks. So, we don't have any drinkers in our theatre now. Our actors have forgotten the word *vodka*. Alcoholism in our theatre has been stamped out. It's too bad we don't go abroad more often.'

'I agree,' I said.

'There was a big fight over the parts,' Dudin continued. 'There's only one opening left – the part of Prince Rama. It's a very important part, because, we're going to be the guests of the Indian government for the anniversary of the Ramayana, but we don't have any young actors in the theatre now. They've all been called up. I even had to take Lenin from street-cleaning duty and make him King of the Monkeys, but we still don't have anybody to play the prince; I truly don't know who could take this part. By any chance would you like to go abroad as a prince?'

'I certainly would,' I answered.

'Oh good, I thought you might not be interested,' Dudin said, smiling broadly. 'I think you should know, this tour is going to be a difficult one – long flights, tiring trips, different climates, and the medical examination preceding the tour will be rigorous. We need actors in perfect health. What kind of shape are you in?'

'Perfect,' I said.

'What's with your eye?'

'Nothing,' I said, 'I just got a little dust in it.'

'And what about your legs? You were walking a bit strangely.'

'Everything's all right!'

'How did you get out of the army if you're in such perfect health?'

'Um . . . it's a long story . . .' I said, rising.

'Just a minute,' said Dudin. 'I haven't finished yet. If it's such a long story, you'll tell me the next time, but there's something else . . . how can I put it . . . There's a policy that bachelors can't be sent abroad; a family member has to stay behind, understand?'

'I understand.'

'I seriously suggest that you find a wife. One with a child would be even better.

'I'll try.'

'There's something else – I trust you don't speak English and, if you do, forget that you do. It can complicate the situation unnecessarily. There's a Ministry rule that says English speakers can't be taken abroad. But that's not a problem; the most

209

important thing is to hurry up and get married so you can file your application as a married man. Is it possible?'

'It's possible,' I said.

'You must realize that the preparation for a trip abroad takes up to several hours a day.'

'You mean the rehearsals?' I asked.

'Rehearsals?' Dudin muttered. 'Party meetings!'

The first Party meeting took place on the stage, behind the closed curtain.

'Dear comrades, let's get started,' announced a man in civilian clothes, introduced by Dudin as a 'representative of the Ministry'. He had a wide rear, narrow shoulders, a long pointed nose, white flyaway hair, white eyelashes, and pink eyes. Actually he looked like a fat albino rat trained to speak. 'Today's meeting is dedicated to an important theme – the conduct of the Soviet man abroad.' The representative of the Ministry pursed his lips, gave a jerk, shot a look back, as if he thought somebody was eavesdropping on him from behind the curtain, then continued in a hushed tone: 'Your theatre has been given the rare opportunity to represent our country abroad. It's a great honour and a tremendous responsibility. You should be aware of the immense confidence the Party, the government, and the KG – I mean, the Ministry of Culture, has placed in you. You will carry the banner of Soviet art. You must carry it through capitalist countries and not soil it with their filth. I've come here to give a little talk to help you hold that banner high, but what I'm going to tell you should not go beyond this stage.'

Once again the speaker pursed his lips, spun around, and suddenly cried out – 'Hey you, over there, open the drapes!'

With a rustle, the curtain rose, revealing the dark auditorium with its empty rows of plush seats. 'That's better.'

The speaker loosened his tie, coughed, and went on, 'My name is Mikhail Mikhailovich. I will be accompanying you on this trip as a representative of the Ministry of Culture.

'We will be meeting every day right up to the day of the trip and, even once you're abroad, it won't be so easy to get rid of me, ha, ha, ha. And so, for this reason, I want you to feel perfectly relaxed with me . . . What was I talking about?'

'Going abroad,' Dudin reminded him.

'Yes, yes, the conduct of the Soviet man abroad. Well, comrades, I'd like to share some information with you, so that later on nothing will come as a surprise.

'I will not hide the fact that a few capitalist countries still exist. Naturally, they are rotting, but, much to our dismay, they still exist, and it is therefore necessary to have contact with them, you know. To avert any incidents, I will attempt to depict what these countries are all about.

'I will start with India. Though this country is hungry, it is probably the better of the two you will see. India, you know, is on the right track; it's going in the direction of socialism. The poverty there is unbelievable, of course, but the people are warm and friendly. They like to beg, but look, don't give them anything. Anyway, you won't have much to give, ha, ha, ha. You will receive three dollars a day. Now, what else? The weather is hot there; the national sport is yoga, and the peasants grow three crops a year, but anyway there isn't a thing to eat. People die by the thousands right on the street, while the holy cows trample on them, ha, ha, ha. Anyway, you'll see for yourself very soon. Oh yes, I want to mention something to the women – if you see a lizard or snake in your bed, don't let out a shriek. Don't panic, or go into hysterics. Show them that Soviet women are not afraid of poisonous animals.' He pumped his white eyebrows up and down to emphasize this fact.

'Right, that's it for India; now we come to the most dangerous country. India is just India. But America, as you know, is the United States. This is where danger beckons at every corner. America, you know, is multinational. By a turn of fate, many Slavic people wound up there. Ukrainians and even Russians live there, much to their disgrace. Mostly traitors to our native land – white officers, and Vlasov's soldiers. You can't imagine how crafty they are; what ingenuity they will use to compromise Soviet actors. They will give you presents; ask you to their homes; invite you to restaurants; try to separate you by giving you single rooms in your hotels. Be careful, comrades! Stay in pairs, walk in threes, eat in fours, and, above all, remember your high status as citizens of the Soviet Union.

'Now, I will attempt to familiarize you with the enemies' tactics so you're not caught off guard. Recently, the Russian Folk Instruments Ensemble went on tour in America. The orchestra's soloist, talented though irresponsible, stole away from the group and made a dash for the nearest department store. I don't know exactly what he was looking for, but the fact is that the provocateurs, in a matter of minutes, slipped a frying pan into his balalaika case. It's no laughing matter, comrades. The soloist was caught at the door and a nasty scandal ensued. A crowd gathered; the police came; and the next morning, his picture was in the paper; what muck! Naturally, we claimed he fell prey to the white officers but, anyway, he will never again go anywhere, that's for certain. When he came back to his native land, he was thrown out of the orchestra. Now let him go ahead and play the pan in his kitchen, ha, ha, ha. But let's move on, it's not funny, comrades. The dance ensemble called The Birches got mixed up in something bigger. I'm telling you about this, comrades, so that you know where danger is lurking.'

'Where?' several actors asked.

'Everywhere, comrades! But what was I talking about?'

'The Birches,' Dudin reminded him.

'Yes, that's right. The Birches went on a long trip by bus from one city to another. The dancers were hot and tired; it was the summer. Finally they arrived at a smart hotel. There was a swimming pool with clear, blue water awaiting them. Without giving it a second thought, the weary dancers flung themselves into the pool. It's perfectly natural; they wanted to revive themselves, to swim and splash around. Suddenly, can you imagine, the water around our girls turned black. It was a horrible, unexplainable sight. Again, there were pictures in the newspaper and filthy lies about the Soviet Regime. It came to light that the enemy had put a chemical in the pool which reacted to the presence of urine in the water. I don't understand why you're laughing, comrades; it's not funny, it's frightening. You yourselves can see to what lengths the enemy will go – they use illegal chemical weapons that make it impossible even to pee in a swimming pool after a rough trip. That's why I have told you over and over – be careful.

'I can assure you the planning of the tour in the U.S. will be perfect. Possibly in India there will be a slight mix-up with the hotel or transport, but in America it's impossible. America is a finely tuned machine. That's why you've got to be doubly careful – don't be late; don't get anything confused. You will have to take responsibility if there's a problem. They won't give you the opportunity to put the blame on them. Well, what was I talking about?'

'America,' Dudin said.

'Yes, America is our most dreadful enemy, the strongest and most insidious, too. Let's be honest – it's a pretty advanced country. I'm not going to tell you that Americans chew gum to kill their hunger pains. No, in America you won't see the incredible poverty that's in India. On the contrary, America will try to impress you with its apparent wealth, to dazzle you with its modern technology. But you should always remember that the most significant difference between capitalism and socialism is that, in our country, life gets better and better every day, but there, worse and worse. So, if you are impressed by their luxury, don't be too impressed. Remember, it's already rotting, and if it doesn't decompose on its own, we will help.

'Work it out, how can a country with the motto "In God We Trust" last for a long time if everybody knows that there is no God? How can a system with a constitution that sets the interests of the individual above those of the state be effective?

'And so, don't get too excited about America. Its days are numbered, and we will wipe it out anyway. Recognize your own strength, don't be afraid to engage in open discussion, and always stick up for the Soviet point of view. They will toss out something like: "You don't have any freedom." You'll return with: "But we have free medicine." They'll pose the sneaky question: "Is it true there's no meat in Russia?" And you will respond: "But we have free education." Don't be afraid to put them on the spot. Remember, the best form of defence is offence. We're well aware that we have certain shortcomings, but why should they know about them; these are internal matters. Think of yourselves

213

as Soviet propagandists. Don't be tricked by their provocative questions. When they ask you: "How much do you make? What's your salary?" don't panic, tell the truth, such and such, but don't make it clear that it's only for a month. It's okay if they think it's per week. If they ask you what kind of apartment you have, don't be afraid to tell the truth. Your apartment has plenty of rooms, but don't go into details about how many families live in that apartment.'

'What should you say if you don't have an apartment?' I blurted out.

'Who said that?' the representative of the Ministry of Culture asked.

'It's that young actor who played Lenin's brother,' Dudin hastened to say.

'Is he married?'

'Yes, of course,' Dudin replied.

'Well then, young man, we'll give you an apartment. For this trip, you can say you're living in a large apartment. You will be, when you get back,' the speaker said, and pursed his lips. 'I'd like to conclude with a few words. Russian theatrical art is well loved all over the world. Naturally, you will be a great success and will be invited to many parties in your honour; but here I must warn you, don't hiccup, don't lick your plate, and most of all, don't drown yourself in alcohol. We don't want any pictures in the newspapers with the caption "Russians are used to eating on all fours." Don't laugh, comrades. First, this already happened one time and, second, it's quite natural for your theatre where half of you play animals. Control yourselves and remember, your friend here will always be watching you.

'And now for the last item. Tomorrow, each of you must go for a checkup at the theatrical clinic. I hope you're in good shape, because this will determine whether you will participate in the tour or not. Perfect health is an absolute must. Be aware that this tour is no joke; it's a very costly affair, a huge expense for the state, but we don't have extra funds for transporting actors' corpses from one country to another.'

With these words came a giggle from the auditorium. Mikhail Mikhailovich gave a jerk, turned around, and peered into the darkness. 'Turn on the lights,' he shouted. When the lights went on, we saw a little boy and girl in the back row of the auditorium. They were the first members of the audience, who had come to the theatre nearly one hour before the start of the children's performance, but they got to see a performance for the adults.

'What's going on?' the Ministry representative screamed in a terrifying voice. 'This is secret information, who's spying on me? Close the drapes!'

The next morning I was lying under portraits of Lenin and Brezhnev, behind a white plastic curtain in the theatrical clinic. A nurse (if Andrewlka had seen her, he would have called her a pussycat), her hands soft and white, hooked me up to the electrocardiogram machine. Beside the machine, on the desk, lay my medical folder.

'Don't move,' the nurse said, 'what's all the looking around for?'

'What a fascinating machine,' I said, staring at my folder, which surely contained the report from the Recruiting Centre. 'How can you understand such a complicated machine?' I asked.

'I don't need to understand it; I just have to get a graph. The doctor is the one who must understand it,' the nurse said softly, placing a metal disc against my heart.

'Oh,' I said, 'it's cold.'

'No, it's you that's hot,' she said timidly, and blushed. 'Is it true that you're going to America?'

'I hope so,' I replied.

'But you're so young! All the other actors in your theatre are so old. It's obvious that they won't defect. How did you get permission?'

'I haven't got permission yet,' I said. 'I have to pass the physical.'

'Don't worry, you'll pass. You're so strong,' the nurse said, lowering her eyes.

'Who knows,' I said.

'Let's see what the electrocardiogram says; it shows everything,' the nurse said, and turned on the machine. The apparatus began to chirp and emit a tape. 'Relax, breathe evenly; now hold your breath; okay, relax. Just lie here and relax. I'll go for the doctor. Be back in a minute,' the nurse said, and left the room.

I knew this would be my only chance. When the nurse went into the corridor, I jumped off the bed and dashed toward the desk. My legs got tangled in the electric wires and I nearly fell down. I grabbed the edge of the curtain; it sailed off to the side, but fortunately didn't get torn. I reached for my file and began to rifle through the pages. It was difficult to comprehend anything – half the words were in Latin. My heart was pounding. The machine buzzed, spewing its tape furiously. I came across sicknesses from my early childhood which were recorded in the beginning of the file – measles, whooping cough . . . I flipped the pages over and started checking the file in reverse. One of the pages fluttered out of the file and slid beneath the table. I dived after it, and when I finally grabbed it I saw the red star of the Recruiting Centre. I stuffed the page into my trouser pocket and crawled out from under the table. Here, I became fully entangled in the wires like a fly in a spider's web. I carefully attempted to get free, but I heard footsteps approaching. I rolled the curtain back into place and bounded onto the bed, knocking the metal disc off my chest. I frantically placed the disc back on the same spot and tried to calm my breathing. Nobody came. I waited for some time. Just when I was about to get up again to straighten out the papers in my file, the door opened.

'Here's the cardiogram report,' came the nurse's voice from the other side of the curtain.

'Uh huh,' said the doctor, 'when did the patient die?'

'He's not dead,' the nurse said, confused, 'he's going to America.'

'What's this about America? This reading clearly indicates a heart attack and death.'

'Oh no, he was so strong!' the nurse cried, and threw aside the curtain.

I tried to breathe evenly and methodically – in . . . out . . . in . . . out . . .

'See, he's not dead,' the nurse screamed, 'he's breathing!'

The doctor bent over me. His face was stern and grim; of course he was in glasses. Why do all doctors wear glasses? I mused. I smiled at him, trying to convince him that I belonged to this life.

'I don't understand,' the doctor said, taking my wrist. 'The pulse is fine, a bit rapid, but sound.'

'I told you,' the nurse muttered under her breath.

'Do you drink?' the doctor asked.

'No!' the nurse replied, with a start.

'Not you!' the doctor said, slightly annoyed. 'Do you drink?'

'I used to,' I said.

'How much did you drink?'

'Normally, like everybody.'

'If it was like everybody in your theatre, I wouldn't call that normal,' the doctor said.

I kept quiet.

'Where's his file?' the doctor asked.

The nurse handed him the file.

'Why is this such a mess?' the doctor said sternly as he put the pages together.

At that point, I stopped breathing.

'I don't know,' the nurse said, 'that's how it was.'

'Hm , everything seems to be all right. I really don't understand why the cardiogram turned out like that.'

'Maybe something went wrong with the machine,' the nurse suggested.

'Hook him up once more,' the doctor said as he got up and walked over to the electrocardiogram machine.

The nurse bent down till her breast touched my chest, and whispered: 'I told you the cardiogram shows everything. Why were you running around like that?'

In . . . out . . . in . . . out . . . I kept breathing through my nose.

'I heard that in America even prisoners walk around in jeans,' the nurse whispered in my ear, 'but in our clinic, nobody has them.'

'You'll have them,' I said.

'Breathe, hold it, breathe,' the nurse said out loud, then added softly, 'You're doing fine. Don't worry, death comes only once.'

After a perfect reading, I walked out of the examination room,

217

descended the stairs, went into the toilet, took the farthest cubicle – the one near the window – put on the latch, took out the paper that stated I was a lunatic with high blood pressure, and ripped it into the tiniest pieces, threw them into the toilet bowl, and flushed the toilet. The second dragon's head, hissing swirling, was sucked down the drain.

After a successful medical, an in-depth conversation with a Comsomol commission about self-discipline, an intricate analysis of my political ideology with a Party commission, daily lectures by the representative of the Ministry of Culture, and nightly rehearsals, I was ready to fulfil the ultimate requirement for a trip abroad – to become a married man.

My second marriage to Lena took place in Moscow's Wedding Palace, a town house built of grey stone, here and there painted green. Prior to the Revolution, this building served as a funeral parlour; now it was a Wedding Palace – concrete evidence of the positive influence of the Soviet Regime on Russian life.

In the large foyer, along the wall, sat dozens of brides in white, looking happy and satisfied. Beside them stood the grooms in black, shifting from one foot to another, looking lost. There was a long wait, since the ceremony for each couple took thirty minutes. The ceremony entails signing the registry; hearing a congratulatory speech by a female civil servant; sharing the requisite bottle of champagne (paid for in advance by the groom); and being entertained by three musicians – an accordionist, a violinist, and a drummer – playing Mendelssohn's Wedding March. Herein lay the problem – during the break between each ceremony, the musicians would polish off the bottles. With this, the music for each ceremony dragged and droned increasingly. Just before it was time for us to sign, the musicians broke into an argument over who was responsible for butchering the Wedding March. The fight grew heated and came to an end only when the drummer hit the accordion player over the head with a bottle of champagne. Nothing happened to the head, but the accordion got soaked, and the band had to be discharged for the day. We waited another twenty minutes until the civil servant got hold of a record player and a record of the same march. When everything was set up, she ushered us into the Wedding Hall. The walls of the hall were a dark oak. Across the parquet floor ran a red carpet which led to a high platform – most likely used previously to hold a coffin, but now it held a ledger. When we were about to sign our names on the graph paper, she asked, 'Where are your witnesses?'

'Nobody told us we had to bring witnesses,' I said to the woman.

'You're supposed to know that. When you make babies, you don't need any witnesses, but you need them when it's a legal proceeding.'

'What should we do?' Lena asked.

'Come back the next time with your witnesses.'

'When is the next time?' I asked.

'Let me check the book,' the woman replied. 'Ah-hah, we're all booked up. I can give you only one day next month, early in the morning.'

'It can't wait till next month,' I said.

'She doesn't look pregnant.'

'No, I can't wait,' I said.

'If you can't wait, then don't get married,' the woman said, turning away.

'I'm going to America in a few days,' I cried.

'Rubbish,' the civil servant said, turning back. 'Nobody would let you go to America at your age.'

'I'm going on tour with my theatre.'

'What about her?' the woman asked.

'I'm staying here,' Lena said.

'Ah, now it's clear. The wife is staying. Now I see. All right, since it's official business, I'll try to round up some witnesses. What a pity that the musicians have left already. If you have no objections, I'll call the cleaning man and woman.'

'Terrific,' I replied.

'Write your names here. I'll have them sign later.'

Lena took the pen.

'Are you going to take his name?' the woman asked.

'No,' Lena said.

'Do you have rings?'

'No,' I said.

'What kind of wedding is this? You don't have anything. There isn't even any champagne left. If you want to be reimbursed for the champagne, you'll have to send a letter to the Wedding Palace.'

'I don't need to be reimbursed.'

'Anyway, by the time you get it you'll probably be divorced,' the woman mumbled, setting the record at the wrong speed.

The march moaned slowly, but the woman didn't take notice because it sounded just like the rendition by the three musicians before their fight.

'Congratulations. Your marriage is now legal,' the woman said. 'I hope you'll be a happy Soviet family. If you wish to go to the Tomb of the Unknown Soldier or the Lenin Mausoleum, a limousine is waiting at the entrance. You pay separately.'

'Thank you,' I said. 'We're not planning on going to the graves.'

'Right, that'll be all. Sign here that you had champagne, and you'll be all set for America.'

We put our signatures on the document and left the palace. Just outside the door, on the front steps, Lena said, 'Defect. The moment you get abroad, defect. Don't worry about me, I'll find some way to get out. Maybe later, you'll send me an invitation.'

'They'll never let you go,' I said.

'Defect anyway. You can't miss a chance like this. Defect!' Lena said and smiled, but her eyes were as green as seawater.

'I'm not going to defect without you,' I said.

'You've got to . . . anyway, you don't really need me . . .'

'That's not true,' I said.

'I beg you, defect! I'll only be a burden to you.'

'Lena, you're just getting a little hysterical after that ridiculous wedding.'

'Maybe I'm hysterical, but at least I have feelings. You don't have any feelings. I looked at you there at *our wedding* and all I noticed on your face was that silly little smile of yours. You don't care about anything. With you, everything's okay. You're like an outside observer. You've got to run away; maybe that life will shake you up. Nothing can help me; I'm not sure things will be better for me there. My life is shot. I'm burned out. I'll just live like an old lady with Aunt Sonia.'

'Lena, I can't defect without you because I love you,' I said, trying to hug her.

'You don't love anyone,' she said, pushing my hands away, 'neither me nor your friends. They love you – Andrewlka because he's crazy; Stas because he's a queer and he can't bear to live without your blue eyes. But you're as different to them as you are to everything and everybody. Get out of my sight!'

'Lena, you're all wrong.'

'No, I'm not. I don't want to see you anymore,' she said, and ran down the steps.

'Where are you going?' I shouted after her.

'Don't bother trying to find me.'

I didn't see Lena for the two weeks before my trip abroad. She wasn't at her aunt's; she wasn't anywhere . . . Who said that death only comes once?

9 America? America!

Domodyedovo International Airport is a huge glass and nickel complex. It was designed to impress foreign tourists with its modern architecture and technology. There was even one accordion passageway leading to the departing planes but, of course, we actors didn't get to use it – we were led outside across the landing strip.

It was as if half of Moscow came to see us off. The crowd stood behind a chainlink fence separated from the airfield. They cheered and waved and bade us luck and a happy journey. They all had the same fiery gleam in their eyes, all with the same goal, hoping that this elaborate send-off would be a constant reminder that we were not going abroad to display our theatrical talents, but to bring back gifts and souvenirs for the thoughtful friends and relatives behind the fence. Yes, almost half of Moscow came, but not the half I needed, because Lena was not among them.

I won't try to tie my travels together into a smooth story, but will simply render my impressions like camera flashes, as they were imprinted in my memory's diary.

Our flight to India was twelve hours of nervous expectation. We arrived in New Delhi at 2 A.M. The first sight of the terminal when we disembarked was a cockroach the size of a rat, crawling to meet our delegation. As previously instructed, not one of us screamed, but a couple of actresses silently fainted, and Mikhail Mikhailovich jumped so high he almost landed back in Russia. Close behind the cockroach, two buses stood waiting to deliver us not to the hotel, to our surprise, but to the Russian Embassy in order to be briefed.

The huge Soviet Embassy stood like a fortress surrounded by

stone walls. It is rumoured that even if a bird flies over the embassy it is ordered to be shot down unless, of course, it's a Russian bird. In order to keep government security the people living on the grounds, such as secretaries, typists, electricians, plumbers, and a cleaning staff, all are imported from Russia and are all well-trained spies.

We arrived at the embassy at 4 A.M. and were escorted to an auditorium and seated in the first two rows. Lo and behold, on stage stood a huge bust of Lenin, to the left a table covered with a red cloth, to the right a podium bearing the hammer and sickle. It was as if we had never left Russia. The auditorium was still alive with anticipation, but nothing happened for about half an hour. Then Mikhail Mikhailovich stood and explained that because of our early arrival we would have to wait for the Ambassador another hour or two.

Due to our mental and physical exhaustion, we all fell asleep, one by one, like ducks on a pond. We were awakened by the sound of a cowbell and someone screaming at the top of his lungs, 'If I had known no one would wait up for me I never would have rushed here an hour before my normal work day.'

The rage of that voice filled the auditorium, as we greeted this fat, crumpled little man (the Ambassador) not with applause but with snores. Mikhail Mikhailovich stood up and immediately apologized for us all.

The Ambassador proceeded to brief us in the same scolding tone as his greeting, laying down the rules we were to follow for the duration of our stay in India. Never walk alone or leave our group for any reason, never drink water from the taps, never buy food from street vendors, never give anything to beggars, and, most important, speak to no one and never do anything without the approval of Mikhail Mikhailovich.

In order not to be tempted by the local surroundings, our three-dollar-a-day allowance was withdrawn. Instead, we were given one carton of American cigarettes per week, all our meals were paid for by the Indian government but, due to prohibition, there was no wine or any other alcoholic beverage.

The Ambassador continued, 'As you know, your group was invited on a cultural exchange, to celebrate the two thousandth anniversary of the *Ramayana*. The *Ramayana* is regarded as a sacred text by the Hindus, therefore I expect a perfect performance. If it's a failure, we will be desecrating their sacred text, bringing shame and disgrace upon ourselves, and perhaps even endangering political rapport between our two countries.'

He suddenly stopped and stared at us with a dark look. Then, scanning our faces, he slowly said, 'Whoever is acting the part of the Rama, please stand.'

As I stood, the Ambassador asked, 'How old are you?,' looking at me through doubting eyes.

'Twenty-six,' I replied hesitantly.

'No! It's impossible! What were you thinking of?' the Ambassador screamed at Mikhail Mikhailovich.

'What were you thinking of?' Mikhail Mikhailovich screamed, turning in the direction of Dudin.

'What are you talking about, comrades?' Dudin replied meekly.

'Your Rama is twenty-six years old. That's what I'm talking about!' said the Ambassador, flushed a deep red with anger. 'There's a law in India that says that Rama, a supreme being and national hero, cannot be portrayed by anyone older than seventeen. He'll be torn apart!'

'What can we do?' said Dudin. 'He's the youngest actor we have in our company. The next in age is a fifty-three-year-old actor portraying the King of Monkeys.'

'This is a catastrophe. Someone is trying to sabotage my position here,' moaned the Ambassador, with one hand on his heart and the other holding on to the podium. 'I knew from the start that this tour would be the end of my career. I will not accept any responsibility for this disaster, and I am not going to attend this evening's premiere performance . . .

'I suggest you run through the play as quickly as possible without an interval. If nothing bad happens, two buses will be waiting at the fire exit door for your escape. Good luck, comrades.'

'Can we go to the hotel?' asked Dudin. 'We haven't slept for twenty-four hours. The actors need some rest.'

'Who needs rest before death? Go directly to the theatre,' ordered the Ambassador.

As we left the auditorium the words of the Ambassador echoed in my brain. The thought occurred to me to defect on the way to the theatre, before the performance, but soon I realized my escape would be impossible. I was under constant guard, like a sacrificial lamb, watched by the electrician and plumber who were sent by the embassy to accompany us to the theatre.

As we approached the theatre we saw that it was extravagantly decorated with garlands of flowers. It frightened me because it reminded me of a funeral (my funeral). Surrounding the building were huge crowds of people. Intermingled in the thick of all that humanity were sacred cows. Those huge masses who came to gawk at their Russian guests made any evacuation of our troupe after the performance a pipe dream.

We organized and reorganized our positions on stage, checking and rechecking our entrances and exits. In our exhausted state, every movement of our bodies was a painful one.

When the time came to begin, there was a mad confusion backstage which only contributed to our nervousness. How we ever ended up wearing the correct costumes is still a mystery to me.

We started the play as a runner would start a hundred-metre dash: with tension and fear, which compressed our performance from three hours to one and a half without an intermission. For the poor audience, this tempo came as a complete surprise, and must have looked like a speeded-up film. There wasn't a cough, a sigh, a whisper, or a click of a trigger (which I was expecting).

We were in the middle of the second act when the King of the Monkeys forgot his lines, and from fear he recited Lenin's monologue at the railway station. At this point we were all soaked with perspiration, our eyes fixed on stage trying not to meet the stares of our audience.

We crossed the finish line of our play and, without changing, continued our run off stage through the darkened halls towards the back exit to the waiting buses. Pushing my way through stagehands, leaping and jumping over wires, cables, and lighting fixtures, I somehow managed to get ahead of my fellow actors. Turning down another corridor, which I hoped was the last, I flew by the watchful eyes of the KGB plumber and electrician and reached the exit in what I thought must have been record time. But near the door I froze with fear, realizing I was alone. What had happened to my fellow actors? I had turned in search of my group when, suddenly I was hit with an incredible force that took me crashing through the door. The King of Monkeys crashed into me, hurled me through the fire exit, and landed on top of me. His weight was like a slab of lead pinning me to the ground.

Dazed by the impact, I kept blinking in disbelief as I found myself in the middle of the street. And to my shock and horror, the buses were nowhere in sight. Instead, the streets were filled with thousands of people all shouting something in unison, like an army of enemy soldiers.

The next moment I was pulled by the crowd from under the King of Monkeys, and, in a flash, there was something around my neck. I grabbed for it, expecting the roughness of a rope, but instead my fingers surrounded the tenderness of flowers.

I was suddenly hoisted up in the air and carried away by the elated crowd. They started a caravan towards our hotel singing and chanting 'Ramachandra, Ramachandra'. I couldn't understand at first what had changed their minds about killing me, but the answer was simple: I was the first foreigner to play the part of the Rama and, thank God, the age-limit did not apply to non-Indians. The crowd reached the hotel steps and there I was proclaimed a living god.

The key to the success of our performance was, without a doubt, *not* my acting of Rama but the condensed version of *Ramayana*. Indian actors usually mimed the *Ramayana*, telling the story with gestures that can take as long as three days to perform. Our version was a cultural shock to the Indian audience, but newspaper headlines were all in favour of it. They said if Indian actors learned the Russian version of the *Ramayana* it would not only open the doors to new theatre, but also help save time and enrich the country's economy. They said that the Russian acting school was superb; that for real art there is no language barrier; that the audience understood almost every word and was moved to tears by the monologue of the King of Monkeys . . .

The day after our premiere performance, the Soviet Ambassador reappeared, and from that day forward, he never left our side. In every new city the Ambassador stood pompously on stage and talked about friendship among nations, and the bond between India and the USSR, always getting lost in his own self-importance, and always forgetting to introduce us.

As we travelled from city to city, our audience grew larger and larger; tickets were sold out days in advance. But of course we didn't profit from that success. All the money we made was taken in by the Soviet Embassy. That's when we realized the importance of the American cigarettes as our currency. It was all we had.

We could trade these cigarettes for almost anything; one pack of Camels could be traded for a bronze antique scorpion, one and a half packs for a leather whip, two packs of Winstons for three pornographic postcards, and for one carton of Marlboros, a little milky emerald.

We were nearing the end of our tour of India, and what could I say about that country? In the north of India the men are tall and beautiful and the women are not, in the south of India the women are tall and beautiful and the men are not, and everywhere we were met with smiles. It seemed that hungry Indians smiled more than Muscovites waiting to buy bananas.

What else? The blaze of the Penjur Gardens at sunset was magnificent and its night air was thick and black and warm like the Black Sea.

What else? I was convinced that I had been wrong about the Taj Mahal. There is nothing in this world more beautiful than this monument to love and death. We all fell in love with that country. A country of dreams, fairy tales, and mysteries.

Departure day came much too quickly. In the few weeks we spent there we only saw a fraction of this great country, only skimmed over its beauty and its great culture. Even though our tour was a success, we weren't completely satisfied. One of our biggest disappointments was that we heard so much about yoga, which is practised by the Hindu culture, but we never had the pleasure of experiencing or even seeing it.

We boarded our buses in silence and sadness. 'Good-bye, India, we'll never see you again,' was written on all the actors' faces. But not mine. I had another thought.

En route to the airport we crossed a flat valley which was disturbed only by a couple of elephants which we left behind in a cloud of red dust. Watching the billows of dust swallow everything behind us put us all in a state of calm serenity, which was disturbed by the sudden movements of Mikhail Mikhailovich. He stood up and started shouting with incredible enthusiasm, '*Stop the bus, stop the bus*. Look, a Yogi! A Yogi in nirvana!'

We ran out of the bus to the left side of the road in order to get a better view. There was a group of half-naked Indians crouched in the gutter. Once we calmed down from all the excitement, we realized they were naked from the waist down and not exercising yoga, but defecating. The group of Indians, pleased with our attention, all smiled and waved, never disturbing their concentration on the business at hand.

'Come on. Come on,' shouted Mikhail Mikhailovich with embarrassment, herding us back on the bus.

We arrived at the airport and drove to the designated terminal. The bus drivers, already knowing we had no money and were out of American cigarettes, refused to unload our luggage. So we had no choice but to wait for airport porters. I took this opportunity to evaluate the situation. In the shadow of the first bus was Dudin with half the group. Near the second bus with the rest of the actors was Mikhail Mikhailovich, fully recovered from his embarrassment. With mistrust in his eyes he organized the removal of our luggage. There was no way of passing either in front of the first bus or behind the second bus without attracting someone's attention, but between the dark shadows of the buses I saw a glimmer of light which signified a space for my escape.

Pretending not to know which bus my luggage was on, I wandered in the direction of the first bus. Halfway there I stopped and looked around. Mikhail Mikhailovich was busy, trying to keep order among the actors. They were scrambling around in a mass of confusion, fearful of losing their souvenirs. No one seemed to notice me. If there was ever a right moment, I thought, this was it. There was no reason to wait any longer.

My heart began to pound with such force it felt as though my chest would burst with each beat. My hands were shaking, my legs were weak . . . I sighed and made my first step towards the sunlight between the buses.

Suddenly the light was covered by a shadow.

My passage to freedom was blocked by a boy about thirteen years of age in a turban and torn robe. In one hand he held a basket, in the other a flute. He quickly sat, crossing his legs, carefully placing the basket in front of him, and brought the flute to his lips.

I didn't know what to do.

A whining melody floated from the flute and in the same rhythm from the basket appeared a huge cobra keeping in time with the music. The swaying snake stood in my way. I had to get past it . . . but then I felt someone tugging at my sleeve. I almost fell from weakness when I heard the piercing voice of Mikhail Mikhailovich demand, 'What the hell are you doing just standing there? It's as though you'd never seen a damned snake charmer. The entire group can't wait for you forever, you know.'

'Okay, okay, I'm sorry, I'm sorry,' I said, and started towards the boarding gate, Mikhail Mikhailovich in close pursuit.

I lost my chance to defect in India. But to be honest it wasn't such a great disappointment. India wasn't the place where I wanted to live, even though for an entire month I was a living god there. I would not want to stay in a country with prohibition. I didn't want to experience for the rest of my life the kind of yoga I saw on the route to the airport. I'd defect in America.

As a 'reward' for our great success in India, we were sent towards America on the cheapest economy flight, which took us through Ceylon, Hong Kong, Tokyo, Toronto, to Montreal, where we were to spend one night and then continue our trip to the U.S.A. by bus.

To make our endless flight to Montreal more comfortable, Mikhail Mikhailovich reiterated again and again the rules and regulations for Soviets abroad. He was certain that review of these rules would prevent all unforeseen problems through our North American tour. But life always brings human problems, which our inhuman attaché didn't seem to understand, and unbeknownst to him, they awaited us right at Canadian customs.

To cut our personal expenses in America, many of us brought food which we saved from Indian restaurants where we had eaten for free. We had bags full of coconuts, bananas, curried chicken and shrimp. Unfortunately, though, U.S. and Canadian law did not allow anyone to bring food across their borders. There was nothing we could do. We had to give up the food which we hoped would help us save those precious three dollars a day. The only exception was the dried, pressed, concentrated pea soup which we had brought from Moscow and never used in India. It was in the shape of large green bricks, only harder. Not one customs official accepted that this was a form of food in Russia.

Another problem came with the spiral water heaters we had each brought for boiling the soup. During a half-hour discussion, we explained to the customs officials that it wasn't any kind of weapon, that Soviet actors, for cooking purposes, always travel with a small pot and large electric spiral. Finally, we were allowed to take the heaters with us.

After customs, we were driven to a charming little hotel in downtown Montreal. To avoid any sexual activity, we were given two separate floors, one for women and one for men. It wasn't necessary. We didn't want sex; we were too tired and too hungry. We were enraged at the memory of having our food taken away from us at the airport, but we wouldn't dare buy food or go to a restaurant to spend money that was meant for blue jeans and pantyhose for family members and friends waiting back in Russia. So, instead of a restaurant, all the actors went to their rooms, locked the doors, and began to cook their pea soup at the same time.

The procedure for cooking hard, bricklike concentrate is a very tricky business. First, before boiling it, you have to crush it with something heavy like a hammer. But how are you supposed to find a hammer in a little hotel where you couldn't even find a sickle? In such a situation, Russians use ingenuity. Without hesitation, we started throwing the blocks of pea soup against walls, sinks, bathtubs, floors and doors, sometimes chipping a piece of concentrate, sometimes a part of the room. We were hungry and couldn't care less that a great thumping noise came from our floors.

The noise suddenly stopped when, simultaneously, all forty of us placed pieces of concentrate into our pots and started to cook our dinner. This practice required a lot of coordination – with one hand you have to dip the spiral water heater into the liquid, and with the other you stir the chunky lumps into smooth soup. This process was very delicate in sound, but not in scent. The smoke and stench began to seep out through the cracks in our doors and then everything went black! This small hotel, with its limited power system, was not able to handle forty spiral water heaters all at one time.

I don't know what the manager of the hotel thought about his Russian guests' activities, but in a state of panic he called the fire department and the police for safety's sake.

In the blackness of our rooms, we continued our cooking until we realized the spiral water heaters were no longer operating. But we weren't discouraged, we had just started a search for another source of electricity when the dark silence was pierced by the sound of sirens and the screech of tyres. The next moment there were footsteps pounding up the stairs, coming from all directions, and someone began to open our doors. Automatically, we followed men in uniform and filed out of our rooms into the corridor. Only one door on our floor still remained closed. With great force the fireman and policeman broke in that door and raced into the room. At the end of their flashlight beams, in the smoke-filled bathroom, was the King of Monkeys huddled with a spiral heater the size of a yardstick in one hand and a spoon in the other, stirring a green lumpy liquid in the toilet bowl!

The police immediately took charge, handcuffed him, confiscated the sabotage weapon, and dragged him out into the corridor. They were ready to take the King of Monkeys to the police station when Mikhail Mikhailovich burst onto the scene, demanding an explanation for the outrage. The police described the entire situation in great detail. Mikhail Mikhailovich, shocked by their explanation, ran into the bathroom to see it for himself. When he came out, the veins in his neck were swollen to three times their size as he screamed at the King of Monkeys: 'What in hell were you doing in the toilet bowl?'

'Cooking soup,' came the shy reply.

'Are you crazy? In the toilet bowl?'

'I washed it very carefully first,' whispered the King of Monkeys.

'Where in the world is your pot?'

'I forgot it in Russia.'

'Why didn't you use the sink like I did, you idiot?'

'I couldn't. I was soaking my socks in the sink,' replied the King of Monkeys, now embarrassed to tears. Mikhail Mikhailovich translated every word to the police, hoping to gain their understanding. A silence came over the corridor. The policemen looked at each other, then without another word they quietly removed the handcuffs from the wrists of the King of Monkeys and left the hotel in a mournful procession.

Early the next morning, Mikhail Mikhailovich called a meeting. He was terrified of the possibility of press action against us. He informed us that we would be leaving Montreal immediately.

We took our seats on the bus, which drove us down the avenue of St Katherine. This avenue was filled with big and little stores. We stared longingly into their windows, even though there was no hope of owning anything that these beautiful shops had to offer. At least we would always have the memory.

The quality of merchandise was the best I had ever seen. But there were no queues. At first I thought the stores were closed due to the early hour, *but no . . . there just weren't any queues.*

If only Boris could see the architecture of this city. Its combination of the new and the old was in full balance because of its great beauty and quality.

What else is there to say?

Cars stop to give pedestrians the right of way and don't even blow their horns impatiently – it was unbelievable, but I saw it with my own eyes.

Never in my life have I seen so many young, beautiful people as in Montreal. They looked relaxed and happy, and that was reflected in their colourful clothing. Not like our black, angry, tired Muscovites.

What else is there to say about Canada?

The morning air of Montreal was crystalline, cool, and fresh, like all of that young country. I didn't have an opportunity to defect there, but I accepted this as a sign of fate. Anyway, to me Canada was only the green lawn in front of the mysterious house of the United States of America. I desperately wanted to visit that house, to look inside and maybe even live there.

On the way from Montreal to New York State we weren't aware of the border between Canada and the U.S.A. No one checked our documents, we weren't searched, questioned, or detained for even a moment. Only when we saw not *one* car in front of each house, but *three*, did we know we were in America. It was difficult to believe. Who would have thought that it was so very simple to enter into another country and that country being the United States of America.

Contrary to our belief, which was that the United States was filled only with skyscrapers, metal bridges, concrete roads, and rubbish tips, this road took us through the most beautiful raw, natural wilderness – a beauty comparable with a Russian forest, but enhanced by a richer assortment of pine, birch, oak, and all the trees we thought only grew in Russian soil.

'Look! It's exactly like Russia.'

'Over there! It's like our native land,' remarked one actor after the other in amazement, no longer sleepy or tired. They were alert and excited. Their tone also insinuated, how dare the tricky Americans copy the wild Russian beauty of nature.

We had only five performances scheduled for the United States and all of them in Saratoga. Saratoga is a well-groomed resort about two hundred miles from New York City. Some of its riches are mineral water, horse racing, and an open-air theatre.

The theatre was the most extravagant I had ever seen. It was built on the side of a hill with a stream and waterfall just behind the stage. The decorative roof was the shape of an open fan, which covered five thousand seats. For very large rock 'n' roll concerts the open side of the hill could accommodate another fifty to sixty thousand people. But we were not the Rolling Stones. We couldn't possibly hope to fill even half of this grand space. We were nervous, very nervous. Never had we performed in such a huge auditorium. Who would come to see *Sleeping Beauty and the Seven Worriers*? Even though it was a Russian version of 'Snow

White' and Americans didn't need a translation, we were sure we would play to an empty house.

Our professional nervousness was nothing compared with the representative of the Ministry's. Just moments before our performance, Mikhail Mikhailovich carried on like a madman, referring to the noise of the waterfall as some sort of sabotage, built behind the stage especially to humiliate us during our production by drowning out our dialogue. He was pacing up and down the stage screaming uncontrollably when a well-dressed man tapped him on the shoulder and asked in broken Russian, 'What's the problem?' Mikhail Mikhailovich explained, referring to the waterfall as an annoyance which would destroy our Soviet production. The gentleman smiled a bright white smile; he was conservative in appearance but under dark-rimmed glasses his eyes were soft and tender.

'Oh! Don't worry about the waterfall. This is America, just relax, it's automatic,' he said, and, with an elegant sweeping gesture of his hand, he pushed a hidden button which stopped the running water. Then he introduced himself to Mikhail Mikhailovich: 'I'm the director of this Art Center. Let me take the opportunity to welcome you. I'm a great admirer of Russian art and I have also studied your language.' Then before walking off stage he said, 'Oh, by the way . . . we're completely sold out, the theatre is filled to capacity. Congratulations! You can start whenever you're ready.'

Our show was constantly being interrupted by whistles coming from the audience, but we couldn't understand what we were doing wrong. In Russia, whistles are like throwing rotten fruit at the artists. When the finale came and the entire audience whistled simultaneously, we were in a state of panic. Now the waterfall would have been a welcome sound, but even Niagara Falls couldn't drown the whistles of so many thousands.

The director of the theatre reappeared backstage after our performance with his smile intact until he saw the mask of tragedy written on our faces. 'What's the problem?' he asked.

Mikhail Mikhailovich responded: 'It's the whistles . . . in Russia they mean complete failure.'

'Don't worry,' the director said, flashing a new smile. 'Here it means success, complete success. Your worries are over; this is America, enjoy yourselves.'

And oh, how we enjoyed ourselves at the end of the week at the banquet given in our honour after our last performance! We were so very proud that we had won over an American audience. We walked on air at our celebration, which took place in a most elaborate restaurant with its own fountain in the centre of the floor, framed by colourful flashing lights. The room was filled with hundreds of people, including the press, who never let their cameras rest. They followed our every move. The buffet table was overflowing with the most exotic assortment of food I had ever seen. It was all so perfect that it looked like plastic made to look real; the glasses and silver looked real, but they were just plastic.

We toasted each other, a lasting friendship between countries and a united flight to planet Mars. Why was it that from childhood we were taught to think of Americans as the enemy? All our lives we were told that Americans are the aggressors who think only how to kill us Russians, and here we were laughing together, drinking together, wishing each other well. They seemed so honest, so genuine; they truly seemed to want to be our friends. We were having a wonderful time – they showed us how to carve ham and turkey; we showed them how to drink champagne, vodka, whiskey, and cognac all at the same time.

We acted like kings, with little fingers extended and our heads held at a proper distance above our plates. Our table manners were impeccable, everything was going smoothly. Not one of us had got drunk enough to fall asleep on the floor or been sick in the fountain.

Our host was very pleased to see that we enjoyed our food. All the food. Confusion came over his face only when he realized that, not just all the food had disappeared, but all the paper plates, the plastic glasses, knives, and forks. There was no rubbish after the party and there was no way he could have imagined that these Soviet actors had taken all of it with them and for many years to come they would be eating off those American dishes to impress their relatives and friends.

The atmosphere of this evening grew more and more friendly.

A young man at the far end of the room started playing a guitar and soon there was a group of people around him singing and clapping hands to the music. The songs they sang were sweet to my ear. Though I didn't understand the words, the language of music is the same everywhere. They sang several songs, all beautiful and all in full harmony.

After the third or fourth song, Mikhail Mikhailovich nervously came over to a group of us and with a jerk asked if anyone knew how to play the guitar. Obviously annoyed by the American display of talent, he was positive they were trying to provoke us by showing us how well their amateurs could sing. Again he asked, 'Who can play?' All eyes turned in my direction. 'Go and sing,' Mikhail Mikhailovich said, '. . . that is an order.' I sheepishly walked towards the group of singing Americans.

I stood in front of the young guitarist and spoke in an international language, a smile and a point of a finger. The young American smiled back at me and without any hesitation handed me the guitar. I stood staring at it for a while. Never had I seen a guitar with twelve strings, let alone played one. I plucked a few chords, testing the sound; it was as rich as a complete orchestra. I looked up to see Mikhail Mikhailovich staring back at me with arms folded and a demanding look in his eyes. I had no time to learn all the chords, so I used only the ones I knew. When I finished my song, whistles and applause filled the room. Mikhail Mikhailovich rushed towards me with the theatre director in tow in congratulatory excitement.

'Great!' said the director as he patted my shoulder. 'I would like to set up a concert for you here in Saratoga, how much do you make in salary?'

'Seventy-five rubles,' I replied.

'A day?' he asked.

I was confused.

'It doesn't matter,' he replied. 'A two-month tour, how would you like that?'

'He can't do it,' answered Mikhail Mikhailovich, stuttering as he tried to compose the next line. 'He . . . he . . . has to . . . sing in . . . Moscow at the . . . the Comsomol Conference.'

236

'All right then, another time. Here's my card. Call me on your next visit.'

Next visit?!

He had no idea that for a Russian this was one chance in a lifetime. There was no possibility for a next visit, I thought as I watched him turn to address my comrades. He was tall and lean, his greying temples gave him a distinguished and intellectual look, and his smile was sincere as he spoke to his guests: 'If any of you would like to refresh yourselves, I invite you for a swim.'

'Where?' some of the actors asked mistrustfully.

'Right here,' he said, pointing to the fountain in the floor.

Everyone laughed, thinking it was a joke. But he then pressed another button and the fountain sprays vanished beneath the water. The colourful lights rose up into the ceiling and before our eyes the fountain was transformed into a swimming pool. It was unbelievable. We were awed by the mystery of this change. Still distrustful, we looked at each other and then at the transformed pool and then at Mikhail Mikhailovich, his white eyelashes fluttering in a violent rhythm.

'Don't be shy,' said the director. 'There are swimsuits waiting for you in the lavatories. You may keep them after your swim as a memento of the Saratoga Art Center; enjoy yourselves.'

Hospitality or provocation? was the question on our faces. The silence was broken by the voice of our forty-five-year-old Snow White, when she asked, 'Where's my suit?'

The director pointed to a door with the letter L. Snow White zigzagged toward the door and, within seconds, reappeared wearing a white, very tight-fitting nylon suit which hugged every inch of her chubby body and exposed her three-tiered waist.

Mikhail Mikhailovich made a move towards her in an attempt at preventing . . . But it was too late. Our Russian Snow White took a pelican dive into the pool. The flashbulbs from our photographers' cameras were blinding as they snapped a shot of her strokes – which were more like small tidal waves. Holding our breath, we all watched the foamy bubbles in between her large thighs, waiting for our silent question to be answered: will it turn black, or not – yes . . . or . . . no?

If there were any chemicals in the water, they weren't working;

237

the only discoloration floating on top, other than our pelican, was her stage make-up. Now knowing the water was safe, all the actors parted and ran in the direction of the doors marked with the letter *M* or *L* and returned with the most colourful bathing suits, almost as colourful as the oversized bodies in them. As one, all forty of us jumped into the pool but, unfortunately, as we jumped in, all the water jumped out. It flowed over the rug, in between the tables and chairs, and continued its way through the entire restaurant. The photographers seemed very happy about the flood; they took photographs of everything and everyone; the director also seemed pleased as he stood laughing hysterically. In fact, we all laughed.

The only one who didn't seem pleased or happy about this situation was Mikhail Mikhailovich. 'Provocation,' he screamed with a rage that made his pink eyes bulge.

'You'll pay for this. You did it especially to spoil our success!' he said, shaking his finger at the director. 'Out of the water, comrades, give back the swimsuits, we're going back to the hotel!'

The next morning, silence was our only companion. We still felt the vibrations, not of the bus, but of the night before. The four-hour trip to New York City was unbearable in this cold tomb of silence. Only when we saw the outline of Manhattan from the approach to the George Washington Bridge did our blood flow again and fill our bodies with warmth. Mikhail Mikhailovich used the highest point of this bridge as his podium, as he stood up to announce that virtually all of our New York City sightseeing trip was being cancelled because he felt we could no longer be trusted. He ignored the crushed look on our faces and continued to outline the day ahead, which consisted of just a three-and-a-half hour stay in Manhattan. All that time would be spent at the Metropolitan Museum, then Kennedy Airport and back to Russia.

The bus stopped in front of a grand building with a staircase that looked as if it led to heaven. There was a festival of sunshine, colour, joy, love, music, and art on the faces of the young and old people who filled the steps of the museum. We, however, were like a dark gloom passing through happiness, as we climbed up to the entrance and made our way into the lobby.

Once inside, we understood why Mikhail Mikhailovich had chosen the Metropolitan Museum. There was no admission charge, only a donation request. Mikhail Mikhailovich dug into his pocket and came out with three dollars and twelve cents, which he handed to the admission clerk. In return, he asked for forty buttons. The buttons were purple with a white 'MMA' imprinted in the centre; these buttons guaranteed our passage throughout the museum. And now Mikhail Mikhailovich arranged us in a circle to be sure that he had our undivided attention as he set down more rules and regulations to be followed. He started by saying, 'You have permission to view any exhibit you want, of course with the exception of abstract art. You are not permitted to speak with foreigners. At five o'clock you are all to meet at the bottom of the museum steps. For every minute you are late, not you, but your families back in Russia will be punished, the later you are, the greater the punishment. Am I clearly understood?'

Never seeing our heads nodding in acknowledgement, Mikhail Mikhailovich disappeared into the distance of the museum. His warning still ringing in our ears, we walked through several rooms in a trance, looking and yet not seeing. Snow White shook us out of our hypnotic state when she voiced her desire to see impressionist art. Several of my comrades joined in with the excitement of her suggestion. Another part of the group expressed a desire to see Egyptian mummies. I stood back and watched as they divided themselves into two groups parting in opposite directions. One half went to the right, the other to the left, I went straight ahead. I found myself in a room with El Grecos. I was drawn to a small painting entitled 'View of Toledo.' This painting was woven with shadows, light, and nervous expectation. The Spanish city crouched under a stormy sky, but to me it was just like Tula and a last look at Russia. 'Good-bye,' I whispered. 'Good-bye . . .'

I moved towards the arched doorway, but then a strange feeling came over me. I stepped back in the corner, but the walls did not give me a feeling of security. I stood for a while trying to regain a strength I wasn't certain I had. I felt as if someone was staring right through me. I looked around and saw a group of students, but they were more interested in the paintings than in me. I let my eyes search the room slowly and then I saw him there, right in front of me. My body was taken over by his overpowering stare. It made me feel as if I was in a lift, my head going up, my legs going down, and my stomach being sucked out by a vacuum. If I stayed here under his spell any longer I would surely lose my will to defect. Hanging on the wall across from me was the portrait of the Grand Inquisitor, draped in red, staring through round-rimmed glasses. It was time to run before fear overpowered me.

I was watching the group of students walking towards me, when I heard a voice say, 'Where is the room of Socialist Realism?' It was the voice of Mikhail Mikhailovich. I didn't dare turn in its direction. I joined the group of students as they passed me and followed them out of the room and into another. I had no idea who the artists were or what the art was like or in which direction we were going. My only concern was not to be caught by any of my comrades. Again we entered another room. I had no way of knowing how long this group intended to stay. I thought maybe I should break away and go on my own, but decided to stay with them just a little longer. We walked through another room and then to my relief we were crossing the lobby. This was it! My opportunity. I made my way to the door.

Once I was outside, all my fear left, a relief came over me and then a calm. I lifted my face up towards the sun, closed my eyes, and breathed in freedom. I felt rejuvenated, I felt new, I felt free. I walked down the steps through the maze of people, jugglers, singers, dancers; they all seemed to be rehearsing for something, there was even a young man performing pantomime. Oh! what a world, a new world, and all of it on the steps of a museum. As I walked carefully in between the bodies that seemed to make these steps their home, they seemed to say to me, 'Come . . . join us . . . be happy.' I made my way down the steps and onto the pavement.

I stood on the pavement for a while, not knowing in which direction to go, turning occasionally to see if anyone was looking for me. I had stepped closer to the kerb, thinking maybe I should cross the street, when a bus pulled up just in front of me. Its centre doors opened and several people walked off. I instinctively held open the doors and climbed on. The bus was filled with very respectable-looking people. I didn't think I looked very much different than they did, but as I sat down I felt them scrutinize me. I realized no one had asked me to buy a ticket or pay my fare when I boarded the bus. Only at the next stop did I see that in America, people board the bus by the front door and pay the driver. In Russia, it's the opposite. Everything in this world doesn't go according to Soviet rules, I thought, as I looked back at the passengers' inquisitive stares.

As the bus moved down Fifth Avenue, it felt as if we were moving between two pages of a giant book of fairy tales. One page of this book was green with trees, grass, flowers, rocks, cliffs, and pathways that could take you and your imagination to your life's dream. The other page of the book was white, a solid wall of beautiful, immaculately clean buildings, each with its own uniformed guard at the entrance. What or who were they guarding? What kind of people lived in these buildings? Who were they? What did they do? They couldn't be just ordinary people. Nine hundred and thirty-five, nine hundred and twenty, eight hundred and seventy, these numbers passed me like pages in a book. My mind reeled, trying to picture the residents of these glorious buildings. The bus stopped to pick up a few passengers across from eight hundred and thirty-four. I watched as the guard ran to a white Rolls-Royce. He stopped and stood like a soldier beside it, then bent down and opened the door for a lady. She was tall, young, and very beautiful. She stepped out of the car like a gentle breeze and floated to the entrance door, which was opened by another uniformed man, and disappeared into the lobby. Now I knew what kind of people lived there.

Contrary to the fast movement of the bus the people in the streets moved slowly. What day is this? I wondered. The tour made one day melt into the other. With a little calculation, I worked out that it was Sunday, which explained the traffic-free avenue and the slow pace of the people. I pressed my nose against the window and watched the smiling faces, but my face wasn't smiling. I wasn't one of the heroes in this book, I was just a reader, who couldn't even understand the full meaning of the words.

The park stopped at a street sign which read Fifty-ninth Street.

The avenue seemed to become wider as it turned into a chain of stores which lined both sides of the street. The windows were filled with everything imaginable and on a much greater scale than in Canada. I hadn't thought that was possible. Everything was here . . . right here . . . on one avenue. Linen, clothing, shoes, rugs, china, crystal, silver, gold, perfume, cameras, tape recorders. The black marketeers of Russia would be blinded by the quantity and availability of all this merchandise. The greatest Russian dreamers could never hope even to create dreams of such things. All of this was much more than their imagination could handle – and you could actually buy these things! In Russia the stores sometimes display very nice imported merchandise, but it's only for show. To impress the tourists. The things displayed can't be bought because they don't exist.

I was mesmerized by the continuation of this endless avenue. I could almost see its length as it narrowed to a pinpoint. And still more and more stores, except that these stores were smaller and not as sophisticated. The windows were not as neatly displayed and there were red signs posted on the windows of these stores which read, SALE, SALE, SALE. I didn't understand the meaning of this word, but it must have been important, it was repeated as often as Lenin's quotations on the streets of Moscow.

I finally tore myself from the bus window and the drastically changing city. I had been so engrossed in the changes taking place outside that I never noticed the transformation inside. I was taken aback by the appearance of the remaining passengers. They were no longer the same well-dressed people as when I boarded this bus. These people were tired, their faces filled with pain and empty of hope. These were not the same optimistic faces I had seen on the steps of the museum.

Just as I turned back to the window the bus stopped. All the passengers stood up and started leaving by the centre doors. I looked to the front of the bus and saw that the bus driver had also gone. I didn't have a choice, this was it, the bus wasn't going any further. I hesitantly stood up and walked toward the exit, my hands trembling as I held open the doors and thought, This . . . is . . . the . . . last . . . stop.

I got off the bus and walked blindly for many blocks, sometimes turning left, sometimes right.

There was an eerie silence around me. I found myself in another world. A dirty, silent, ugly, gloomy world. It looked exactly like the America depicted in Soviet films. There was rubbish all around me, newspapers flying in the wind, broken bottles under my feet. The decaying buildings in this world of grey gloom were like tortured spirits. Even the sun hid from these decaying skeletons.

The people in this world were also grey and gloomy. They walked unsure of their steps, with cracked, painted smiles that showed a rotting from within. But these smiles were somehow familiar to me. The more faces I saw, the more I understood the familiarity; these were the same smiles as the Moscow dissidents'. Just as in Moscow, the alcoholics here also had to hide their bottles, except here they used brown paper bags. In Russia they used the pockets of their coats, because in Russia a brown paper bag is more difficult to get than a bottle of vodka.

The familiar feeling of knowing this part of the world stayed with me as I walked through it in search of a street sign. As I reached the corner I saw it hanging from a metal pole. It wouldn't have surprised me if it had read Arbat.

B-O-W-E-R-Y. I read it letter by letter. Bowery. It was called by another name, but New York also had its Arbat. My shoulders slumped as I turned the corner and, putting one foot in front of the other, began to count each step. I had walked for many blocks when I realized I had already counted nine hundred and forty-two steps. It was time to stop counting. I had to find a police station, announce my defection, and ask for political asylum. Then I thought, once I found it, how would I ask for asylum? The only other language I was familiar with was German, which I had studied in high school. The only word I knew in English was SALE, which I learned while riding down Fifth Avenue. Again I saw this word when I passed a stand with someone selling blue jeans, but what did it mean? Maybe 'attention,' I thought.

People walked by me as if I didn't exist. I wanted to stop them and ask for help, only I didn't know how . . . but then I didn't really try. I was afraid; this feeling of fear held me from all sides. It was the same fear, lost loneliness, and sadness that I had felt when I looked for the garden at the Garden Circle. Again I was like a helpless baby, again I was completely alone.

A sad melody filled the air around me. I turned around almost in a complete circle in search of the sound. And there he was leaning against a mesh fence, a tall, thin, bearded black man, thoughtfully engrossed in playing a saxophone. His music lured me closer and closer till I stood just in front of him. His clothing was tattered and dirty, on the ground next to him was the instrument case, which was shredded and torn with a few silver coins scattered inside it.

Across from him was a young girl standing inside a telephone booth, she wasn't talking on the telephone, just standing there. She was wearing very short shorts, I can't use enough *verys* to describe how very, very tight they were, and so deeply cut into her body and in between her legs that it was almost painful to look at.

Next to the musician, on the steps of an abandoned building, was a man dressed in a black winter coat. This seemed odd since the weather was very warm. He sat biting his nails; it looked as if nothing could or would distract him. He moved from one finger to the other in deep concentration.

I looked thoughtfully at the musician, then the girl in the telephone booth, and then the nail-biting maniac. Which one should I ask for help? The musician was obviously too involved in his music. The girl must have felt my silent plea for help; she took a step towards me and smiled. Her dark painted eyes so openly and clearly expressed how she wanted to help me that, without hesitation, I turned to the nail-biter in the black coat.

'*Ya Ruski*,' I said to him, '*pierebezchik*.' Never reacting to my words, he just sat there and kept biting his nails. I had to use some ingenuity here, so I pulled on his sleeve. Again no reaction. Then I thought I would try some German, so again I pulled on his sleeve and, pounding on my chest, screamed, '*Polizei! Polizei!*' Ah, finally I had his attention, I thought, when he stopped biting his nails. So I repeated, '*Polizei! Polizei!*' Suddenly he jumped up and out of his coat and ran down the street. I was shocked to see he was completely naked. I just stood with his coat in my hand watching as he leaped over the fence. I wanted to stop him but I didn't know what to say. That's when the only English word I knew came to me. 'Sale!' I screamed after him, but he vanished behind a row of buildings.

I stood for a while, puzzled at what I might have said to upset him so, then I turned to the telephone booth. The girl was gone. She was nowhere in sight, vanished with the wind. It was as though she had never been there.

'Now what?' I pondered the question that a paralyzed Lenin posed when he lost his bedpan.

The black musician, still untouched by the moving world around him, continued his own painful outcry through his saxophone. His music was filling me with an exquisite sadness. It flowed so easily, so smoothly, so naturally, that it seemed an extension of his being. He was incredibly talented; the best jazz musicians in Russia could never dream of reaching his professional level. What was strange, though, was that I noticed his saxophone case still had the same coins scattered in it; not one coin was added. That's when I realized, not only in my walk this day, but during my entire American tour, not once did I find money lying in the street. There were a lot of things on the pavements and in the gutters, but never the shimmer of a coin. It looked to me that in America it was difficult to find money easily. I shivered. It wasn't that I was afraid of struggling all over again; I believed that I could come through the hardest of times and win. But to fight for a new beginning alone and only for myself was a terrible thought. I didn't know if I could stand the loneliness. But even if this new beginning could be easy and lucky for me, I didn't want it alone. I wanted to share my happiness with someone . . . someone special, someone I loved. I couldn't leave Lena in that jail on the other side of the earth and be happy. But what could I do? She had insisted that once I was abroad I should stay there and not come back. Isn't it crazy to wait so many years for the right moment and then not take advantage of it? But again, there is no right moment without the one you love. To lose one's native land is frightening, but to lose your land and your love is like death itself. Was this sudden weakness of mine fear or love?

I felt as if I was truly going out of my mind until an idea came to me. Many years ago, when I was trying to decide if I should go to Moscow to study, I let the ace of clubs decide my fate. Once again I placed my fate on a card. I pulled out the business card given me by the director of the Saratoga Art Centre. Looking at it was confusing; the only part of it I could read was the telephone number, but I clenched my jaw and bravely walked to the telephone booth.

I took out several coins from my pocket and examined them carefully. They all had a Liberty sign, but they all were different in size. Some looked too small, some too large, and, to my surprise, they didn't have any numbers on them, only pictures. I chose the one with the embossed relief on the eagle. It seemed to be right and it fitted into the slot of the telephone perfectly. So I let it drop in and then dialled the number. The telephone rang several times and then I heard a woman's voice, which surprised me. I suppose I expected the director himself to answer the telephone. The woman on the other end was saying something that I didn't understand. She kept repeating it over and over, but I just couldn't respond. I didn't know what to say or how to say it. Feeling helpless and lost, I tried and tried to speak, but nothing came out – my voice box was severed by a language barrier.

Tears ran down my cheeks. The card had decided my fate. I put back the receiver and stepped out of the telephone booth feeling weak and defeated. Still holding the odd-sized coins in the palm of my hand, I went over to the musician and threw them into his saxophone case. Then, barely able to carry the weight of my own body, I crossed the street to the blue-jean stand which displayed the word SALE. I bought a pair of jeans for the nurse as promised, giving the man what I thought was a big bill. With the change he gave me I had eight dollars and five cents left. I wasn't sure this would be enough for the taxi fare back to the museum, but there was no other way to get back in time. Thank God that, unlike Moscow, the street was filled with taxis. I raised my arm and immediately one stopped right in front of me. I barely had

246

the strength to open its door and get inside. The driver turned to me and asked me something. I just sat there and pointed to the purple pin with the white 'MMA' on my lapel. He nodded his head in understanding, pulled down the handle on the meter, and we were off.

All the way back I prayed that no one had noticed my disappearance. What if something had happened there while I was away? What if Mikhail Mikhailovich got a crazy idea to leave the museum earlier than planned? What if I didn't get back in time? What would they do to Lena, to my mother, to my sister? How would they punish them? I prayed for the taxi to go faster. I didn't know how to tell the driver that I was in a hurry, so I had no choice but to pray.

What seemed like an endless trip, in twenty minutes came to an end. It was five dollars and fifty cents on the meter when we pulled up to the museum. I didn't have time to get my change from the driver, for when I stepped out of the taxi I saw my comrades already outside gathered around a young man miming a monkey.

At first I couldn't move, but I told myself not to panic and, seeing them totally involved in watching the pantomime, I quickly turned to the museum stairs and ran up, taking two steps at a time. When I reached the top I turned back to the pavement to see my group still enjoying the young entertainer's show. I started my climb down slowly, taking my time so as not to draw anyone's attention. Halfway down I saw Mikhail Mikhailovich turning and looking around. When he saw me he made a gesture to hurry up, but not in anger. His face showed a tired relief; this tour brought a lot of pressure on him, too. Sometimes we forget that KGB officers are also human. And I felt sorry for him, he was also a slave to the Regime, just like us.

'Where were you? We've been waiting for you,' he said.

'I was looking for the Socialist Realism exhibit,' I replied with sincerity.

'I looked for it earlier and I couldn't find it,' said Mikhail Mikhailovich.

'I found it,' I said with a smile.

'Where? Where? Where?' my comrades asked, turning away from the mime one after the other.

'Just a few rooms away from El Greco,' I replied.

'That was Salvador Dali, that's surrealism,' someone said.

'Oh, I thought it was the same,' I said innocently.

'Okay, now that we're all together, let's board the bus,' said Mikhail Mikhailovich, once again in control. Like mechanical dolls we all followed his order and boarded the bus, as so many times before. Except this was the last time. Our trip was all but over. The doors to this prison on wheels closed for the very last time.

I sat silently watching freedom outside. I was no longer a part of it. Now I was an outsider and the city looked different. Maybe it was because of the shadow Mikhail Mikhailovich cast on all of us under his control, or maybe it was just the restlessness of nature. The sun was going down and the shadows from the park trees were like barricades crossing Fifth Avenue. There were fewer people on the street now, which made it look almost deserted, even the uniformed men near the doors and the numbers on the now darkened buildings no longer stood out as before.

The only ray of sun was when we approached the number eight thirty-four. It peeked through the trees and fell onto the white Rolls-Royce like a spotlight on that part of the book that I had started to read but didn't finish. The bus turned down a side street and the book was closed.

On the way to Kennedy Airport, I understood that Mikhail Mikhailovich obviously had a weakness for bridges, because again he took advantage of the highest point of the Triboro Bridge to stand up and make another speech. He stood with legs spread apart for balance, and started to outline his newest order. He began by saying, 'I want each of you to write a report on this tour, for example: what you thought of it, what you did, what you wanted to do, what your comrades did that you think I should know about . . .'

I could hardly hear him, because I didn't want to hear him anymore. Now that our tour was over, I knew more about myself. I knew more about the world, I knew more about its people. In this part of the world some people lived better than others, but it

248

seemed to me they all had a choice, not as in Russia, where the Government makes the choices. Another thing I was sure of now was that nowhere do people live more repressed than in the Soviet Union, because in the free world the law of the country is above everyone and everyone is under the law. In Russia the law is in the hands of the government and people like Mikhail Mikhailovich, who can do with it whatever they want, as now in the confines of this prison on wheels. I watched Mikhail Mikhailovich's lips moving, but I still heard nothing, because I knew he wasn't saying anything I hadn't heard before. I no longer felt sorry for him, I now felt sorry only for myself.

I looked back at Manhattan for the last time. The steel needle of the Empire State Building glittered on the background of a red sky, injecting my heart with pain at the thought that I would never travel through this city again. The bright sun setting behind this beautiful city will stay with me forever. It was like a shiny diamond pin on the chest of the planet earth. I asked myself, what could create such a power, such a beauty? It had to be a force unknown to us . . . *freedom*. I hadn't had time truly to taste it, but I held the hope that one day I would.

North, south, east, west, my cross, my blessed destiny. India was my soul, Canada was my youth, America is my hope, Russia is my pain. I'm going home, but I'm not giving up. I'm going home, but just for a visit, because it is not my home anymore.

The plane circled over Moscow and made a smooth landing at Domodyedovo Airport. The same airport that only a month ago amazed us with its extraordinary modernity now, after we had seen Kennedy Airport, looked like a crooked little matchbox tossed in a dump.

A bus took us into the city. Moscow was grey and depressing to me, even the red coloured flags and slogans looked faded and dirty. Behind this faded red the architecture was provincially pompous. What was even worse was seeing my people walking through the streets of Moscow like empty shells, which filled me with pity and sadness. I asked the bus driver to let me out at the Metro. Riding down the escalator made me feel better, I saw that the Metro was still the same, still beautiful, still clean. Hello, my Metro! Hello, my motherland!

I changed trains at the Circle Line to Arbat. Once on the street I was slapped in the face by a cold wind but on my street it felt more like a friendly pat. I ran to the wooden castle, which welcomed me with its warmth. Each carved swirl seemed to smile at me. I raced up the stairs without tripping once and held my breath as I opened the door to my room.

Lena was sitting on the windowsill.

'Hi!' I said.

'You came back!' she said, throwing her arms around me.

'I'm sorry,' I said, 'I couldn't . . .'

'That's good. It's so good,' Lena whispered, her tears burning my cheek.

'But why are you crying?'

'I was so afraid you'd stay there without me. I was so afraid.'

'Don't cry, I'm here.'

'Tell me how it is there. The way we thought?' she said.

'No,' I replied, 'better, much better, but completely different. Lena, I promise you to find the way out for both of us, and when we leave . . . I know where to go.'

'America?'

'America!'

1 I Have an Idea

I returned to Moscow after my foreign tour with the intention of staying just long enough to find a way for Lena and me to escape together. But my intended 'short visit' soon stretched to more than three years.

Strangely, the more I wanted to leave Russia, the more my career seemed to blossom. After the great reviews *Pravda* gave to our tour abroad, I got a leading part in a TV show; then I was invited to Kiev film studio for an audition and was accepted. After this came Mosfilm's motion picture about the life of the gymnast Olga Korbut, where I played her boyfriend. This role made me famous and soon I was considered a star.

By Soviet standards, I was rocketing to great heights and my credits were the envy of many a young actor, but the more successful I was in the business of propaganda – so-called 'Soviet Art' – the more I hated being a part of it.

My life with Lena had hardly changed. She still didn't have government approval to work and even though she managed to get some parts here and there, these jobs always ended in a disaster because of her nervousness due to endless complications with her documents. Thanks to Dudin I had temporary permission to work (which I got while playing Lenin's brother, and which Dudin managed to prolong every year). So I was in Moscow legally, even though I still didn't have propiska. This problem could have been solved only if the City Council gave me a room to live in, but in spite of Mikhail Mikhailovich's promise of a new apartment, we still lived in the same room at Toilik's wooden castle.

After promising Lena three years earlier that I would find a way for us to get out, I was beginning to feel like a failure. I could see no way for us to escape. No way at all.

We burned many candles through sleepless nights plotting every conceivable means of escape. One idea we had was to take a tourist trip and defect once we were out of the country, but it was impossible to buy a ticket any farther than Bulgaria. Our ideas became wilder and crazier. We even planned to hijack a plane, but this would mean weapons, and weapons always meant having to use them. We didn't want to hurt anyone. We just wanted to get out.

As the endless days and nights passed, the shape of one of our plans became clearer. We decided that when summer came, we would visit Lena's grandfather in her hometown on the Black Sea. We would rent a boat and take provisions for several days. Though the Black Sea coastline was heavily guarded by military ships, we planned to head towards the other shore at night in the hope of being saved by a Turkish fishing boat. Of course we understood that our chance of success was one in a million. But the positive part of this plan was that if we were caught we could say that this was a tragic accident and pretend we were lost.

It wasn't much of a plan, but we had nothing else. So we waited for summer . . . and while we waited, two events occurred that would change our lives forever: one was an increase in the price of vodka, the other was the start of Jewish emigration.

For the average citizen, like Lena or me, these two events seemed absolutely unrelated; but for social scientists (like Toilik, for example), the second was an outgrowth of the first.

By order of the government, vodka made from grain and potatoes was taken off the shelves and a new vodka made from petrol was put in its place. That switch could have passed unnoticed if the price of the bottle hadn't been unexpectedly raised from 3.12 rubles to 4.12 rubles. This was accompanied by a national campaign to rationalize the price hike – the fight against alcoholism, but it's not easy to break the will of the people. 'It's better to die drunk than to live sober,' goes a Russian folk saying, and it's better not to mess about with people who have such folklore.

Who wouldn't resent such an increase? Maybe the insensitive

ones who don't touch the stuff. But the sensitive ones, who wake up with a hangover every morning out of love for their country, were deeply affected by this event.

Toilik was the first to protest. He began to hold dissident meetings in the wooden castle. The people who showed up for these meetings were the ones known as the political avant-garde of Moscow, its notorious 'Top Ten'. They were inveterate dissidents, arrested hundreds of times, repeatedly dragged to the Sober-up Centre, subjected to compulsory treatment, but, in spite of all this, they remained forever faithful to their principles.

Toilik was cautious by nature and never let anyone into his apartment without first checking his loyalty to the club. He would shout a series of questions out the window, and the guest would shout his answers back in a secret code.

'Who's there?'

'The prick of a bear!'

'What do you want?'

'A cunt!'

'Ah, it's you you cock sucker!'

'Yes, it's me, you mother-fucker!'

The code was rather primitive and it seemed easy for enemies and informers to use, but therein lay its complexity: nobody would dare scream such words in the middle of the street, except a club member.

After the first test came the second. The dissident would have to climb the labyrinthine stairs in total darkness to Toilik's door, knock the traditional knock with his head, and, only after succeeding at this, encounter the final and most crucial test – downing a glass of tooth elixir or mouthwash, a drink that can be imbibed only by men who are irrevocably dedicated to social causes.

After each member went through the mandatory tests and ordeals, the meeting was officially called to order.

The themes of the meetings varied from the simple – the difference between promiscuity in a democratic cabinet and impotence in the communist Politburo; to the complex – how to divide 4.12 (the new price of vodka) by three persons.

Everyone in the Top Ten had shown up for the latest meeting, except for one or two dissidents who couldn't cope that day with the steep slope of the staircase. Even a few feminists came, true daughters of the women's lib movement. They were stern women. I've seen them so many times before, their faces looked as if they were hewn from wood with an axe, never touched by rouge or lipstick, rather adorned by natural paints – black and blue marks, brown scabs, and bloody sores. These women seldom smiled, and then, only out of the side of their mouths – the special Arbat smile, which coyly covered up their missing teeth. These feminists were trained never to expose the black gaps in their mouths in a foolish, senseless grin and, if it happened that they couldn't keep themselves from laughing, their strict etiquette demanded that they fling up a hand with its broken nails and slam the trap shut.

When all the activists had arrived and taken their assigned seats, Toilik began his introductory remarks.

'Friends, you, of course, are well aware of the reason we are here today. All of you, I hope, understand the serious nature of this meeting, the Soviet government has cheated us again!'

Through the thin plywood partition, Lena and I could hear each word of this historic meeting, smell the bracing scent of alcohol, and almost see those brave individuals, so vibrant was their spirit. The dissidents knew, of course, that we were listening, but they didn't care; they trusted us – our presence was like the silent minority at their meetings. They aligned themselves with us through the partition, probably because we never encroached on their drinks, which were strictly counted at each meeting. As for ideas, the dissidents never hesitated to share them.

'Friends,' Toilik continued, 'let me start today's seminar with this question. Why does the government see vodka as an economic staple and label us, the consumers of this vodka, as the enemy? Vodka is the basis of life in Russia – what else could fill the yearning emptiness of the Russian soul? For vodka you can be killed; for vodka you should also be pardoned!'

'Right!' one dissident screamed. 'Yesterday, with my very own eyes, I saw a man get beaten up in the supermarket for breaking a bottle of vodka, his own bottle, not somebody else's. The whole

254

line kicked him and trampled on him for his deed. Then, we all took up a collection and bought him a new bottle!'

'Vodka is sacred!' came a deep bass voice through the partition. 'I hate it when somebody asks me: "Which vodka do you prefer, the new or the old?" What a silly question. What's the difference – there are only two kinds of vodka, good and very good.'

'Yes, good answer!' the dissidents cheered the bass on. 'Good vodka and very good vodka!'

'Stop it,' shouted Toilik. 'I'm talking about a totally different thing – how the Party plays on our love of vodka. For you, vodka is good at any price, and this is how the government patches the holes in its economy. Vodka was always expensive, but three of us, with a ruble each, could get together and buy a bottle. Sure, somebody had to pay 1.12 rubles, but at least he got the empty bottle. But now? Just try to divide 4.12 by three. It's a mess! Simple people dislike such complications. It got them angry. They started talking about human rights, freedom of speech, and the democratization of our country. It was a perfect chance to attack the government. The smell of revolution was in the air. All Moscow was living in anticipation of an insurrection or a demonstration. Moscow was in turmoil. Everybody was waiting for the moment; everybody was waiting for the sign . . . Matches and salt disappeared from the shelves of the supermarkets and this is a sure sign of a civil war. And then what happened? Nothing. How the government cheated us! How craftily the tables were turned at the last moment! It became clear that there was to be *no* insurrection, *no* democratization; instead, there was to be *Jewish Emigration*.

'Emigration?! . . . a long-forgotten word in Russia. The very concept is a mystery to the modern Soviet man. How could it be possible to leave a country where life gets better and better every day; where medicine is free; and only for a plot in the cemetery one needs to pay. How could one emigrate from a country where all people, even Jews, must love their native land according to the laws of the constitution?

'But, as the government says, Jews don't love anything. For a Jew it is bad everywhere. This is precisely why they are wandering Jews. Jews don't need democratization; they need emigration!

255

And so, this emigration has become known as The Jewish Emigration.

'On the other hand, why should it be all right for Jews to leave, but not all right for other people? Are they special or something? How deftly the Party turned the people against the Jews! People forgot about democratization. They forgot that vodka used to cost 3.12 rubles. They knew only one thing – all problems started with the Jews.

'We dissidents must not swallow the bait. We need to fight, either for a reduction in the price of vodka, or for emigration for everybody!'

Through the partition resounded applause and the gulping of drinks.

'We want cheap vodka and emigration!'

'I want emigration and democratization!'

'I'm for blood and freedom! My plan is simple – kill all ladies of the Party! Take their Party membership cards and kill them indiscriminately,' stated the basso.

'Kill them individually and collectively!'

'Why not kill men too?' somebody shouted, probably wishing to go even further into this theoretical discussion.

'Because men drink, and that means they are with us. Ladies first!' said the basso, his words steeped in applause.

'I agree! I agree with everything!' came a drunken woman's voice above the applause. 'I'm not a Party member. I drink and I'm not exactly a lady, but if anybody wants to kill me, he can kill me right now! I will die with a light heart! I'm happy to sacrifice myself for our cause.'

'Friends!' somebody screamed, 'Friends! Give me the floor. That's enough theory. Let's get to the practice; let's drink while we still can!'

This proposal went over well. Everybody quieted down, anxious to get to the practice. But just then came the angry voice of Toilik, who, as the host, had the power of veto.

'No!' he said sternly. 'Under no circumstances should we deviate from our tradition. I propose that we sing!'

The room became silent. Then came the shuffle of moving chairs, and the traditional knock (with the head) at *my* door. . . .

'Come on, Toilik,' I said.

The door flew open and Toilik's back came storming into the room. After the third bottle, he always walked backward, as if he had just got off the Moscow-Tula Express.

'Sash . . . gimme the guitar,' said Toilik, weaving around the room.

'Take it,' I said, 'it's over there, in the corner.'

Toilik turned at a treacherous angle but, contrary to the laws of physics, didn't fall down. He scooped up the guitar, spun around, and backed out of the room.

'Please don't hit anyone with the guitar,' I said.

'Thank you,' Toilik muttered, shutting the door.

Generally, if the evening didn't end in a fight, it was perfectly safe to give Toilik the guitar. His style of playing was unique – he never touched either the keyboard or the strings; he simply moved his hand near the guitar without any rhythm or system. As for his singing – he always sang the same song, the 'Internationale'. But if in the morning he sang in a loud operatic voice, at night he sang the same words, strangely enough, in a whisper. The dissidents at the meeting chimed in cautiously, as if the 'Internationale' were an illegal, underground song. They sang in strict unison, except for a basso profundo, who always sang one stanza ahead of the others.

The chorus finished up the last stanza after the bass. They got to the coda and then came a cacophony of noise.

CLANG went the glasses, forks, and knives.

SPLASH went the jugs, bottles, and vials.

SCREECH went the chairs, table, and bed.

BANG went the fists, heels, and knees.

The revolutionary rhapsody came to an end and everybody, exhausted from their responsibility for their country, began to get ready to leave. This did not necessarily signify the end of the meeting or the prospect of peace and quiet, though; I knew that from experience.

'Friends,' Toilik started his farewell speech, 'where are you going in this dark night? What delirium is dragging you from this warm place out into the freezing cold? Stay here, brothers, there is enough room for everybody.'

'No, Toilik, no.'

'Why do you never want to stay?'

'Because you always invite us to stay and then you wind up throwing us out.'

'When did I do that?'

'Always!'

'I'm sorry if I ever did that. Don't worry, it won't happen again. I beg you with all my heart, stay, pick a spot anywhere in this cosy room – under the table or near the radiator. It's freezing outside. You'll never make it to the Metro in this storm.'

'Are you sure you won't throw us out in the middle of the night?' Bass asked.

'What are you talking about?'

'Are you sure?' Bass insisted.

'I'm sure.'

'You swear?'

'I swear, or I'll never take another drop.'

'All right. You've talked us into it.'

We could hear Toilik's friends settling down. For a while, it was quiet; then there was some mumbling and snoring here and there. Somebody moaned; another sighed; somebody wheezed, and then, just when all became quiet, at exactly a quarter to one, the night's silence was pierced with Toilik's frightful scream:

'I can't stand it! I can't sleep when there are strangers in the house. Everybody out! Get the hell out of here, you homeless alcoholics!'

The response to this sudden barrage was but a faint murmur, a wheeze, a moan.

'What I am saying is – get out of this apartment, you parasites!' Toilik wailed. 'This is not a hotel! You'd better get going before I call the police! Do you understand me?'

The stubborn dissidents refused to understand anything. Somebody tried to explain that the Metro would be closed by the time they got there.

'That's not my problem!' Toilik persisted. 'Get out of here, you tramps.'

'But you promised.'

'What did I promise? Get out!'

258

The script was always the same. It was a mystery why Toilik had to throw the dissidents out exactly fifteen minutes before the Metro closed; the poor fellows, in their exhausted condition, always found it impossible to get there on time.

Somebody attempted to express his disagreement with Toilik's policy; somebody else tried to resist; somebody begged the host to let him sleep in the hallway; but Toilik was adamant. He dragged the dissidents to the staircase and pushed them down, one after the other. Though the stairs were antique, they were designed with such precision that nobody got stuck at the turns and each one automatically went flying out of the front door of the wooden castle. This was the product of the ingenious Russian builders who, even back in the nineteenth century, had found a way to facilitate the descent of the besotted guests of the house.

The dissidents made their way home through snowy Moscow, forgetting Toilik's insults in the wind and snow, and praying for some truth to the saying that the freezing cold doesn't harm drunks.

'Sash, Sashka,' Toilik's voice rang out when he finished seeing his guests to the door. 'Come here! I want to talk to you. I won't let you sleep all night if you don't come here. You know me.'

I knew him well enough to take him seriously. I threw on my clothes and went out in the hall. There, my way was blocked by Toilik holding a bottle of port wine.

'Let's have a drink, Sash.'

'Okay, let's.' I gave in without a struggle, knowing from experience it was better to accept his proposal immediately.

'I want to talk to you. Let's go to the kitchen.'

'Listen,' Toilik said, climbing up on the stove, bottle in hand, 'do you know why I throw my friends out in the freezing cold? I do it because I don't trust them for a minute, and because I know these meetings are a complete waste of time. There wasn't one meeting in history that ever brought results.'

'You're right,' I said. 'I understand you perfectly. Now can I go to sleep?'

'I understand this perfectly, too,' Toilik said, ignoring me. 'But nevertheless, I continue to call these absurd meetings. Why? Out of loneliness. Let me tell you, loneliness is the worst thing in the world. It was out of loneliness that I rented you a room, not for money. Remember you didn't pay me rent for a few months. Did I ask you for money? No, because money is something I have never had and never will have. You're okay, you have Nefertiti, and Nefertiti, let me tell you, is a good fellow. Where is she?'

'She's sleeping,' I said.

'Nefertiti!' he screamed. 'Come out and drink with us. I want to talk with both of you.'

'No, Toilik, thank you. It's late,' returned Lena's voice. 'Sasha, come back here.'

'Listen, Toilik, I've got to go.'

'I understand,' he said, 'but I've got something to tell you. I got an idea. I want to help you. Both of you.'

'What do you mean?'

'Don't think you're the only one who can listen through the wall. I've also heard a few things.'

'Toilik, what are you talking about?'

'I overheard your conversation.'

'What conversation?' I asked nervously.

'That's not important. The important thing is that I know how to help you. I got an idea! But first, let's have another drink.'

'Okay, let's make it a fast one,' I said softly.

Toilik took a slug from the bottle and then passed the port over to me.

'Sasha, don't drink any more. Come back here,' Lena cried from our room.

'I've got to go, Toilik,' I said.

'But I have to tell you something.'

'Tomorrow,' I said. 'Tell me tomorrow.'

'As you wish,' Toilik said as he lay down on the stove.

'Don't burn yourself,' I said.

'Don't worry about that. Just remember, I have an idea.'

2 A Dead Man

I didn't see Toilik the next morning when I left for the theatre. With rehearsals all day and a performance in the evening, I completely forgot about him and his idea.

After work, I walked home along the boulevard. As I stepped on that path, familiar in every detail, I thought – as I often did – of that first time I had walked this way with Lena. It was seven years ago. No, more – almost eight years! The time . . . the time . . .

That night with Lena the snowflakes were dancing, swirling all around us. And the boulevard, pure white with snow, was clean and fresh – as fresh as our young, exuberant love of life. Now, as I looked back, the only similarity I saw with the past after nearly eight years was that our lives were just as cold – maybe colder.

There were no snowflakes this night. Instead, there was a bright half-moon in an otherwise dark sky. Through the frost-covered branches the moon looked like a goldfish trapped in a white net.

I turned off the boulevard to Arbat. The moon, keeping pace with me, leaped out of its net and floated above the roofs of the buildings, lighting my way. I walked a few more blocks, stepped onto the icy porch of the wooden castle, opened the door, and went inside. On the first step, I bumped into something dark and formless. I stepped back and opened the front door to let in the moonlight. I recognized Toilik lying in a heap. His face, partially turned toward me, looked pale and yellow.

'Toilik,' I called to him.

He didn't move.

'Toilik, are you okay?'

'Yes, I'm okay.'

'What happened?'

'Somebody pushed me down the stairs.'

'Who?'

'I don't know.'

'Why?'

'I don't know. What about my bottle?' he asked.

'What bottle?'

'I was carrying a bottle. Did I break it?'

'Where is it?' I asked.

'Somewhere around here,' he said. 'Under me.'

I bent over and slipped my hand under him. My fingers felt something sticky on his clothes and on the stairs.

'Was it port wine?' I asked.

'What, are you kidding? You think I'd get myself killed for port wine? It's supposed to be vodka.'

I dug deeper and struck something sharp like the edge of a broken bottle. I touched it gingerly, trying not to get cut. Toilik moaned and rolled on his side. The moonlight lifted a terrible picture out of the darkness: Toilik's hand, clutching an intact bottle of vodka, was twisted around, and through the torn sleeve of his jacket, wet with blood, protruded a chip of bone.

'You've broken your arm,' I said, feeling suddenly nauseated.

'Who cares! What about the bottle?' Toilik demanded.

'It's okay,' I replied, taking it out from under him.

'Are you sure?'

'I'm going to call an ambulance,' I said.

'No ambulances. They'll take me to the Sober-up Centre,' Toilik said. 'Take me by taxi.'

We couldn't get a taxi but some driver pulled up and agreed to take us to the hospital for half a bottle, which he drank on the way. Blood poured from Toilik's sleeve all over the back seat, but not once did Toilik moan; he feared the driver would turn him out if he saw that the car was getting soiled.

When we got to the hospital, there was nobody in the emergency room but, anyway, it still took more than an hour before the doctor and his assistant appeared. The assistant removed Toilik's clothes. The doctor adjusted his glasses, took a large hypodermic needle, jabbed it into Toilik's arm, and began to draw blood.

Toilik screamed violently, 'Hey, you mudak, what are you sucking my blood for? I've lost enough already.'

'Don't budge,' said the doctor gruffly, continuing his bloody business.

'What are you trying to do, kill me!' Toilik roared. 'Get that needle out of there or I'll bust your glasses.'

The doctor jerked the needle out of Toilik's arm. The syringe was nearly full and on the tip of the needle was a big red drop.

'Give me back my blood or I'll kill you,' snarled Toilik.

'Shut up,' said the doctor. 'The hospital needs this blood for transfusions.'

'I need that blood for myself!' cried Toilik.

'You need a cast, not blood. Keep quiet, patient, or we'll send you to the Sober-up Centre.'

The doctor and the assistant put a splint on Toilik's arm and proceeded to put on a cast. When they were through with his arm, they kept going and put the plaster on his torso, neck, and even his other arm. When the plaster hardened, the doctor snickered, 'Now we will see who will kill whom, you alcoholic.'

'I'll complain,' screamed Toilik. 'I'm a hero of the Soviet Union!'

'How are you going to prove it? We put your medal inside the cast,' laughed the assistant.

They held him, one on each side, and lugged him towards the door as if he were a plaster bust, but Toilik spread his legs apart and got stuck in the doorway. The assistant forced his legs together and they dragged him into the corridor.

'Hey,' he screamed, 'don't leave me alone. They'll kill me.'

'I'm coming, Toilik,' I shouted, and ran after them.

There was no space for Toilik in the wards, so the doctor set him up in a hideaway bed at the end of the hallway where the linen was stored. It was good and bad – bad because it was terribly drafty; good because, in that dead end, we could drink the rest of the bottle of vodka Toilik had miraculously saved.

'Look at what that bloody doctor did to me – I can't even do my own drinking now. You're going to have to feed me like a baby.'

'Okay, here you are,' I said, holding the bottle to his lips.

'Sit down, relax. You look tired,' he said.

'Okay, Toilik, but I can't stay very long. Lena's waiting for me,' I said.

'Nobody's waiting for me,' he said sadly, gazing at the linen.

'Come on, Toilik. Let's drink to your health.'

'No,' Toilik said, 'let's drink to those who are no longer waiting for me.'

I knew I was trapped, but I decided to give it one more try.

'Okay, Toilik, let's drink to those who aren't waiting for you, then one for the road, and then I'm going.'

'No,' Toilik said, 'you're not going anywhere until I tell you why nobody is waiting for me. Do you know I have a wife and daughter?'

'Yes, I do,' I said.

'You don't know anything!' he said. 'Do you know how we went our separate ways? Do you know why? If you want to hear the saddest story in the world, stick around and listen; if you don't want to, you're going to hear it anyway, because this is connected with what I wanted to tell you yesterday.'

'All right, Toilik. I'm listening.'

'You know I used to be a pilot at a military base. One day, it was payday in fact, I'd finished flying and was about to go home, when my boss summoned me and said, "Listen, Toilik, we've got a special mission for you here, but let me say from the outset that it requires absolute secrecy." "I understand," I said, "Comrade Chief." "All right," he said, "as of this moment, consider yourself on this mission. Remember, never breathe a word of this to anyone, is that clear?" "Clear, Comrade Chief," I said. "Right, this is it – I want you to fly to point 47. There you will be met and given instructions on what to do next." What was I to do? I got into my MiG, took off, and arrived at the designated spot in no time. As I approached a small landing strip, to the left, I saw a little town surrounded by a forest.

'The very moment I touched the ground, a grey limousine drove up the runway and a colonel stepped out. He was a young man, but his hair was already grey. On one hand he wore a black glove. Later I realized that he had an artificial hand. "Good day,

Comrade Colonel," I said, and saluted. He smiled and tapped me on the shoulder with his real hand and said casually, "How's it going?" "Perfect, Comrade Colonel." "Glad to hear it," he said. "I know you're one of our best men, Toilik, an expert pilot, but I have a question for you. Have you ever flown an American jet?" "No, never, Comrade Colonel," I said. "How could I?" "But can you?" he asked, peering into my eyes and smiling. "As long as it has fuel!" I joked, wondering where he would get an American jet. He laughed and said, "You'll get all the fuel you want." Then he took my arm gently, as if he were holding a girl, and said, "Let's go. I'm going to show you something."

'We crossed the airfield, entered a hangar, brightly lit up, and inside was an American F-14, pretty as a picture. "Where did you get her?" I asked. "It doesn't matter," the colonel said. "Now, she's all yours." I couldn't wait – I jumped in, took a seat, got comfortable, examined the dials and knobs, and played with them a bit. Everything was different. I knew I needed at least a week to get used to it, but to save face I said, "It's nothing special. There is no reason to wait around. I'm ready, Colonel." "All right," said the colonel. And off I went.

'To cut a long story short, that beauty had a mind of her own. I wouldn't dare to fly her a second time. But that day, I flew her up to eight thousand metres when the dials on the instrument panel went wild and the plane started to shake, but I managed to get her back to the airport and even land somehow. When I rolled her to a stop, I jumped out, lay face down, covered my head with my hands, and waited for the plane to explode. Nothing happened. I had made it.

'People came running up to me from all sides. The colonel hugged me with one arm and whispered tender words in my ear.

'"Toilik, you're a hero! You did the impossible – you flew a plane nobody else was brave enough to fly. Go right ahead and consider yourself a Hero of the Soviet Union. Tomorrow, you will receive the Gold Star." "It was a pleasure to try," I said. "Now I have something else planned for you," the colonel announced. "I'm going to take you somewhere special. Get ready for an adventurous programme." "I'm always ready, Comrade Colonel, but I've got to get home soon. My wife is waiting for my salary." "I will take you to your wife in due time," the colonel said. "But now let's go and change our clothes. Where we're going, it is impossible to be dressed like Soviet officers. Also, I must warn you, don't talk with anyone there, except me." I was intrigued. We got into the car, made a stop at the terminal, where we changed into civilian clothes, then drove out of the airport. We passed ten barbed-wire fences and ten patrol units. Our documents were checked ten times, and then, believe it or not, we came upon an American city! It was a real American city; of course, it wasn't New York, and not exactly a city, but a small American town with a few streets. The buildings were American, the cars were American, the billboards were American, the restaurants were American, and there were Americans all around chewing gum, smoking cigars, and chatting in the American language, which is called English.

'At first, I thought perhaps I was seeing things after that rough landing, but the colonel just kept laughing as he made his way through the town. We headed straight for the bar. There the waiter came up to us and asked us something very politely in English. The colonel replied sweetly, also in English, and we took a seat at the bar. Above the bar, a colour TV showed cowboys riding mustangs and shooting each other with Colts. The colonel, seeing that I was in shock, took pity on me and explained the whole thing. As it turned out, that town was a special place – it's where spies are trained before being sent to America. There, they are prepared to deal with affluence, so they don't go crazy when they get to the States. That town has even more pleasures than in America. It's probably to make the spies disappointed when they get abroad.

'The bar was only the beginning. After a few drinks, we ate steaks the size of an elephant's ear, then we played roulette, then we rolled into a cinema where we saw everything from the waist down, then came another bar, where we saw the live version of what was in the film, and then, when everything in my head was jumbled from the flashing neon lights, the colonel took me to a brothel, but they call it a "massage parlour".

'The massage parlour had a heart-shaped swimming pool and there were attractive girls everywhere. We went for a dip in the

266

pool with a few of the girls. They washed our private parts while other girls, something like waitresses, danced on the edge of the pool and served refreshing drinks. They were dressed in black tailcoats and bow ties, nothing more. As they carried martinis back and forth, they swivelled around in such a way that their naked behinds were temptingly displayed beneath their tails. Each one had a number on her rear so, if you were interested in one of them, you could request her by number for a massage.

'Yes, there I was, with the colonel in the swimming pool, sipping martinis, checking the numbers, and little by little getting thoroughly drunk. Soon, I sensed that Number Eight was giving me the eye and motioning to the stairs with her knee. I got the message and whispered to the colonel, "May I be excused for a moment?" He just laughed, his artificial hand in the black glove bobbing up and down in the water. Taking this for permission, I got out of the swimming pool, wrapped myself in a towel which displayed the American flag, slipped my wet feet into my shoes (where my salary was hidden), and pattered after Number Eight up the stairs. Even now, this number dances before my eyes at night.

'We came to a door also numbered eight. The room was tiny, about the size of my bedroom. There, the girl looked into my eyes, chirped something in English, and smiled as if to say, "You follow?"

'Of course I didn't follow, but I nodded anyway. Then, while doing a tantalizing dance, she began to take off her tailcoat. Let me tell you, I've never seen such a beautiful girl, before or since, even in the films. She tossed off her tails and, in only her bow tie, she flitted over to the bed. I, of course, kicked my shoes off, lowered the flag, and drew closer to her. When I climbed onto the bed she stared at me uncomprehendingly and chirped some more English. Naturally, I again nodded my full consent and attempted to hug her, but she pulled away, crouching against the wall, and told me through gestures, "Where is your money?" Let me tell you, this West is really corrupting people!

'I worked out that, according to their rules, you must pay in advance. I leaped onto the floor, grabbed one shoe, fished around inside, and pulled out my soaked money. I took two fives and

267

held them out to that beauty. Suddenly, she started clawing the air and, forgetting that she was an American whore, cried out in perfect Russian, "No! No! Anything but that!" At first I thought she was repulsed by the wet bills and, in order to calm her down, I said, "Don't worry, sweetie, they're not dirty; they're just wet. My feet were wet from the pool." But again she cried, "Oh no! Anything but that!"

'Then, thinking that, for some reason, she didn't take fives, I pulled out a ten, offered it to her, and said, "I'm sorry, but this one also got a bit wet." At this, she burst out crying.

'Here, to tell you the truth, I was at a loss. I put twenty rubles in front of her, but again she said no. Then I put two and two together and, trying to control myself, asked, "How much do you need, dear, fifty? What do you want – to gobble up my whole salary for one night? Isn't that a little too much?" Tears rolled down her cheeks. I was getting more and more enraged. "Ah, you've decided to use tears to get me? You scum! It will not work! This just will not work, you unscrupulous prostitute!"

'When she heard these words, she stopped crying and said in a crisp tone, "Fuck your mother, comrade. I'm no prostitute. I'm a third-year student in the spy school. So, dear comrade, put up your *dollars*, or I'll have to ask you to leave the classroom!"

'This speech cut me to the quick. "Eh you, whore," I said to her, shaking and stammering. "Take this money. How could it be that a prostitute won't accept Soviet rubles? It's printed right on them that they're accepted on all Soviet territory." "No," she said, "I'm not taking them, that's it. In this town, you can't even buy a Coke with your rubles." This drove me crazy.

'If you don't want to take this Soviet money, you tramp, then I will have you without any money!' I said, and pounced on her. But here, that lovely lady did something with her hands – just a fleeting movement – and I passed out. They call it – karate!

'When I came to, I realized I was lying on a bed in the dark and felt the warmth of a woman beside me. The woman was lying with her back to me. She was stark naked; the whole blanket was wrapped around me. I lay still for a few moments in thought. Then I carefully unrolled the blanket and without a second

268

thought, jumped on her, pressing her against the wall, knowing that the only way to overcome a trained spy is by surprise.

'I attacked her from behind. In her sleep, she couldn't figure out what was going on; she was panting, and puffing, and pawing the wall. I didn't let up one bit until I finished my business. What's true is true – I never tasted anything sweeter in my life; it was everything and even a little more.

'Next, I jumped off the bed, rummaged around in the corner for my shoes, took all the money that was there, laid it on her shoulder, and whispered in her ear, "Take my rubles, Contagious. I haven't got anything else." She grabbed the notes and, still facing the wall, asked, "What's with you, Toilik?," her voice so familiar it was frightening.

'I dashed over to the lamp, turned on the light, and stared unflinchingly at her naked ass. Instead of the number eight, there was a mole on the left side, just like my wife had. When she glanced over her shoulder at me, I froze – her face was also exactly the same as my wife's, only she was squinting because of the bright light. I looked around, the room was mine!

'Only then did the light in my head go on. I realized that, when I was knocked out, the colonel took me home, as promised. So, I had raped my own wife and had given her my entire salary down to the last kopeck. When I grasped this in all its magnitude, there and then, I began to beat my wife-spy with deadly blows – for the rubles, for the dollars, for dancing without any panties, for the English, and for the sexology exam I took with her near the wall, and for everything remembered and for everything forgotten. To be perfectly honest, I wanted to kill her; and maybe it was a mistake that I didn't, because in the morning, she informed on me, and I was arrested. A gaol term was inevitable, but that was the very day I was awarded the medal of the Hero of the Soviet Union, as my friend the colonel had promised. The colonel intervened and I was just fired from my job instead of being sent to gaol. Naturally, the Gold Star was taken back the same day it was given. The one on my chest isn't mine. I bought it from a real hero for a bottle on the black market. Such is my fate – one day up, the same day down.

'After this scandal, my wife and daughter left me. My whole

269

life was in shambles, and I wound up a dissident. How could one not be a dissident in a country where a medal can be given and taken away the same day, where whores are spies, and spies are whores, where only a raped wife will take rubles, but a prostitute must be given dollars!

'This society is rotten; it stinks. We need change, but there will never be any changes in Russia. Sash, run away from here. Nefertiti was right – you've got to run away before they kill you.'

'I don't know what you are talking about, Toilik,' I stammered.

'Don't give me that rubbish. I have ears, you know. I've heard your conversations through the wall. I'm on your side. I want to help you get out.'

'How?' It was useless to pretend anymore with him. 'We can't go across the border, they'll arrest us.'

'I know how.'

'You mean hijack a plane? No way. There is a KGB agent on each plane.'

'Emigrate,' he whispered.

'It's impossible. We're not Jews.'

'Aren't you persecuted all your life without reason? Aren't you looking for the promised land? You are a real Jew. You just need to get an invitation from your relative in Israel.'

'I don't have any relative in Israel!'

'So get one,' said Toilik, smiling.

'How?' I asked, dumbfounded.

'First, you've got to believe with all your heart that you're Jewish. Then you've got to find a foreigner – '

'Where am I going to find a foreigner? I've met only one in my life, and he was just from the Sudan.'

'What's he doing here?' Toilik asked, growing animated.

'He's a student at the Architecture Institute,' I said.

'How long have you known him?'

'We met about seven years ago, but then he went to Africa for a while, and I haven't seen him since he got back.'

'When is he going to finish school?' Toilik asked.

'He's supposed to graduate this spring.'

'Can you trust him?' Toilik whispered.

'I think so. I heard that he changed a lot after his trip to the Sudan, but he's still one of us.'

'Is he a good drinker?' Toilik asked.

'The best!'

'Then you can trust him. The next time you see him, ask him, when he returns to the Sudan, if he would stop over in Israel – there, half the country is from Russia. He's got to find somebody who will pretend to be your relative, and send you an invitation to Israel.'

'And then?'

'Getting an invitation from a Jewish relative makes you Jewish and gives you the right to emigrate. Once you get out of the country, you can go anywhere you want. America was just one day's dream for me; for you, it can be a lifetime reality.'

'How come you don't do it yourself?' I asked.

'I'm not sure I'll even get out of this hospital,' said Toilik quietly. 'I'm a dead man.'

3 We Need a Foreigner

From the loss of blood, the too-tight cast, and the lack of movement, Toilik's health went from bad to worse and his lungs gradually swelled up. He was put on the operating table, where the cast was cracked and his Gold Star – somewhere inside the plaster – was dumped in the dustbin. An incision was made in Toilik's chest. Here, his heart stopped beating. He was clinically dead for a couple of minutes. He was given heart massage, electric shock therapy, and oxygen through a tube in his mouth. Much to the doctors' surprise, Toilik was resuscitated. Following surgery, his heart worked fairly well, but he developed a cough. Every day the cough worsened. The doctors, certain he had caught a cold from the draught in the corridor, moved him into a ward and treated him with doses of penicillin – six shots a day. From the shots, his rear end turned blue, but the cough did not subside, and his temperature rose. One morning, just as Toilik began to sing the 'Internationale,' he went into a coughing fit and died. The doctors were certain he had died because he was allergic to penicillin, but this was not so. The autopsy revealed that in the right lung of the hero was lodged Toilik's own tooth. This had caused the inflammation of the lung. The tooth had been knocked out during the operation when the oxygen tube was inserted in his mouth. The absence of that one tooth hadn't been detected by either the doctors or Toilik himself, who, prior to the surgery, didn't exactly have a full set.

After Toilik's body was cremated at the Moscow Crematorium, his wife, her boyfriend – another alcoholic – and her daughter moved into the wooden castle. There was no longer room for Lena and me in that house. What were we to do? We took the bronze candelabra as a memento and left.

272

The next six months were spent moving from place to place. First, we stayed with our old friend Andrewlka, then with Boris, then with their friends, then with friends of their friends, then with casual acquaintances, and then even with strangers.

Lena, for all her admirable loyalty, wasn't accustomed to a life of constant moving. She had a terrible time with it, but I never heard her complaining. She would just bitterly joke that I had given her propiska, not for an apartment but for a crocodile suitcase, a gift from Andrew. The continual packing and moving had Lena so trained that with only one lock on the suitcase open, she could slip her arm in and, without looking, pull out whatever we needed.

Packing and moving . . .

We got to know the drifting, homeless life of sailors. Trains, trolleybuses, and trams were our ships. How many times we traversed Moscow, seeking islands of repose. We soon discovered that finding shelter was considerably easier with a guitar than without. We sang in student dormitories and workers' quarters; in modern cafés in the centre of town and tumble-down log cabins on the outskirts. We sang in the luxurious apartments of academics, and the basement nooks of banished poets and artists. We became natives of the Moscow underground.

In the morning, I would play a decadent prince in the theatre or a union activist on TV. At night, Lena and I took our guitars and lived another life – a life distant from official art where, for the first time, we were happy and proud to be performers.

We got to know the sweetness of underground art, its freedom and its beauty. For so many years we had been looking for a breath of fresh air and, what a paradox, we found it in the Moscow underground. Here, we first sensed that we hadn't produced our imaginary records in vain. Here, in that underground, there was a brotherhood of people moving in their own orbit, like the Metro moving beneath the earth. We jumped aboard this train and got caught up in the rhythm of its wheels.

> We hurtle, lonely, in a cramped car,
> Passing the Kremlin's ruby star,
> Spitting out minutes like cherry stones,

A grey crowd of destiny's drones.
The day's complete, the work is done,
Station stop 'Crematorium' – somebody's gone.

Smell of corpses, odour of charring flesh –
Curl joyfully, the smoke of our strife,
Ah you, Mother, Mother Russia,
Crematorium of human life.

Our reputation as singers who had melodies for outlawed thoughts spread swiftly. We found ourselves facing audiences of fifty and sixty, when ten or twelve had been promised. It was a great feeling, but at the same time it was frightening. We could very easily come to station 'crematorium' ourselves.

How many times had we decided, before a concert, not to sing certain songs to strangers, or at least to change some of the words? But then it somehow seemed foolish to be afraid when we were surrounded by friends, and even more foolish to hide some words from them. In the end, we always wound up singing everything.

They were strange concerts. No admission fee, no applause, and no bows. We would just sing through the night; nobody wanted to go to sleep. But come the morning, the people would leave and the sense of danger returned. We would curse each other for our carelessness; maybe there was an informer in the crowd. With pain, we tried to recollect who was sitting there in the dark corner and whom did he come with? And we went into a panic, scared to death, promising each other that we'd be more careful. But the next night, we would be singing again, our promises forgotten.

The tension soon began driving us crazy. Danger was getting too close; it would take only one person who would whisper something about us to the KGB. It was a miracle that one still hadn't come to our concerts . . . or maybe he had, and they weren't going to touch us till the right moment. How long could it continue? We were tired of trembling; we were tired of walking on the edge of a cliff. There was only one thing to do – stop all our concerts until we had found a way out of the country, and then, once abroad, we would send our songs back by radio and tapes.

But how could we stop our life on the road? It was impossible to break our contract with these people as long as we still had no place to live. Finally, in desperation, I sent a letter to Dudin:

Dear Comrade Director,

Three years ago I was promised by the representative of the Ministry that after my trip to America I would have an apartment. I don't think that a man with such a high position could possibly lie to me. I would not bother you about this promise if my wife and I hadn't had to live on the street these last six months.

If the representative of the Ministry has forgotten his promise, maybe you can help me by giving me permission to sleep on stage in our set of the palace.

With all my respect to you, Sasha K.—

In just a few days, I was invited into Dudin's office.

'Do you want some tea?' Dudin asked me.

'No,' I said. 'Thank you.'

'So, *where* do you live?'

'On the street, as I said.'

'It shows. You look ten years older,' said Dudin thoughtfully. 'Soon you won't be able to play a prince, you'll have to play a king,' he said with a wry smile.

'Good,' I replied. 'Maybe I'll get the key to the palace.'

'You might,' said Dudin, looking at me mischievously.

I didn't say anything.

Dudin drank his tea as if he were alone in the room.

'A holiday is coming,' he finally said, 'and you know that holidays are always . . . oh, by the way did I offer . . . do you want some of my tea?' Dudin asked, staring at me with his childlike blue eyes.

'Yes, please,' I said.

Dudin slowly and carefully poured half of his tea into another glass. 'Do you mind? It's all I have,' he admitted.

'It's fine,' I said. 'Thank you.' The tea was hot, strong, and sweet.

275

'So,' Dudin continued, 'you know that holidays in Soviet Russia have a magic power, and even though this holiday is not particularly Soviet, I always thought – maybe because I'm old – that Easter is not so bad. I have an apartment for you – better than the palace which we finally got for Lenin's family. So I thought you should have it. After all, you were part of Lenin's family at one time,' he said with a smile and began to drink his tea.

'Thank you!' I cried.

'Don't rush to thank me. Here comes the usual catch. It's a pretty big apartment – about twenty square metres – and it's for three people, not for two . . .'

'Does that mean I have to invite my brother, Lenin, to live with us?' I asked bitterly.

'Don't be stupid,' Dudin said sharply. 'There is another way to extend your family.'

'Ah, I see . . . but that takes nine months, as I heard.'

'No. It's enough if you show the official document from the hospital stating the pregnancy of your wife. Don't use a false paper. They can check.'

'Well,' I said, 'I need to speak with Lena.'

'Tell her if she has a miscarriage or something like that later on, it will not change anything after the apartment is already yours.'

'Thank you,' I said, offering him my right hand.

'You're welcome.' He took my hand and shook it. 'Good luck.'

Lena and I did everything Dudin said. For the first time in my life I discovered that even lovemaking, when ordered by the government, didn't bring much pleasure. But, as we say, there is nothing bad without something good. We got an apartment. To be precise, it wasn't an apartment, but one long, narrow room, like a railway carriage with a single window at the end. The best part was that the carriage was not stuck somewhere halfway to Tula, but was located in one of the high-rise buildings right on Arbat. From its window, we could see our past – poor old Toilik's wooden castle.

It was probably the most unexpected victory that came out of our fight with the dragons – obtaining our first legal apartment won us the right for *Permanent Moscow Propiska!* How many years we had lived outside the law, with the hope of having our own place! Now we had it all!

We had beaten the dragons; we had cut off all three heads; we had come through the three magic doors to Soviet happiness. We got it all and what we felt was just emptiness and indifference. We both knew that having this place would not stop us from giving up our underground concerts. Sooner or later we would probably be arrested in this very apartment and sent from Moscow to Siberia.

'I don't want my child to live here for a day,' said Lena. 'I don't want another crushed life.'

She went to the doctor who had performed her appendectomy and this time he had much more success. I didn't say no to Lena when she went to the clinic, I agreed with her. We didn't want a new Soviet citizen. We wanted an invitation abroad. We needed a foreigner.

4 The Time Has Come

Youssef had returned from the Sudan a different person. Instead of being in blue jeans, he walked around the Institute dressed in just a long white shirt, barefoot, with bracelets on his ankles and a ring in his nose. He was no longer an ordinary son of a diplomat; he was the grandson of a king. He was a real prince, not a counterfeit theatrical prince like me; he didn't need white gloves – he was a prince of the powerful Tukbu tribe, which encompassed 450 people, not including women, of course.

His grandfather, a great African leader, liked Youssef's proposal to build a palace for him and his wives. And so, after putting Youssef on the right path, he sent him back to the Soviet Union to continue his studies at the Moscow Architecture Institute.

This time, as Boris told me, Youssef was a model student – he never cut classes, never came late, routinely turned in his projects before the deadline, and, most important of all, didn't drink. The only time he had any trouble was in his sculpture class, and that was only in the very early days of his return. Who knows, perhaps it wasn't his fault, but the fault of the instructor who announced that, for the first class, the students were free to do whatever they felt like – they were to let their fantasies guide them. Youssef was the last one in the class to complete his work, and when he finally presented his sculpture, there was an outburst in the room. One girl even went charging out of the classroom with her hands over her eyes. Right on the teacher's desk, Youssef placed his creation – a huge clay phallus, rigidly pointing up at the ceiling. It was evident that the student had worked earnestly and knowledgeably. The phallus was fashioned very naturally, in the best tradition of Socialist Realism. There wasn't even a hint of the abstract, so there was nothing for the professor to do but give the conscientious
278

foreigner a well-deserved A. But after the class the prince was summoned to the dean's office. To avoid any misunderstanding, Boris, as a friend, was called in as well. The conversation commenced on the periphery – friendship between nations and the international significance of the Third World. Gradually, the dean started coming to the point and gingerly asked Youssef why he had chosen such a narrow approach to art when there were so many other avenues for self-expression. Youssef replied that in his tribe, the phallus was a godly object, and the creation of any other sculpture constituted blasphemy. He said that in his culture, the phallus is sculpture, and sculpture is the phallus, so, when they say phallus they mean sculpture, and when they say sculpture they mean phallus.

The dean, an intelligent man, made no attempt to correct Youssef's foreign view of the world and damage relations between friendly countries. He simply informed Youssef that he was already such a mature sculptor that it would no longer be necessary for him to attend the sculpture class. He went on to say that he would arrange for Youssef to get an A in the course and, instead of the art class, Youssef would take Party History. Youssef demurely thanked the dean; the incident between the two nations came to an end, and by his senior year was completely forgotten.

Who could recall the barefoot prince in the white shirt with a ring in his nose in the graduating Youssef? Once again, Marx proved he was right when he said to Engels that environment changes human behaviour. Youssef had got himself warm boots and a heavy coat, and walked with his head buried in his shoulders, like all Russians. He wore an ordinary suit from the 'Bolshevik Factory,' and even shared vodka for three (not four) in the lobbies. He attained freedom of expression by using the best Russian swear words only and, all in all, he was no different from the ordinary Soviet student, except for colour. Youssef was doing well in all his subjects, including Party History, and finished as one of the top students in his class. It was even proposed that after graduation, he be invited to join the Comsomol as an honorary member.

The theme of Youssef's graduation project captured the attention of all the architects in Moscow – it was somewhat unusual for a future Comsomol member to present a project called 'My Father's Winter Palace'. Rumours circulated that Youssef was preparing something unbelievable. Students, professors, and other architects packed the auditorium. One of the ministries was keenly interested in building that palace in the Sudan and, for that reason, members of the Ministry and specialists on Africa were on the Commission which was to judge the project.

Boris, Lena, and I were there also. This was the first opportunity I had had to see Youssef again. He presented fifteen boards with the façade and interior of the palace for the Commission's review. The very first board met with whispers of approval – it was an aerial view of the palace which looked like a red five-cornered star. Tension mounted with each new presentation of Youssef's boards. To protect the palace from rival tribes, the structure was surrounded by a high fence which brought to mind the Kremlin wall – a detail that didn't go unnoticed by the Commission. When Youssef unveiled his final board, the front view of the palace, a simultaneous cry and round of applause rang out in the auditorium. The tower of the palace was crowned with a gold hammer and sickle.

Youssef waited for the applause to die down, then announced that that wasn't all. He said that, as a sign of gratitude to the Soviet Government for giving him the opportunity to study for free, on his own initiative he had decided to built a twenty-metre monument in front of the palace. He went on to say that he had built a maquette of the monument (one sixth of actual size) with his own hands. He said that he had worked on the project throughout his years of study, and it was to be called 'Lenin, Stalin, and Free Africa'. The door opened, and four students brought out a huge construction covered with a white sheet. It was obvious that beneath the sheet was a three-figure composition. The audience took a deep breath.

Youssef swiftly yanked one corner of the sheet. The sheet slipped onto the floor soundlessly, revealing an incredible sight. From a base of mango wood projected three huge erect phalluses – a white phallus, a red one, and, between them, the biggest of all, a black one.

It's better not to describe what took place after that. It will suffice to say that the talk about admitting Youssef to the Comsomol ceased, and if Boris hadn't been in the audience the African prince would have been dragged out into the street and beaten by the Commission. Youssef, who was in shock, was led by Boris through the fire exit, who then took him on a honeymoon.

The honeymoon wasn't Youssef's, of course, but Boris's. It seemed that Boris rescued the prince, not out of human compassion, but because he wanted to use Youssef's Volkswagen on his honeymoon. I suppose he didn't want to be alone with his new wife, for he had also invited Stas, Andrewlka, Lena, and me along for the ride.

I don't know how American students manage to fit thirty people into a Volkswagen! With Stas in our group of six, the car was pretty packed. For quite a while, we tried to work out the best arrangement, and finally we got it – in the front seat sat Youssef, who was driving; Boris, who was giving directions; and Andrewlka. In the back seat, the only one who actually had a seat was Stas; through all these years he had become even fatter, so Lena and I were practically sitting on his lap.

The cause for this journey was, as I said, Boris's recent wedding to Mashka, the daughter of an old general of the Soviet Union. The itinerary included the religious sights on the river Nerl, which is two hundred kilometres east of Moscow. But first, we had to make a detour to pick up Boris's young wife at the Kremlin dacha where she lived with her famous father. The road to that dacha was a wide and well-paved highway, probably the best in the country. It felt good to be moving along that highway in a Volkswagen. It was the first time I had ridden in a foreign car. The sound of the engine was different from Russian cars; the tyres rolled along the asphalt with hypnotic smoothness.

The landscape along the route wasn't typical – we didn't come across one poster with the sayings of Lenin. Either the Party bosses knew all the lines by heart, or their generation was already experiencing the completed form of communism.

Soon the green fences of the dachas sprang up along the highway. First, we passed dachas with low fences, which belonged to Soviet writers.

Then we passed dachas which belonged to Soviet ministers.

The fences were a bit higher and, behind them, big, grey dogs on chains raced back and forth.

Then we made a right turn off the highway and, for a little while, followed a meandering road. Eventually, we came upon a red gate surrounded by barbed wire and soldiers, separating the dachas of the top Soviet generals and Politburo members from the rest of the world. Guards in civilian clothes were positioned at each side of the barrier. There was a stir when they spotted the foreign car. When we started jumping out of the little Volkswagen one after the other – Youssef, Andrewlka, Boris, Lena, Stas, and I – the guards were stunned by our number. They apparently took us for a band of foreign terrorists. They ordered us to stand still near the car with our hands up. After they had searched us and found we were not armed, the guards calmed down and entered into lengthy negotiations with Boris, who had to give detailed explanations of who we were collectively, as well as individually, and whom we had come to see. The exchange was a tense one, but ended successfully. Apparently, the turning point was the introduction of the black prince. Boris claimed that Youssef was a renowned African communist, the younger brother of Patrice Lumumba. After this, the guards saluted and opened the gate to the hidden kingdom of the Party.

We stepped through the gate. For a few minutes we walked through an ordinary green forest, except that the grass in the forest had just been cut, and lamp posts were scattered among the trees. The paths were asphalt and at the end of each path, there were shoe-shine machines. We took one of the paths down to the river. It was a small, clear river with reeds lining its banks and lilies on the water. We asked Boris what the lovely river was called. Much to our surprise, he replied that it was the Moscow River. Here, upstream, the water wasn't covered with petrol slicks and black oily patches but was, instead, clear and blue. Across the sparkling stream, among white lilies, floated rowing boats carrying well-rounded Party workers. This idyllic landscape was enveloped in silence. For me, at least, there was no peace in that silence.

Following Boris, we headed up a hill and stepped on a path of crushed bricks, which soon turned into steps lined with large cement vases filled with little yellow flowers. The stairs took us to a grey, architecturally nondescript, three-story building. The construction seemed solid enough – the foundation was a grey stone, the rest, grey bricks and grey stucco. There were terraces on the side of the building that faced the river. There were tables on the terraces, and scattered about on the tables and under the tables were empty bottles of vodka and Pepsi-Cola. So these were the legendary Kremlin dachas? Sensing our disappointment, Boris revealed that the outside wasn't the main attraction, it was what was inside, namely, the bathroom and the kitchen. He said that the sinks and toilet bowls in each dacha were French – all from an international exhibition of lavatory equipment. He told us that workers and engineers from Finland had been summoned to install them, not because the Finnish work better and drink less, but because our workers would undoubtedly try to take those treasures home with them.

We went inside. Apparently, the hallway was decorated by a colour-blind decorator. The floor was covered by an orange rug with green flecks. The drapes were a lemon-coloured velvet. The walls were painted the colour of three-day-old borscht. And, in the place of honour, where one would expect a fireplace, there was a painfully bright blue lift. Boris didn't take us in the lift; he said he would show us the lift and toilet bowls another time. He led the way straight down the dark corridor through the building and flung open a heavy emergency-exit door.

The garden was a clearing with high, uncut grass, burdock, and weeds. When our eyes grew accustomed to the bright sunlikgt, we were able to make out, at the far end of the field, in the shade of a sprawling oak, a hut from behind which came the clang of a balalaika.

'Don't let my father-in-law scare you,' said Boris. 'He's a little cuckoo. He resists change and continues to live in the Civil War days.'

Our group followed a nearly imperceptible path through the clearing and came to the hut. Behind the hut, with his back to the oak, sat the famous general – famous not so much for his heroic deeds, but for his tremendous moustache. He was dressed in long johns and a military shirt. In the general's hands rested a battered old balalaika. Beside his outstretched feet lay an army saddle and a revolver. A copper cartridge from a rifle was standing on the saddle. The general peered at the cartridge forlornly, played the balalaika in the measured rhythm of cavalry prancing, and sang:

> Oh, my cartridge, little cartridge,
> Bloody wedding, lonely start.
> In the morning in my carriage
> Love like a bullet struck my heart.

As he spotted us, the general shouted as if he were on horseback, in a voice surprisingly loud for his age:

'Hey, Mashka! Your man is here. Drag yourself out.'

Buxom Mashka looked the same as when I saw her near the wooden castle a long time ago. With a red kerchief on her head, she came crawling out of the hut. She had bits of straw all over her. In one hand, she held a military boot; in the other, a brush. It wasn't quite clear from her puffy, pillowlike face if she was pleased to see her husband or not.

'What the devil are you standing there staring for?' the general shouted. 'Haven't you ever seen men before? Come on, take care of your guests. Go and get the milk.'

Mashka vanished inside the hut and reappeared momentarily, a jug of milk in her hands. She passed the milk to the general and stared at us once again.

'Hey, Mashka. How you doin'?' Boris said nervously.

'Hello,' said Mashka.

'Are you feeling okay?' Boris asked with a note of concern.

'Oh, I feel all right,' replied Mashka.

'Hey,' cried the general, 'that's enough chitchat. You never get full on words. Who wants milk, soldiers?' the general said after taking a slug. His moustache got all wet, and white threads of milk fell from its drooping ends back into the jug. 'What are you so quiet about, soldiers? Last call!' He looked from one person to the next and said, 'Hey you, the last one on the right. Come over here and have some milk with me.'

The last one on the right was me. I followed the order and walked up to the general.

'Drink!' the veteran commanded gruffly.

I raised the jug to my lips and drank. The milk was cool and tasty – definitely not from the supermarket. I took a few big sips when I felt something touch my lips. I quietly lowered the jug and peered inside. It seemed to me that somebody was sitting there looking up at me. I placed it at an angle so I could see better and nearly dropped dead . . . in the milk floated a large green frog.

'What's the matter, soldier? Scared?' The general chuckled.

'There's a frog in the jug!' I said.

'And what do you think is supposed to be in there, a piece of shit?' the general asked, his moustache twitching.

'Did it fall in there accidentally?' I tried to ask politely.

'Accidentally, my eye! It's always in there,' said the veteran, his moustache rising.

'How come?' I asked, not quite sure if he was joking or not.

'So the milk doesn't turn sour, stupid. It's an old Russian custom,' the general said pedantically. 'I don't believe in all that modern stuff, like electric coolers. It's better to have a frog in your milk than cancer in your stomach. We always kept frogs in the milk during the Civil War, and we always had fresh milk. The frog is a clean, useful animal. Besides, it warns you if somebody has slipped poison in your drink.' At that point the general turned his gaze upon Mashka. 'I have nothing against poison. I personally enjoyed putting it in the well in 1919, for the White Army officers. But I don't want it for myself, of course. Why did you stop drinking? Don't worry; there's no poison in there. If the frog is all right, it means you'll be all right.'

'No thanks, I've had enough,' I said, handing the jug to the general.

'As you like. Who else wants milk? How come you're so quiet? This is your last chance,' he said, travelling around the group with his eyes. It seemed that only then did he notice Youssef.

'Who is that black officer? Come on over here, you!'

Youssef stepped up to the general. He flashed his teeth and the whites of his eyes and held his hand out to take the jug.

'Oh no!' swaggered the general as he held the jug off to one side. 'I didn't offer you my milk. I didn't offer it to you, shit

285

face. I'm not going to drink with you. I'm not going to give you my milk!'

'Fuck you!' the black prince said in a dignified manner.

'What?' exclaimed the shocked general.

'You're an old mudak!' Youssef returned, assuredly.

The next moment, the general's revolver flashed menacingly in his hand.

'Get up against the wall,' the general growled at Youssef, his moustache and gun trembling.

'Father!' screamed Boris, 'don't! Youssef doesn't know any other words. He's a foreigner.'

'Shut up!' the general commanded. 'We wiped out the white officers in the Revolution, but now blacks come crawling to us from all sides. You nigger, get up against the wall.'

Youssef spun around, slowly walked up the dacha, and positioned himself against the wall.

'What's your rank?' the general demanded.

'Prince,' replied Youssef.

'A ha!' the general said, brightening. 'I knew he was an aristocrat.'

'Papa,' Boris pleaded, 'is this really necessary today? How about some other time?'

'Yes, it is necessary today. It's necessary all right!' muttered the general, raising the gun and aiming. 'It's necessary to finish off the Czar's family. Fire!' he ordered himself abruptly.

The silence of the forest was pierced six times. Pieces of brick and plaster crumbled all around Youssef, but he remained standing without even a shudder. He was a real prince. The general placed the smoking gun on the grass, looked at Youssef, and said, 'I respect such bravery even in the enemy. Hey, Mashka, drag my box over here.'

Mashka dived into the hut. The first thing to be seen emerging from the hut was her round rump, then her bent back, and finally the rest of Mashka lugging a wooden box in which danced and clanged six bottles of grain vodka. The general whacked her on the rear crisply.

'Ow!' Mashka said.

'Drag that case over to the black officer; he has passed the test of fire,' the general said. 'I didn't give him milk, but now I'm paying him with vodka.'

'Come on, Mashka,' said Boris hurriedly, 'we've got to get going.'

'I don't want to go,' said Mashka, smiling at Andrew. 'I'm not in the mood for a honeymoon right now. I've got to finish cleaning these boots and then I have to rush to the village for more milk.'

'Andrewlka thinks he'll stick around too,' Andrewlka said. 'He wants to hear some more of the general's playing. Besides, it's too crowded in the car.'

'As you like,' said Boris.

'Bye-bye, everybody, have a nice time,' said Mashka, and waved her hand. Andrewlka waved, too.

'Bye-bye,' we said.

Youssef and I took hold of the case of vodka and headed for the car.

'A honeymoon without a wife!' whispered Boris, coming behind us. 'What luck!'

With two in the front seat and three in the back, we headed north-east.

'What do you think of my papa-in-law?' Boris asked when we reached the highway. 'What a character, eh? He shot at me, too, the first time he laid eyes on me, accusing me of being a Chinese spy. He sprayed bullets all around me; you heard him – he calls it a test of fire.'

'He's a mudak, that father of yours,' said Youssef.

'First of all, he isn't my father, he's Mashka's; and second of all, he isn't such a mudak considering his age. He'll be hitting ninety soon, but he's still as strong as a horse. He eats bread and milk exclusively. He never touches a drop of vodka, although he can get it for free. There's nothing modern in his life-style – he spends the whole summer in the hut; it's impossible to coax him into using a toilet; he always goes in the bushes. He uses my Mashka as a batman. Yes, he's a tyrant, but what strength, what hardiness; why, he even has a lover!'

'Come on, pull the other one,' said Stas.

'Stop pissing around,' said the prince. 'Sorry, Lena.'

'You don't believe it?' said Boris. 'All right then, I'll prove it to you. Did you notice that cartridge on the saddle beside him?'

'What about it?' Stas asked.

'His lover is hidden in that cartridge,' Boris said, beaming.

'What the hell are you talking about?' Stas asked.

'Bollocks!' the prince said.

'Listen,' said Boris, lowering his voice. 'I didn't want to talk about this, but since I've already brought it up I might as well tell you; but don't go telling anyone else; it's a government affair, understand?'

'Sure, sure,' we all said.

'Swear?'

'We swear.'

'Right, listen. But this isn't for your ears, Lena. My papa-in-law always carried that cartridge around with him even when he was getting washed. It aroused my curiosity, I thought it was a memento from the war, and once I asked him why he always had it with him. "Come along with me and you'll see for yourself," he replied. "It's time to share the family secrets with you." (It was just before the wedding.) So, he went to wash up, and I followed him. Behind the hut, there was a tub and a barrel of rainwater. He stripped and got into the tub, and I poured the water from the barrel over him. The old man moaned and dipped himself into the cold water, leaving outside only his head, hands, and the tip of his penis – a sad sight.'

'Penis!' the prince echoed, getting excited.

'With one hand he held his penis,' Boris continued, 'and with the other, he let an immense cockroach out of the cartridge and placed it on his penis. Yes, a cockroach! "It's my favourite lover," he said. The cockroach began to dash around on its little peninsula like mad, racing up and down and from side to side, but there was no place to go. The old man's moustache was fluttering, his eyes rolling in orgasm, and, all the while, he kept repeating that there was no better lover in the whole world. He told me that it was way back during the Civil War that he became addicted to this; that he would get bored raping girls, but he never tired of his cockroaches. He said that in general, humans didn't interest him; in his lifetime he had killed so many people that human

288

beings were nothing to him. Animals, cockroaches and frogs, were much more precious in his opinion. But that's not all; he revealed that among his friends in the Politburo, many of them get their kicks the very same way. As for impotence, there is supposed to be no better remedy than the fast legs of a cockroach. He said that nearly all of them have their own little darling, and that he was the one who had set the trend. Youssef, keep to the right; you're not in England!'

'Fuck your mother, you liar,' said the heir of the king of Tukbu.

'I'm not lying, I'm just repeating what I heard. If you saw their wives, you'd believe me for sure. They're better off with the cockroaches!'

'I'll have to try that,' Stas laughed.

We all chuckled, but it occurred to me that perhaps the whole thing was true. If I hadn't seen the cartridge with my own eyes, I might never believe it, but now, I believe everything and at the same time nothing.

'Do you love your Mashka?' Lena asked Boris.

'Oh, come on. How could I be in love with her – I don't even know if she was born of a cockroach or a frog!'

'You dirty son of a bitch,' Youssef said.

'What did you marry her for?' Lena pursued.

'Because it's the only way I'll get out of building matchboxes or military forts on the Chinese border for ninety rubles a month all my life. But now that the wedding is over, I can build a dacha for myself, or go anywhere – even to Paris!'

When the fiery wheel of the sun had rolled to the end of the day's path and lazily fallen down behind the horizon, the four wheels of our carriage carried us to the Nerl River. There, we turned off the highway and descended into a dark green field which looked like a huge billiard table dotted with haystacks. On the left side of the table, like a cube of chalk, was the ancient church, Pakrava, which was surrounded by the water.

The river Nerl, near the edifice, had washed the foot of this holy church for eight centuries. How many rains poured down on that river in all those years! How many drops rippled in its clear mirror! How many thaws sent it water! With what touching constancy the water has retained the reflection of the clear-cut beauty of the oldest Russian church. That evening, lit up by the last rays of the falling sun, the cupola of the little church glowed in the river like a pink pearl. Yes, its beauty was like nothing on this earth.

But right behind the church swayed the black snakes of high-voltage wires, on which even birds feared to bread. Across the expanse, electric poles, like iron giants, crossed the valley in kilometre-long steps. It was as if there were no other spot in all Russia to put the rusty, wide-open legs of those metallic monsters in the shape of a cross – as if in mockery. It's difficult to kill centuries-old beauty, even with electricity; but they did manage to kill the peace.

Hoping to induce peace in our own souls, we set ourselves the task of polishing off three bottles of vodka before heading for the church. We knew that the church was not on an island, but that there was bound to be some path that led up to it. But no matter how hard we tried to find that path, it was hopeless. The water would always wind up blocking our way. We drank two more bottles, made another attempt, and came up against the river again. As we downed the sixth bottle, the feeling that the path was nearby became heightened, but we simply couldn't find it – the water was everywhere and we were getting hysterical. . . .

At this point, Stas announced that if everyone got out of the car and we let him drive, he would find the way in no time. We obliged him and got out. He took the seat behind the wheel and started the engine. Youssef, shouting that he couldn't trust his car with a drunken driver, leaped onto the roof of the Volkswagen. The roof sagged in, but this didn't stop Stas. The engine was revving, and the car lurched forward.

We laughed and cheered as the Volks circled around on the green field, with Youssef still balanced on the roof and screaming that he loved Russia and didn't want to go back to Africa; that it was too hot there, and that he loved snow.

'Only foreigners can live here,' said Lena, and we all stopped laughing.

The red ball of the sun disappeared and night came. It was

turning damp and sad. The vodka had run out. We couldn't decide what to do next – go back to Moscow, or stay where we were and have dinner. After lengthy debates, we decided to build a fire and make dinner first, then head back for Moscow. We started looking around for kindling wood. We came upon some branches and reeds near the water. We piled them up and attempted to set them ablaze, but to no avail – they were wet. What on earth were we doing there in the middle of the night, and how had we happened to be blown that way?

Just then we heard a sound. At first, with the rustling of the wind in the grass, we didn't realize exactly what it was. Then it came closer. Then there was a flicker of light, and it began to draw near along with a song. We still couldn't grasp the words, but the melody sounded happy. We peered into the darkness, guessing at what it could be. The tiny flame came closer and closer and soon seemed to be very near us. Out of the darkness came two hands – one holding a thick wax candle; the other, glowing at the edges, protecting the flame from the wind. It was a man dressed in a black cape with a hood.

'*Christ will rise in the summer!*' came the words of the song, as a chill ran down our spines. The man passed us as if he hadn't even seen us, then took the path leading to the water. His dark back blocked the candle, but the light outlined the departing figure with an alluring glow.

'Oh my God, today's Easter!' Lena said, going after the man.

'That's right! Easter!' I repeated. 'How could I have forgotten!'

The luminous figure went around the water and, without a word, we all followed.

'*Christ will rise in the summer!*' flew across the river. The water rippled in tiny waves and each wave, like a liquid mirror, reflected the light in its own way. We followed that light and found ourselves beside the church walls. It was so simple that it was a mystery why we hadn't been able to find that path in daylight.

The man in black slowly ascended the church steps and stopped near the door, which was fastened shut with large nails. We stood quietly, looking at him. The monk knelt down and said a prayer. I can still remember those words –

Christ will rise from the dead,
Through death he will conquer death.

When the monk finished praying, he rose and turned towards us. Though the candle lit up the entire church, his face remained in the shadow of his hood, but we felt that he was smiling. He switched the candle to his left hand and, with his right, blessed us, then motioned for us to draw near. We went closer to him. From somewhere in the folds of his robe, he took out thin candles and distributed them among us. When we each had a candle, he stepped down, made the sign of the cross over us again, and lit our candles with his own. When all the candles were burning, he broke into song and made his way around the church. We followed him quietly, encircling the little white church as if we were a chain. The monk was up ahead, behind him was Lena, then Stas, Youssef, Boris, and me.

The flames of the candles illuminated the white walls of the church, one after the other, cutting them out of the night's darkness. We went around and again came to the entrance. The monk hastened up the steps and proclaimed joyfully:

'*Christ is risen!*'

We peered at him in silence. He turned to us and said:

'*Christ is risen!*'

We wanted to respond but, not knowing what to say, we remained quiet.

'*It is true, the Lord is risen*,' he said, and repeated the refrain. Raising his hand holding the lighted candle, he blessed the door which was nailed shut and uttered softly:

'*These doors will soon be open.*'

Then he descended the steps, came up to each of us, embraced us, then went away from the church and vanished in the night.

The candles burned down and the lights went out. A heavy fog came towards us from the river, slowly it crept to our feet, then surrounded us completely. We groped our way back to the car, took our seats, and drove away in silence through the deep, enveloping fog. We listened to the tyres rolling across the grass. There was no road. Everybody was getting sleepy. Lena put her head on my shoulder and dozed off. I wanted to sleep too, but was afraid that if I moved I'd wake her.

We seemed to go a long way, but there was still no road in sight. Soon the fog was so thick it became impossible to make out anything – it was like driving through cotton. The light given off by the headlamps ended abruptly one metre from the car. When the car began to lurch and vibrate, we realized we were in trouble. Lena's head hit my shoulder, and she awoke.

'Where are we?' she asked.

'On the road to heaven,' Boris replied.

At that very moment, the car hit something and stopped. The impact was soft; it felt as if we had hit the fog. We crawled out of the car one by one. Beneath our feet was a freshly cut field. The car had ploughed into a haystack. There wasn't much else to do but pick a haystack, spread out, and go to sleep.

Lena and I lay down on the soft hay, wrapped in the curling fog. As we looked up, at first the world around us was black, then, eventually, it turned grey, then white. The fog was thinning out, revealing a sliver of blue sky, then another, and another. In the blue to our right, in the rays of the rising sun, glittered the cupola of the Pakrava church! For all our driving, we hadn't got anywhere.

The wind carried the fog along, and it felt as if we were floating on a cloud past the church. The haystacks appeared like mountain peaks jutting into the clouds. On a neighbouring haystack, we saw Youssef standing, like a statue fashioned from ebony, silently peering at the cupola shimmering in the sun.

'What do you think?' Lena said.

'I think that's our foreigner,' I said.

'I was thinking the same thing,' Lena said. 'I never expected to find him at the Pakrava church. It's fate.'

'You know,' I said, 'it looks as if I'm starting to believe.'

'In what?' Lena asked.

'In God,' I said.

Lena was silent.

'And you?' I asked.

'You're a funny man,' said Lena. 'I've always believed.'

We sat quietly for a few minutes, staring at the clearing sky. There was no fog any more.

'When should we ask him to send the invitation?' Lena asked.

'Today,' I said. 'The time has come.'

5 It's Not Easy to Be a Jew

One September morning the postman entered the back courtyard. On his way to the lobby, his steps could be counted by the crunching of partially frozen puddles under his feet. He climbed the stairs to the second floor and knocked on our door. I opened the door a sliver, but the postman requested my signature for a long white envelope. It was an unusual envelope: it had a clear plastic window, and through this window I saw my name.

Slowly, letter by letter, I signed the receipt. The postman left me standing, still staring at the envelope. Lena came to me soundlessly, embracing me from the back, and looked over my shoulder, her hands finding their way down my arms and into my hands and squeezing them almost painfully. This was it, our letter from abroad.

It happened four months after Youssef's departure and we were shocked, but not because we didn't anticipate it. We had done nothing all these months but wait; we never even bought furniture for our apartment in anticipation, we continued to live out of our crocodile suitcase with our guitars in tow, and still we weren't ready. It was just that it happened so matter-of-factly. We, who were so used to the complexity of fate, were mesmerized by the simplicity of this outcome. The most fantastic and sophisticated plans we created never looked good enough and suddenly the most primitive and idiotic plan of Toilik's seemed to be working.

I carefully opened this strange white envelope. It contained a letter with a red raised seal. I read it almost fainting from nervousness. It was an official invitation from someone called Dim Haviv, who wanted to reunite our family in Israel. We had it! Here in my hand was what we'd been waiting for. But it wasn't the end of our problem – it was only the beginning. The real risks were just about to start, because the moment we received that letter we changed from being citizens of the Soviet Union to traitors.

Now what? flashed in my mind. It was Lenin's question one minute before his death.

It would be a lie if I said I was never scared in my life; it would be a lie if I said I was scared only once or twice. The truth is I was scared many times, but I have never experienced such an animalistic fear as the moment after I received that letter. It was as though a cold snake crawled into my stomach and began to eat my flesh, piece by piece, and drink my blood, drop by drop. I looked at Lena . . . her frail body trembled and her eyes were like frozen seawater. The fear tied us by its cold chains and dragged us back inside the room.

Looking into each other's eyes, we undressed slowly, and then, with the passion of our disappearing youth, we threw our bodies onto the floor and into the flame of lovemaking, which through all our illegal years had turned into a wild desperation. We went crazy with a hungry need. Our kisses were more like bites, our embraces like a deadly vice, our fingers were like sharp claws. We were angry and rough, as if we wanted to hide within each other's bodies, as if only there could we find peace, as if we wanted to destroy each other so as not to face the threatening reality. We were fighting the entire icy world around us and to win the battle we had only the heat of our bodies. Bodies of longtime lovers, lovers who didn't need comfort, who had already forgotten the meaning of the word.

Our entire beings convulsed with the release of our simultaneous screams, as we rolled back and forth on the parquet floor . . . Our lovemaking slowed down to a gentle rhythm. The battle was over, the fear was dead.

We gained strength from each other; we now had the urge to fight, to act. Reality brought some questions; if only we knew what our next step should be. Who could we ask? Who could we trust?

'We mustn't trust anyone,' said Lena. 'It's too risky.'

'We can trust our friends,' I said. 'I'll phone someone.'

'No! Don't, the phone is probably tapped,' Lena said, 'and I still don't think we should tell even our friends until we have permission to leave.'

'If we don't trust our friends, I'm afraid I don't know how to live. Who knows how long this will take? We can't live a lie among our friends!'

'If they don't know,' she reasoned, 'it will be easier for them as well as for us. If they know what we're planning, they may not be able to deal with the idea of what can happen to them because of us.'

'I still don't believe we can make it without them. Mistrusting our friends . . . it's impossible. They've helped us all these years; I'm going to phone.'

'Please don't! I have a terrible feeling,' pleaded Lena, and she began to cry.

Just then the phone rang.

'Don't answer it! There's something wrong,' Lena cried.

'Don't be silly. It's too early for bad news,' I tried to reassure her, but the ringing phone unnerved me too.

'It's the police. I feel it,' said Lena hopelessly.

'The police wouldn't ring in the morning, they come at night,' I said, forcing myself to pick up the receiver.

'Please don't – '

'It's Andrewlka,' I said, turning to Lena with relief.

'Don't tell,' Lena mouthed to me.

'Hello,' said Andrewlka, 'did you get your white envelope?'

It caught me off balance.

'What?' I asked. 'What white envelope? . . . How in the world do you know?' I was relieved, I didn't need to lie.

'Andrewlka knows everything, because Andrewlka has friends everywhere,' he said playfully.

'Well, if Andrewlka is so informed, what does he suggest we do?'

'Andrewlka suggests you go to the nearest police station and ask for application forms – emigration forms, that is. Then fill them in very carefully, because just one mistake and even Andrewlka with all his power and connections will not be able to help. But don't delay. This is the *right time* . . . do it now.'

'What do you mean, the right time? The right time for what?'

'Andrewlka can't explain, just don't forget where he works part-time, trust him, Andrewlka is always right.'

'Okay, but may I ask you to keep this a secret?'

'Andrewlka's the best secret keeper, but it's too late. He's already told everyone and we're planning a bon voyage party with "Ciao Bambino Potatoes" every day till you leave.'

If we leave, I thought.

Following Andrewlka's instructions, we went that same day to the local police station on Kutuzov Prospekt. The fact of this reality still made me nervous. By asking for an application to leave the USSR, we proved that we were enemies of the people, fully aware and responsible for our actions.

The clerk at the station put his glasses on his long, sharp nose and looked over our invitation very carefully, glancing back and forth, from the letter to us, with leery, mistrusting eyes. Then he asked for our passports and checked our propiskas. Thank God, for the first time we had everything in order, and he handed each of us an application.

'Can I have an extra in case I make a mistake?' I asked.

'You'd better not, Jew boy,' the clerk said, smiling.

I shivered at his remark, then replied, 'You have no right to speak to me that way.'

'You have no rights in this country, you Jewish weasel. Now go to your job and ask for a *character reference*. It's the first thing to do, because I'm not going to accept your application without a reference. Get out before I arrest you! Get out, you circumcised prick!' he suddenly screamed.

I felt helpless and beaten. There was no possibility of fighting back and, most of all, it was painfully embarrassing. All my life I had heard the same words, but they had never touched me, it never occurred to me that they could hurt so very much, because they were never directed at me. Thinking back, I felt dirty with guilt. I wasn't much better than that policeman. Now I had to learn to be patient and to swallow these insults. I had to learn to accept everything that came with my new nationality. I turned to Lena and took her hand in mine, and we both left in sad silence.

With a heavy heart, I went to the theatre to tell Dudin of my emigration plans. When I arrived, his secretary informed me that Dudin was out at a meeting and should return in one hour. So now I had an hour with nothing to do but roam through the theatre with its many memories.

I didn't know how, but everyone already knew my plans to leave the country. I couldn't have received more attention if I'd gone there with a yellow star on my chest. In the hour that I spent waiting for Dudin, I learned how much we depend on the friendship of others, especially in a time of need. 'Hello,' I said to a group of actors, but just a few responded, with half-angry, half-smiling faces. Though I was the same person, I was regarded differently. This is when I understood that truth is not reality, but what others perceived as reality. I felt that I was not just a Jew, but a Jew liar, a Jew hiding, embarrassed about his nationality, and this kind of Jew is regarded in the worst way. I never felt more lost than in that hour.

I once read about an American reporter who, while looking for a sensational story, painted his face and hands black and moved into the streets of the city in the hope of getting a clear and honest picture of the racial problems. It took him on a journey of experiencing terrible insults, injustice, and pain. He was beaten, arrested, and treated as the lowest caste of human. He was stunned by the sudden and drastic changes brought him by his new skin colour. He was so horrified and crushed by his experience in a true hell that he was unable to complete his experiment.

In Russia, you don't need to change the colour of your skin to experience the same pain of prejudice. You need only to change one word on your document, which states your nationality. And if this word is placed on your birth certificate, you will face a journey of misery to your death. You will be tortured by insulting remarks, sarcastic smiles, sharp elbows poked in your ribs while waiting in endless queues, by not being accepted into the University, being harassed on your job, being beaten on the streets, being arrested and then killed only because of the star of David, which hangs around your neck.

You don't have to be black in Russia to experience a racial hell, you have to be a Jew.

I became familiar with that hell while walking through my theatre among my comrades. I felt persecuted by everyone I came in contact with. I felt responsible for and guilty of crimes I hadn't committed. I was beginning to know what it was to be a Jew in Russia and only one hour had passed since my nationality had been changed, only one hour of a traditional Russian game called 'Beating the Jew'.

I was drained and weakened by my experience when the time came to return to Dudin's office.

'I've come to ask you for a character reference,' I said in the doorway.

Dudin greeted me with 'I know, I know, you don't have to tell me,' his eyes paled by sadness. 'I've already been informed. Sit down.'

I sat down and focused my gaze out the window; it was easier not to look directly into Dudin's troubled face. For the first time, he didn't offer me a cup of tea.

'Well,' he said, 'let's get straight to the point. You've put me in a very difficult position. I was responsible for hiring you to work in this theatre. I made certain that you got an apartment, and I took you on tour abroad. If I had known you were Jewish, none of these things would have been possible. I think you remember the fifth question on your application form to this theatre. It referred to your nationality. I hope you understand that by lying on that form you've made it look as though I've collaborated with you, and if I prove that I knew nothing, I'm still responsible for not checking more thoroughly. My superiors will use this situation against me. You're the first and only actor in this capital to emigrate. I should have listened to Comrade Silver's warning.

'Ah,' he continued with a rueful smile, 'I liked you, though . . . I liked you very much. Only because of your talent have I treated you as a superior in my troupe. This special singling-out makes my problems even greater. My only solace is that you didn't defect while we were on tour. I thank you for that; I know it must have been an incredible temptation. . . . So what am I going to do with you?'

'I don't know,' I replied.

'No matter what the outcome, I'm in trouble. But as I've told you before, there was only one person that I feared and he is dead, so . . . let's do it this way. . . . My position here requires that I fire you today, but I won't. I'll try to keep you here as long as possible, but I hope you understand it can't be for very long. I was told to try and talk you out of your decision, but my conscience tells me not to. Who knows what I would have done if I were young. . . . Well, let me ask you – what about your family, have you considered them and the possibility of their being harassed?'

'My mother is a senior citizen and doesn't work, and my sister is married and also does not work. There is nothing that could happen to them – at least I hope not.'

'You understand you also will not work soon. I'm truly sorry about this. You had everything to look forward to. You're a rising star and you could be the biggest and the best. Now, you're finished as an actor. . . . If you get permission to leave you'll probably never work as an actor again, because there will be a language barrier, and, if you don't get permission to leave, you will never be allowed to work in any capacity ever again, not even as a street cleaner. Do you understand this?'

'I understand, but I'm willing to take the chance.'

'I've always thought of you as more than just an actor; you're an adventurer as well, and in Russia all the adventurers wind up in jail. Be very careful when filling out your emigration forms; I hear they're very tricky and complicated. Let's hope that everything works out for you and they let you go.'

'Let's hope,' I whispered.

'Here's your character reference. I've made it simple so as not to bring on any more suspicion than I already have to deal with. You can go now. This is, I'm afraid, our last conversation. I'm not allowed to speak to you after this . . . so . . . good-bye.'

'Goodbye,' I said with deep emotion, 'and thank you for everything.' I stood up and prepared to leave.

'Come over here,' Dudin said, and motioned with his finger. I came to him. He stretched out his arm, grabbed the back of my head with his hand, and pulled me even closer. While embracing me, he whispered, 'If I were young . . . I would also run away. Good luck, my son.'

When I reached the door, he called out to me, 'Tell my secretary I've run out of tea.'

Walking out of the theatre through a path made in a deep snow, I suddenly bumped into the ex-King of Monkeys, ex-Lenin. After the pea-soup scandal in Montreal, he was back working as a street cleaner, shovelling snow.

'Hello,' I said.

'If I had known you were a Jew, I would have pushed you into the orchestra pit long ago,' the response came clear and loud.

'No, you couldn't have, Comrade Lenin, you were too busy stealing,' I replied.

'One more word from you and I'll use this shovel on your head,' he said, walking up to me.

'Don't do it,' I said, smiling friendly. 'Would you like anything from Israel?'

'I hope they don't let you go, and I'll have a chance to bash in your Jewish skull,' said Lenin, his face now red with rage as he approached with shovel in hand.

'But if they do, I know what I'll do for you, Comrade Lenin. I'll send you an invitation from Israel.'

After that day, rumours began to circulate in the theatre that I was working for the KGB and was going abroad on a special mission. It explained to everyone why I wasn't arrested or even fired. But the real reason for my good fortune was the 'right time' – the political game called détente. Two great leaders, Brezhnev and Nixon, as in the best tradition of the Egyptian Pharaohs, had a secret agreement to exchange a few hundred thousand Russian Jews for a bunch of American technology.

Now that I had my character reference in hand, my next step was to prove in writing on my emigration form that I was a full-blooded Jew, and that I had lived a lie as a Russian. Peering at the papers, I knew I had taken a perilous path. All the answers on the six-page form had to fit together into a cohesive story. Since the KGB had information about each family, going back at least three generations, this was no easy task. Each answer given on this form could be used as evidence against me; each line, an indictment; each page, a guilty verdict – and with it a trip not to the west and freedom but to the northeast and prison camp.

The forms were prepared like a crossword puzzle, every square a KGB prison cell. Each question was trickier than the last, particularly because we didn't know anything about Dim Haviv, except one thing. It was important that that person had left Russia before the Revolution, first because the KGB wouldn't have records of that time, second because nobody could say that *he* or *she* was anti-Soviet.

Was Dim Haviv a man or a woman? Dim Haviv, Haviv Dim . . . What was Dim supposed to mean and what was Haviv? Which was the first name and which was the last? When and where did destiny separate us? What holocaust split our 'family' apart, and how did our names become so drastically different?

We decided that Dim Haviv was a woman – my aunt Haviv. It was better if she was a woman, we thought. Her name could have changed through marriage. Next we decided that I was Jewish on my father's side – first of all, because he was dead, and nobody could ask him; second, because he was an orphan, so the KGB wouldn't have any records on him. We wrote a dramatic family saga:

My father was born in 1910 in Kahovka, South of Russia. His father, a Russian, was killed in 1914 during World War I.

His mother, a Jew, fled from Russia to Poland in 1915, to escape the Czar's pogrom.

She took her baby daughter Dim with her, but left my father behind.

During World War II, my Jewish grandmother was killed by Fascists in a ghetto in Poland.

After the war, my aunt went to Israel, where she married David Haviv.

They had a happy life together, but then he died suddenly.

She was all alone in the world and she started to search for her relatives.

She found me and sent me an invitation.

According to Jewish law, my father was Jewish, because his mother was Jewish; according to Soviet law, since my father was a Jew, I am also a Jew.

Therefore, I have the right to emigrate to Israel.

My father was a devout communist, he served his government whenever called upon. On his deathbed he told me of a secret he planned to take to his grave. I was very young then and didn't have a full understanding of what he was saying. He repeated himself several times in these same words, 'You are a Jew, my son, you are a Jew.' I knew then I must also keep this secret. He also told me I must go to the land of my ancestors, he had a sister there whom he hadn't seen since he was a boy. His sister's name was Dim and she lived in Israel. So, to fulfil my father's last wish, I feel I must find my roots, even though I love Mother Russia.

It took Lena and me three full days and nights to create this story, and to answer all six pages of questions. We read and reread them hundreds of times. We alternated asking each other all the questions, to make sure our answers were believable, and to make them sound as spontaneous and truthful as possible. Finally, everything seemed right; we now felt confident enough to seal these forms with our signatures. The next step was to deliver the documents to the police station.

There the same clerk checked each and every question and answer on our documents, running his finger under each line in order not to lose his place. We stood watching intently as he read. His finger finally stopped moving, he looked up at us with eyes that could almost kill with contempt, grabbed the papers, and left the room. We didn't dare move. We stood waiting for about half an hour and when the clerk returned empty-handed he was wearing a sly grin.

'What should we do now, comrade?' I said with my most charming smile. This was a good test for my acting ability.

'I'm not a comrade to a traitor to *my* country,' he said, looking right through me.

'I'm sorry, sergeant, but we don't know what to do now.'

'Wait,' he said.

'For how long?'

'By the generous law of *my* country, you will be notified by the Emigration Office within three months,' said the clerk. Then, as though he were talking to a couple of lepers, he added. 'Today is September the twenty-second. If you don't receive a postcard with the answer by December the twenty-second, it means your case needs special attention, and special cases have *no* time limits. Do you understand, Jew boy?'

'Yes, sir,' I said.

'So go and pray in your Jew synagogue for an answer before that deadline.'

'Thank you, sir,' I replied, swallowing my pride.

Once we were out in the fresh cold wind, I let out a sigh of frustration and looked up to the pale blue sky. Among the frozen clouds were a flock of birds flying south. They were the last lonely group to migrate. I took a deep breath of icy but invigorating air. Exhaling slowly, I turned to Lena and put my arms around her, trying to protect her from the angry wind. I held her closer and whispered, 'You know, Lena, it's not easy to be a Jew.'

6 Gained One, Lost One

Life in Russia was of course a constant wait. Waiting to move to Moscow, waiting for propiska, waiting for a job, waiting to go abroad, waiting for an invitation, still waiting for permission to emigrate, and the everyday waiting with fear of arrest.

With each month of waiting for permission, I lost parts in the theatre. Dudin tried to slow down that process, but he couldn't do it forever. Somebody was putting pressure on him. The day was coming when I would no longer be a prince but an unemployed actor, and then . . . it was better not to think what was going to happen.

So, during all this waiting and anticipation we drank. Our friends were always there supporting us with the strength we all got from a bottle. Lena was wrong; they didn't abandon us. Andrewlka, Boris, and Stas organized bon-voyage parties every night to help keep our minds free of worry. In October, we bade farewell to our illusions. In November, we toasted each other and our disappearing youth. By December, we were consuming more vodka than in the previous two months, and yet we were more sober than ever, while toasting a farewell to life itself.

And so came the morning of December twenty-second. The shortest day of the year and the longest night. The night of our waiting but the beginning of the end for us.

We were awakened by the telephone; it was Boris. 'Hello,' he said, have you received your mail yet?'

'No,' I said.

'Good luck, and don't forget there's another farewell party at Andrewlka's. He has something very special for you.'

'All right, we'll be there,' I said, and hung up. Now I busied myself on the lookout for the postman. He was late. This was the last day for a yes answer, tomorrow would be too late. Then it could only be no.

When I saw the postman crossing the courtyard, my heart stopped beating. I heard the entrance door squeak open and slam shut. I heard him walking up the stairs, but I didn't wait for him to knock. I couldn't stand the anticipation any longer, so I opened the door. He was a bit startled when I asked him if I had any mail.

Yes, he had mail for us.

Yes, it was a postcard.

Yes, it was an official postcard.

No, it wasn't a postcard from the Emigration Office.

It was a postcard from Lena's aunt Sonia, who was in the Kremlin Hospital. Even though Lena never saw eye to eye with her, she worried about her and kept in touch. After all, Sonia was her only relative in Moscow.

The postcard said that Sonia was critically ill, near dying. As a rule, Aunt Sonia would die a few times a year, so we didn't take the postcard very seriously. But we did take very seriously the fact that we hadn't got our notification from the Emigration Office. It meant that our case would be given special attention – and we knew exactly where that would take us. We were crushed. To keep our minds off this disaster, we decided to visit Aunt Sonia in the hospital.

We got dressed in silence and went outside. The day was grey and gloomy, the wind piercing. Banks of snow lined the walls of the houses, covered the streets, and kept coming down. The Kremlin Hospital was just a few blocks from Arbat, on Granousky Street, but it took us forever to get there. The wind was vicious and we walked the whole way turned around – one step forward and two back, like Lenin's theory.

When we got to the main entrance, we saw an extraordinary limousine parked out front – a gold Lincoln Continental. Men in grey hats, smoking cigarettes, stood beside the car. When we approached the entrance to the hospital, one of the men took a step towards us and said, 'Stop. You're not allowed to go in there.'

'I have to. My aunt's in critical condition,' Lena said.

'In ten minutes, it'll be possible to go in, but not now.'

'Don't you understand, my aunt is dying.'

'I told you, in ten minutes – '

'Maybe she'll be dead in ten minutes, or maybe she *is* dead,' Lena shouted back, losing control.

'If your aunt is alive, she can wait a little longer; if she's dead, there's no reason to hurry,' the grey hat said philosophically, as he blew smoke in Lena's face and edged us over to one side.

Just then, there was a stir in the group positioned around the car, as if someone had turned on a mechanism beneath the pavement. All the smokers, in one movement, threw their cigarettes down on the pavement and went into a strange, but well-coordinated routine – two of them blocked the pedestrians on the right; two did the same on the left; one went up to the hospital entrance and opened the door; another opened the door of the limousine; then they held their positions for a few seconds. Nobody emerged either from the hospital or from the car. Then the grey hats, as if on a silent command, shut the doors, opened up the flow of pedestrians on the street, and, as if nothing had happened, took out new cigarettes and resumed smoking. We attempted once again to enter the hospital but, not being part of that still-unfinished performance, we were stopped. Two more times the hats replayed the scene with the invisible man. Throwing their cigarettes on the pavement, blocking the path of the pedestrians, opening the doors, closing them, and lighting their cigarettes again. When they did their routine for the fourth time, and we had already stopped watching out of boredom and the freezing cold, two new faces appeared in the doorway of the Kremlin Hospital – a man in a dark suit with a brown bag under one of his arms and, after him, a woman with a heavy face and big breasts. They crossed the pavement, slipped into the waiting car, and sped off. All the men in the grey hats disappeared at the same time. If it weren't for the cigarette butts still smoking on the pavement, we might have thought we had dreamed up the whole thing. Driving off in that gold Lincoln Continental was the First Secretary of the Politburo, the leader of the Soviet Union, Comrade Leonid Ilyich Brezhnev, and his beloved daughter, Galina.

The entrance to the hospital was now open. We went up to the information desk, where a policeman and receptionist checked who we were and whom we were visiting. Then we were given visitor's passes and were told to follow a nurse.

The Kremlin Hospital looked more like a lavish villa than a clinic. There were marble columns, marble floors, and marble staircases. Sonia was in a private room, half pink marble, half painted green. She lay on a bed made of flat boards. There were no pillows or mattresses, only two sheets – one under Sonia, the other over her. Even in such a bed she was almost dimensionless, like a flower pressed between the pages of a book. Her puffball of hair and her dark wrinkled hands resting on the sheet were practically the only evidence that someone was in the bed. The old woman lay there perfectly still. Her eyes were shut, she wore headphones on her head, and held some sort of tickets with a red stripe on the diagonal which looked like little playing cards in her hands. On the wall behind the head of the bed hung an attention-getting poster of Lenin with the words of Mayakovsky inscribed at the top:

LENIN LIVED,
LENIN LIVES,
LENIN WILL LIVE FOREVER!

As for Aunt Sonia's life, that wasn't so definite.

'Hello,' Lena said quietly.

Sonia didn't respond but fidgeted with the tickets in her hands.

'How are you, Aunt Sonia?' Lena said a little louder.

'What?' Sonia said without opening her eyes.

'Hello,' Lena shouted.

'Who's there?' Sonia said.

'It's me,' Lena screamed.

'Who?' Sonia asked.

'It's us, Sasha and me,' Lena cried.

'Come in,' Sonia yelled fairly clearly.

'We're already here,' Lena screamed.

'What?' Sonia shouted.

'We've already come in,' Lena cried.

'Who?' Sonia screamed.

'Sasha and me,' Lena repeated.

'Where are you? I can't see you.'

'Your eyes are closed, Aunt Sonia!' Lena screamed.

'What? I can't hear you,' Sonia yelled.

'Take those headphones off,' Lena cried.

'I don't need a phone.'

'What do you need?' Lena shouted.

'A pillow!'

'The nurse told me the doctor said you're not supposed to have a pillow,' Lena screamed.

'Give the doctor a bottle of champagne,' the old woman added to that cosmic conversation. 'Do you hear me?'

'Yes,' shouted Lena.

'Don't leave me alone, don't leave Russia. I'll give you caviar,' Sonia yelled.

'Thank you, Aunt,' Lena screamed.

'Look out of the window,' Sonia cried. 'Check if the ferry is on its way.'

'It's on its way,' Lena shouted with tears in her eyes. There were no windows in the room.

'Take these coupons and go by ferry to get caviar for yourself and champagne for my doctor. Then he'll give me back my pillow.'

Sonia moved the coupons around on the sheet. Some of them said 'lunch,' some said 'dinner'. She piled up the coupons, but when Lena went to take them, she suddenly hid the entire pile under the sheet. One of the coupons slipped out of her hands and fell down on the floor. I picked it up. On the coupon was written 'lunch'.

'Hurry up,' wailed Sonia. 'Take the ferry! Go to Kremlyovka, but not to Israel! Do you hear me?'

'Yes,' Lena screamed back.

'Can you see me?'

'Yes,' Lena cried, 'I can see you and I can hear you perfectly.'

'Why can't I see you?' Sonia shouted.

'Open your eyes!' Lena screamed.

'What? I can't hear you!' Sonia yelled.

'Would you take those headphones off!'

'No,' Sonia cried. 'Don't take away my radio. The next programme is a reading from *Pravda!*'

There was no need to take the ferry to get to Kremlyovka, the Kremlin Health Food Store; it was in the other wing of the hospital. We went out of the back door, crossed the courtyard where, here and there, brown frozen asters stuck up through the snow. We went up the steps and opened the heavy oak doors. Inside, there was a vestibule with huge man-sized Chinese vases in each corner painted with dragons. As soon as we took a few steps, a robust man in a grey uniform emerged from behind one of the vases. His frame was exactly the same shape as the vase he stood behind.

'Hello,' Lena said. 'Do you remember me? I used to come here with my aunt.'

'Where is your aunt?' the guard asked.

'She's in the hospital. She couldn't come today.'

'So?'

'Can we go inside? We've got to pick something up for her,' Lena said.

'Okay, but just this once,' the guard said. 'The rule is, the coupon can *only* be used by its proper owner.'

Down the hall, there was a large room with two pink marble tables on which were sheets of brown paper and balls of string. On one wall hung a bulletin board covered with tacked-up pieces of paper. I read it with amazement.

HEALTH-FOOD LUNCHES (Lunch coupons)

			special
1. salami herring horse radish Bolshevik biscuits	2. cod liver khalva pickles Pepsi-Cola	3. salmon bird's milk ketchup	4. red tangerines, 3 kg.
2 coupons	*1 coupon*	*2 coupons*	1 coupon

HEALTH-FOOD DINNERS (Dinner coupons)

1. Polish ham Portuguese anchovies Hungarian apples	2. shrimp pineapple olive oil	3. sturgeon sausages Soviet cheese	4. red caviar black caviar gum drops
2 coupons	*1 coupon*	*1 coupon*	*2 coupons*

There was no possibility of getting caviar with our single lunch coupon. We decided to take the tangerines, and went to the counter. There were three windows at the counter, but only one was open. From that window stretched a long line of people. Yes, there were even queues in the Kremlin Health Food Store! It was a queue of loyal Party members – in their coats with muskrat collars and reindeer hats. Their faces were padded with fat, but their mouths were haughty nevertheless. The Party mouths would come up to the window and state a lunch or dinner number. After getting their cans and bottles, they would go to the marble tables. There, with professional adroitness, they would wrap their food in the brown paper, fasten the packages securely, place them under their arms, and proudly walk away with their precious food – food which had a very special value – for such food the Revolution took place, millions of people were killed, and prison camps were set up. Yes, all this happened for those packages of food. To be able to eat food which the rest of the population has never even smelled, to sit on French toilet bowls, and to drive an American limousine. What a victory!

And we too had a coupon; and we too were standing on that line, and we too went up to the window and called out our number. And we too got our precious food – tangerines, not orange ones, but special red ones. And we too wrapped them up in the brown paper. How easy it was to become one of *them*, I thought with a shudder. 'Let's get out of here. We have to go to Andrewlka's,' I said to Lena.

'Next time, don't come without your aunt,' the guard said when we passed the vase on the way out.

But next time never came. Though the selections from *Pravda* were short, Sonia never heard the end. All that was left of that old communist was a bag of tangerines as red as blood. So it goes – life in its circles. We found an aunt in Israel, we lost an aunt in Moscow. Gained one, lost one. Or had we lost both?

7 So Long

There wasn't just a cold wind when we set out for Andrewlka's, but wind with snow, and there wasn't just snow, but snow with rain. The Kremlyovka package got soaked and nearly fell apart — I wasn't able to wrap it as well as the Party bosses. Worried that the tangerines would scatter any second, I hugged the package all around with my left hand. My right hand was frozen stiff, I had lost one of my leather gloves somewhere, probably in Kremlyovka. Bloody tangerines, no luck with them: one death . . . one glove . . . what next?

December the twenty-second! The day had hardly started yet, but the longest night was already rolling in. Oh, how nasty it was that night of December the twenty-second, and what a wind. Right from Siberia and so tricky. When we went to the hospital it was in our face, and when we went back it was again in our face. Why is it that in Russia the wind is always in your face?

Exhausted and frozen, we reached Andrewlka's house. We tumbled into the foyer, where we caught our breath. Then I gave Andrewlka's door a good kick, but it didn't open. I put the soggy package of tangerines on the tile floor and banged the door with my shoulder. It didn't budge. Then, summoning all my strength, I hit it again harder, and only then realized that the door was locked from the inside. It was the first time Andrewlka's door had ever been locked. I looked at Lena, Lena looked at me. We both looked at the door . . . and slowly backed up toward the entrance.

'The package,' Lena whispered. 'You left the package there.'

I went back to the door and started pulling the package up. But the string snapped, the bundle fell down on its side, brushing against the door, and a few tangerines popped out, hitting the floor.

'Who's there?' came a hushed voice from behind the door.

'It's us,' I said.

'Who's us?' the door inquired.

'We are us,' I said, 'who are you?'

'An emigration inspector,' came the reply as the door opened wide. There, on the threshold, stood a neatly groomed Andrewlka in sunglasses and a grey tweed suit.

'Oh,' Lena sighed, 'you're crazy. I nearly died of fright.'

'Surprise,' Andrewlka cried, 'Andrewlka loves to surprise his friends.'

'Please, don't ever do that again,' Lena sighed.

'Five minutes ago, Andrewlka was proud and happy, but now he's steeped in depression because nobody likes his surprises.'

'Have a tangerine, but no tears, please,' I said, picking up the fruit from the floor and holding out the package to Andrew.

'Tangerines!' Andrewlka shouted. 'Sashulka presented Andrewlka with tangerines. Now Andrewlka feels better – much better. Tangerines – the missing link to Andrewlka's happiness. Sound the trumpets, beat the drums. Andrewlka smells the scent of the Kremlin. Let's hurry and wash them off. We've got to wash the Kremlin dust off them,' Andrewlka said, shoving me toward the bathroom.

'Throw them in the bathtub,' Andrewlka continued. 'Oh no! It's already full!'

I looked at the bathtub and was stunned. The entire tub, up to the edge, and even over the edge was filled with red tangerines, just like mine.

'Where did you get them?' I said.

'What?' Andrewlka asked naively, taking his sunglasses off.

'The tangerines.'

'You just gave them to me.'

'Not these, the ones in the bathtub!'

'Oh, those!' Andrewlka looked down and finally worked it out. 'Andrewlka took them from the living room. There are a lot of them there.'

'What the hell are you talking about?'

'Nobody ever believes Andrewlka. Even his best friend, Sash-ulka. Go and see for yourself.' He exhaled heavily, putting his sunglasses back on his nose.

Andrewlka was right once again. The whole living room was festooned with tangerines. In the corners, they climbed halfway up the walls. The entire floor was covered with bright red balls except for an island of rug. On the middle of the rug was Andrewlka's crystal bowl, filled with a brownish-yellow liquid. From the strong smell, fighting the smell of tangerines, I guessed it was Chacha. Around the bowl, sitting with crystal glasses in their hands, were Boris, Stas, and someone else in a cap whose back was to us. Stumbling over the tangerines, I made my way to the rug island. The man with his back to me stood and turned. I stopped dead on my way from the shock. First I thought it was Lenin from our theatre in full make-up, but no, it was a real face . . . and only then did I realize who it was.

'Let Andrewlka introduce you to the Infamous Wolfkiller. The entire police force is looking for him to put him in jail, but he prefers to stay here. Isn't it a marvellous decision?'

'Kepi, how are you?' I said in disbelief. 'I'm so glad to see you again.'

'Who are you, how do you know my name, ha?' Kepi asked mistrustfully, staring at me.

'The Tula-Moscow Express, about ten years ago, remember? Vodka, beer, and dried fish?'

'My God! It's you. I forget your name . . . ah . . . ah . . . Sashka, right?'

'Right!'

'You told me where to buy the weapons, ha? I remember!'

'How did you wind up here?' I asked.

'Business . . .'

'We'll get to the business later,' said Andrewlka. 'The Chacha's getting cold. Let's take our seats and get started.'

We sat down on the rug around the crystal bowl. Andrewlka poured everyone a full glass, asked Stas for his lighter, lit the grape's alcohol in the bowl, and in the twinkling light of burning Chacha, proposed a toast:

'Andrewlka wants to drink to friendship. His life is his friends.
316

He is so proud to have the best and most famous friends in the world! He was blessed by his mother to have this little place where every great has a chance to meet another great. Cheers!'

We drank to everybody present. Then we drank the next round for everybody who was away.

'It's amazing,' I said to Kepi. 'I would never have expected to meet you here.'

'I told you, I'm here on business.'

'What kind of business?'

'To make an exchange with two Georgians, Goga and Voga. I give them some metal from Tula, they give me these tangerines.'

'That's funny,' I said, 'I also brought some.'

'Where did you get yours?' Kepi asked with surprise.

'Kremlyovka.'

'It looks like tangerines on the black market and tangerines in the Kremlin come from the same tree,' Stas quipped.

'The only difference is that for them it's communism, but for us it's capitalism,' returned Andrewlka.

'You talk too much.' Kepi cut Andrewlka short. 'You'd better tell me when we're going to finish this deal, ha? I don't have much time. I brought my stuff, so I'm taking the tangerines.'

'Sorry, but Andrewlka can't allow it without Goga's or Voga's permission.'

'I can't wait. I have to exchange the fruit for something important.'

'What's the problem?' I asked, trying to ease the growing tension.

'I had a contract with two Georgians,' said Kepi angrily. 'They wanted some weapons. So I brought heavy stuff from Tula. He,' Kepi pointed at Andrewlka, 'put it in his cupboard and now tells me I can't take *my* tangerines.'

'You can take them any time you please but only after Goga and Voga give their permission,' said Andrewlka, sipping his Chacha.

'Where are they, anyway?' I asked.

'There's a rumour that they were arrested two days ago,' Boris said softly.

'There's something fishy about this,' Kepi said, looking at Andrew with mistrust.

'Let's not talk about the sad things of life,' said Andrewlka, pouring Chacha from the bowl to the glasses. 'Let's drink to Sasha and Lena and their happy trip abroad. Bon voyage, dear friends!'

'I'm not sure about this toast,' I said. 'We didn't get our postcard and today was the last day. Let's drink to something else.'

Everybody put his glass down. They all knew what it meant not to get permission in three months. People who had 'special cases' waited for years, lost their jobs, apartments, all they owned, were turned down again and again, and finally they just disappeared.

'Please don't cry,' I said. 'Maybe we didn't get permission, but we had an invitation and three months of hope. It's something anyway. Let's drink to the man who sent us the invitation, the man of his word. There is no need to keep his name secret any more. Let's drink to Youssef.'

We didn't have a chance to clink our glasses before Boris stopped us.

'I'm afraid there is more bad news. I didn't want to mention this before, but there was some kind of *coup d'état* in Sudan. Youssef was killed during a massacre of communists.'

'Why?' Lena cried in shock. 'He wasn't a communist, he was a prince!'

'That hammer and sickle on the palace roof betrayed him. Youssef was arrested and then tortured to death. But he never asked for mercy, he was a true prince. Let's drink to him, and don't clink the glasses.'

We Russians get used to death, but the death of a foreigner, especially a happy foreigner like Youssef, seemed impossible. But what could we do? We drank to Youssef's peace in Black Heaven.

We were silent for a long moment until Lena suddenly cried out, 'I can't stand it any more! Everything connected with this country brings death. I'm not going to sit and wait till they come and kill me. We have to do something. I'm ready for anything!'

'If you're ready, I know what to do,' said Kepi very seriously.

318

'But I'm warning you, if it gets around you will all be very sorry. Cross your hearts, all of you, that what I say now will stay between us. Swear!'

First we drank, then we swore.

'I have a plan to hijack a plane, and I need partners.'

'Forget it,' I said. 'We thought about it; it's suicide.'

Kepi didn't answer for quite some time. He took his cap off his head, put his big hand on his sweaty bald spot, and only then did he speak, separating each sentence with a long pause. . . .

'I'm ready for suicide. . . . My daughter was poisoned by rotten moose meat and died . . . I have nothing to lose . . . I think you also have nothing to lose . . . They will get you very soon . . . I invite you . . . any one of you who is ready for action . . . *to get them* . . . and who knows? Maybe my plan will even work!'

'What's the plan?' Lena asked eagerly.

'Tell us about it. You can trust us,' Stas said with a crazy look in his eyes.

'It's simple . . .' Kepi lowered his voice. 'Right in this room, in that cupboard, we have two machine guns and a rifle. Plus, tomorrow I can exchange these tangerines for a bomb. Ha! After I get the explosives, we'll take the weapons and make our move to the highway. We'll stop a big truck and give the driver two choices, the bottle or the bullet. No doubt he'll choose the bottle and will drive us to the airport. We'll crash through the fence and make our next move right to a plane getting ready for an international flight. We take over the plane and give the pilot three choices: bullet, bomb, or a flight to the West. I hope he'll choose the last one. If not, we have to make a big boom!'

'That might be fun!' said Stas, obviously excited. 'I like this plan. I'm in with one condition: you'll give me the bomb. I love the bomb. I love a big boom!'

'Don't leave Andrewlka alone. Andrewlka is going with you. All the American film stars are waiting for him. Let's go right now. Why should we wait? Andrewlka is pleased with this new idea . . . Sound the trumpets, beat the drums! Andrewlka goes to Hollywood!'

'Are all of you nuts?' cried Boris. 'Pretty soon there will be nobody left to drink with. Stop this theatre. This is your native land, Holy Russia. Somehow, I can understand Sasha and Lena – they're fighting for freedom of art. That's the goal of their life. But you! Why do you want to go? Why would you want to leave your country? What's your problem?'

'There is one big problem here,' said Kepi. 'I despise this country! I hate Russia and its people.'

'Hey, don't confuse Russia with our Regime,' Boris interjected.

'I don't see the difference,' said Kepi, stiffening. 'I have equal hatred for the Soviet Regime, Russia, and all Russians.'

'Why Russians? It's communists who created this repressive system,' Lena said.

'Russians always suppress somebody – even themselves – whether czars are in power or communists. Minorities can always complain that the Russians torture them, but what are we supposed to say – who tortures us Russians? Whom do we have to run away from except from ourselves? I hate Russians. The Jews can justify their escape by saying they're going back to the land of their ancestors. I envy Jews because they are the only ones who can leave this country legally.'

'I hated Jews all my life and now my best friend is a Jew,' said Boris. 'I hate Jews! They're too clever.'

'I hate Russians!' said Kepi. 'They're too stupid.'

'Andrewlka hates Ukrainians, because they're Ukrainians,' said Andrew.

'I hate blacks because they killed Youssef,' said Stas.

'Is that what we've come to – a republic of hatred?!' Lena cried.

'This is a communist democracy. Let's drink to the Soviet Union, the only country where all people hate each other equally,' Stas quipped.

'The worst crime of the communists – they planted hatred in our hearts,' Lena sighed in despair.

'You shouldn't talk like that about your country. It's Holy Russia!' Boris repeated stubbornly.

'It's not our country and it's not our Regime,' Lena nearly screamed. 'The communists have taken everything away from us – our land, our culture, and our religion. If they had even left us with hope, but no, they took our hope too, and now there's nothing left, nothing . . .'

'You're wrong, Lena,' Stas interfered. 'Your point of view is too depressing. Let's look at the Soviet Regime from an optimistic angle. Communists took everything from people and now they give it back to them gradually, so the people appreciate whatever they get; they are grateful for every piece of meat or fish. They've learned to relish the tiniest things, and they've found real happiness in this.'

'Don't joke about it, Stas,' Lena said quietly. 'How did we get to this point, we, the children of Great Russia. We would turn to prostitution for a pack of foreign cigarettes; commit murder for a pair of jeans! Is this Holy Russia? Is this what we call the deepness of a Russian soul? I want to cry out to the whole world, "Save our souls!"'

'Why bother saving such a worthless thing?' Stas chuckled.

'The West should help us to fight the Soviet Regime!' Lena said.

'You're taking their side? You'd become traitors?' Boris asked angrily.

'No, saviours! There are only two sides – Life and Death,' Lena said emotionally. 'If the West doesn't help us to free Russia, all that is good in it will die! And then communists will take over the world.'

'Nobody is going to help us Russians,' Kepi said very confidently. 'We're being punished for our pride, our hatred. This pride of ours can only be washed away with blood. Maybe then love for our native land will return, and with it will come faith!'

'What faith? Who has faith?' Boris asked.

'I do,' Lena said.

'I do,' I said.

'Andrewlka does,' said Andrew, taking off his sunglasses.

'Oh, come on, that's going a bit too far – Andrewlka believes in God! Now I've heard everything,' Boris shouted. 'I suppose next you'll be saying that we're all God's children. We are all brothers.'

'Yes,' Andrewlka replied. 'We're all brothers.'

'So, what's mine is yours, and what's yours is mine?' Boris demanded.

'That's right,' Andrew said.

Boris picked up a crystal glass, took a long hard look at Andrew, and said: 'So you can do whatever you want with my stuff, and I can do whatever I want with yours, right?'

'Right,' Andrew said.

The very next moment, Boris flung the crystal glass with full force against the ceiling, and a shiny shower of broken chips rained down on us.

'Bravo! Andrewlka liked the noise,' said Andrewlka.

'Are we still brothers?'

'Yes,' Andrewlka replied without batting an eyelash.

Everybody watched in wonderment as a second glass was smashed, then a third and a fourth . . . When all the glasses were gone, Boris reached for the crystal bowl of burning Chacha.

'Put it down,' Andrew's voice rang out coolly.

'How come?' asked Boris. 'You said what's yours is mine.'

'If you're Andrew's brother, you should know that he never drinks without fire. Put the bowl down!'

'If this isn't mine, then my wife isn't yours,' Boris shouted hysterically.

Everybody sat motionless, wondering what was going on. Tiny crystal stars twinkled among the tangerines. Boris hid his face in his hands and stayed like that for a few minutes, his sandy hair sticking out through his fingers. Then he leaped up and, stumbling over the tangerines, bolted out of the room.

Everybody fixed his gaze on Andrew.

'Everything's okay,' Andrewlka said with a smile. 'No problem. Andrewlka deserved it.'

'What was that all about?' Kepi asked. 'I didn't understand. What happened, ha?'

'*Cherchez la femme*,' Andrewlka said. '*C'est la vie.*'

'Translate,' said Kepi.

'It means that Andrewlka had an affair with Boris's wife, Mashka,' Stas said.

'You son of a bitch! You slept with your friend's wife?' Kepi flared up.

'Andrewlka has such a big heart; he can't say no to anybody,' Andrewlka said.

'You bastard!' Kepi shouted. 'You double-crossed your friend. What did I have to go and get involved with you for? I never trusted you! I bet you're the one who sold out Goga and Voga. I bet you informed on them!'

'Andrewlka doesn't inform on friends,' said Andrewlka.

'I don't trust you. Listen,' warned Kepi, 'if you inform on me, I swear I'll kill you!'

'How?' Andrewlka inquired with curiosity. 'Like a wolf or like a moose, with the machine gun or with the rifle?'

'I'm not going to use a bullet for an informer. I'll kill you with anything that comes to hand – strangle you with a string, crush your skull with a stone, or stab your heart with an awl.'

'It's not easy to kill Andrewlka. Andrewlka is strong like his lilacs. Your string will break on his neck, your stone will crack on his head, your awl will snap against Andrewlka's big heart.'

'No, it won't.'

'Yes, it will. Do you want to make a bet?'

'For what?'

'Anything you want.'

'Your life.'

'That's too cheap. Andrewlka's life isn't worth anything. How about something more valuable.'

'Like your stupid lilacs, ha?'

'No, they're too expensive. How about Andrewlka's garden knife? If you kill him you can take his knife.'

'I can't listen to this any more. They must be drunk,' Lena said. 'Let's go.'

'No, don't leave us. What about our plan to hijack the plane?' Andrewlka pleaded.

'That's tomorrow,' said Stas, getting up. 'Tonight Sasha, Lena, and I have a concert in the Palace of Art. We really have to go; we're late already. Are you going with us . . . what's your name, comrade?'

'No, no, Wolfkiller stays here. Andrewlka's going to put him up for the night.'

'I'm not staying here with you, you informer,' Kepi snapped.

'Yes, you are; don't forget we have our business to discuss,' Andrewlka said sweetly. 'All Moscow has slept in Andrewlka's apartment, except Andrewlka's killer. Tonight, even he will sleep here.'

'Are you sure it's all right? There won't be any trouble?' I asked.

'Don't worry . . . There won't be any trouble as long as Andrewlka has Chacha to burn and he's going to burn it till dawn. Hey, Stas, how about a tangerine for the road? There are some left. Catch it! All right then, so long.'

'So long,' Stas said.

'So long,' Lena said.

'So long,' I said. 'So long.'

8 The Concert of the Century

'Thank you for getting us out of there, Stas,' Lena said. 'You're welcome,' he replied with the wink of an eye.

'The concert was a perfect excuse,' I said. 'I just hope there won't be any more trouble tonight. I don't know who to worry about more, Kepi or Andrewlka.'

'Forget about it,' said Stas. 'We really don't have much time, you'll probably want to change your clothes.'

'For what?'

'Oh, if you want to perform like this, it's all right with me,' Stas called out as he rushed into the middle of the street with the obvious intention of catching a taxi.

'Wait a minute, Stas, what are you saying?' Lena asked.

'I told you already, we have a concert tonight!' screamed Stas from across the street, trying to block the traffic.

'Come over here,' I shouted. 'What is it? What do you want from us?'

Stas came back on the pavement with a big innocent grin. 'Remember that concert I used to talk about – the Concert of the Century? Remember?'

'What about it?'

'I finally organized it and you two are going to be in it! Congratulations!' he said, patting my back enthusiastically.

'Forget it!'

'No, you don't understand – '

'Stas, you're out of your mind. We might be arrested any day, maybe tomorrow, and you're talking about a concert?'

'It's not tomorrow. It's tonight. Come on, aren't we going to have fun anymore or what? Just do me a favour. After all, I was the one who discovered you. I opened all the doors for you.'

'I see,' said Lena sharply. 'Now you want to open one more door for us – to a Siberian prison camp!'

'I've been planning this concert for years, waiting for just the right moment. I was counting on you, and now, when everything is ready, you want to spoil all the fun.'

'Stas, don't you understand? We are not in a position to take the risk!'

'You're wrong. You're still in a position to show Them who's in charge. You still have something to say, and as that fellow in a kepi said, you have nothing to lose. We have to do it as a last hurrah! Tonight you are going to the concert with me; tomorrow I'll go with you to the airport to hijack a plane. We'll really get these reds by their balls. Let's have our last fun. . . .'

'Where is this concert?'

'At the Palace of Art.'

'How did you arrange to have it there?'

'Through Anna Ivanna.'

'Who's going to be performing?'

'Anna Ivanna and you. I tried to invite the general, Boris's papa, with his balalaika and the cockroach, but he refused. You see, now I really need you. With you in the second part it will be a sensation!'

'What's in the first part?' I asked.

'Anna Ivanna and her Encounters with Lenin.'

'You are crazy, Stas, completely crazy,' Lena said, shaking her head in disbelief. 'Who'll let us sing in this concert?'

'Don't worry. This is a different type of concert. There won't be any censorship or commissions.'

'You know such a concert doesn't exist,' said Lena.

'I told you, this one is special. Anna Ivanna is a star. She will tell her story about how she met Lenin, then play the piano, and then dance. And I mean she's *really* going to dance,' he added with a sly grin.

'I have to see it,' I said. 'You've got me.'

'Me too,' Lena agreed, and we all laughed.

'What time is the concert?' I asked.

'It's a late show. After the film about eleven-thirty. We still have time. All we have to do is pick up your guitars and lyrics to your songs. I'll make a selection on the way. Oh, wait a minute, I do have to make one telephone call and then I'll stop a cab.'

Anna Ivanna was, by now, well known all over Moscow due to her dramatic recounting of her meeting with Vladimir Ilyich Lenin. Her every day began or ended with this story; she covered all Moscow – from school to school, from university to university, from factory to factory – resurrecting the memory of the unforgettable leader. With years, her performance took on more and more expressiveness and strength. At first she used to tell her audience that she had spotted Lenin with her binoculars in a crowd at the Petrograd Railway Station standing on top of the armoured car. Later, her story was embellished with colourful details, as if her binoculars had placed her at Lenin's feet. And finally, she had herself standing on the running board of the armoured car, grabbing Vladimir Ilyich's coat when a gust of wind nearly knocked him down. At that point in the story, even if it was her third performance of the day, her eyes moistened and a tear, always just one, gushed out of her right eye and trickled down her cheek, beating a hard path between her warts. It was no accident that Anna Ivanna was a teacher in the Theatre Institute! Compared with her, other Lenin storytellers were like amateurs, with their boring tales of how they shook the great leader's hand in some dark Kremlin corridor. Anyone could make that up, but to touch the leader's fleece coat, dusty and dirty; to feel the holy dirt coming under your nails; to shiver from the touch of the cloth – this is the kind of thing that goes down in history books. This was why Anna Ivanna always had a full house. And the concert in the Palace of Art was no exception; the auditorium was filled to the rafters; there wasn't even room to drop an apple, as we say.

During the last few minutes before the concert, Stas stayed with Anna Ivanna in her dressing room, preparing the star for her performance. Then, like a true impresario, he walked out on the stage. His dark blue suit, starched white shirt, and plaid bow tie made him look bigger than ever and more important. His round, happy-go-lucky face, lit up by the projectors, expressed total satisfaction with the turnout. He paused on the stage to give the audience an extra minute to look him over, then commenced his introductory remarks:

'Dear comrades, dear friends. I am happy to see your fiery eyes in the darkness of this auditorium; I'm happy to hear the rapid beat of your hearts; I'm happy to share in your excitement over this concert starring Anna Ivanna.'

The audience burst into a round of applause. Stas beamed and went on:

'Comrades, friends, I can tell you with confidence that this evening's performance will not disappoint you. More than that, I'm not afraid to say that tonight you are going to see and hear something out of this world. Every one of Anna Ivanna's concerts is an extraordinary event, but tonight, she is going to be more than just a storyteller; she will reveal herself totally, presenting something thoroughly new from her repertoire . . . she will tell you about her encounters not only with Lenin, but with other great people as well – and not only with words but with music. And now for the first number of our programme, the incredible, incomparable Anna Ivanna!'

Stas took the microphone and went backstage. The projector lights went out, bringing silence.

A round shadow rolled out from backstage and stopped near the piano. A bright light flashed. In the middle of the stage stood Anna Ivanna.

Her shoulders were draped in a heavy black cape; on her head was a black beret with a bright red feather – a rather unusual costume for a teacher of Party History. 'A Conversation with Comrade Chopin!' she screamed in a hoarse voice, then leaped onto the bench beside the piano and placed her hands on the keys. A tender, romantic melody, Sonata No. 7, flowed through the auditorium. Just as the audience calmed down and got ready to listen to the sugary trills, Anna Ivanna smashed the keys with her fists. The instrument cried like a wounded animal; the audience stirred, anticipating the worst, but then the piano stopped crying, and the auditorium was once again filled with Chopin's tender music.

The conversation went like so – Anna Ivanna played a couple

of familiar bars in question form, then let herself go and, with her unleashed fists, improvised her Party answer to the apolitical question.

The first conversation was followed by a second one, with Comrade Mozart. In her conversation with that genius, Anna Ivanna loosened up by using not only her fists, but her elbows as well.

When it was Comrade Beethoven's turn, the audience realized that real art had no limits. To make contact with the deaf composer, Anna Ivanna used every resource in her body and soul. After playing the first few bars of the Fifth symphony, representing the knock at death's door, Anna Ivanna answered the pessimistic German with a response that was full of life. She leaped onto the stool, her back to the piano, and pounded on the keys with her huge backside, producing an astonishing sound.

Lena and I stood backstage, unable to believe our eyes. Stas stood there too, smiling his enchanting smile.

'What is she, crazy?' I said to Stas.

'She's all right. She was a bit jittery before the performance so I had to give her some pills. Now she's in good shape. Look at how she's performing.'

Anna Ivanna had crawled inside the grand piano and was plucking the strings with her fingers. She didn't exactly fit inside the instrument, and the stick that held up the top of the piano was knocked out of place by her hips. With this, the top came crashing down. The piano cried out one last time, driving the audience wild. Stas screamed into the microphone, above the noise:

'And now for the final number in the first part of our concert – "A Conversation between Comrade Lenin and Isadora Duncan!"'

The audience quietened down. From within the piano came a tinkling of strings, which a trained ear would recognize as the theme from the 'Appassionata,' Lenin's favourite composition. Slowly but surely, the faint music grew into a stormy cacophony, then died. The top of the piano opened slowly and, as if from a black coffin, rose the figure of a woman. Here Anna Ivanna bared her true self – she tossed aside her black cape and beret, and stood up inside the piano in the light of the projector, wearing only a pink negligee.

'Isadora,' Stas whispered into the mike.

Anna/Isadora fearlessly leaped onto the stage. Her jeté was followed by the sharp-as-a-shot sound of the piano top falling down. The noise distracted the ballerina and she fell down, landing on all fours. Anna/Isadora wasn't daunted in the least; she got up, wiped her hands on the negligee, and flung herself into a wild dance. Words cannot describe this show, just as words cannot describe a hippo prancing in a slip or a jellyfish dancing the tarantella. It was at the same time lascivious and blatantly naive. Above all, it was great.

When the solo was over and the curtain came down, the audience was roaring, screaming, and shouting, begging Isadora for an encore, but the temperamental ballerina wouldn't come out of her dressing room.

'Okay, we can consider the first part of the concert a rousing success,' Stas said, rubbing his hands with pleasure.

'Stas, tell me the truth – how did you get her to do it?' Lena asked.

'A little training in Stas's Method and a few choice pills. Do you want some too? No? Well, anyway, her part of the concert is over; now it's your turn.'

'I hate to tell you, Stas,' I said, 'but we're getting out of here before the police surround the place.'

'What are you worried about? I'm not going to use your real names; I'll introduce you as Hungarian gypsies. I've already picked out the right songs. They're – '

'Stas, forget it. We're leaving. Give me back my songs.'

'Didn't I give them back to you?'

'No.'

'Let's check the dressing room. They should be there.'

We went to the dressing room and searched everywhere – the drawers, tables, closets, and guitar cases. The songs were nowhere to be found.

'Stas, try to remember where you could have left them. This is a serious matter; if anybody finds them, we could wind up in gaol.'

'Oh yes, now I know where I put them – in Anna Ivanna's dressing room.'

'Don't tell me,' Lena gasped.

'Let's hurry,' I said.

We found the door to Anna Ivanna's dressing room locked. We knocked; nobody answered, but we could see a light from under the door.

'Anna Ivanna,' Stas said in a singsong voice, 'come on, sweetheart, open up, it's me.'

Anna Ivanna didn't open the door. Stas called her once more, then he took a step backward and rammed the door with his shoulder. Anna Ivanna was seated in front of the mirror at the make-up table. Her eyes glared at us from the mirror. The lyrics were in a messy pile in front of her on the table. Stas took a step toward her, but she snatched up the papers, clutching them to her breast.

'Congratulations, Anna Ivanna, you were fantastic!' Stas said in his charming way. 'The audience is still applauding. But now, Sasha and Lena have to sing. They need their songs. Give them over, okay?'

'You scoundrel!' Anna Ivanna said icily into the mirror. 'How dare you get me, a good communist, mixed up with these traitors and their anti-Soviet . . . anti-Soviet . . .' Her nervousness prevented her from finding the right word.

'Anna Ivanna, my dear. You don't understand . . .'

'I understand perfectly,' she said, waving the papers. 'And I put a roof over your head!' she said, rising and turning her angry face toward us.

'Give me the songs,' Stas said, going up to Anna Ivanna.

'Get away from me, you scoundrel.'

'Anna Ivanna, what do you need these lyrics for? You're a ballerina!'

'Shut up! I'm handing them over to the police right now.'

'Anna Ivanna, I can't believe you would inform on your students. Do you want to be like Murka, whom you sang about? Do you really want to have us locked up for these papers?'

'Ideals and Party membership are what's important to me,' Anna Ivanna said, losing her breath. 'Now get out!'

'Anna Ivanna, don't get yourself all upset. Here, take a pill.'

'You've already given me your drugs, and now I don't remember what I did on stage. Get out of here or I'll call the guard.'

'Anna Ivanna, let's make a deal – you give me the papers, and I'll . . . give you a tangerine; a lot of tangerines like this one.' He took a bright red tangerine out of his pocket.

'You'll get your papers tomorrow at the police station,' said Anna Ivanna coldly. 'Now, for the last time, get out of my way; I've got to get dressed.'

Instead of going toward the door, Stas turned to the clothes rack where Anna Ivanna's things were hanging. He grabbed Anna Ivanna's Aeroflot bag, opened the zipper, and took out a red card.

'No,' Anna Ivanna cried, 'don't touch my Party membership card. Put it back.'

Stas took a cigarette lighter from his pocket.

'No! No! Give it to me,' Anna Ivanna said, lunging for Stas.

Stas held the card up over his head. Unable to reach that height, Anna Ivanna jumped up and down, screaming:

'Give me my card! Give me – '

'Give me those papers or I'll burn your membership,' Stas said, flicking on the lighter.

Anna Ivanna kept jumping around Stas, like a frog around an oak.

'Give me, give me, give me,' she cried.

'The papers first,' Stas said, lighting the corner of the card.

'Take them, take them, you drug addict, you queer!' Anna Ivanna screeched, shoving the papers into her torturer's face.

Stas grabbed the papers and handed over the burning I.D. card. Holding the still-burning card over her head like an Olympic torch, Anna Ivanna raced out of the room, leaving behind a strong smell of singing hair.

'Anna Ivanna, you forgot your tangerine,' Stas screamed at the open door.

'Fire!' someone cried in the corridor. 'Fire!'

People started racing through the hall.

'Let's get out of here,' Stas said to Lena and me. 'It looks like the Concert of the Century is over.'

332

When we left the dressing room, we saw people running every which way, and a stagehand unsuccessfully trying to take a fire extinguisher off the wall. We headed for the stage door, but ran right into a guard.

'Who are you and what are you doing here?' the guard demanded.

'Did you see an old lady?' Stas asked, ignoring his questions.

'What?' the guard said with confusion.

'An old lady, an arsonist, in a negligee.'

'Has she got any distinguishing marks?' the guard inquired.

'She's in a negligee.'

'That's not a distinguishing mark,' the guard replied drily. 'Does she have any special marks?'

'No, she doesn't have any special marks – she's just an ordinary babushka. An old lady is an old lady,' Stas muttered, circling around the guard, getting closer to the door. 'Her eyes are . . . something like . . . I don't know what colour they are . . . like no colour at all; her hair is sort of . . . it's hard to say what colour . . . probably kind of grey, very thin around the temples. Oh, now I remember, she has a wart right here, yes, right here . . . and here too . . . and here, and here. She has lots of them; I can't remember all of them, but the biggest one is here on her nose and it has a hair growing out of it, a long black hair . . .'

'Fire!' screamed the stagehand, running towards us, the fire extinguisher in his hands. 'Fire!'

'We'll try to catch her on the street,' Stas said to the startled guard. Before he could react, we ran outside and headed for the Metro.

It was a quarter to one, only fifteen minutes before the Metro closed. We had to take the Circle Line to get to my place. On the down escalator, Stas, trying to make us laugh, juggled his tangerine with two vials of pills.

A train had just pulled into the station. As we walked down the empty platform, Stas tossed the tangerine to Lena, she threw it to me, and I passed it back to Stas.

Two conductors, standing in the cabin of the first car, scrutinized us with piercing eyes.

'You think we have all night to wait for you idiots?' one shouted.

We went into the first car. Three weary passengers with shopping bags frowned at us; a fourth, dressed in a military uniform, slouched in the corner, too drunk to notice anything. The doors closed and the train pulled out.

We plunked ourselves down and almost immediately our merriment fizzled. I felt as if exhaustion had glued me to my seat. As the train was passing station after station, heavy thoughts were passing through my head. It was clear now that we had gone about it all wrong from the start. Emigration wasn't such a good idea after all. We should have tried to sneak over the border on the Black Sea. It seemed that now we had no choice but to try Kepi's plan for hijacking the plane. . . .

The train ground to a halt. The doors opened. Every time we stopped, one of the conductors pranced out of his cabin onto the platform and sneered at us through the open door.

'If he keeps on looking at us with that evil eye, we'll have to hijack this train,' I said absently to Stas.

'That way, we could go abroad together,' Stas said, laughing. In that moment his eyes locked with mine and he said, 'That might be fun.' The silent but electric communication that can occur only between two old friends took over.

'No,' I said. 'Don't do it.' But it was too late. I knew Stas well enough to know that when he was in a mood like that, nothing could stop him. The next second he suddenly grabbed my black leather glove, which was resting on my knee, stuffed something inside, and rushed over to the conductor. My heart skipped a beat as I jumped up and chased after him. Lena didn't know what was happening but immediately picked up the guitars and followed close behind. Before we knew it, Stas was shoving the conductor into the cabin.

'Don't panic, comrades. Get inside. I can explode this any second,' Stas threatened, brandishing a black object, his voice sombre and menacing. 'I warned you. Now follow my orders – go ahead!'

I grabbed Lena's wrist and pulled her out of the car. 'Don't get mixed up in this,' I shouted at her. 'Go away!' But she didn't go. I had to push her away from the train.

Lena stumbled onto the platform and looked up at me with eyes full of terror. 'What about you?' she cried.

I had no answer. It was as if I no longer existed except in this nightmare.

'You'll be sorry you didn't stick with us, Lena,' screamed Stas through the cabin door over my shoulder. 'The concert continues!'

The passengers were sticking their heads out of the train doors to see what was going on. Even the head of the drunk officer could be seen among the curious passengers.

'Close the doors!' Stas commanded. 'If you don't, I'll blow up this train. One . . . two . . .'

The conductor hit the switch. The doors hissed shut and a passenger's mesh shopping bag and the officer's head got caught in the doors' pinch. We pulled out. The last thing I saw in the rearview mirror was the officer's hat rolling down the platform and Lena running after the train clutching the guitars. The next moment was blackened by the darkness of a tunnel.

'Faster, faster!' Stas roared above the roar of the engine.

In the tunnel, lights flashed green . . . red . . . yellow . . . white . . . yellow . . . white . . . It was stifling in the cabin, and the sweat-covered faces of the conductors also flashed red . . . yellow . . . white . . . yellow . . . white . . .

One of the conductors had a moustache which twitched diagonally in fear. The other one, much too scared to turn in our direction, could only mouth the questions he wanted to ask 'What's going on? Where are we going?'

'We're going to America,' said Stas as he held the concealed weapon under the conductor's nose. 'Why are you shaking? Don't you want to go to America? Everybody wants to go to America! Faster! Faster!'

We flew out of the tunnel into the bright marble expanse of the station.

'Don't stop!' Stas warned the conductors. Then he took the microphone off the hook and announced: 'The train will not be stopping here, comrade passengers; this is an express train with one destination. Next stop, America!'

The people on the platform jumped back in unison. Their faces transformed into one elongated, shocked face, like a smudged line. With the noise of the train, it was impossible to hear, but a long mouth opened in a silent gasp.

Again, darkness and lights – green . . . red . . . yellow . . . white . . . yellow . . . white . . . yellow . . .

The wind whistled by the open door against my back but, inside, it was impossible to breathe. *We hurtle, lonely, in a cramped car . . . we hurtle, lonely, in a cramped car . . .* The words reverberated again and again in my head. The train galloped along on the circumference under the sleepy city in an absurd and endless circle.

Around the bend there suddenly appeared two ominous red lights – an unknowing train was at the next station. The conductors turned to us mechanically.

'Brake!' Stas and I screeched simultaneously.

Shriek! Squeal! Grind! We were dashed against the windscreen, but the trains didn't collide. A split second before, the train in front of us pulled out. For some time, both trains moved like one along the platform, then split apart – ours stopping dead; the other one zooming into the tunnel.

'Thanks for the ride, comrades,' Stas said, pushing me out the cabin door. Holding the black weapon up over his head on the platform, Stas shouted, 'Keep going!'

He didn't need to repeat his command. The train shot forward and, as it whirred past, something hit us – sausages tumbling from a net bag squeezed between the doors. Next we saw an officer's hand pressed against the glass. His eyes were bulging, his hatless, beet-red head caught in the guillotine of the doors. The head wailed frantically as the train rushed for the tunnel. The long echoing *AhAhAhAhAhAhAhAhAh* . . . faded in the well of the tunnel.

Running along the platform, we laughed madly. Old women in blue uniforms were mopping the spotless floors. The station was wet and empty. We were running on a shiny, slippery, marbled mirror. Our reflection was running upside down, a warped pose in the water. It was as slippery as ice and every second I thought my feet would be taken out from under me. Near the escalator I

336

turned back. Stas ran puffing like a locomotive on skates but didn't fall down. On the opposite side of the station I saw two grey uniformed figures clumsily dancing towards us on the slippery floor. Had the conductors already radioed in a report on our hijacking attempt? No matter. it seemed as if we could get away. I got ready to leap onto the up escalator but suddenly stopped in my tracks. The two escalators on each side were going down. The one between them was immobile. The long unending stairs, closed off by a red velvet rope, disappeared into a three-hundred-metre passage. I was paralyzed, but not wholly out of fear. I recognized these stairs – this Metro station – it was the lost Metro from my childhood!

'Stop!' screamed the female escalator operator with a greyish-green face as I jumped over the red rope and ran up.

'Stop!' she screamed louder as Stas unhooked the rope in which he had become entangled. Flinging the rope down, almost losing his balance, he pounded up after me. The end of the stairs wasn't within sight.

The secret passage was long, like life.

On both sides, smoothly and lazily, slid down the last few people. How was it possible that when the Metro was about to close, two down escalators were working and nothing was going up? It was absurd and funny, but we weren't inclined to laugh. We were climbing and climbing, puffing like asthmatics. By the middle, we were already dying. Glancing back, we saw that the policemen hadn't given chase. It was strange. They stood at the bottom of the stairs with the operator, coolly watching us with their heads tilted back. Relaxed and smiling, their three faces, one female and two male, were like a triangle. We continued to struggle up the stairs. We could see the end at last; there was only a little way left but we had no strength. We fought against strained muscles. Like mountain climbers near the peak, we needed oxygen. 'Stas, would you happen to have a respirator on you?' I asked in a hoarse voice. At this point, we were almost at the top. But something happened, something we didn't understand right away – a strange fateful movement under our feet. We were running but the top of the stairs was no closer. Now, when the end was only ten metres away, the escalator started up and was going down!

We ran harder but we were no closer to safety.

We ran still harder, but we were losing ground fast.

This was it. The triangle smiled. 'Now you understand why I never liked stairs?' Stas exhaled. It was the first time I didn't laugh at his joke. I screamed out in frustration. Just then I leaped for a lamp post, frantically trying to maintain my grip as the steps moved under my feet. I made it up onto the partition and saw Stas jump after me.

I ran up in a reverse slalom, grabbing each post from bottom to top. Suddenly the last light bulb exploded near my face. The shot came from the triangle. Then another shot. I looked down; I was covered with gooseflesh – Stas was lying on the stairs in a foolish pose, his arms and legs up in the air, a red spot on his ruffled white shirt. Straining to lift his head, he mouthed some words: 'Go on,' or maybe it was 'Good-bye'.

Down the partition faster and faster tumbled the black leather glove, its deformed fingers spread apart. On the way, the glove hit one of the lamps and its lifelike fingers hooked onto the lamp post. From inside, a small bright tangerine popped out and playfully bounced its way down.

I couldn't look at it. I turned, jumped down from the partition, and ran away.

'Good-bye, Stas. Forgive me and farewell. The Concert of the Century is over.'

9 The Biggest Russian Fence

I ran through a cold, dark Moscow, wind tearing at my coat, sleet and snow whipping at my face and eyes. I was hot and cold at the same time. My body was burning hot, my soul was as cold as ice. Sweat and melted snow ran down my cheeks, mixed with the salt of my tears, and left a dead taste on my lips. Run, run, run, I kept pushing myself.

The storm was getting stronger and the snow was now like a solid white wall that was impossible to penetrate. My body became weaker with every move, my breathing more and more laboured with my fight against the wind. I turned left down a dark side street which looked quiet and ran along a long brick building. The wet snow was now almost up to my knees as I trudged through the storm with legs of lead. I turned right on a narrow empty street surrounded by grey matchboxes on both sides. Run, run, run, I repeated to myself, but the buildings were passing me more and more slowly, their black windows like eyes watching my every step. Soon I just couldn't go any farther. I stopped on the corner right in front of a laundry with a blue sign. I stopped there not just because of loss of strength, but because of a frightening realization: I found myself back where this terrible night had begun . . .

Recalling the long brick building a few blocks back, I understood that it was the hospital where Tanya took my blood pressure, and this laundry, this was where I took Andrew's bed linen. Now it was clear to me: the train had brought me back. The station of my childhood was only one stop from Andrewlka's. I could see the grey matchboxes which surrounded me on all sides and then I knew I was now only a few blocks from Andrewlka's apartment.

Filled with fear and exhaustion, I tried to calm myself. I needed to hide, not only from the police, but from myself. I needed to see a familiar face, I needed to speak to someone who could give me comfort. Lena! Oh my God! I must ring her, and tell her that I'm still alive. I'll ring her from Andrew's, how good it is that a place like Andrewlka's with its doors always open exists for fugitives like me.

I set out in the direction of Andrewlka's apartment feeling a little better. Arriving at the entrance of his building, I looked around to make certain I was still alone. I entered the building with great caution, tiptoeing up the stairs, using the wall as a shield against the unknown. Reaching his apartment, I pushed in the door and, still tiptoeing, I made my way down the hall which led to his living room. It was still filled with tangerines. Oh, how I hated those tangerines!

In the twinkling light of the remaining Chacha, I could see the silhouettes of four men standing among the piles of tangerines. Andrew was not among them. It was strange to me that they stood there wearing their hats and coats. I recognized one short figure wearing a heavy winter coat and a kepi, the others wore dark grey autumn coats with fur hats.

Who are they? I wondered. But my tired brain was unable to react to more fear. Instead, it gave me a comfortable answer: they must be friends of Andrewlka's who arrived late for the party. Yes, just a new group of guests. I couldn't see their faces and their eyes were just black holes in their shadowed heads, but they had to be friends, I reassured myself. One of the shadows raised his arm in my direction and there was a dull shimmer of metal at the end of it. I blinked several times, not being able to believe the sight in front of me; in his hand – aimed at my head – was a pistol.

'Don't move,' the man with the gun ordered.

'Who are you?' asked the second man.

I didn't answer, hoping to steal some time to organize my thoughts.

'Who are you?' he repeated.

'Is this your apartment?' asked the third man.

'No,' I answered, my voice almost inaudible.

'Then what are you doing here?'

While I was trying to construct my answer, the third man came up from behind me and very professionally searched every inch of my body. His search travelled from under my arms down my sides to my ankles and back up the insides of my calves and thighs, leading to my groin, which he also checked very carefully.

'Where are your documents, and what is your name?'

'I don't have any documents. I just came to visit my friend,' I said, trying to avoid the question of my name.

'Is *he* your friend?' asked the first man, pointing his gun at Kepi's head.

'No,' I said.

'So what's his name? Is it Wolfkiller?' asked the second man.

'I don't know,' I replied. 'I've never seen him before.'

'And do you know him?' The third man directed his question at Kepi. Kepi didn't answer. It was obvious that he hadn't answered any of their previous questions. In the dimness of the light I could now see that his face was covered with blood.

'Answer the question,' said the man with the gun pointed at Kepi's face. In a sudden surge of anger, the man grabbed at Kepi's beard and jerked it till he had a handful of hairs. Kepi only moaned from the pain.

'He and his beard remind me of someone,' said the first man thoughtfully.

'He reminds me of a corpse, a burning corpse,' said the second man, and walked over to Kepi. He held him from behind in a tight grip, which left Kepi immobile. 'Is your name Wolfkiller? Answer me or I'll turn you into ashes!' he screamed in Kepi's ear, while the other pulled Kepi's hands down towards the bowl of burning Chacha.

'Are you going to talk or burn?' Again there was no answer. Then both men slowly forced Kepi's hands into the burning Chacha. As they lowered his hands into the fire, the hair on his hands quickly disappeared into the orange flame. It burned his flesh and continued its way up his sleeve, the cuff of his coat now in flames. 'Stop it!' I screamed, and made a move towards him, but was stopped by the third man, who pulled his gun and rested its cold metal against my temple. 'Stop it! Please!' I pleaded.

'Don't move,' he ordered me. 'Watch! His bearded face is next.'

I froze, but because of my move the two men stepped away from Kepi as he clutched his singed hands to his chest.

'Let's start on that one, he looks more talkative,' one of the men said, and they all turned in my direction.

'What are you doing here at this late hour?' asked the first man.

'I came to pick something up that I left here a while ago.' I sighed with relief; I now had a story.

'What did you leave here?'

'Icons,' I said.

'Tangerines, Chacha, icons; it looks like we uncovered a rose garden here.'

'When did you leave these icons?'

'Some time ago,' I said. In another life, I thought.

'Where do you suppose these icons are?'

'I think they're in that cupboard,' I said without hope, but trying to sound confident. I saw Kepi shiver at my answer.

The first man made a step in the direction of the cupboard, but was tripped by tangerines and almost fell. Perhaps I could learn to love the fruit after all.

'Go and get your own icons,' he ordered.

I walked slowly through the maze of tangerines and, unable to avoid them, felt their plump firmness under my feet as they sprang with softness. It was like walking on a woman's body. Trying not to lose my balance, I reached for the doorknob on the cupboard and held on to it tightly.

I paused for a moment, deliberating whether or not to continue my pretence of searching for icons. I slowly opened the cupboard door, still undecided. I didn't dare look up. I heard the silent tension and felt the burning stares of eyes upon me. I didn't know what my next move would be until the sound of shattering glass wiped out my thoughts. I quickly turned to see the entire rug aflame. Just one look at Kepi told me he had taken advantage of an unguarded moment. The fire from the alcohol of the remaining Chacha now covered the floor, creating a flow of blue and red curls which enhanced the pattern of the Persian rug. For

342

a second I was mesmerized by its new beauty – and then suddenly I knew what I had to do next . . .

The undercover men tried stamping out the fire to no avail. Next, they threw off their grey coats and used them to smother the flames. With great speed and concentration, their efforts were a success. Their success also left the room in complete darkness. In the darkness someone screamed, 'Get some damned light in here!' The search for a light wasn't easy. I heard the tumbling and tripping of bodies, the squish of tangerines, the profanities which came without any effort. Finally, someone said, 'I've found the lamp . . . but I can't find the switch.'

Now it was my turn. I allowed my instinct to take over. I found myself in the cupboard in a desperate search for something – I didn't quite know what – until my fingers caressed the cool, long body of metal. I firmly placed both hands tightly around it and held on as if to life itself.

'I found it!' came a joyful cry as he pulled the switch. The brightness of the light was almost blinding. I stood in the shadow of the cupboard and watched the KGB men trying to regain control. They brushed themselves off and straightened their ties, almost pleased with themselves as they made their move towards Kepi. But Kepi had a sly grin on his face. It puzzled them and they turned in search of its cause. That's when I stepped out into their view. The colour drained from their faces and their eyes bulged with fear when they saw me pointing a huge Stankov machine gun at them.

What they didn't know was that I was more scared than they were. If this situation hadn't reminded me of a film I had done – a war film, where I held a top-loading machine gun just like this one – I don't think I'd have known what to do . . .

'Hands up,' I ordered, repeating a line from the film. Their eyes shifted from one side to the other. I don't think they'd ever had such a gun turned against them.

'Down on the floor,' I said, continuing my role. I never saw more obedient men than these; they were trained to follow orders. All three flung themselves down on the tangerines. Kepi came towards them and very cautiously collected their pistols, putting them in his coat pockets.

'Give me the machine gun, and take the sub and rifle from the cupboard.' I did as he said.

'Now, you bastards, stand up . . . very slowly,' sang out Kepi. They moved as ordered, in almost balletlike movement, showing that their intentions were only to follow commands. Kepi directed them into the cupboard, one by one, but only two of them fitted inside; there was no room for the third. Kepi's steady hands held the machine gun to their every movement. This required a little reorganization, so he had them back out while he thought over the situation. He took a look into the cupboard and saw there was room for them to lie down, one on top of the other, which was now his next directive. For his own pleasure he had the smallest of the undercover men lie down first, the second largest on top of him, and the largest was the last. He obviously felt special satisfaction from knowing the KGB used this same method in transporting prisoners. The door to the cupboard closed easily, the lock was flimsy, but good enough.

'I don't want to hear one sound from you animals,' screamed Kepi through the door. 'You come out only when I say so.'

We had started to walk away when Kepi had a second thought. 'Open the cupboard door,' he said. I obeyed; he was now in control. I unlocked the door and held it open to see these sandwiched men again. Kepi took a step towards them and pointed the machine gun at the temple of the top man.

'You're right, I'm Wolfkiller, and before I pull this trigger, tell me who informed on me.'

'I don't know,' came the reply.

'Then how did you know I was here? Don't tell me that you're dogs in disguise, and your noses led you here! Tell me! Who informed?'

'We had an anonymous call, I don't know who it was.'

'Was it Andrewlka? Answer me!' Kepi was now pulling back the trigger.

'I don't know, I don't know, please don't shoot!' The plea was now filled with tears.

'This is it, I'm counting to three, one . . . two . . . three . . .'

Now hysterical and sobbing uncontrollably, the KGB man cried, 'Oh my God, I don't know!'

344

'Don't tell me the KGB believes in God,' retorted Kepi sarcastically. He shrugged and lowered his gun. 'Close the door,' he said. After I locked the cupboard, Kepi knocked another warning.

'Don't move until I say so.'

Their silence told us they understood. 'Let's go,' whispered Kepi, and silently we stepped through the maze of tangerines toward the hall.

'Where's Andrewlka?' I whispered to Kepi.

'Your friend the informer left while I was asleep and called the KGB.'

'Andrewlka would never do that.'

'Who else would have done it?'

'I think I know, but I can't tell you until I know for sure.'

'Well, I'm sure it was Andrewlka, and he'll pay for it,' he said in a low voice.

There was a rustling coming from the cupboard. Kepi cupped his hand around his mouth and in the direction of the sandwiched men, screamed out another warning. 'I said don't move, or I'll start a shooting spree!'

'Let's go,' I mouthed silently.

We moved quietly towards the hall, went out onto the stairs, and cautiously made our way to the front door.

As soon as we opened the door we knew we were in trouble.

The snow had stopped; there was a thick white blanket covering the city. The angry wind was no more, the sky was clearing, the moon was peeking out through the remaining clouds. It was so beautiful it made Moscow seem pure and peaceful . . . so unlike reality. We knew we didn't have much time. We had no choice; we had to run. We understood very clearly the lock on the cupboard door was too weak to hold the three men. We also knew reinforcements would join in the search for 'Wolfkiller' and his accomplice. So we ran, leaving a trail of suicidal tracks. In the moonlight they were like black ink spots in the white snow. There was no way back, we had to go ahead. Kepi ran first, his round little body now smaller as he sank into the snow, still cradling the machine gun as if it were a child. I followed in his footsteps in the hope that we could fool the KGB. Following

345

Kepi's steps was not a problem, the problem was the added burden of the sub and rifle. This whole night had been like a marathon for me; I must have covered a hundred kilometres – my entire body throbbed.

Kepi seemed to be picking up speed, his little legs carrying him faster than I ever thought possible. We were approaching the laundry. It was like a backward dream for me. He made a right at the corner; I was in close pursuit. Then he made a left onto another deserted street. We were now at the hospital. We ran in its shadow, thinking maybe our tracks would be less noticeable. After another turn we came to a dark narrow street; the narrow darkness felt safer. We continued our run for several more blocks. Our marathon ended when we were faced with a tall iron fence. Beyond it was a park. It felt good to stop; my legs were pulsating like a fast heartbeat, but then my entire body seemed as if it was about to bleed.

We approached the gate. It was open. We were both relieved by the calm of these surroundings. As we walked under the arch and into the park, I broke the silence and asked Kepi if he thought they had escaped yet.

'It's possible, that lock was worthless.'

'I hope not, I'm scared,' I admitted.

Kepi didn't answer. We continued walking, the reflection of the moon on the pure white landscape created an iridescent glow all around us. The snow-covered trees were like crystals shimmering in the moonlight. As we neared the centre of the park we saw a figure, it was a bust of Lenin. The plaster head was capped with a hat of white snow. Looking around, we saw that nothing was untouched by the whiteness except the black iron fence which surrounded the park. From different sides, we circled Lenin's bust, and again I saw the resemblance in Kepi's and Lenin's profiles. There was an important difference: Lenin was dead, Kepi was *still* alive.

We walked to the far end of the park and found that the snowdrifts were almost waist high. I thought surely I would lose Kepi in the deep snow. We looked for an exit; there was none . . . we were trapped. The iron fence was about three metres high, with each spearlike bar divided by a ring. It surrounded us like a cage. Oh! Mother Russia! a country divided by fences.

The only route we could take was over this fence. I threw my rifle and submachine gun in between the narrow spaced bars and started my climb over. It was difficult; I had very little strength left. The cold iron stuck to the skin of my palms; its rusted edges were like thorns that pierced through my trousers when I wrapped my legs around them to help boost myself up. Nothing could stop me now, not now. Halfway up I couldn't get a good enough grip on the narrow spears. My fingers were frozen, my legs aching, my heart beating much too fast. I took a deep breath of icy air and, with whatever strength I had left, gave myself another boost. My fingers reached the ring. I grabbed it and held on. I had the leverage I needed and slowly I raised myself to the top. I flung one leg over the fence for added balance. Carefully, I raised the other leg over in between the sharp spears and lowered myself down the other side. I had started gathering up my weapons when I realized that Kepi hadn't even started climbing. He stood on the other side, still cradling the machine gun.

'Kepi, what are you waiting for?'

'I can't climb up with the machine gun.'

'Then hand it to me.'

'It won't fit through the bars.'

'Then leave it there. We haven't much time.'

'*No.*'

'Okay, try to throw it over to me.'

Without a moment's hesitation he took two steps back and, with his entire body and strength, sent it soaring into the air. It fell short, hitting the tips of the spears.

'Pick it up. Hurry! Throw it again.'

He stood narrowing his eyes in concentration and, with a groan, sent it back into the air. This time the machine gun got caught on top of the fence in between the spears and Kepi started his climb. It was made more difficult with the pockets of his coat filled with pistols, but his fat little body moved up with an ease I didn't think he was capable of. Obviously he was much stronger than he looked. His wide peasant hands hung on to the fence with a sure grip. When he reached the top, he positioned himself on the

347

fence and, balancing between the spears, he proceeded to unhook the machine gun. Then, before my eyes, he started to sway . . . I couldn't watch, I closed my eyes, thinking the worst. After a short silence, I persuaded myself to take a peep and see what had happened. I looked down, expecting an outline in the snow marking the descent of my round little friend, but all I saw were our old footprints. A short moan led my eyes up the fence. There he hung, on one of the spears, which held him under his heavy coat like a beetle on a pin. He had managed to unhook the machine gun. It was back in his arms. I had started to move up in order to free Kepi when, through the bars of the fence, I saw them.

There they stood, under the arch of the entrance gate – three silhouettes, heads lowered and eyes focused on the ground, like three black dogs following our tracks. I knew then this was the end – and I knew the only way to save myself was to leave Kepi and run. But my body was unwilling to accept the logic of my mind. I just couldn't do it again; I couldn't for the second time in one night leave a friend in the hands of the KGB.

I watched them as they neared the bust of Lenin. They were like three shadows of death in the white square. They were so engrossed in our tracks they hadn't bothered to look up; if they had, they would have surely seen us.

One of the shadows strayed from the pack, still bent over, following the indentations in the snow. The other two stood studying the divided steps around the bust of Lenin. The stray moved a little slower now, scratching his head in confusion, and then stopped . . . and so did my heart as I watched him straighten up and follow the remaining tracks with his eyes. I couldn't see his eyes, but I knew they were looking straight at me. And he saw me . . . I felt his eyes follow the length of my body up the fence. He raised his arm, pointed his finger to Kepi, and turned and said something to the other men. I watched as they all straightened at attention. Any hope I had was gone . . . we were doomed. But . . .

In a flash of lightning and a clash of thunder, the pointed finger of the stray undercover man was gone. The tracing bullets from Kepi's machine gun found their target. The man raised both

348

arms in startled surprise and was cut down by the power of the dotted green line of fire. One of the other men dived into the snow, hoping to hide under its whiteness. He was cut in half while in flight. The third man tried to steal refuge behind Lenin's bust, but even the Great Lenin couldn't save him. The plaster bust disintegrated into a cloud of dust, as if it had been hit by twenty hammers and sickles. There was no way to hide from the green lightning. The third man lay dead next to his own head, covered by plaster dust, his fur hat rolled over next to him like a dead cat.

I fell to my knees. I was sick. Never had I wanted to be a part of such a slaughter. There was no other way, I told myself. It was either them or us. I pulled myself up, using the fence to support my weakened body and soul.

'Sash, help me down,' I heard from above. I looked up to see the man behind the thunder and lightning still dangling in mid-air.

'Here's the machine gun,' he said, as he dropped it only inches from me. I put my arms through the bars of the fence and my hands under the soles of Kepi's wet boots. This wasn't going to be easy, I realized, when I felt the weight of his body. I pushed up with all my might; it wasn't good enough. With each push I sank deeper and deeper into the snow. This required a little more thought. I told Kepi that when I said lift up, he would have to try and swing himself up if he wanted to be freed. I wedged my feet into the snow so they felt secure and gave it another try. 'Ready . . . lift . . . up!' He strained I strained. Slowly, with a groan that came from both of our throats, he was freed from the spear. He held on to one of the rings in between the bars, which enabled him to straddle the fence and ease himself down.

As soon as Kepi landed, he started digging in the snow in a frantic search for his weapons. First the submachine gun, then the rifle.

'Kepi, let's go. Throw away all that metal, just throw it away.' He turned to me with a crazed look in his eyes that told me, 'Not another word,' then went back to digging for the machine gun. When he had them all he was visibly pleased. The smile on his face said, 'I'm ready.'

Not even making an attempt to run, we walked towards the highway of the Circle Garden in silence. I couldn't accept the reality of what had happened, it all seemed so unreal, so horrible. My insides turned and twisted at the unwanted memory. The highway snow was wet and dirty and partially eaten away by the heavy night traffic.

It was time to part. We stood looking at each other, not knowing what to say. Kepi's face took on a more serious look as he said, 'Well . . . I'm sorry I spent all the bullets, but I told you once I start I can't stop. I think we should leave the plane hijacking for another time.'

'Good-bye, Kepi.'

'Good-bye, Sash. You have to admit it was a good fight! What a victory! Ha?' he said, gloating with pride. He looked silly standing there hugging his arsenal.

'You'd better hide those weapons or cover them with something before you're arrested.'

'Let them try,' he said defiantly. He turned and walked away with the barrels of his guns sticking out in every direction.

I stood for a while trying to decide which route to take home. Finally, I chose the shortest route, which was right through the centre of Moscow, directly to Arbat. When I crossed the highway I saw the snow on this side was virgin and pure – unlike my night of bloodshed. The cleanliness of snow can camouflage the appearance of anything, even rubbish, and make it look and smell clean. But it's only a temporary cover. I'd been through so much this night and yet Moscow was serene and untouched by my experience. I didn't want to run through this city any more. I wanted to walk in this serenity admiring the white beauty around me, feeling the silence and peace, but instead, hidden, unexplained fear was growing inside me. Oh, Moscow, my love, my hate, my Christmas city without a Christmas.

I slowly made my way to the Red Square. It was surrounded by bright lights which marked its existence like a tiny village of monuments. It made me smile to see Lenin's tomb looking like a four-layer wedding cake topped with an icing of snow. The only difference was that the two figures were not on top of the cake but on the bottom.

The Spas tower clock rang out three bells. The smile on my face vanished when I realized that the guards changed every hour on the hour. This was not the time to be seen here. I slowed down and hid in the shadow of the St Basil Cathedral, hoping nobody would spot me there. I watched three more figures outside the Kremlin Gate march towards the Lenin's tomb like wooden soldiers . . . I was relieved when they passed me and I was unnoticed. I quickly crossed the square and followed the path along the Kremlin wall.

In front of me was the Moscow River. I stopped to rest and leaned over the wharf to look into the thick, black water. It was filled with the remains of people's lives: parts of wooden boards, rusted wires, pieces of newspapers bobbing up and down between dirty chunks of ice. Right under me I saw a dead cat, its head bobbing against the granite wharf. Its lifeless body reminded me of the hat near the headless man in the park. I retched with pain as my stomach heaved, eliminating every bit of sourness left inside me. This is what I thought of our victory as I faced the Kremlin wall – the biggest Russian fence.

10 Never

On my way home I kept going over the succession of the night's events. I couldn't believe what had happened, but it was too late to change anything.

I couldn't get my mind off Stas. I knew I couldn't have helped him, but that didn't make me feel any better about leaving him wounded and bleeding on the escalator. What did they do with him? Was he arrested or was he dead?

I couldn't help Boris either. Where had *he* gone? I saw how terribly he was hurt. Not just by the adultery committed by his wife, but by the betrayal of his friend.

And then there was Kepi. What was he going to do now? Was he really going to get even with Andrewlka?

I couldn't stop thinking of Andrewlka either. Did he inform on Kepi or not? And if he didn't, who did? This was the most frightening question of all, because I thought *I knew the answer.*

The longest night of the year finally came to an end, but the morning light didn't bring me peace. In fact, it brought more worry, more fear. When I opened the door to my apartment, I was afraid to go in. I stood for a while listening . . . There was no sound. I stepped in, trying not to make any noise. I walked through the hall to the door to our room and saw Lena sleeping on the bed. I decided not to wake her.

Hoping to wash away the memory of this terrible night, I went to take a shower. I undressed, put my sweaty clothes in a pile on the bathroom floor, and stepped into the bathtub. I turned on the tap, but no water came out. The pipes began to wail and shake, and a little mirror hanging on the wall behind the pipes slipped and fell, then shattered in the bathtub. A bad omen, I ruminated, seven years' bad luck. The mirror wasn't ours; it was left by the previous tenants, so I couldn't be sure who would get those years – they or I. Weighing this unpleasant thought, I bent over to gather up the chips of glass. As I reached down, a cascade of ice-cold water suddenly hit my back. Crouching there in shock, I watched helplessly as the water and glass ran between my toes. That's when, through the scratching noise of the glass scraping against the enamel bathtub, I heard the ringing of the telephone. I jumped over the side of the tub, my toe throbbing, and, leaving a trail of wet, bloody footprints, ran out to the hall.

After hearing the first words over the phone I forgot about my toe.

'Comrade Sasha K—?'

'Yes.'

'I'm a Special Investigator for the Committee on Government Security . . .'

The seven years were going to be mine, I thought.

'Are you there?' he said.

'Yes, Comrade Investigator.'

'I'd like to have a little chat with you.'

'When?' I asked.

'In forty-five minutes,' he replied.

'Where?' I asked.

'At the Metro stop – Revolution Square.'

'It's a big station, Comrade Investigator.'

'There's a statue of a soldier with a gun . . .'

'All right, I'll be there,' I said, feeling the pulse in my cut toe.

'Don't go!' Lena said, emerging from the doorway.

'They'll come here.'

'They can come, but you're not going!'

'What's the difference? They'll get me sooner or later.'

'Later is better,' Lena said.

I shook my head, defeated.

'Is it because of last night?' she asked.

'I'm afraid so.'

I arrived at Revolution Square on time, but nobody was there to meet me. There were several bronze soldiers with guns standing beneath the arches at the station. I walked from statue to statue, feeling as if all these soldiers had come together for my execution. I wandered away. If somebody was watching me, I wanted to show that I didn't care. I coolly walked along the edge of the platform. In the darkness of the tunnel, the tracks glistened like knife blades. A train emerged, pumping air in front of it. Just when the wind hit me, somebody grabbed my arm and said:

'It can be dangerous on the edge of the platform. Let's go upstairs, my friend. Do you remember me?'

I remembered him – it was Mikhail Mikhailovich, the representative from the Ministry of Culture.

He led me up Marx Prospekt. We passed my theatre, the Bolshoi Theatre, the Maly Theatre, and came to Dzerzhinsky Square, its metal monument to the first Secret Police chief pointing straight up in the middle of the square like a bayonet.

'How come you're limping, my friend?' my companion asked.

'I cut my foot this morning,' I said.

'You should be more careful when you're shaving,' he chuckled.

He took my arm and we went on walking around the square. We reached a huge, black granite building, the main office of the Secret Police, famous for its underground cells which nobody gets out of.

'We've got time, my friend,' said the representative, 'let's go for a walk. How's your foot?'

'It's okay,' I said.

We went up the street, passing the buildings of the Secret Police. They were well known to Muscovites. I would be able to figure out how serious my crime was depending on which building he took me to.

When we were near the black building, I was sure they had picked me up for last night's Metro ride to America and the shooting. When we came to the brown building, I reckoned it was time to pay them back for my songs and underground concerts. Near the blue building, I decided I was being arrested for avoiding the call-up. Next we came to a dirty yellow building. My companion tugged at my sleeve. I realized that the walk was over. My counterfeit invitation from Israel had done me in. My companion interrupted my thoughts, poked his elbow into my side, and said, pointing at a girl crossing the street:

'What an arse that one has. Look! You couldn't run around it in three days!'

'Yes, you're right,' I mumbled.

'Let's turn back,' the representative from the Ministry said.

Now all the buildings came in reverse order, and I felt a chill. Did they know about Kepi and last night's shooting, or not? If they did, then I'd surely become a 'guest' in the black building. I knew that all the buildings were linked by an underground passageway, so they could lead me into one and then drag me beneath the earth to another, nevertheless, any colour would be preferable to black.

'Hey, look – that one's even bigger,' Mikhail Mikhailovich whispered.

It seemed that my companion was so preoccupied with the rear ends of the girls on the street that he didn't want to go inside any of the buildings. When we got to the black one, though, he stopped me right near the door . . . then swung around and continued his stroll once more. I began to believe that they knew not only about the concerts, the counterfeit invitation, Kepi's shooting, and the Metro hijacking, but every single thing in my life.

I felt another jab in my side.

'Nice, she's nice,' I said, trying to put as much excitement as possible into my voice.

'That's enough girl-watching,' the representative said with surprising stiffness. 'It's time, my friend. Let's go.'

I didn't know where to go. We were standing near a low fence which surrounded an abandoned garden between the blue and brown buildings. My guide opened the squeaky garden gate. We went in and walked along the fence. At first it wasn't actually a fence, but twigs sticking out of the snow. The twigs grew taller, to my waist, and their ends became sharper. The fence rose over my head, but I could still see the street and moving silhouettes between the slats. The boards became more dense, the fence strong and high like those at the ministers' dachas. Then they were higher and higher like the ones around the Politburo dachas.

355

Then they looked like the fences at Brezhnev's dacha, with barbed wire on top; then the fence became so huge that it completely blocked the sky. The paths became so narrow that we couldn't walk side by side, and my guide stepped behind me. Here, when I was already anticipating a shot in the back of my head, we reached the end of the path and came to a five-storey building – an ordinary, grey residence – a matchbox standing vertically. The windows of the building had charming curtains, and flowers and cactuses on the windowsills.

We walked up to the entrance, wiped our wet shoes on the rubber mat, and my guide knocked at the door. The door opened. Behind the door stood a soldier, a pistol strapped to his waist. He looked at me, then at my companion, and motioned for us to come in.

Seen from the inside, this was no ordinary matchbox. Instead of the usual small, gloomy foyer painted half-green, half-white, there was an immense hall lined with grey and black granite. The hall, three or four storeys high, made one wonder how it fitted inside that matchbox. Despite what I had seen from the outside, there was no window inside. There were a few iron staircases, and my guide led me up one of them. After several flights, we came upon a landing with a lift. We went into the lift, my guide pressed four, the door closed, and we went down. The lift continued going down quite some time – longer than it took to walk up. We got out on the fourth floor, underground. There we encountered the same huge granite hall as above ground, except without the stairs. We went to the right; there were many doors; we stopped near door number 49. My companion knocked, then opened the door and let me go into the room. I never did see him again.

It was a bright room with a window on one wall! In front of the window, behind a desk cluttered with files, books, boxes, and a tape recorder, sat a man dressed in civilian clothes. His face looked familiar, but I couldn't place him. I had already met too many of that sort. He had a round, potato face, small eyes the colour of lead, and was a little fat.

'Sit down,' he said. 'Do you smoke?'

'No,' I replied.

'Right,' he said. 'It's not good for your health. I'd like to quit, too, but I don't have the willpower. Tell me your secret. How were you able to stop?'

'I never started,' I said.

'Smart,' he said, taking a cigarette out of one of the boxes. 'But if you're really that smart, you've probably already guessed why I invited you here today.'

'No,' I said.

'You don't have any idea?'

'No, I have no idea.'

'Think a little harder.'

I didn't answer.

'So, you're not so smart after all. I'll tell you why; but first, if you don't have any objections, I think I'll turn on the tape recorder. I hope the microphone won't make you uncomfortable.'

'No. It's all right. I'm used to microphones,' I said.

'What a pleasure to work with professionals,' he said, switching on the tape recorder and moving the mike towards me.

The reels began to turn slowly.

'I need some information.'

'About what?'

'About one of your friends.'

'Who do you have in mind?'

'You mean you have so many friends on whose account you could be invited here for questioning?'

'No,' I said, 'I don't have any friends like that.' He knows everything, I thought morosely.

'What an actor! Now I see that you really are an actor! You work in the theatre, don't you?'

'Yes.'

'On TV too?'

'From time to time.'

'Have you been involved in concerts?'

'Sometimes,' I said, finding it hard to get the word out.

'What's happening to you?' he asked gently.

'Nothing,' I said, and, for the first time in my life, felt like smoking. 'Nothing.'

'If you say so. Well, we were talking about the concerts you've sometimes been involved in. Right?'

'Right.'

'But the concerts aren't very important, for today. Tell me about the film business. Have you made any films?'

'Yes.'

'Which studios did you work for?'

'Mosfilm, Lenfilm, Dovzhenko.'

'Is that all?'

'That's all.'

'Have you ever worked at the Military Studio?'

'What?'

'I asked you if you've ever worked at the Military Studio?'

'Yes,' I said. 'Sorry, I forgot. I worked there many years ago.'

'There we are – it seems we've got to the main point,' he said, pulling his chair closer to the desk.

It seems we've got off the track, I thought. 'What would you like to know?'

'How was the salary there?' he asked me.

'Not bad,' I said, wondering what he was driving at.

'Can you be more precise?'

'It was good, but not very regular,' I said.

'Is this your signature?' the investigator said, handing me a batch of receipts.

'This is my signature here and here; the others aren't mine.'

'Good! That's just what I expected. You know, we're conducting an investigation of that studio. A group of film makers has been arrested. Can you imagine, they cheated the state out of several thousand rubles. The director has already conceded his hand in this; but the cameraman denies any involvement and puts the blame on somebody else – your friend, who used to work as his assistant. Do you know who I'm talking about?'

'Yes, I do, but it's a lie.'

'I agree, but the cameraman is stubbornly sticking to his story that your friend stole, not just money, but also a military uniform.'

'That's a lie, too,' I said. 'He wound up wearing that uniform because they took off with his clothes, they abandoned us in the forest – '

358

'You were in a stolen uniform, too?'

'I had no choice!'

'Don't get excited, comrade. I understand you perfectly. It's just a formality. I know that your friend stole nothing. In fact, I know him personally. He used to work here at the Ministry. Yes, he was sweeping around here all the time. It was a riot. Forget about the military coats. It's not a major issue. I just needed official verification. Could you sign here – it's about the forged signatures and the uniforms.'

I read the paper and signed it.

'Is that it?' I asked.

'That's it. When you see your friend the next time, tell him it's all over. No, I think I'll give him a call myself, right now. Anyway, I need to talk with him about something.' The investigator winked at me, drew the phone closer to himself, dialled the number from memory, then put his hand over the receiver and whispered to me:

'You're free to go, but if you have a minute why don't you wait for me to finish . . . Hello, can I speak with Andrew? . . . When will he be back? . . . I've got to talk with him . . . Right, when he gets back, tell him to call the Ministry in Dzerzhinsky. He'll know who it is. Tell him we need his services once again. So long.' The investigator put the receiver down and, with a slight smile, said, 'Without that apartment, life in Moscow would come to a halt,' then added thoughtfully, 'do you know by any chance who's living at his place now? He has a strange accent . . .'

'I don't know,' I said.

'You don't seem to know much,' he said, smiling, 'but that's all right. Anyway, thank you very much for stopping by . . . Good-bye.'

'Good-bye,' I said, rising.

'Uh, just a minute, please. I have one little question left for you.'

'Yes?' I said, freezing.

'It's not exactly a question . . . it's more like a conversation, private stuff. What are you standing for? Sit down. We probably don't need the tape recorder any more. This is just a friendly chat,' he said, switching off the recorder. Leaning back in the

359

armchair and looking at me with a not-so-friendly look, he said: 'So, you're getting ready to emigrate.'

I sat down.

'I'm interested in knowing why you decided to leave your native land.'

I didn't know what to say.

'Who is this Dim Haviv?' he asked.

If only I knew! I thought to myself, and said, 'My aunt.'

'I think you didn't understand me – this is a private, friendly talk. The tape recorder is off; what's the point of the charades?'

'It's true; I have a sick, old aunt in Israel who needs my help.'

'Don't lie. It doesn't suit you. We both know perfectly well that you don't have an aunt in Israel and that you're not a Jew. But that's not the point. I'm trying to understand you. I want to grasp what, or maybe who, led you to take such a step. I want to bring you back to your senses. I'm your friend. Don't get the idea I talk to everybody like this. From what I've heard, you're the hope of the Soviet film industry.'

Hope? There's no hope in this country, I thought.

'The majority of those who are leaving are criminals who want to get away before they are caught and punished,' he continued.

Everybody's a criminal to you, I thought.

'But what are you leaving for? This is something of a mystery to me. You are from a communist family. Your father was an important man. I just can't figure it out. Why?'

'It's very simple – I love my aunt!' I said.

'Come on! What's this talk about loving your aunt when your mother remains here!'

'My mother has my sister, Natasha, but my aunt Haviv is all alone. She needs my help.'

'Please, cut it out. I've had enough. Perhaps you think I have another tape recorder working? Maybe you're right. Let's check.' He opened his desk drawer, looked inside, and said with a grin, 'You're right! I forgot to turn this one off.' He pressed a button. 'There you are. I give you the word of a KGBist – I don't have a third one; even our ministry could not sustain such expenses. Now you can talk freely. I'll never tell a soul. I'm your friend. I want to help you understand what a mistake you're about to make. You will leave the country and regret it all your life.'

I never regret what I do, only what I don't do, I thought, and said, 'It's too late; I have promised my aunt. She's expecting me.'

'Why do you think one thing, but say another?'

It's Soviet training, I thought, but said nothing.

'You're stubborn, really stubborn,' he said. 'If you keep it up, you're going to wind up in gaol.'

I've been in gaol all my life, I thought.

'Your whole generation is made up of stubborn idealists,' he went on, 'and the funny part is that we communists made you idealists. Soviet education trained you like that because there is no communism without idealism. But now this very idealism is turning you against communism. And you artists are the worst. The problem with artists is that everyone in art is a genius nowadays. We have so much trouble with these geniuses; they keep us busy all the time. It's becoming harder to find an average man than a genius. And the funny thing is that our Regime doesn't need geniuses; it needs workers, and so, our goal is to turn geniuses into normal folks. When the Party needs a genius, it will appoint one and set the appropriate salary. We don't pay very well, but it's regular money. So maybe you call our art propaganda; but the good part is that you don't have to sweat too much over it; you just have to follow orders. Why can't you go along with this like the others?'

Because your propaganda is repulsive and provincial, and I've spent my whole life trying to run away from the provinces, I thought. 'I can't concentrate on such complicated things when my aunt is dying from loneliness in Israel,' I said.

'What's all this about Israel? You think I don't know you're going to America? But tell me, what are you going there for – to find happiness? What is happiness in America – to have everything you want? You know, when you have everything, you don't want anything.

'Many go to America for riches – to pick money from the trees. But I know you're not like them – money doesn't interest you. You're an idealist. So, what are you going for – for freedom? What is freedom except weakness? Where there's freedom, everything is permitted; everything is good. That's their philosophy. They're fools, your Americans. We call them our deadly enemy, but they only respond with a toothy grin because we are their potential customers. That's their weakness and that's why we will eliminate them. The world needs a strong hand because freedom didn't give anything to anybody except decadence; control gives everything.' He stood up, went around the table, stopped near me, and, peering at me with opaque grey eyes, said, 'Tell me honestly, when Soviet tanks roll down Broadway, which side will you be on?'

On the side of freedom, I thought. 'I don't know why you're telling me about America. I've already been there; but now I'm going to Israel,' I said.

He made an abrupt turn, walked away from me towards the window, and, staring out the window, said in a strange, flat voice:

'If you could only understand what it's like to be an emigrant. It's poverty, hunger, dirt, and injustice . . .'

I've had it all my life, I thought.

'. . . we gave you a happy childhood . . .'

My mother gave it to me.

'. . . we gave you bread to eat . . .'

God gave me bread.

'. . . we gave you a free education and free medicine . . .'

And now you want me to pay for it with my freedom.

'. . . we gave you everything. We made you a winner in our country . . .'

The only winner in Russia is the one who escapes out of here.

'. . . You're throwing away a successful career, an apartment in Moscow, and your motherland for the abstract word – freedom. I'm asking you for the last time – do you think it's worth it?'

I don't know. I've never had it. But I want to find out, I thought, and said, 'I have an aunt who may die at any moment.'

'Yes,' he exhaled, still looking out the window. 'I can see that you've made up your mind. I'm wasting my time. All right, go – but why do you have to leave as a Jew and lose forever the possibility of ever coming back? Listen, I'm going to make you an offer. I can arrange it so that you can go straight to America as a Russian, with a Soviet passport. You'll look around for a few years, and see how things are there. You'll get to know what freedom is through experience, and when you realize that what I told you was the truth, and you decide to come back, you'll be able to come home. Naturally, we might ask a favour of you before you return. What do you think?'

I let it pass.

'You are the last person who should want to be a Jew,' he said sharply as he turned towards me.

'I don't want to be a Jew, I am a Jew, you must try to understand the call of kin,' I replied softly.

'In your passport it says you're Russian,' he said.

'In my passport I'm a Russian, but in my soul I'm a Jew.'

'You're about as Jewish as I am!' he said, turning his face towards me.

'No, I'm really a Jew,' I said.

'Go to America as a Russian; it was never good, in all of history, to be Jewish. Renounce your Jewishness!'

No! I will never renounce this nationality. They have given me hope, they have given me the chance to get out of this cage, I thought, and said, 'I love my Jewish aunt.'

'I suggest you reconsider or I can reopen the stolen military uniform case.'

'I love my aunt more than life,' I said.

He looked at me with a weary smile and said, 'Our conversation is over. It would have been different but for the special political situation now – which won't last long – but now you can go.'

'Now what?' Lenin's last words echoed in my brain. Which way to go?

'Here's your exit pass, you'll be escorted out.'

I stood up to leave, but the sound of his voice stopped me.

'By the way, here are your approved emigration papers.'

'What about my wife's papers?' I asked, hiding my emotion.

'Here are her papers, too. I hear she's very beautiful. Are you sure you don't want to leave her here with me? After your questioning by the CIA, you may be sorry you brought her along.'

I turned and left the room without saying good-bye. I'll never be sorry, I thought. Never.

It had taken many years of waiting to find a way out of Russia, but now that we had approval, we had only two weeks to leave. These two weeks were filled with formalities connected with our departure, forfeiting our passports to the Emigration Office, picking up our visas, reserving our tickets, seeing lawyers to verify our signatures, having their signatures notarized, having both the lawyers and our notarized signatures approved by the Ministry of Jurisprudence, and paying . . . and paying . . .

Leaving the Soviet Union was not just difficult; it was costly. We had to reimburse the Government 3,500 rubles for our free education, relinquishing our citizenship cost 2,500; our one-way tickets cost 2,000 rubles; there was also a tax for our musical instruments of 1,200 rubles. We could have bought new ones for less. The tax on our bronze candelabra was 980 rubles. It could have been gold for that price. The only thing we weren't asked to pay for was Lena's appendix, but only because we left it behind.

By anyone's standards, our total expenses were astronomical. The little Lena and I had managed to save wasn't nearly enough to pay for our exit tax. Every ruble we ever earned in films and television appearances was now spent. In desperation we resorted to selling our clothes, and yet that wasn't enough! I sold all my souvenirs, which I had collected while abroad, and that wasn't enough! My mother donated her life's savings, and it wasn't enough! The total that came from selling part of our lives and our memories finally paid for everything but our tickets. With only a few days left before our departure, we felt that we were at the end of a dark tunnel that had suddenly been sealed shut. We had no other resource, no place to turn, no route of escape. All we needed was to pay for one-way tickets out of the Soviet Union, but our shortage of funds was about to keep us from leaving Russia forever.

When there was just one day left before our departure, Lena and I became numb, not knowing where to find or even steal the money we needed for our plane tickets. As if in a trance, in the hope that by some miracle we would be leaving tomorrow, I walked to the theatre for the last time to bid farewell to my fellow actors, even though they no longer admitted to my existence.

As I walked through the theatre doors, I discovered a great change in the attitude of the actors. They seemed to forget about my nationality and they greeted me warmly. This drastic change made me wonder why? Was it because I now had approval to leave the country? Maybe they just respected me for my victory against the government. Whatever the reason, they couldn't have expressed their support for me more openly. Everyone seemed to be in a holiday spirit.

One by one each actor took me quietly into his dressing room. They considered it their duty to drink a toast to my courage and strength against the system. This private time also gave them an opportunity to ask about my aunt.

Was she young or old?

Was she rich or poor?

Was she weak or strong?

Was she sick or healthy?

In order not to disappoint them, I tried to fulfil their curiosity with a fairy tale that would stay with them like a dream.

I told them my aunt was very rich, almost a millionaire, and that she was very old and in poor health. This response excited them, for they knew that I would most definitely be her heir and that once I got to Israel I would then send them blue jeans, boots, suits, furs, or even cars, when I remembered their kindness. We drank to my aunt's existence, health, and of course a special toast to her wealth. But now, sadly, it was time to leave. . . .

The entire theatre group gathered around me to bid me a safe journey and, to my utmost surprise, a miracle happened; they handed me a bag of rubles! They had collected the money earlier, knowing that I couldn't pay for my airline tickets. I was overcome by joy and pride in my comrades. It wasn't important to them that I was a Jew, they just wanted to help me in fulfilling My Dream. I promised to send them everything they asked for and, even though as a prince I lost my Kingdom, they made me feel like a King.

Our room was empty.

'Sit down for a minute,' said Lena.

We sat down on our crocodile suitcase and kept still – it was an old Russian custom to sit and reflect before a trip. As we had lived with one suitcase and two guitars, we would leave the same way. Many years we had waited for this trip, but now, with our tickets in hand, we wanted to cry.

Through the window, snow fell like crumbling plaster and, in that white sadness, Toilik's wooden castle on the other side of Arbat melted and vanished. There would be no more of this life; we were heading for a new one and away from something we hadn't done – crimes committed by our country – crimes our country makes its people pay for.

When I looked at Lena, I was struck by the change in her hair. Long ago, when we first met, she had a grey streak. At the time I thought of it as an accent of fashion. Now her dark strands were almost outnumbered by grey ones, and I knew for sure that this change wasn't caused by fashion, but by life itself.

'Once you told me you couldn't see yourself here in ten years. Now I know why – you're not going to be here,' I said to Lena.

'Yes,' she said, 'it's hard to believe that nearly ten years have passed.'

'We're right on schedule.'

'Let's go, Americanets,' Lena said with a smile.

'Let's go, Americanka,' I said, rising to go.

For the last time, we went down to the Metro. For the last time, we took the Circle Line. It was the longer way, but that's what we wanted. I never did like good-byes, so we had arranged with those who wanted to see us off to meet us in the last carriage on the stations of the Circle Line.

At Kiev Station, Lena's father came aboard, hunched over and worn out, with her grandfather, straight as a soldier. At Kursky

367

Station I embraced my mother, her near-sighted eyes smiling; she was followed by heavy-stepping, sad-looking Natasha. We were supposed to meet Boris at Comsomol Station and Andrewlka at Prospekt of Peace, but nobody came into the car at either station.

'Where is Boris?' Lena asked me.

'He probably couldn't come; you understand his situation . . .'

Lena understood. The secret police would be taking pictures of the well-wishers. For Boris, with his new family, it was better not to take a chance.

'What about Andrew?'

'I don't know . . . I haven't seen him since *that* night, but he was supposed to be here at this station. I hope we'll see him at the airport. He probably just left home late.'

Andrewlka wasn't late that morning. He put his new white sheepskin coat on and left his apartment to go to the Prospekt of Peace Station right on time. He was going along whistling 'A Hard Day's Night,' thoroughly out of tune, when suddenly on the stairs his whistling came to a stop. On the right side, beneath his window, there were no longer any lilac bushes. They had been cut down and were lying on the snow in bunches.

Andrewlka leaped down the stairs and reached out to take a frail branch in his hands. But, at that moment, something sharp and cold struck him on the back. He turned around; in front of him stood Kepi, the handle of an awl in his hand. his eyes raced from Andrewlka to the broken awl, and from the awl to Andrewlka.

'Why?' Andrewlka cried, trying to keep his balance on unsteady legs. 'Why did you cut my beautiful lilacs?'

'Because you ratted on me, you dirty informer!'

'Andrewlka doesn't inform on friends,' Andrew said, swaying from side to side.

'You informed on me!' Kepi insisted. 'But you're lucky that my awl broke. I lost the bet.'

'No,' said Andrewlka, 'you won. Take the garden knife.'

'But I didn't kill you.'

'You did,' Andrewlka said.

'No!' fumed Kepi. 'No!'

'Nobody ever believes Andrewlka,' said Andrewlka, smiling dreamily as he stumbled alongside the grey buildings. 'Nobody ever . . .'

The hospital was one stop away by Metro or one stop by bus. Andrewlka headed for the Metro but, as he was crossing the street, he caught sight of a bus approaching.

Andrewlka turned around in the middle of the street and headed for the bus. He hesitated at the door; the bus was packed. He was wondering whether to squeeze in or not, when a crowd of workers suddenly scurried up behind him and, with a heave-ho, shoved Andrewlka in. Andrewlka needed to get off at the next stop, but he found himself squashed between backs and stomachs deep inside the bus. There was no way to squeeze through the crowd to get to the front door, so he tried to cut a path to the back door.

'What the hell are you going to the back of the bus for? You're breaking the law!' shouted the ticket-taker over the passengers' heads. 'And where is your ticket? Don't let him out, comrades!'

Andrewlka wanted to pay but his money was in his left pocket, and his left arm had become numb.

'Andrewlka never buys a ticket,' said Andrewlka, smiling unabashedly.

'Don't let that ticketless citizen out the rear door!' screamed the conductor.

Several of the comrades didn't have tickets either, but they were glad they weren't the ones caught, so they closed ranks on Andrewlka and didn't let him get off. At the next stop, even more workers squeezed into the bus.

'Andrewlka is dying. Let him out . . .' Andrewlka moaned.

'First you have to buy a ticket, then you have the right to die,' a huge hulk said into Andrewlka's face, the smell of wine on his breath.

At the next stop, with more passengers boarding the bus, Andrewlka found it harder to breathe. Everything grew dark around him. He could no longer hear anything. His body was sinking, his legs dangling lifelessly, but he wasn't able to fall down. The crowd was proceeding to carry him from the back door to the front, as prescribed by Soviet law.

369

Soviet law would not be violated – Andrewlka was thrown out the front door of the bus at the last stop. He lay on the street beside a telegraph pole. The atom of his consciousness rolled into the farthest and darkest recess of his skull. Nobody took notice of him lying there in the freezing cold for quite some time. They thought he was just another drunk. Eventually, two men took pity on him and propped him up against the telegraph pole. For that service they took his money, his wallet full of I.D. cards, his sheepskin coat, and his watch. Some time later, a babushka walking her dog spotted Andrewlka and called an ambulance. It wasn't an ambulance that showed up, but one of the Black Ravens, to take Andrewlka to the Sober-up Centre. There, he was undressed and thrown into a cold shower. The water washed away the blood on his back, making him indistinguishable from the other drunks the policeman dragged from the shower to the barber.

The barber had shaved half of Andrewlka's head, and was about to start on the other half, when he stopped his work.

'Hey', he called out to the policeman. 'Come over here. Take a look.'

'Uh huh,' the policeman said, nodding.

'What do you think – finish it up or not?' the barber asked.

'Finish it.'

'What for?'

'It'll look a little funny at the funeral.'

'Why should I trouble myself with a dead one when I have so many live ones?'

'Does he have any documents on him?'

'No.'

'Okay, then don't bother with him. When did he croak?'

'Just now.'

'Did he say anything?'

'Some gobbledygook about trumpets and lilacs. . . .'

When Lena and I went through customs at the airport, we were searched extensively. Two female customs officials told Lena to go with them to a private room. Two male officials searched me and my crocodile. They didn't find anything illegal on me, save a forgotten five-ruble note in my pocket. They ordered me to hand it over to my well-wishers. In the suitcase they didn't come across anything special, except the bronze candelabra. They checked its accompanying document, tossed it back into the suitcase, X-rayed the suitcase, and when they saw nothing but the candelabra, they began to laugh over the fact that all our possessions fitted in one suitcase.

The customs officials had laughed in vain. We had managed to smuggle out our contraband goods. On pieces of white cotton, sewn into the cuffs of our trousers, were written the words to our songs – an SOS from the people we had left behind.

After customs, we were informed that we no longer had the right to see our relatives and well-wishers. Hoping to get around this, I asked them how I was supposed to give away the five-ruble note. I was told to go upstairs and throw it down.

We went up metal steps to the second floor. At the top of the stairs there was a small platform from which we could look down and see, perhaps for the last time in our lives, the faces of those dear to us. We smiled at them and waved good-bye. They smiled and waved back. I squeezed the five-ruble note in my pocket. I took it out, made it into a paper aeroplane, and tossed it down. It flew, twisting and turning in a wide arc across the lobby, past the information booth, then towards the bar and over the heads of the long line of people waiting for beer. All the heads looked up at once. The five rubles veered downward, disappearing among the feet. All eyes looked down; only one pair of eyes went on looking up at us – the slanty eyes of Boris. He came to see us for a last time. He *came*.

And suddenly I knew! Boris never informed on Kepi, Stas did, as he probably informed on Ali many years ago for the same reason – just for fun!

Lena and I sat on the plane in silence, being very careful not to speak. We knew that all Aeroflot planes had hidden microphones, and that for just one wrong word planes had been turned back and passengers arrested.

The plane moved slowly, paused for a second, then, little by little, picked up speed, creeping its way down the runway, the wheels clinging to the Russian land as if unwilling to part with it. Then, with a great surge of power, the plane tore away from the ground and soared into the sky, ripping through the dark grey clouds. We finally found our way into the clear, blue, peaceful space.

Several months later, in New York, I received an unsigned letter. I knew the handwriting well enough to recognize who wrote it. The letter wished us good luck in our new country, told of a bitter divorce, and then, at the end, described Andrewlka's last trip. Maybe it wasn't exactly the truth about his death, but what was the truth about his life? A frightening picture of it came to me, as if I had been there. I felt sorry, terribly sorry, but I had left all my tears back in Russia. What could I do, except wish that Andrewlka had taken the Metro?

Also available in Methuen Paperbacks

Vladimir Volkoff   The Set-Up

Psar wanted to go home. A White Russian, living in Paris, he is not the most obvious immigrant to the Mother Country. But there is a way – if Psar will only collude with the KGB in a dazzling plot to confound both the dissident movement and Western liberals alike. Psar must agree, and so begins a nightmare of manipulation and obscure but increasing danger, as the steely web of the KGB's all-pervasive disinformation network is revealed in its ruthless complexity.

Seldom has the seamy and dangerous world of espionage been so relentlessly explored as in this brilliant and disturbing award-winning novel.

'This book may be pure entertainment, but it gradually builds up a picture of world politics as a great amoral game of chess in which the Russians are supreme masters' John Weightman.   *The Observer*

Irving Stone Depths of Glory

Depths of Glory spotlights one of the most brilliant and important figures in the history of art – Camille Pissarro, father of the Impressionist Movement. From a childhood in the West Indies, through a forbidden marriage to the Pissarro household maid and a life of considerable hardship, he never deviated from his commitment to his art, an art which created outrage and scandal and condemned him and his Impressionist colleagues to years of neglect, poverty and misunderstanding. Yet what a group they were – Manet, Degas, Van Gogh, Renoir, Cezanne and other giants of art all have their place in Irving Stone's vast and marvellously detailed narrative canvas.

Against a background of Paris at the moment of its pre-eminence as art capital of the world, *Depths of Glory* pursues the absorbing story of one man's indomitable courage and, without losing any of the authenticity of his life's story, turns the dramatic events into a rich, vivid novel in which the world of the Impressionists comes vibrantly alive.

'*Depths of Glory* is a feast for the followers of Stone and readers of the genre established more than three decades ago with his novel of Van Gogh, *Lust for Life*' *Publishers Weekly*

Antonia Fraser   Oxford Blood

A programme on the Golden Kids at Oxford University seems a frivolous prospect, and Jemima Shore, renowned TV investigator, feels she has better things to work on. But a startling confidence from a stranger changes her mind, and draws her to Lord Saffron, at the centre of the closed world of Oxford Society and its peerage. Handsome, disreputable and overprivileged, he is in fact not what he seems: for Jemima has it on excellent authority that he is a changeling, and no true heir to the Ives' title and fortune.

As her investigations probe deeper, Jemima becomes involved in Saffron's adopted world of expensive pranks, balls and weekend parties, and finds it thick with sinister intrigue and envy. But none of this prepares her for the shock of an attempt made on Saffron's life, and – it seems – her own . . . .

'With deft, wry prose and a credible plot, Fraser holds our interest and leaves us clamoring for more Jemima Shore adventures' *Publishers Weekly*

'Dare one say the best Jemima Shore yet . . . Some acid characterisation, much excitement, and lots of fun' *Sunday Telegraph*

'[Antonia Fraser] is, as always, rivetingly readable' *London Evening Standard*

'Elegant, witty writing, sharp observation mixed with genuine sympathy . . . and not a few thrills' *Sunday Times*

These and other Methuen Paperbacks are available at your bookshop or newsagent. In case of difficulties orders may be sent to:

Methuen Paperbacks
Cash Sales Department
PO Box 11
Falmouth
Cornwall TR10 109EN

Please send cheque or postal order, no currency, for purchase price quoted and allow the following for postage and packing:

UK	55p for the first book, 22p for the second book and 14p for each additional book ordered to a maximum charge of £1.75.
BFPO & Eire	55p for the first book, 22p for the second book plus 14p for the next seven books, thereafter 8p per book.
Overseas Customers	£1.00 for the first book, plus 25p per copy for each additonal book.

While every effort is made to keep prices low, it is sometimes necessary to increase prices at short notice. Methuen Paperbacks reserves the right to show new retail prices on covers which may differ from those previously advertised in the text or elsewhere.